Fitz looked out the window and saw below, on the practice grounds, his daughter trying to swing a sword. Gerald joined him at the window.

"It seems we have a budding warrior, my lord," said Gerald.

"Mmm," the baron replied, thinking deeply. "I wonder if we might encourage her a bit?"

"Encourage her, my lord? You want your daughter to be a warrior?"

"Why not?" he turned to face Gerald. "I daresay she has the determination."

"Isn't that a little dangerous?"

"My dear sergeant," the baron said after a brief pause, "I think it's apparent by now that if Beverly wants to learn to fight, she's going to do it with or without us. I'd rather she learn to fight properly."

Gerald saw the look of resolve on his lord's face. He knew how this was going to end, but he had to play his part. "And how, my lord, are we to proceed in this manner?" he asked, knowing full well the answer.

"I think it's best," said the baron, "that you 'discover' her training, and offer a few tips, don't you? She has to think it's her idea."

Gerald sighed, "Very well, my lord, I shall see to it at once."

"Thank you, Gerald," said Fitz. Then added, "Oh, and Gerald?"

"Yes, my lord?"

"Train her properly, real training, not pretend."

He was about to object but saw the look on the baron's face. He swallowed his pride, "Yes, my lord."

And so Gerald Matheson, the Sergeant-at-Arms of Bodden Keep marched down to begin training his newest protégé, a seven-year-old girl.

∾

Also by Paul J Bennett

SWORD OF THE CROWN

Heir to the Crown: Book Two

PAUL J BENNETT

Paul J Bennett

Fourth Edition: April 2020

ISBN: 978-1-7751059-7-8

This book is a work of fiction. Any similarity to any person, living or dead is entirely coincidental.

Dedication

Dedicated to my buddy Brady

2007 to 2018

ONE

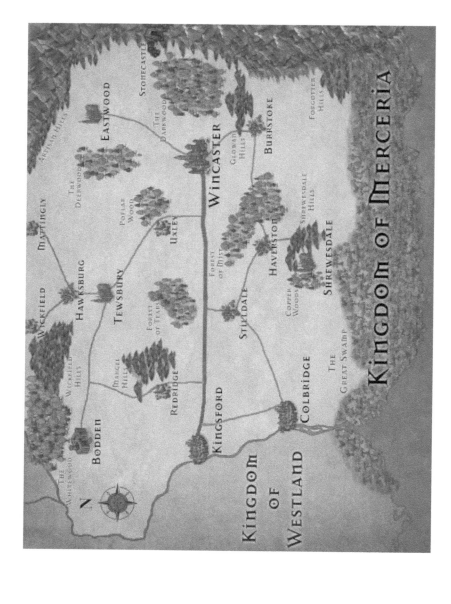

Bodden

WINTER 935 MC* (MERCERIAN CALENDAR)

⁓

T he wind howled in from the west, driving the snow into great sheets of white, blocking everything from view. The horses struggled to make their way through the deep drifts, forcing the riders to slow their pace. Ahead, periodically, they spotted the Keep, its beacon lit to guide them home. Another gust swirled around them, temporarily stealing the scene from view. The leader, encrusted in snow and weighted down with the responsibility for his men, pushed on. "Almost home," he yelled, but his voice was carried away by the relentless squalls that stole the very words from his lips.

The wind died down revealing the welcoming gates of Bodden before them. He looked behind him to see his men strung out in a single line, following his trail through the deep snow. The horses were breathing heavily, and he felt the cold seeping through his thick clothes. This was no time to be outside, but even in these severe conditions, the land must be protected. They had come across the raiders by accident, stumbling into them in the worst weather they had seen for years. It had been a quick and bloody encounter, with the enemy fleeing, leaving behind two dead and carrying off three more wounded. Now the patrol struggled to make it back without freezing to death. One of their own, Jack Anderson, had taken a brutal cut to the arm, and now he slouched in his saddle, tied in place with some straps that they had managed to cobble together.

The gate drew slowly closer, and it seemed that winter threw its last gasp at them with a massive crosswind that threatened to blow them off their horses before they reached home. Sergeant Gerald Matheson, the leader of the frozen group, clung to his saddle, his hands growing more numb by the moment. Just a little further, he thought, and they would be safely within the walls.

They passed through the gate, and suddenly the wind dropped. Almost like magic, the sky cleared as if portending some great event. He knew the weather here could be fickle; he had served for years in Bodden and had seen clear skies turn dark with little warning.

He dropped to the ground, taking a moment to shake the snow from his cloak. Ice crusted his thin beard, and he rubbed it, trying to warm his face. He stroked his horse's neck absently as he watched his men trail in behind him, two of them carrying Anderson to the surgeon. They had worked hard today, in harsh conditions to protect this land, now they deserved a rest. With no thought to his own respite, he led his horse to the stables. The stable boys came to take everyone's mounts, but he insisted on taking care of his horse himself. He owed his life to this creature, the least he could do was look after it.

It was late, and darkness was just starting to fall as he made his way into the great hall after tending to his mount. He saw Sir Randolph standing by the fire, sipping a cup of wine, and nodded his welcome.

"Sergeant," the knight said, "how went the patrol?"

"We ran into some raiders, but we managed to drive them off," Gerald replied. "I doubt that particular bunch will trouble us again, but Anderson took a hit."

"How bad?" the knight asked.

"I'm afraid he won't be able to swing a sword again," Gerald paused. Bodden was chronically undermanned, and even the loss of this one man would have far-reaching ramifications. He needed to find the baron. "I must report to Fitz, is he in the map room?"

Sir Randolph held up his hand to halt him and walked over, stopping to fill a second cup along the way. He handed it to Gerald. "I'm afraid," he said solemnly, "that the baron is otherwise engaged."

Gerald took the cup, looking Sir Randolph in the eye. "The child?" he asked.

Everyone knew that Lady Evelyn Fitzwilliam was due any day now. He could only assume she was delivering this evening.

Sir Randolph smiled, but there was a sadness in his eyes. "The child lives," he said, "but Lady Evelyn will likely not see morning."

Gerald grew silent. It had been only three years since the loss of his own family, and he knew the pain that Baron Fitzwilliam must be going through.

Outside the master's bedchamber, the wind was howling and shrieking, but the shutters kept it at bay. Candles dimly lit the room while Baron Fitzwilliam mopped the forehead of the pale woman lying in the bed.

"I'm sorry, Richard," said Lady Evelyn, "I failed to give you a son."

Baron Fitzwilliam's eyes teared up. "You have failed no one, my love. You have given me a daughter."

"But a daughter cannot inherit. You must remarry and have a son."

"Nonsense. I never wanted the title in the first place. If my brother hadn't died, I'd still be a soldier. I shall never remarry. Our daughter will carry on the name." He noticed her strength draining, her face growing paler by the moment.

"But the family name?" she whispered.

"Will remain in safe hands," he finished. "I promise you, our daughter will grow up to be the mistress of this Keep, and she shall remember the great love her mother had for her."

"What shall we call her?" he asked, desperate to keep her with him, if only for another moment.

She smiled briefly, "Beverly, after my grandmother."

Her eyes closed. He saw her take one more breath and then lie still. Outside, as if recognizing the solemness of the occasion, the wind died down. Lady Evelyn Fitzwilliam, the Baroness of Bodden, was dead.

Baron Fitzwilliam walked over to the midwife, gently removing the baby from her arms, gazing at the infant through tear-stained eyes. The baby looked up at him, squirming in its wrappings. "You," he said, his voice breaking with emotion, "are Lady Beverly Evelyn Fitzwilliam, and your mother was the most wonderful woman in the kingdom. I promise you that I will do everything in my power to make you happy, and one day, when you're older, you will rule Bodden, I will see to it. On your mother's honour, I pledge to give you the life you deserve."

TWO

Child

SUMMER 939 MC

Baron Richard Fitzwilliam rode through the gate, followed by his soldiers. They had been patrolling the countryside on the lookout for raiders, which were common this time of year. He dismounted, and while he would normally tend to his own horse, today he handed it off to the stable hand, his mind already working on the next task he had in his busy day. Walking across the courtyard, he heard a familiar cry, "Papa!" He turned just in time to see his daughter, red-haired like her mother, charging across the courtyard without a care in the world, her arms held out, waiting for the embrace of her father. Fitzwilliam grinned, it was hard to keep a stern expression where his daughter was concerned, and so he knelt down, waiting for her hug. She jumped into his arms, and he held her tight, standing up to spin her legs through the air. He held her close, not wanting to let her go, enjoying the moment and forgetting all his troubles. He looked down at her, and she smiled back at him. "Well, what have we here?" he said to her. "Lady Beverly Fitzwilliam, I do believe."

She laughed, and the sound was like magic. He was enjoying the moment immeasurably when he caught sight of his sergeant nearby. Still clutching his child, he turned to face him.

"My lord," the man said, "did you get a chance to check in on the Claytons?"

"Yes, Gerald," the baron replied, still wearing a smile, "they're fine, though why they wanted to farm way out there is beyond me."

"It's the dirt," Gerald explained.

"The dirt?"

"Yes, it's very fertile, excellent for growing crops. Far better than what we have here."

Fitz looked thoughtful for a moment while holding on to his daughter. "You were a farmer once. Just how good is this dirt?"

"It's very good, actually. It's near a river, and the runoff brings all the good soil to the area."

The baron looked around at the outer Keep. The village was growing, and soon he would need to expand the outer wall, to ensure the people's safety. Perhaps they could put this dirt to good use. "How difficult would it be to move the soil?" he asked suddenly.

Gerald was taken aback by the unexpected turn of conversation. "Move the soil?" he asked incredulously.

"Yes, it's just soil, we should be able to dig it up and move it. It would be much better to have the farms nearer to the Keep, keeping the farmers safe. How many have been killed by raiders in the last five years?"

"Too many," Gerald answered, "and we have few enough as it is. As you know, it's hard to convince them to come out to the frontier when it's so dangerous."

"Precisely! We'll need to mark out some areas. We'll give each farmer a plot and then draft some people to start hauling the soil while we build the houses."

Though taken by surprise, Sergeant Matheson reacted quickly, setting his mind to this new task. "We'll need to build some more wagons first."

"How long will that take?" the baron asked.

"We only have the one wagon maker, so it'll take at least a year, and then we'll have to relocate people in the spring before the crops are planted."

"So we're looking at spring of '41 for the great soil move?"

"Aye, my lord," Gerald agreed.

The baron continued moving towards the Keep, his daughter still tucked securely under his arm, while Gerald followed along. She played with her father's beard and moustache as they walked, a chuckle escaping from him. They made their way up to the top of the Keep. The baron referred to this as his map room, for a large map was spread out across the table in the centre of the room, weighed down by various rocks. He sat Beverly in a chair by the window, and then he and Gerald turned back to the map to start discussing their plans.

Not content to sit idly by, Beverly walked over to the table, peeking over its top. The map had always enthralled her, and now she watched with great excitement as Gerald and her father discussed things beyond her comprehension. She could just see the edge of the map, but from her angle it was indecipherable. She began pushing her chair towards the table.

The baron turned around at the sound of the chair scraping along the floor. "What's this?" he said, smiling in amusement. "Does someone want to see what we're doing?"

"Yes, Papa," she chimed in.

Gerald lifted the chair and brought it to the table, then picked Beverly up and placed her standing on the chair. "How's that?" he asked.

The young girl smiled brightly, "Thank you, Gerald."

He tried to correct her, "Thank you, Sergeant."

It was Fitz's turn for a correction, "Don't be silly, Gerald. You might be a sergeant to the men, but you're like family to us. Let her call you by your name. I can't see it would do any harm, it's not as if she's one of the troops."

"Very well," said Gerald, resigned to his fate. He turned to Beverly, "You're most welcome, m'lady," he said with an exaggerated bow.

Beverly, now with a better view, began casting her eyes about, seeing the room from a whole new perspective. "Papa, I can see out the window from up here!"

Fitz understood her sense of wonder. One of the reasons he liked this room so much was the location. Here he was, at the top of the Keep, and by opening the shutters, he beheld the whole barony. The vista was magnificent, and on a day like today, the fresh air and light breeze brought a pleasant scent into the room.

Fitz walked over to the west window and gazed out upon the land, his land. "Ah, the fresh smell of roses, it so reminds me of Evelyn. She always loved roses, you know."

Gerald walked over to the window, to stand beside him. "She would have been proud of you, my lord. You always do what's needed for the people. Not too many lords would be willing to haul dirt."

The baron kept gazing out the window. "You know, Gerald, I've always believed in the nobility, but not the way most believe in it."

"What do you mean, my lord?"

"Well, most people, most nobles, believe it's the right of the nobility to be served by the people." He detected a look of confusion on his sergeant's face.

"Isn't that how it works?" Gerald asked.

"No, at least it shouldn't be. Nobility bestows the duty of the noble to look after the people. It's their obligation. Do you understand?"

A small voice chimed in from the table, "Yes, Papa, the nobles must look after the commoners."

Fitz smiled at his daughter, "That's right, my dear, remember, we serve the people. Oh, we're in charge, but if we lose the support of the people, we are nothing."

Gerald wondered at the keen mind of the baron. He would never consider himself a scholar, but he had learned so much from his mentor.

"There are many in the capital that would disagree with you," Gerald warned.

"Hah!" the baron snorted. "I dare say you're right. But we know better, don't we, Beverly?"

"Yes, Papa," she chimed in again.

"Anyway," he continued, "I digress, let's get back to this map. I was thinking the north field might be the place to start."

They migrated back to the table and began discussing the situation in more detail. Beverly watched them, as they examined the map and talked. Her eyes fell on some wooden figures. Bodden Keep had been attacked on numerous occasions and kept a fairly substantial number of troops. The baron had found it expedient to represent these troops with wooden figures, which he would then place on the map when giving orders. Now these figures fell into the eye-line of Beverly, and she was spellbound. She looked up at her father as if she was guilty of something, but he was busy pointing at the map. She reached across and grabbed a soldier, holding it up to the light to see it better. It was supposed to represent a knight, though the carving was somewhat crude. She detected the likeness of a horse and decided it was interesting.

Gerald was deep in discussion, "...and then the north wall could be extended, but we'd need another sally port."

"I thought about that," the baron continued, "but the problem is the amount of stone we'd need." He took a breath to continue with his discourse and was interrupted by a strange sound. They looked across the table to see Beverly, playing with the knight, making horse noises as she galloped it across the table.

"I think," said Gerald, in the sudden silence, "that it's time your daughter learned to ride."

"So it is," the baron agreed. "Well, that's enough planning for one day. Come along, my young dumpling," he said picking her up, "it's time we get you on your very own horse."

Gerald followed them down to the stables where the stable master suggested a pony for Beverly. Some time was spent selecting tack, and Gerald watched as the baron, with great care and patience, led her around while she sat in the saddle.

He had only gone a few steps when the stable master interjected, "My lord, she must ride side saddle."

The baron stopped the pony and looked at Beverly, then back at the stable master. Gerald saw his lord wrestling with the problem. At last, Fitz turned back to Beverly and asked, "How would you like to sit? Like this?" he lifted her off, placing her back on the saddle sideways. "Or like this?" he returned her to her previous position.

"Like this, just like you, Papa," she quickly answered.

"But that's no way for a lady to sit, my lord," the stable master protested.

"This," he said, turning politely on the man, "is no ordinary lady. She is the Lady of Bodden Keep and if she wants to ride like a man, so be it."

Gerald smiled. This wouldn't be the last time the baron would be at odds with his servants where his daughter was concerned, of that he was sure.

THREE

Respect

AUTUMN 940 MC

~

Beverly grew accustomed to the saddle rather quickly, and now it was common that when the baron left the Keep on horseback, she tagged along on her pony. It was Gerald's duty, as Sergeant-at-Arms, to look after the safety of the baron and his family, and so, whenever Beverly rode out with her father, an extra contingent of soldiers followed.

Bodden had a variety of soldiers within its walls, far more than usual for a Keep of its size. It was an important stronghold on the border, the guardian against the raiders that came from the north. There were the usual footmen, mostly armed with spears, but some with swords and shields. Then there were the archers, whom the baron prized. Most used a regular bow, but a small number of them were armed with longbows that would pierce the breastplate of a heavily armoured knight. Lastly, were the horsemen, of which there were two types; soldiers of common birth, armed with swords, shields and mail, and the knights, who were a mixed blessing.

Of the knights that were in Bodden, some were outstanding, particularly the ones that had past experience, but more often than not, they were sent by the king with little training and no discipline. Most of them resented Gerald, for the baron had made it clear to all that his Sergeant-at-Arms was to be obeyed as if the baron himself had given the orders. This didn't sit well with the spoiled nobility of Merceria, they knew full-well that Gerald was a commoner, worse, he was a farmer.

On this day Gerald had decided to assign two new knights to the escort. The baron was riding out to examine the grounds where the great 'earth move' was going to take place. Beverly was trotting along beside him, with two knights, Sir Barston and Sir Leyland, filing dutifully behind.

As they headed out the gate, Beverly turned in her saddle. "Good-bye, Gerald," she shouted, waving her hand.

The two knights, witnessing this, turned in their seats to look at him. "Yes," said Sir Barston, "good-bye, Gerald." Both men snickered.

They were suddenly jolted forward as their horses halted. Baron Fitzwilliam had stopped his mount and the smile on his face from watching his young daughter suddenly turned into a scowl.

Beverly looked up at him, "Did I do something wrong, Papa?"

He smiled down at her, "No my dear, you did nothing wrong at all."

"Then what's wrong?" she innocently asked.

He looked down at her, leaning slightly in his saddle so that he could talk in a softer voice. "In an army, my dear, it's important to maintain discipline and the chain of command. A soldier must always respect their leader, and when someone fails in that respect, they need to be reminded. Do you understand what I mean?"

"Yes, Father, I shouldn't call the sergeant by his name."

"No, you misunderstand, my dear," he said kindly. "You may call him Gerald whenever you like, just as I may. But the men under his command…" he pointed to the two knights who were oblivious to what was coming, "must treat him with respect."

"If I was a soldier, would I have to do that too?" she asked.

He thought about that carefully before answering. "When performing your duty, yes. But at home, in the Keep, he is a friend, and you should call him by his name."

"One day I'm going to be a soldier," she stated.

He looked at her in surprise. "Indeed?"

He heard a snicker coming from one of the knights.

"Do you find something humorous, Sir Barston?"

Sir Barston, not being the brightest of knights, decided to speak frankly. Gerald stood by, waiting to see the man sink himself with his own words. "Well, my lord, the idea's quite funny, don't you see?"

The baron was not amused, and his face displayed his displeasure. He was a fair man, however, and believed it best to give the knight the opportunity to speak his mind.

"I mean," Sir Barston continued, laughing in between talking, "a female knight? I've never heard of such a thing, it's absolutely preposterous!"

The baron turned his horse around carefully and rode up beside the man. As he moved, he looked over to Beverly, "My dear," he said, "would you be so kind as to ride over to the sergeant, and wait there?"

"Yes Papa," she said, guiding her pony back through the gate. As she rode past Sir Leyland, she looked up at him and stuck out her tongue. The young knight hadn't a clue how to handle it and just sat there with a stunned look on his face. She rode over to where Gerald was standing and turned her pony skillfully to face the same direction as he.

"Saxnor's balls, Papa's about to give it to them," she said.

Gerald looked at her in surprise. "Such language, from one so small," he scolded.

She returned the look, "It's the same language that you and Papa use, isn't it?" she asked with her innocent eyes.

He coughed to cover up a laugh, "I suppose it is," he admitted, "though it seems strange coming from one so-"

"Female?" she interrupted.

"No," he corrected, "I was going to say from one so young. I've certainly seen my fair share of cursing women over the years, take Cook for instance." The cook's penchant for cursing was legendary.

She chuckled, then turned back to watch the performance in front of them.

The baron, now beside Sir Barston, was looking the knight's horse up and down. "Your horse looks particularly well-groomed, Sir Barston," he said in a friendly tone.

The knight, confused by this turnabout in the baron's tone merely said, "Thank you, my lord?"

"What type of brush do you use?" the baron asked.

"Brush, my lord?"

"To brush your horse, what type of brush do you use?"

"I don't know, my lord," Sir Barston looked confused. "I don't brush my horse."

Gerald knew where this was going and turned his head slightly to speak to Beverly, still keeping his eye on the drama unfolding before him.

"Watch this closely, Beverly," he said, "you'll learn an important lesson."

Baron Richard Fitzwilliam was a soldier's soldier. He believed that if a man looked after his horse, the horse would serve him well in battle. The mere thought that a knight, who relied on his steed far more than an ordinary soldier, should not even know how to brush his horse, was unconscionable.

"Dismount, Sir Barston," the baron said evenly, "you too, Sir Leyland."

The two knights dismounted. The baron called over to his sergeant, "Sergeant, would you be so kind as to come and take these two away?"

"Yes, my lord," he responded and walked over, ready to march the knights away.

"No, not those two," he said looking at the knights. "I'd like you to walk these two magnificent beasts back to the stable, please. At least I know YOU understand how to treat a horse."

Gerald kept a straight face as the baron added, "And when you return we'll discuss extra duties for these two…" he paused as if deciding on the best words to pick, "soldiers."

Gerald walked the horses back to the stables and handed them over to the stable boys.

He marched back to the baron, deciding it was best to play this as professionally as possible. Walking up directly in front of the baron, he stood to attention. "Horses returned, my lord," he said in an official tone.

The twinkle in the baron's eye told him that Fitz had appreciated the performance. "I believe Sir Barston here, has something he wants to say to you, Sergeant." He looked at the older knight with a stern countenance. Sir Barston still looked confused. It was a wonder, thought the baron, that these rich nobles' sons didn't seem to grasp even the basic aspects of life. By and large, they were incredibly stupid, or lazy, or, in this case, both.

"Sir Barston here," the baron continued, beginning to relish this tactic, "has decided that he'd like to learn more about looking after his horse. Would you kindly see to it that any spare time he might have be put to just such a purpose? Perhaps start with the basics, you know, mucking out the stables and such?"

"It would be my pleasure, my lord," Gerald replied, "and what of Sir Leyland?"

"Oh I think his horse skills are quite adequate," the baron said. Then, as Sir Leyland began to relax, he added, "He's volunteered to lend his strength to cleaning out the waste pit. I think you'll find that our intrepid engineer is overseeing that operation. I'm sure he'll appreciate the extra help."

Beverly watched the entire exchange, absorbing it all. The baron observed them head off, each in their separate directions, and then turned to Beverly, "Come along, my dear, we still have to ride out."

"My lord," Gerald burst out, "you cannot go without an escort."

"Oh, very well. Go and get your horse, Gerald."

He ran over to the stables, rushing to saddle up his horse and returned shortly, out of breath, but ready to go.

"We'll need another guard, my lord," he said.

"Just how many guards do you think we need, Gerald?" he asked.

"At least two, my lord."

The baron looked around the courtyard, then turned his horse, riding over to the smith, who was oiling some weapons. "Master Grady," he said, "pass me that sword and scabbard there," pointing to a short sword.

The smith passed it up to him, and he rode back to where Gerald and Beverly were waiting. He pulled his charger up beside Beverly and leaned towards her. "Put your arms up, my dear," he said, and as she did so, he took the scabbard and buckled it around her waist.

"There," he said at last, "now we have two guards, Gerald and Beverly."

They rode off through the gate, Beverly's grin bigger than it had ever been before.

FOUR

Council

SPRING 941 MC

～

The great soil move, as it came to be known, started in the spring of '41. The baron had gone to extraordinary measures to carefully and meticulously plan the entire operation, keeping everybody busy throughout the past two years. It had taken some work to convince the farmers of the whole idea. Fearful of losing their land, the baron had guaranteed them title to the new plots, and so when the day finally arrived, they were eager to begin. With the wagons built and houses constructed, all that was left to do was move the soil. There were more wagons than horses, so the plan was for the horses to travel back and forth, dropping off empty wagons, and then picking up the ones full of dirt. In this manner, they would move things much faster.

All the manpower they could muster was on hand, with several men standing by to run messages. Sergeant Matheson was his voice and ears, for even the baron was not able to be in two places at once. Beverly spent her time riding everywhere, racing with the wind on her fleet little pony. It was hot, and the work was gruelling, but aside from small, easily solved problems, the operation went smoothly.

It was late afternoon one day as Gerald returned to the land around the Keep. He had just come from the Clayton's where the next shipment of soil had been loaded into wagons. They were merely waiting for the horses to return to complete the last trip of the day. Beverly was riding up and down the rows of farmers, watching them work. She saw Gerald approaching and

trotted towards him then stopped. Something had caught her attention on
the ridgeline to the north. He cast his eyes in the direction she was looking
and saw a glint of light reflected off of something.

He instantly knew what it was and spurred his horse into a gallop.
"Alarm, alarm," he shouted at the top of his lungs. "We're under attack! Back
to the Keep!"

He pushed his horse to the limit, riding straight for Beverly. She was
looking northward when the raiders came into view. There were two dozen
of them, and they charged over the hill like a small swarm of ants. The
workers, spurred on by Gerald's warning, were rushing to the safety of the
Keep. He saw Beverly, small as she was, spur her pony and start galloping
for the gate, but he realized the raiders were going to get to her first.

Beverly looked over her shoulder and saw the horsemen approaching.
Her pony, fitting for a six-year-old, was far too small to outrun a raider. She
stopped her mount, turning it sideways to the attackers, and then drew her
sword clumsily. The weight in her hands felt cumbersome, and she had no
clue how to use it, but she was determined to show no fear. The horsemen
got closer, several breaking off to attack the other tenants, while four of
them headed straight towards Beverly, who sat calmly waiting with her
sword in front of her. They laughed in amusement as they got closer, soon
surrounding her, taunting the small child. It was great sport for them, to
tease a young girl so easily, but they lost their focus, forgetting that things
were happening around them.

Gerald rode straight past the first rider, slicing with his sword as he
went. A deep cut appeared across the raider's lower back, and he screamed
in pain, but Gerald didn't pause. He continued directly into the next rider,
turning to sideswipe the mount. His own warhorse was used to this tactic
and kept its feet, snorting as it moved, but the raider's horse lost its footing,
sliding to the ground, the rider flailing awkwardly as he landed. Gerald
kicked his horse forward and thrust with his sword, feeling the point bury
itself into the stunned-looking raider. "Run!" he yelled to Beverly, who then
turned her pony and spurred the animal forward. He felt a slash across his
own back and was thankful he had worn his chainmail today, for he would
have a bruise, but no cut to his skin. Without looking, he swung out with a
backhanded blow and felt the sword bite flesh. The third raider let out a
scream, clutching his face.

Turning his horse about, he spotted Beverly, still astride her pony,
making her way to the gate of the Keep. Glancing left, he noticed another
group of riders bearing down on the farmers who had been laying out
stakes to mark the land. He spurred his horse forward, passing by Sir
Barston who was on the ground dead, his skull crushed by a hoof. His well-

trained horse responded instantly to his commands, and soon he was thundering down towards the farmers. Cutting in front of them, he placed himself between the villagers and the approaching attackers, attempting to draw their attention. They took the bait and angled towards him. He spurred his horse onward with the raiders in pursuit, leading them away from the farmers. Being familiar with the area, he made for a small copse of trees, ducking as he entered. The raiders followed, rewarding him with the sound of at least one rider being hit by a tree branch. Clearing the trees, he turned to surprise two riders who were using their arms to shield their faces from the stinging branches. It was a simple matter to dispatch them, so intent were they on their safety that they never expected an attack as they exited the grove.

He picked his way back through the trees, returning to the original scene of the attack. The workers had all made it back to the Keep, leaving the attackers riding about in frustration, seeking revenge for their dead. They had expected to find something valuable, and Gerald laughed, all they had found was dirt. It didn't take long for them to give up the search and leave, finally allowing him to ride back through the gates and report that the attackers had fled.

The people inside the walls were relieved with this news, and the baron ordered the work to wait until the next day. Tonight, he announced, they would celebrate with spirits, and the mood quickly turned festive. Fortunately, only one man had died, Sir Barston. They had been lucky, but he knew the baron would not count on that luck a second time. They couldn't afford to be surprised like that again.

Gerald saw to his horse and then headed to the map room, where the baron was, no doubt, discussing the situation with his most trusted advisors. Taking the steps two at a time, he arrived at the door only to find a young Beverly, her ear pressed against it, listening.

"What have we here?" he said, and she turned around, startled. "We can't have people spying on us now, can we?" he chided.

Beverly looked terrified. He reached forward, pushing the door open, holding out his other hand for hers. Never one to shirk responsibility, she placed her hand in his, and he led her into the room.

Baron Fitzwilliam was standing at the map table along with Mason, the head archer, Tumly, the leader of the Bodden Foot, and Sir Garant, leader of his knights. "What have we here?" said the baron, turning at the sound of the door opening.

"It appears, my lord," said Gerald gravely, "that we have a spy."

The baron walked over to Beverly, looking down at her. "Have you been listening at the door?" he asked.

"Yes, Father," she said.

"And what did you hear?" he asked in a stern voice.

"Nothing, Father, I couldn't hear a thing!"

He stepped back and stared at her for a moment, stroking his beard with his fingers. "Well, we can't have that can we." He looked towards Gerald, who was still holding her hand. "Get her a chair, Gerald, she can't hear a thing from the hallway."

Her face lit up as if by magic. Gerald dutifully grabbed a chair, bringing it over to the map table. The baron pointed to it, "Sit there and pay attention, my dear, these are important matters that we discuss."

She sat down, a diminutive figure amongst the large men, while they discussed what to do. Late into the evening they talked and planned, the baron making sure she was fed along with the others. Beverly was entranced with the proceedings, continuing to listen as the night grew darker and the candles were lit. They discussed what happened, why the raiders were here, where they had come from, who might be leading them. The conversation seemed to be going in circles.

They were debating what to do to guard against future attacks, and the consensus appeared to be to increase their patrols, but they didn't have enough horses.

Sir Garant and Gerald were debating this very fact when a young voice spoke up.

"What about a tower?" she said, navigating a small gap in the conversation.

"A tower?" said Sir Garant. "What do you mean a tower? It would take months to build a tower."

Beverly stood in her seat as all eyes turned towards her. "Not a stone tower, a wooden one. Tall enough to see far away, on the hilltop here," she said, pointing at the map.

The baron was suddenly inspired. "By Saxnor's beard, she's right. We'd only need a few soldiers to man a tower. If we build a number of them, we'd see anybody coming from miles around. We can make simple observation towers, no defences, with a fire standing by to set them alight if we need to abandon them."

The room exploded into a cacophony of ideas, and soon the plans began to take shape.

Baron Fitzwilliam looked over to his daughter, proud of her suggestion, only to see she had fallen asleep. She was lying, half on the table, one of the tiny wooden knights clutched in her hand. He could have called a servant and ordered them to take her to bed, but this was Fitz the Elder, and he liked to do things himself. "Keep them going, Gerald," he said, "I'm going to put Lady Beverly to bed." He picked her up carefully, carrying her in both arms and excused himself. They all watched him go, touched by his tenderness, and then, as soon as the door was closed, erupted into conversation again.

He carried her down the stairs to her room and lay her on her bed. He tucked her in, looking at her sleeping face. On her bedside table was a portrait of her mother, and he gazed at her image longingly. "Oh Evelyn," he thought out loud, "how proud you would be of your daughter."

"Papa?" the little girl's voice enquired, breaking his reverie.

He turned to see the sleepy-eyed child before him. "Yes, my dear?"

"Are they going to make the towers?"

"Yes, Beverly, they are, and it's all thanks to you."

"That's nice," she said, and then lapsed back to sleep.

The next day the garrison rose early to get to work, and much to the baron's surprise, Beverly was up with them. Bodden's engineer, a humourless man called Stevens, worked out the details of the towers with a little trial and error. Soon, a practical design was created that would have the towers going up quickly. The work, though relatively easy, was messy. The characteristic spring rains had come and turned the ground into a soggy quagmire. The baron was there through it all, insisting on helping raise the beams they would use for the towers. They elected to put a horseman and bowmen in each tower, the horseman's job being to ride them to safety should an attack occur. The bowmen would stay in the tower, watching for trouble. By taking shifts, they would cover the area much more efficiently than running patrols.

At the baron's insistence, they had left Beverly at the Keep, and she now took time to explore. She knew the entire place by heart, of course, but there were some areas where she wasn't normally allowed to go and these, she discovered, were not guarded when all the men were out working. The most interesting one, to her mind, was the armoury. Here she discovered all manner of weapons, arranged in neat rows. Most were far too big for her to handle, but she could imagine heroic knights wielding these tools astride majestic horses. She was mesmerized by it all. The armoury was gated, of course, so she couldn't touch anything, but she stood at the iron gate that blocked the door and looked on. It was then that she decided to pay a visit to the smith.

Bodden had a number of smiths, but of these, only one was reckoned a master swordsmith. Old Grady, as he was called, had been with the barony for years. No one knew precisely how old he was, but he had served her uncle and when he died, her father after that. He was a dour man, constantly grumpy, but Beverly found him amusing. She wandered down to his smithy, drawn by the sounds of hammering.

As she got closer, the hammering stopped, and she heard the telltale sound of quenching. She turned the corner to see him holding a red-hot blade in the water, his face turned towards his apprentice, yelling, as was normal. Grady's apprentice was a man named Martin, but never was a man more ill-suited to his profession. Martin had originally been a farmer, and when his farm was destroyed in a raid, he was taken in by Grady as an apprentice. He had been at it for many years and yet he still hadn't mastered the most rudimentary of tasks.

She stepped into the room, looking at everything. There were half-finished blades on tables, spearheads sitting on the workbench, all manner of strange tongs and hammers hanging on the wall. This place was magical to her, and she loved seeing how everything worked.

"Hello, m'lady," Martin greeted her.

Grady looked at her, but only grunted a greeting.

"Hello, Martin," said Beverly politely. "What are you working on today?"

Grady snorted. "Nothing," he blustered, "he can't even manage to fire up the forge properly. He's only been here six years, you'd think he'd of managed to learn something by now."

Beverly ignored the smith's bluster. She looked at a large set of tongs hanging from the wall. "Oh, those are large, what do you use them for?" she asked.

To her surprise, it was Grady who stepped around from his workbench. "These," he said, lifting them down from the wall, "are for shields. A sword is easy to hold in the forge, but a metal shield is quite unwieldy when you're pounding it with a hammer."

Beverly knew that Grady could be downright poetic when talking about his craft, so she spurred him on. "How do they work?" she asked.

Sure enough, old Grady fell for the bait and soon he was talking at great lengths about how he forged shields. He was mainly a weaponsmith, of course, but had mastered the art of mail years ago. Once she had him talking about shields, it was a relatively simple matter to get him to switch topics, and soon the idea of armour came up.

"So, you make the armour for the knights, don't you?" she asked.

"Actually," he grumbled. He liked to sound like he was complaining, "Most knights bring their own armour with them. I just repair it. I haven't made mail in a couple of years."

"Is it hard? Making mail?" she asked.

"Time-consuming," he answered. "Chainmail isn't difficult, but the metal plates we cover it with these days require a different skill set. The breast-plate is perhaps the most difficult as it has to be custom fitted, you see."

Beverly was fascinated, and now came to the question she really wanted answered. "How would you make armour for a woman?" she enquired.

"A woman? Don't make me laugh," the smith roared.

"What's so funny?" she said, upset at his behaviour.

"You can't make armour for a woman," he said, trying to catch his breath.

"Why not?" she asked innocently.

"Well...because," he answered hesitantly.

"Because why?" she pressed.

"Because women aren't built for combat, they're too...delicate."

Beverly made a sour face. Grady looked amused.

"Sorry, my lady, but it just can't happen. Women are all the wrong shape."

"But what about the legends," she persisted, "or the Elves?"

The old man smiled, "The legends were written years ago, long before we had metal like this to work with. And Elves? Trust me you don't want to wear what the Elves call armour."

Disappointed by this news, she decided she'd had enough. "Thank you anyway," she said politely, "you've been most illuminating."

She left him, heading back into the Keep. So he wouldn't make armour for a girl. She would have to figure out something else if she wanted to be a knight. It was then that it became cemented into her mind. She would prove him wrong! She would become a knight, a valiant fighter, a beacon of justice, a warrior to be spoken of in years to come. Of course, first she had to learn how to use a sword.

FIVE

Playing with Swords

SUMMER 942 MC

⁓

T he great movement of soil the year before had been successful, and with the planting of the season's first crops, an even better harvest was expected this year. The new watchtowers had proved useful since their construction, not only to spot enemy raiders before they were too close, but to deter them from future attacks. On three occasions alarms had been sounded, giving the troops time to respond, preventing the raiders from coming any closer. Each time the baron sent out a group of horsemen to hunt them down, even leading one sortie himself.

The Keep became a busy place during this time, for the farmers were now closer, and the village that existed within the outer bailey grew to accommodate the increased trade. Beverly enjoyed walking through the village. It was a comfortable place, where people knew each other, and she soon recognized many of the villagers by name.

It was a particularly hot day, late in the summer when Beverly was walking once more through the streets. She stopped to look at some nice fabric and was discussing it with the shopkeeper when she heard a sound in the distance, a distinctive thud of wood hitting wood. Not quite able to discern what was making it, she left the dressmaker with a promise to return and followed the sound which led her around the corner and away from the shops.

Here, was a group of boys, close to her own age. They were fighting with wooden swords, daring each other to attack, and then swinging wildly.

She recognized some of them as the sons of soldiers, while others, she assumed, must be related to the villagers.

Leaning against the wall, trying to look nonchalant, she watched them play fight. One of them would lunge forward, striking overhead with their sword. The other boy would then block the swing and do likewise. She was struck by the simplicity of their movements, having seen her father's soldiers in training. It was the responsibility of the Sergeant-at-Arms to keep the baron's men in tip-top shape, and she was sure he would be disappointed by these lad's feeble attempts at fighting.

She was trying to recall the drills she had witnessed the soldiers practise when a voice interrupted her thoughts.

"What d'you think you're looking at?" the tallest boy said.

"Pardon?" she said, shaken from her reverie.

"This fighting's for boys, not girls," the boy said. "Go tend to your sewing."

As the baron's daughter, she was not used to being treated so rudely, but she didn't want to go running off to get help. Something made her want to make a stand, and so she looked back at the boy without moving. "You're doing it all wrong," she told him.

The boy walked over to her, with the two others backing him up. "What would a girl know about fighting?" the youth accused.

She stood up defiantly, "Obviously, more than you."

"What did you say?" the lad's face turned red. "Say it again, I dare you!"

Clenching her first, she felt her anger rising, "I said, you're doing it all wrong. Your strikes are too easy to block, and your attacks have no strength behind them." She was quite prepared to get into a fight about this, so sure was she of her ideas. "Let me show you."

"No girl is going to show ME how to use a sword," he shouted.

She was sure he was about to hit her, saw him make a fist, but one of the other boys grabbed his arm and whispered something in his ear. The boy looked down as he listened, then looking back up at Beverly, his face paled.

He growled something incomprehensible, and then turned around, "Come on," he said, "we'll go find some other place to practise our swordsmanship."

Beverly felt cheated. She had never practised with a sword, but her encounter with the raiders the year before had made her more concerned. She resolved to start practicing today, immediately in fact. She would show those boys how to use a sword!

Making her way back to the Keep, she entered the practise yard. No one was here today. They were all out on guard duty or patrols, so she retrieved her sword and walked to the centre of the yard. She thought about all the times she had seen Gerald train the soldiers and decided to start with some basic drills. Taking up a stance, her right foot in front by about a foot's length or so, she swung the sword from her right-hand side in a sweep and tried to step forward with her left foot, but found it awkward. She tried again, this time stepping forward with her right leg, but once again found the action clumsy. Getting frustrated, she tried swinging the sword in a backhanded motion, but the sword came loose in her grasp, clattering to the cobblestones. Embarrassed, she looked around sheepishly, but fortunately for her, no one was about, and so she picked it up and started again. She soon came to the realization that this was going to be more difficult than she had first thought.

Baron Fitzwilliam was in the map room listening to Gerald, who was detailing the Keep's stores. Ever since the northern wars had begun, Bodden had been a prime target. It had already come under siege on three separate occasions, and the baron was determined to always have sufficient food stores to survive an extended siege if need be. The windows were open, letting in the sweet summer breeze, and as he listened, he moved towards the west window, the better to feel the breeze on his face. Gerald was going on about how many bushels of grain they would need to make up the shortfall when they were both startled by a rather loud clanging sound.

Fitz looked out the window and saw below, on the practice grounds, his daughter trying to swing a sword. Gerald joined him at the window.

"It seems we have a budding warrior, my lord," said Gerald.

"Mmm," the baron replied, thinking deeply. "I wonder if we might encourage her a bit?"

"Encourage her, my lord? You want your daughter to be a warrior?"

"Why not?" he turned to face Gerald. "I daresay she has the determination."

"Isn't that a little dangerous?"

"My dear sergeant," the baron said after a brief pause, "I think it's apparent by now that if Beverly wants to learn to fight, she's going to do it with or without us. I'd rather she learn to fight properly."

Gerald saw the look of resolve on his lord's face. He knew how this was going to end, but he had to play his part. "And how, my lord, are we to proceed in this manner?" he asked, knowing full well the answer.

"I think it's best," said the baron, "that you 'discover' her training, and offer a few tips, don't you? She has to think it's her idea."

Gerald sighed, "Very well, my lord, I shall see to it at once."

"Thank you, Gerald," said Fitz. Then added, "Oh, and Gerald?"

"Yes, my lord?"

"Train her properly, real training, not pretend."

He was about to object but saw the look on the baron's face. He swallowed his pride, "Yes, my lord."

And so Gerald Matheson, the Sergeant-at-Arms of Bodden Keep marched down to begin training his newest protégé, a seven-year-old girl.

Beverly tried stepping, then swinging, then stopped. Her right arm was getting sore, and she rubbed it. She would never get the hang of this, she thought. She would have to watch the soldiers practise tomorrow and learn the basics. Her frustration level was rising at her own inabilities when a voice interrupted her thoughts.

"Every new recruit needs to start with a practise sword," said Gerald walking towards her. He tossed her a wooden sword which she managed to catch. "Put away the other blade. You'll learn to handle it when your arm toughens up."

She leaned the sword against the wall and gripped the practise weapon in her right hand. Gerald guided her out into the centre of the yard and stood beside her. "Now, stand with your feet even with one another, but about shoulder-width apart. When you swing from the right, take a step forward with your right foot."

"But I've been trying that," she complained.

"No, I've been watching you," he said, remaining calm and professional. "You step and then swing, you need to do both at the same time. Your movement will put more weight into the swing." To illustrate he carried out the movement himself. "You see? Now you try it."

It only took a moment for her to get the hang of it, and then he showed her how to do a backhand swing. Soon, she was stepping forward with a forward slash and then stepping again with a backhand swing. He returned her to the middle of the yard and stood in front of her with another wooden sword. "Now do it again," he said, and as she swung, he blocked and stepped backwards, then blocked the backhand stroke, stepping back again.

Before long they were going back and forth in the yard. First, she would attack six times, then he would counter-attack, and then it would be her turn to block. She was having a wonderful time, and he recognized the look of determination on her face that he had seen so often on the baron. She would have kept at practise for hours, he had no doubt, but he also knew her arms would be sore tomorrow, for she had to get them used to the effort. He finished up with some stretching exercises, warning her that her arms would hurt later.

"So, recruit," he said as they were finishing, "are you willing to return tomorrow for more training?"

Beverly looked up at him and smiled, "Yes, please! I mean, yes, Sergeant."

"Excellent. We'll meet here again tomorrow at the same time. We can't really have the new recruits practicing with the regular soldiers, now can we? Take that practise sword with you and go see the swordsmith and get him to adjust the grip on it, you've got smaller hands. If he gives you any guff, you tell him the Sergeant-at-Arms sent you."

Gerald was surprised by Beverly's determination for she practised every chance she got. If only, he thought, his actual recruits were as disciplined as she was. The summer wore on, and the training continued. Soon, he had her practicing different techniques, lower and higher thrusts and swings. She ate it up like a wolf among sheep. By the time the cooler air of autumn had arrived, she had progressed to a real sword, though only a short one. Gerald found the training not too tiresome, in fact, he hated to admit it, but he had fun. Her enthusiasm was inspiring, and he often found himself showing her tricks that he normally wouldn't mention to trainees.

SIX

Survivor

AUTUMN 942 MC

The patrol topped the rise and looked down into the valley before them. It was a cold morning with a mist that drifted into the recesses of the valley like a blanket, obscuring the area below. Baron Fitzwilliam rode up beside his sergeant, with the other riders just behind.

"See anything, Gerald?" he asked.

Gerald looked down into the valley, but didn't speak. He was straining to catch a sound of something off in the distance, removing his helmet to make it easier. "Horses," he finally said, "I can hear them down in the valley."

He replaced his helmet and continued his report, "I think they're waiting for something, my lord, I heard movement. A wagon, maybe?"

"Well," said Fitz, "we'd best be getting a move on if we're going to stop them." He turned to his men, and commanded them, "In line, trotting forward, not too fast, and keep the line straight."

The horses were repositioned, forming a line with Baron Fitzwilliam and Gerald in the centre. They paused while the baron drew his sword, raising and lowering it to signal the advance. The line moved forward at a slow trot. The baron had started using these tactics years ago when he had discovered that the Norlanders who raided the area were ill-disciplined and feared formed cavalry. The line slowly advanced into the valley, the mist enveloping them, but proving to be thinner than expected.

Fitz called the turn, and the right-hand side slowly sped up and began to move while the left shortened their pace and turned left, the result being warming up. This was pretty typical in Beverly's experience. Every knight would go through some drills, and then the real practise would start with the knights breaking into pairs to square off against one another.

Each year the number of knights in Bodden varied. It depended mostly on how active the frontier was along with how many knights the king decided to send. Presently, there were only seventeen knights, with seven of those reckoned as 'new', having not seen combat since their arrival.

Sir Thomas began by walking over to one of the new knights, Sir Miles, and tapping the unproven man's shield with his sword. This was the accepted manner of starting, and Beverly looked forward to seeing how the new knight might fare.

The others stepped back to watch as the two combatants moved to the centre of the yard, circling each other, sizing up their opponent. Sir Thomas was a careful and calculating fighter, one of the better knights here at Bodden. Sir Miles, however, appeared eager to make a name for himself and suddenly lunged out at his older opponent. Sir Thomas, caught off guard, backed up quickly and the crowd 'oohed' and 'aaahed.'

They reset their positions back to the centre to start again, with Miles once again lunging. This time, Sir Thomas simply sidestepped and smacked the other knight on the arse with the flat of his blade.

"That was an insult, sir," said Sir Miles as he turned to face the veteran.

"The insult is that you called that an attack, sir," replied Sir Thomas.

"I must insist that you take that back, sir," the younger knight growled, growing red in the face.

"I must insist that you take that back, sir," mimicked Sir Thomas.

The young man was speechless for a moment. "How dare you, sir! I am the son of the Earl of Shrewesdale. You cannot speak to me in this manner!"

Beverly was engrossed by the exchange in front of her. The Earl of Shrewesdale was a powerful man. The situation would quickly escalate if somebody didn't step in soon. This was going to be most interesting indeed.

"That being the case," Sir Thomas continued the baiting, "I would think that you would have learned some manners, or do they not teach manners in the whore houses of Shrewesdale?"

Sir Miles unexpectedly threw his sword to the ground. Something had just happened, something that Beverly did not quite understand, but the assembled knights all went quiet.

Sir Miles removed his glove and walked towards Sir Thomas, striking the other knight's face with it. Sir Thomas took the blow without flinching, even though Beverly clearly see the red mark on his face.

"I demand satisfaction for your insult," announced Sir Miles.

"Very well," Sir Thomas replied in a sombre voice, "choose your weapon."

Sir Miles walked over to the weapons rack, studying the choices at his disposal. To Beverly, it looked ludicrous, as if he were choosing an apple from a vendor. Finally, he selected a Mercerian broadsword and tossed a second, duplicate blade, to Sir Thomas.

The remaining knights formed a circle, while both fighters leaned their shields against the wall, before entering to face each other.

Sir Edward stepped between them, holding his sword in the air, while each took their stance. Sir Edward waited while everyone went quiet, and then sliced his sword downward, uttering a loud, "Begin."

The first assault came from Sir Thomas, a full body slam that caused the startled younger knight to stagger back, reeling from the blow. Sir Thomas tried to repeat his manoeuvre, but this time Sir Miles stepped to the side, striking a weak blow that careened off the older man's armour.

Sir Thomas bellowed in frustration and wheeled about to face his attacker.

"Enough!" came a roar from behind them, announcing the arrival of the Sergeant-at-Arms, as he stepped into the circle.

"What's going on here?" Gerald demanded.

"This man," yelled Sir Miles indignantly, "has insulted my family honour. I demand satisfaction!"

"This weasel," said Sir Thomas, his temper flaring, "is a snivelling toad who-"

"Shut up! Both of you," yelled Gerald.

Beverly had never seen Gerald so upset, and stood to get a better view.

"This - will - stop - right - now," he emphasized each word as he spoke. "Return to your billets."

"I will not," an indignant Sir Miles yelled. "I have been insulted."

Gerald turned on Miles with a look of fury. "Listen to me you little shit," he said in a low voice. "I don't care if you're a prince of the realm, in this Keep you do as I say. Do you understand me?"

"That's right," said Sir Thomas, "listen to the sergeant."

"Shut up," Gerald yelled, turning on Sir Thomas. "I've just about had it with you lot. You live a life of privilege in the great cities, and then you come out here where people are dying, damn it, and you have the gall to be insulted? I'm not putting up with this shit anymore! From now on, you're on guard duty until I say otherwise."

"You can't do that," they both uttered in unison. Beverly giggled into her hands. It was comical to see great knights acting like spoiled children.

"Knights do not do guard duty," added Sir Thomas, "that's for a job for foot soldiers."

"That's right," agreed Sir Miles, now in accord with his rival.

"I'll take this to the baron," threatened Sir Thomas, his previous adversary now nodding in agreement.

"Fine, let's go see him right now!" declared Gerald, straining to keep his voice calm.

Beverly turned and ran. She knew her father was in the map room, and wanted to be there before they arrived. If they got there first, she might not be allowed in, but he would never kick her out if she were already in the room.

She ran as fast as her legs could carry her, taking every second step on the stairs to shave precious moments off her time. Bursting into the map room, she saw her father sitting at the table and took a moment to catch her breath.

Normally the map of Bodden fully covered the table, but he had rolled it up and was picking away at a plate of meat and cheese as he perused a book. Surprised as she rushed into the room, he looked up and asked, "Something wrong, my dear?"

"No Papa, why would you say that?" She didn't want to reveal the coming storm and tried to look relaxed.

He made a face, "Well, it's not every day I hear yelling outside, and then my daughter bursts into the room. Or did you forget that a window faces onto the training yard?"

"Oh, I forgot," she admitted, "but the knights are coming here, they were duelling, and then Gerald stopped them, and now they're mad at him, and they're coming up here to complain." She rushed out the words, fearful that they would arrive at any moment.

"I see," her father said. "Well, you might as well sit at the table so you can see how punishment is handed out."

"Surely you're not going to punish Gerald?" she questioned.

"No, of course not, my dear. I'm going to punish the knights."

"But they're knights, and Gerald's a commoner. I thought..."

"Yes, Gerald is a commoner, but he is also my Sergeant-at-Arms, and as such, has my complete trust. He's my representative, and any disobedience to him is disobedience to my authority. Do you understand?"

She was about to answer when Gerald and the two knights arrived at the door, which Beverly had failed to close. A gaggle of other knights followed them, and she saw her father put his hand to his forehead for a moment. It was a habit he often did when presented with a difficult problem.

The knights filed into the room, respectful of the silence.

"Well, what's this all about?" said the baron, rising from his chair.

The knights all started talking at once, while Gerald kept his silence.

The baron held up his hand to stop them. "You," he said, pointing to Sir Miles.

"This commoner," the young knight said, "tried to assign us to guard duty."

"And?" enquired the baron.

"Knights do not stand guard. They are the vanguards in battle, the hammer that destroys the enemy on the field of glory."

"I see," said the baron, "and you?" he indicated Sir Thomas.

"I've raised this issue before, my lord. It is unseemly that a commoner should order about knights. Are we not nobles?"

Fitz turned to Gerald, "Might I ask, Sergeant, what brought about this punishment?"

Gerald stood rigid, looking directly at the baron, "They were duelling, my lord."

Fitz turned to look at the two knights, "Is this true?"

They both nodded, "But that's not the point, my lord."

"Oh, I think it is precisely the point, Sir Miles."

Beverly watched her father closely as he wandered about the room, deep in thought. He's already made up his mind, she thought, but he wants them to wonder what's going to happen. She looked at the faces of the knights, faces of concern, of worry, even. Then she looked at Gerald. He looked calm. He knew exactly what was going to happen!

The baron completed his circuit of the room, making direct eye contact with each of his knights. He turned his back on the group of them and winked at Beverly, who was on the other side of the table. "How dare you!" he yelled as he turned to face the assembled group.

Beverly intensely observed the knights and witnessed Sir Thomas and Sir Miles smile. They were sure that Gerald was about to get into trouble.

"How dare you impugn the character of my Sergeant-at-Arms," he said dramatically, pointing at Gerald. "I have known this warrior for years, and he has fought to keep the people of this realm safe. He killed his first soldier at, how old were you?"

"Thirteen, my lord," Gerald replied neutrally.

"Saxnor's balls, half of you weren't even born yet. You, Sir Miles, how many men have you killed?"

The young knight looked embarrassed, "None, my lord."

"I would hazard a guess that Sergeant Matheson here, has probably killed more raiders than the lot of you combined, and yet you have the audacity to complain about him? Let me make this quite clear gentlemen, and I use the term loosely. An order from Sergeant Matheson is an order from my own lips. Do you understand that?"

The knights nodded meekly.

"There will be no more talk of duels, and no more complaints heard about the sergeant. As for the punishment," he paused for dramatic effect, and Beverly watched him smile slightly as he turned to face them again, "I would have let that stand, but since you've complained about it, I think it only fair that I increase it. As a result, you two will not only carry out guard duty at the sergeant's request, but you will also clean out the stables. I shall make sure the stable master is informed that these duties will continue until I say otherwise. You are dismissed."

The knights began filing out of the room, "Not you, Gerald," the baron said, and the sergeant remained behind.

The room emptied save for Fitz, Gerald and Beverly, who was expecting her father to perhaps rebuke the sergeant. It was dangerous to anger a noble. Much to her surprise he poured a cup of wine and passed it to Gerald.

"Were they truly duelling?" he asked.

"I'm afraid so, my lord."

"It's true," piped in Beverly, glad to see her trainer was not in trouble. "I heard them arguing. Sir Thomas doesn't like Sir Miles."

"They're bored, my lord," offered Gerald. "They need something to distract them."

"They could be sent out on patrols?" offered Beverly, eager to participate.

"Hmm," pondered her father, "you may be right." He turned towards Gerald, "Let's add knights to the patrols, and make sure those two don't get put together for now. Perhaps if we keep them tired, they won't have time to argue."

"Yes, my lord."

The baron turned to his daughter. "Well, my dear," he said, "what have you learned today?"

Beverly looked at her father. "Knights are stupid?" she offered.

Her father laughed, and Gerald almost spit out his drink. "I daresay, in this case, you might be right, but not all knights are stupid. They just don't follow a code."

"A code?"

"Yes, a set of rules if you like, guiding principles. I always try to instil a sense of duty in my knights. They must protect everyone, not just the nobles, for without the common people, there can be no nobility. Many of the knights who come here have yet to learn that lesson, and today was a good example of the entitlement to which they have become accustomed. Knights used to swear fealty to a lord, but these days all the knights must take an oath to the king, who then decides which noble they will serve."

"So when... I mean, IF I were a knight, I would pledge my loyalty to the king?" she asked hesitantly.

He smiled at her, "My dear, we all serve the king, but once knighted, you would need to find a worthy sponsor."

"Like you, Father?"

"Your father is a very worthy man," said Gerald, "but you can't serve your own family as a knight, you have to serve someone else."

"Why is that?" she asked.

"Following the farmer's rebellion in '93," explained her father, "the granting of knighthood became the exclusive domain of the king. You see, the king had witnessed the power of the knights in battle, and feared that they might be used against him in the future. It wasn't until about 30 years ago that King Harran relented, and permitted some knights to choose their sponsor."

"But whom would I serve?" she asked.

The baron smiled at her. "You have many years before you have to worry about that. You're an accomplished rider, and you've started training with the sword, but you have a long way to go to become a knight."

Beverly was shocked. Her secret was out.

The baron had spotted the look on her face, "Oh, come on now, we all know that you want to be a knight. There's nothing wrong with that, but it takes time."

"But," she stammered, "I thought women weren't allowed to be knights."

"My dear," he said, "you can be anything you want to be. If you want to be a knight, we shall make sure you're the best knight in the kingdom. Isn't that right, Gerald?"

"Yes, my lord."

EIGHT

The Smithy

SUMMER 945 MC

The crops yield had tripled over the past few years, resulting in a surplus of food that provided the baron reason to celebrate with a grand feast. In the two years since their duel, Sir Thomas and Sir Miles had settled their differences, and the younger knight had matured into a decent warrior. Gerald had no more problems with either of them, and the entire barony was at peace. Even the raiders were thinning out, for there had not been a raid for months.

It was a warm midsummer day, and Beverly had just finished practicing with Gerald. Now ten years old and having a firm grasp of sword basics, Gerald had begun teaching her how to use other weapons, though some were still too big for her to wield with competency. In particular, she liked the warhammer, but found the grip difficult to handle, so after practise she took the weapon down to see Old Grady, with the hope that he might be able to balance it.

Grady, strangely enough, was not at his forge, so Beverly took the opportunity to look around. She was peering into the forge itself, not in use, but still quite hot, when a young voice interrupted her.

"Can I help you, miss?"

She wheeled around to see Aldwin looking at her.

The boy turned red, "Sorry, m'lady, I didn't know it was you."

"That's all right, Aldwin," she said, "I was just having a look around. Is Grady about?"

"He's down at the market, m'lady, waitin' for the new shipment of black iron."

"Perhaps you can help me then," she said. "How long have you been working here?"

"Almost three years, m'lady, ever since the baron rescued me."

"Well, you see," she said, producing the hammer, "I've got this weapon here, but I can't grip it properly. I was wondering if Grady might be able to give it a new handle?"

Aldwin took the hammer and swung it experimentally. "It doesn't need a new handle, m'lady, just a new wrapping. I can do that for you."

She stared at him, trying to detect if he was serious. "If you would be so kind," she said. "How long would it take? Should I pick it up in a few days?"

"It should only take a few moments, if you're willing to wait?" he offered. "Why don't you have a seat, and I'll start on it right away?"

Beverly looked around, but couldn't find a place to sit.

Aldwin looked up from the hammer and realized her confusion, "Just a moment, m'lady," he said clumsily and disappeared into the back room. A moment later he appeared with a stool. He set it down, wiping the seat with a cloth, "There you go."

"Thank you."

She watched him as he returned to the workbench. He placed the hammer into a vice to hold it and removed the end of the handle. "What are you doing?" she asked.

"I'm removing the cap so I can get to the handle wrap. You can see here, the handle is wood, but the end cap helps balance it and stops the wrapping from coming loose," he explained as he worked. The whole process so enthralled Beverly that she stood up and walked over to get a better view.

Aldwin was careful, taking his time, working deliberately. Once he had the cap removed, he slowly unwound the old leather strips that had formed the grip. These were then tossed aside as he looked about the workshop, laying eyes on some new strips of leather. He retrieved these and experimented with them by partially wrapping them around the handle. After one or two tries, he laid the leather down on the workbench and grabbed a sharp knife, then began cutting the leather into thinner strips.

"How will the leather stay in place?" she asked. "Won't it slip off?"

By now she was right beside him, watching closely.

"I'll use some glue to hold it in place, plus it'll be wrapped carefully and be slightly damp."

"Damp? You're going to make it wet? Why would you do that?"

"That way, when it dries, it will shrink and make a tighter fit."

"That's clever, Aldwin," she observed.

"I saw it happen to Grady once, by accident. I thought it might be useful one day."

He finished cutting the leather and then tried a test fitting. It did the job, so he placed the leather in some water. While it was soaking, he fished out a jar, removing its lid and used a spare piece of leather to start liberally painting the handle with the contents. "We have to make sure the leather's not too wet," he said, and Beverly recognized the determination in his face. He was concentrating on the handle, being careful not to make a mess. "Can you hand me the leather strip?" he said, forgetting who he was talking to.

Beverly dutifully handed him the carefully trimmed leather and he starting wrapping it as tightly as he could. As it got to the end of the handle, he cut off the excess, leaving just enough to go under the end cap.

"There," he said with some pride, "how's that?"

He turned to Beverly, with a smile of success. His whole face lit up, and she realized how proud he was of the job he had done.

She smiled back at him, "That looks amazing, Aldwin. You must have practised that many times to be so good at it."

He turned a bright shade of red, "Actually, I've never done it before," he said, then hastily added, "m'lady."

He cleared his throat nervously, and then looked back to the hammer. "If you find it a little unwieldy, I could add some weight to the end of the handle, then it might balance better for you."

"Could you? That would be perfect," she said, still staring at his face.

"The only thing is, I'll have to wait for the glue to set. If you come back later, we can try some weights to see what you like, then make the changes." He kept his eyes on the hammer the whole time he spoke.

Beverly looked at the hammer held in the vice, then looked back at his face. It was still bright red, and she questioned the reason for his discomfort. Was he embarrassed? She suddenly figured out the cause. It had to be her! She was standing very close to him, could even smell him, so she abruptly stepped back.

"Thank you, Aldwin," she said. "What would be a good time to come back to see you," she paused, "to try the weights, I mean."

"I should think by the time the sun goes down it will be ready."

"Won't you be done work by then?" she asked. "I don't want you working longer because of me."

"It's no bother, m'lady," he said, perhaps a little too quickly. "I'd work anytime for you." As if realizing what he just said, or fearing he might have offended her, he turned an even brighter shade of red.

Beverly decided it was best to ignore his embarrassment. "Very well, Aldwin," she agreed. "I'll see you just after dark."

Wandering out of the smithy, she found she was hungry, so she made her way to the kitchen where everyone was hard at work. The Keep provided the meals for the soldiers and servants, keeping the kitchen in full use from before sun up to well past sundown. She wandered through the kitchen and was mostly ignored by the staff, for she was often a visitor down here, usually to retrieve some food for her father. One of the servants looked up from their work and called out.

"My lady, is there something I can get you?" she asked.

"Just a little peckish, Rose," Beverly replied. "What have you got that's not too much work, I don't want to be a bother."

"I've got some ham that's been roasting, why don't I cut you off a slice or two, and maybe some fresh bread to go with it."

"That would be nice, thank you."

The cook led her over to a small table, off to the side and plated up some food. Moments later she was nibbling away at the food absently, thinking about her encounter with Aldwin. Her mind was having trouble processing things, and her look of confusion must have been evident, for after only a moment, Rose returned.

"Is something wrong, my lady?" she asked. "Is the food all right?"

The servant's enquiry pulled from her musings. "Oh yes, everything's fine Rose. I was just…thinking."

"You be careful now," said Rose, smiling, "you don't want to go thinking too much."

Beverly laughed. "Rose," she asked, "can I ask you a question?"

The older woman wiped her hands on her apron and stood, waiting. "Go ahead then," she prompted.

"I was down in the smithy," Beverly began. "I went down to see Old Grady, but he wasn't there, so I talked to Aldwin instead. He helped me with a war hammer that I have, only he was acting sort of strange."

"Strange? How was he strange?"

"Well, he was reworking the handle, and so I came over to watch and he…"

"He what, my lady?"

"Well, he turned red and got nervous."

"That's to be expected, my lady. He's not used to being around nobility; he's just a smith's apprentice. Plus, I doubt he has many friends. Grady keeps him in the smithy all day long. He sleeps on the floor, you know."

"On the floor? How barbaric."

"My lady, it's common for apprentices to sleep in their shop. It's how they look after things."

Beverly didn't think it was very nice, but decided not to say anything else about it. She finished up her meal and headed back into the Keep with the intent of seeing what her father was doing. Running up to the map room, she found it empty and wondered where he had disappeared to. She asked a servant who told her that the baron was in the stables, which she found strange, as her father liked to ride first thing in the morning. Perhaps something had come up? She resolved to discover what had him in the stables at this time of the day and headed over there immediately. She arrived to find her father cleaning a stall with a pitchfork.

"Father? What are you doing?" she enquired.

Her father turned to face her, resting on the pitchfork. "Ah, Beverly," he said, "I wondered what you were doing. Having fun?"

"Yes Papa, but what are you doing? We have a stable master to do that."

"The stable master's wife has gone into labour," he said, "so I thought I'd lend a hand and do his work for him, to free him up for his wife."

"Shouldn't the stable boys be doing that?" she asked, a little shocked.

"The midwife's got them running errands. Look here," he said, "grab that rake over there and lend a hand."

She picked up the rake, and he showed her how to use it.

"It's humbling," he said, "to do manual labour. Nobles should do it more frequently. It helps us appreciate the work that others do."

She joined her father in raking out the stalls and then gathered buckets to draw water from the well to fill the trough for the horses. "You know, I've been thinking," said the baron. "It's about time we got a proper horse for you. You can't ride a pony forever, now can you? What do you think?"

"Really?" she asked incredulously. "That would be wonderful."

"You'd have to learn to care for it yourself. A horse is more work than a pony.

"I promise I'll do everything," she agreed quickly. "Thank you, Papa."

The baron smiled. "Now," he said, "I think we're about done here. I'll just drop by to see how the stable master's family is doing. Why don't you run along back to the Keep? I'll write to your Uncle Robert tomorrow, and we'll see about getting you a nice horse."

"Aren't there horses here, Papa?" she asked.

"Yes, my dear," he replied, "but your Uncle Robert Brandon raises horses, some of the finest war horses in the kingdom."

Her eyes lit up. A war horse! This was almost too good to be true. It would definitely be worth the wait.

The idea of her very own warhorse kept her busy, and it was with some guilt that she noticed the sun had gone down and she had not returned to the smithy. She rushed down the Keep's stairs, hoping it was not too late and came around the corner to the door to the smithy. Just before she entered, she heard Grady talking.

"You soiled rat," he was saying, "what d'you mean by working for free. All the work done here is paid. You think I can afford to give things away for free?"

"But Master Grady," Aldwin was saying, "it was for Lady Beverly."

"I don't care if it was for the Queen of Merceria herself," he yelled, and then Beverly heard a slap.

She opened the door to see a scene she would never forget. Grady was towering over Aldwin, who lay sprawled on the floor, holding the side of his face. She was shocked. She had heard of people beating others but had never seen it for herself.

"What's going on here?" she demanded.

Old man Grady turned to see her standing in the doorway. "Sorry m'lady," he said, "I was just dealing with an internal matter. It seems the young lad is having a hearing problem. Is there something I can help your ladyship with?" his voice was all syrup, but his face was vinegar.

"I came," said Beverly, thinking quickly, "to find out if the hammer was ready and to arrange payment."

Grady was surprised and glanced down at Aldwin who had crawled away from him. He looked back at Beverly. "Yes m'lady," he said and looked around the room. "Go and get the hammer, Aldwin, there's a good lad."

Aldwin retrieved the hammer, removing it from the vice and carrying it over to the table. Beverly looked at him, but he would not meet her gaze. The side of his face looked red and slightly swollen.

"How much do I owe you?" Beverly asked.

Grady looked over the hammer as it sat on the table. "Well, I've wrapped the handle carefully, as you can see, and it's quite a complicated procedure, I can tell you. I've even used some glue?" this he asked out loud, without thinking about it as he glanced again at Aldwin for confirmation. "It'll be about fifteen shillings, m'lady."

"Thank you, master smith," she said. "I trust I can pay later?"

"Of course m'lady," he said. "You can bring the payment any time you like. Or I can add it to your father's accounts if you wish?"

"No, I insist on paying my own debts," she said, for she had a sneaking suspicion that the bill to her father would grow more expensive. "I'll bring it by tomorrow, if that's acceptable?"

"Certainly m'lady," he said as he picked up the hammer and handed it to her.

She looked over the weapon carefully, noticing the fine work that Aldwin had done. She still wanted to balance it but didn't want to get

Aldwin into any more trouble, so she swung it back and forth a few times in the air, then nodded at Grady and left.

That evening, Beverly waited for her father's return. As he stepped through the doorway to the great hall, she charged up to him impatiently, interrupting his conversation with Gerald. "Father," she blurted, "I have to talk to you immediately!"

The baron, stunned by the explosion of emotions, stopped talking in the middle of his sentence, staring back at her, then composed himself. "My dear, what is it that has you so vexed?"

"It's Aldwin," she blurted out, "the smith is beating him!"

"Calm down," he soothed, "and tell me what happened."

"I went down to collect my warhammer, as I was having the grip re-done and Old Man Grady hit Aldwin! His face was all red on one side."

"It's the right of the smith to discipline his apprentice, my dear."

"You don't understand, Father. He took the credit for Aldwin's work, and when I offered to pay-"

"You what?"

There was a moment of silence before Beverly replied. "I offered to pay. He said it would be fifteen shillings."

The baron looked at his Sergeant-at-Arms, and Beverly sensed a moment of understanding between them.

"What is it, Father, I don't understand?"

It was Gerald who answered. "The smith serves the baron, Beverly. He shouldn't be charging the baron anything. After all, it was the baron that had the smithy built."

"Yes," the baron agreed, "and by extension, that includes you. The scoundrel must have decided he could make some quick coin. Probably thought you wouldn't say anything."

"Should I take care of it, my lord?" offered Gerald.

"No, Gerald, I'll see to this myself."

"What should I do, Father?" asked Beverly.

"You wait here, my dear. I'll go have a chat with the smith about his duties," he paused, looking at his daughter, "and his treatment of his apprentice." He left the room without another word.

"Your father's upset," remarked Gerald.

"Without a doubt. What do you think he'll do?" asked Beverly.

"He'll take care of it, he always does. Your father likes to tackle problems head-on. I wouldn't like to be in Old Man Grady's shoes."

The next day when she tried to deliver the coins to Grady, the old man said little, refusing the offer. She couldn't help but notice swelling around his eye, and though she decided not to mention it, she resolved to keep a closer watch on the smith from this point forward. Later, when Grady left for the night, she returned to the smithy to check in on Aldwin.

He was making some sketches and looked up as she approached. "M'lady," he said, a smile crossing his face, "is there something I can do for you?"

She was unsure how to broach the subject and struggled to find her words. "I was just...How are things, Aldwin? I understand my father visited here earlier."

"Yes, he had words with Master Grady."

"Is everything all right?" she asked, concern creasing her brow.

"Everything's fine," he responded. "My master has suddenly developed a concern for my well-being."

"My father can be a very persuasive man."

"So it seems," he agreed. "Is there something I can do for you m'lady?"

"Not really, Aldwin," she said, glancing around the room. "Tell me, what is it you're doing?"

"I've been making some sketches," he said. "I've been examining some of the armour worn by the knights from Wincaster."

She looked down at his sketches, the charcoal image was very lifelike, and she marvelled at his skill. "That's incredible," she gushed, then tried to compose herself. "I mean, you show remarkable skill."

"One day, I'm going to make armour like this," he said, "and become the finest armourer in the kingdom."

He began explaining the details of his sketches, and she soon lost herself in his voice.

She was glad things had improved for him, and remembering what the cook had explained, she resolved to visit more often to keep an eye on him. After all, one day she would need her own smith if she was going to be a knight.

In the end, it was quite late when she returned to the Keep. Her father, sitting in the great hall, watched her enter.

"Where have you been, Beverly?" he queried politely. "I've missed you."

"Oh, I was down in the smithy, Father," she said, "getting my hammer balanced."

"Really? How interesting, let's have a look then." He waited for her to hand it over.

She reluctantly gave it to him, "Well," she admitted sheepishly, "we never actually got around to playing with the weights."

NINE

Lightning

AUTUMN 945 MC

Summer made its way to autumn, with the weather turning into the cooler days that typically precede the coming of snow. Beverly, who once she made up her mind about something carried through, found her days to be busy. She had work to do in the stables every morning, weapons practise every afternoon and visited Aldwin almost every evening. At these visits, she noticed that Aldwin was growing at an alarming rate, so she started bringing him food. Her father had suspected the lad would be a large man when he finished growing, the makings of an excellent smith. The evidence appeared to support it, for word of his work had spread, and now the smithy found more warriors coming to have the grips replaced on their weapons. Old Man Grady was pleased with the influx of new customers, and began to give Aldwin more responsibility and training. He was not yet ready to pound steel, but he pumped the bellows while Grady hammered and even helped with finishing the tangs of weapons that Grady had forged.

On one of the last warm days of autumn, she was in the practise yard with her new shield. Gerald had found her a light shield, suited to her size and she was trying to become familiar with holding it as a counterweight to her weapon. Her skill with a sword had grown, but she tended to favour the hammer. She wasn't sure if it suited her better, or if she was just more attached to it. Voicing her desire to learn everything, Gerald had demonstrated how to use axes, maces, various clubs, and even some polearms. No weapon, no matter how rare or difficult to use, escaped her eagerness, and she began to amass quite a collection of proficiencies. The only weapon that was beyond her present abilities happened to be the great sword, but she was convinced that was only due to her small stature. Although she was still quite young, she had already developed muscles from her constant training and felt that it would not be too long before she could add it to her arsenal. She was sure she was stronger than anyone else her age, with the possible exception of Aldwin, of course.

Gerald arrived at the training yard to find her standing with shield and sword, ready. "We're going to do something a little different today," he announced.

Her interest was piqued. "A new weapon?" she hoped.

"No, a new way of fighting."

"I'm not sure I follow."

"Come with me, and I'll show you," he said mysteriously, leading her through the gate into the village. There, she saw two riders, her father and her Uncle Robert, the Baron of Hawksburg.

"Is she ready?" Fitz asked Gerald.

"As ready as she'll ever be, my lord," he replied.

"Well, bring her over then."

As Beverly walked towards the two of them, they shifted their mounts to reveal a stunning black stallion. The creature was massive, one of the famed Mercerian Chargers that her Uncle Robert was renowned for breeding. The creature was beautiful, she thought, with a glossy black shine to its coat, and a long mane and tail. She walked over to the beast and put her hand on its muzzle, feeling the creature nuzzle her hand back.

"Nice, isn't he?" offered her uncle. "His name's Lightning. He's yours, happy birthday."

She looked at him in wonderment. "But my birthday isn't for a couple of months."

"Well, yes, that's true, but I have to be back in Hawksburg before winter sets in, so I didn't think you'd mind. Give him a try."

The horse was already saddled, and she recognized it as a fighting rig similar to her father's. She stepped into Gerald's cupped hands and hauled herself up into the saddle, in one smooth motion. Lightning didn't budge, standing calmly as she reached forward to pat him on the neck.

"Grab a mount and meet us outside the gate, Gerald," the baron directed. "I believe my daughter would like to stretch her horse's legs."

The three of them trotted through the village, and by the time they reached the outer gate, Gerald had caught up with them. Beverly was enjoying the smoothness of the ride, and how much easier it was for her to sit tall in the saddle when she realized that the saddle had been made specifically for her! Her father had been planning this gift for some time to have a saddle custom fit for both her and Lightning. She surveyed her surroundings and observed how very high up she was, for her new horse was a good deal taller than most of the mounts around Bodden, taller, in fact than even her father's own warhorse. They cantered out into the pastureland, then Beverly, letting Lightning have his head, sprang into a gallop, and she felt the exhilaration of flying through the air at a tremendous speed. The horse was well named, for he was full of energy. She charged across the field, and then made a gradual turn to loop back. Returning to her father, she slowed to a trot, but Lightning didn't even appear winded.

Lord Robert smiled and looked at her, "He seems to like you Beverly, make sure you treat him well."

"I will," she promised. "Thank you so much, Uncle."

Spending most of her waking hours tending to Lightning, she ensured she was the one to feed him at mealtimes and mucked out his stall herself. She worked with the stable master to finish off his training. The horse was already suitable for riding but did not yet know her commands. Being only ten, she found he was difficult to mount, so they trained him to kneel with his front legs allowing her to grab his mane gently and pull herself up. It didn't take long for her to discover she loved riding a horse much more than a pony, and it soon became a difficult task to find someone to ride with. If she had things her way, she would ride all day long.

Lightning was as adept at learning new skills as she was. Over the past weeks, she had trained him to respond to her commands, while in the practise field she mastered all the basic techniques that Gerald could teach her. In an effort to keep her engaged in training, he introduced her to fighting on horseback. The manoeuvres were much more challenging, but to her delight, she never fell from the saddle. Mercerians had invented the stirrups many years ago, and she learned to employ them to her advantage while leaning into a turn, or setting herself up for a charge with a spear.

Her father, a master horseman, taught her to control Lightning with only her legs, freeing up her hands to use weapon and shield. He told her the neighbouring Kingdom of Westland had also adopted stirrups and held tournaments where warriors tried to unhorse each other for entertainment. Beverly found that hard to believe, for practise was one thing, but fighting for pleasure was barbaric.

. . .

It had become the custom in Merceria for knights to take on an apprentice, a squire. The squire would perform the menial duties of looking after the horse, cleaning the weapons and such, and in return, they would receive training in the knightly ways. Beverly thought this custom was strange, for it encouraged laziness in the knights. Bodden, of course, had an assortment of knights, and many of them had squires who were commanded to look after their mentor's horse.

On a cold day, late in the year, with winter threatening to envelop the land soon, Beverly was just finishing cleaning out Lightning's stable while the creature nibbled on a bale of hay. She heard voices in the next stall, and not being able to stop herself, she crept up to the wooden wall between them and listened.

"Have you seen Lady Beverly with her horse? It's so pathetic," said a voice she identified as Reginald Somersby, squire to Sir Augustine. "She dotes on the beast like it's her long lost lover. I'll never understand why they persist in giving her hope that she could become a knight. The whole idea is simply ridiculous."

"I don't know why she's constantly training her horse either," said a second, unrecognizable voice. "What else can you train a horse to do?"

"Agreed," Reginald said, "the creature will probably get killed in the first battle anyway, and then all the training will go to waste." They both laughed at this while Beverly's face reddened with anger.

She made a show of finishing up the work in the stall, deliberately creating noise to get their attention. She hung the rake back on the wall and began saddling up Lightning. I'll teach them to mock me, she thought, I'll show them what a true warhorse can do. She finished with Lightning, and then walked out of the stall, leaving him inside for the moment. The two squires, their conversation interrupted, looked on, trying to gather what she was doing.

Beverly strode to the other side of the stables, picked up a shield and drew her sword. She then began going through the practise exercises that she had been drilling for the past six months; pivot, thrust, block, all the while subconsciously using the footwork she had learned.

The two squires looked at each other, completely confused by her actions. They moved through the stall's door, the better to see the crazy redhead who was apparently out of her mind.

When she knew she had their undivided attention, she let out a loud whistle, and the squires were pushed aside by Lightning, who burst out of his stall and came thundering towards her. The horse skidded to a stop, turned and knelt, while she completed a swing with her sword and then suddenly leaped into the saddle.

The squires stood, open-mouthed with amazement. Using only her legs to command her mount, she left the now silenced squires dumbstruck in the stables behind her. The bond between her and her steed was so complete that Lightning knew instinctively what she wanted.

TEN

Sir Harold

SUMMER 950 MC

～

The summer of '50 was milder than most, and the farmers despaired, for they expected a bad harvest. Beverly continued with her training, but it was becoming apparent that there was not much left that anyone at Bodden could teach her. Her proficiency with melee weapons had grown immensely, and there was little in the way of fighting skills that she hadn't learned. It was now a matter of her growing, for she was still not the tall, towering knight that she yearned to be. She diligently carried out her drills, and Gerald patiently watched her, but found little to critique. He could still beat her in a fight, as she was excellent at blocking but lacked the necessary physical strength to prevent him from knocking her back. This would come in time, of course, but she was growing impatient.

No one questioned her equestrian skills, and even the stable master frequently came to her for help with new mounts. Since that day long ago in the stable with the two squires, she had earned the grudging respect of all the knights. She was brushing down Lightning when an old man rode into the courtyard wearing an out-dated style of armour, seated upon a large horse, similar to her own. She watched him as he dismounted, noticing his weathered face and the ragged state of his clothing, and yet there was a sense of danger about him. Unexpectedly, her father came out of the Keep, walked up to the stranger and shook his hand. Much to her surprise, they came towards the stable, her father breaking into a smile when he caught sight of her.

"Ah, there you are, my dear. Allow me to introduce, Sir Harold of Stilldale."

Beverly immediately recognized his name! Everyone in Merceria knew of him, for Sir Harold was a hero, renowned for his actions at the siege of Colbridge many years ago when Westland had attempted to take the city. Since then, he'd had a long and glorious career that spanned decades. He was looked upon by many as the gold standard of knights. She was overcome by awe and could only stammer out a few words.

"I thought you were dead," she said, and then blushed furiously. She felt so stupid. Meeting a hero of the realm, only to make such an inane comment.

"I'm sure you're not the only one," the man smiled. "You must be Lady Beverly Fitzwilliam of Bodden." He bowed deeply, in the old style, extending his right leg as he did so. It would look ludicrous for a knight to do so in court these days, and yet on Sir Harold, it looked elegant and refined, an echo of days long passed.

"Pleased to meet you," she recovered. "Might I enquire as to why you're visiting us? We don't get many guests in Bodden."

"Sir Harold," explained the baron, "is here to see you."

Beverly was shocked, "Me?"

"Yes, your father wrote to me. Apparently, he can teach you little more, and so I volunteered to come and train you myself."

"You're going to train me?" She was incredulous.

"Yes, if that's all right with you?"

She curtsied, trying to be as elegant as he, "I would be honoured."

"Very well," Sir Harold responded. "Allow me to get settled in and we'll make a start. Have you a regular training schedule?"

"Yes, I'm due to practise melee after lunch."

"Lunch. What an excellent idea. Baron, would you be so kind as to lead the way?"

They headed off to the dining room, with Beverly left behind to ponder this new development. Sir Harold's legacy was inspiring! She realized that her father had gone to extraordinary lengths to arrange this training. She was, she felt, the luckiest girl in the whole kingdom.

With the arrival of Sir Harold, the training ramped up considerably, and Beverly found herself struggling to keep pace. Just as she came to grips with one thing, another would be introduced. Her knowledge and skill set grew by leaps and bounds. He pushed her hard, and each evening she would trundle down to the smithy to see Aldwin, her muscles aching from the day's strain.

She was now fifteen and had grown both taller and broader. Her muscles had hardened considerably, allowing her to handle any weapon with ease, including the great sword, though its massive size still gave her a bit of trouble. Even Lightning no longer kneeled when she mounted, and she leaped into the saddle effortlessly.

Sir Harold was taking her training seriously, had her riding her horse, swinging at targets with a mace, all the while he was watching carefully, quick to notice any errors. Lean back, lean forward, shift weight, it was an endless list of corrections, but Beverly learned and soon the movements became second nature.

She had just completed a run and trotted down the line, preparing to repeat the procedure, when Sir Harold called her over. She rode up, halting in front of him.

He looked up at her and then struck a thoughtful pose, his hand stroking his beard absently. "Come down here," he requested, and she dismounted in a fluid motion.

"Stand there a moment," he pointed while walking around her. Making a complete circuit, he paused in front of her. "We need to get you some real armour, not this padded stuff." He felt her arm muscle, "I think you're ready for it, let's see about getting you fitted. Do you have an armourer here that can make chain?"

"Yes," she responded, "the smith's apprentice has been making chain for months."

"Well, then it's time we go see this apprentice."

They dropped Lightning off at the stables, making their way to the smithy. Entering, Beverly noticed the sudden change of temperature, for though the day was mild, it was like an oven in there.

Old Man Grady was pulling a sword out of the forge and hammering away at it, occasionally quenching it in a pool of liquid. Aldwin came over to the workbench when he saw them enter. This was now the normal routine since Grady did not like dealing with people.

"M'lady," he greeted them, "my lord. How may I be of assistance?"

It was Sir Harold that spoke up first, "The Lady Beverly is in need of a chainmail coat. Can you make such an item?"

Aldwin was, perhaps, a little too eager and immediately blurted out, "Yes, of course, my lord."

"Then you must start taking measurements right away, these things take time."

"Yes, my lord."

Sir Harold turned to Beverly, "Take that leather jacket off Beverly, he'll need to measure you for the chainmail."

Beverly turned bright red, her eyes opening wide. They had just left the practise field, and she was covered in sweat. All she had beneath her jacket was a light linen shirt. She looked at Sir Harold, hoping he would see her embarrassment, but evidently, he failed to grasp the issue.

"I would suggest that the light might be better over there," the knight said, pointing to a window. "I'll drop by later to see how you're doing." He strode off, leaving Beverly with Aldwin, who was getting a strip of leather to take her measurements. She drew a deep breath, then undid the jerkin, peeling it away from her skin, as the sweat had made it stick. She felt a slight breeze on her damp shirt, making her shiver. Aldwin returned and prepared to measure her shoulders and chest, then stopped. She could feel his eyes on her, and a little quiver ran through her body. He immediately looked at her face and cleared his throat.

"I'll have to measure your shoulders first, m'lady," he said.

He walked around behind her, and then she felt the soft touch of his hands on her shoulders. He ran the strip of leather across her back, and she swore she could feel the warmth of his body near her. She felt flustered. She took a deep breath in, closing her eyes as she released the air. In a moment he was finished, and he walked around in front of her. She opened her eyes to see his grey eyes gazing into hers.

"Are you all right, m'lady?" he asked, in a soft voice.

She cleared her throat, "I'm fine Aldwin, please continue."

He stretched the strip out between his open arms and paused. He had to stretch all the way around her chest to make the measurement. He was embarrassed, she could tell.

"I won't bite, you know," she said, trying to reassure him.

He suddenly reached forward, as if to embrace her and her eyes went wide. His arms passed underneath hers and she realized he was reaching around her back to take the measurement. He pressed his face close to hers, looking behind her, trying to mark the measurement on the strip of leather. She felt the heat of him on her cheek.

He stepped back nervously, and she realized she was trembling. She saw a look of concern cross his face and he appeared to be about to say something, so she quickly interrupted him, "It's a trifle hot in here. Can I just get some air?"

He nodded his agreement, and she ran from the room with a quick, "I'll be just a moment."

The instant she entered the courtyard, she gulped in the fresh air. She was shaking, and for a brief moment she wondered if she had a fever, then the fresh air hit her face, and she sat down on a step. This was silly, she thought, she had known Aldwin for years, there was no reason to feel nervous. After all, he had to take her measurements, you can't just wear any armour. And he had to be able to touch her to take those measurements. She sucked in great gasps of air and steadied herself. She wandered over to the water barrel and splashed her face. It was time to get down to business.

She walked calmly back to the smithy where Aldwin was patiently waiting.

She resumed her previous position, ready to start again.

"You may touch me now," she said, then realized what she had just uttered. "I mean you may take my measurements now," she corrected.

It was an awkward situation and years later she would look back and remember it with fondness, but for now, she found it terrifying, and yet exhilarating at the same time.

Aldwin continued measuring her; arm length, body length and a multitude of other small measurements, that were required. Beverly fought to keep control and began to relax. It was near the end that it became obvious that Aldwin was hesitant about something.

"Is there something wrong?" she asked.

Aldwin looked her straight in the eyes. "I have to measure your..." his voice trailed off.

"My what?" she prompted.

"Your chest, m'lady."

"My chest?"

"Yes, if the armour is too constrictive, it won't be comfortable."

"So what's the problem, go ahead and measure them."

"Um...it's not that simple. I have to allow for...growth."

"Growth? What do you mean growth?"

"Well," he rambled, "how do I put this? You're still young, and you haven't fully...developed yet. I have to allow for future growth."

Her jaw dropped open as she took in the full meaning of his words. She snapped her mouth shut and looked him straight in the eyes. She could almost feel herself being drawn in as she stammered out, "You'll have to improvise, make a best guess."

He drew the leather across her breasts and around her back. Once again he had to lean into her, and she closed her eyes, smelling him as his face brushed against hers. She wanted the moment to last, wanted to hug him and hold him, but she knew that could never be, their class difference prevented it.

Aldwin stepped back, holding the strip of leather in his right hand. "I'm all done, m'lady," he said, in a husky voice.

"Thank you, Aldwin," said Beverly, and she ran from the room in a flood of emotions.

That evening at dinner, she was picking at her food. Sir Harold and her father were there, and they had invited Gerald to join them. Beverly was lost in her thoughts as Sir Harold was regaling them with stories of his past. The room suddenly went quiet, and she looked up to see them all looking at her.

"Beverly?" her father prompted.

"Yes, Papa?" she said, oblivious to what they had been talking about.

"How did it go?" asked the baron.

"How did what go?"

"You went down to the smithy today?" he reminded her.

She blushed, "How did you know about that?"

"Sir Harold told me," he explained.

"How did..." she blushed again.

"He said you went to get your armour fitted. I was wondering how it went? What are you talking about?"

"Oh, nothing, Father. I was lost on another subject."

"Well," persisted the baron, "did Grady set you up?"

"No," she replied, "it was Aldwin who took my measurements. He'll be making the mail."

Baron Fitzwilliam looked at Gerald, and then back at Beverly. "I think it's time we had a little talk, Beverly."

"Father!" she was shocked. "Here, in front of guests?"

"No, not that talk, for goodness sake. I told you about that years ago. No, I'm talking about the armourer talk."

"The armourer talk?"

"Yes, my dear, you see when someone makes you armour, they have to measure, well, everything. There has to be a level of trust between the armourer and the warrior. Now for most of us, it's not a big deal, but, well, you're a young woman, and the problem is that Aldwin is a young man."

"Yes, I know that, Father."

"Er, well, there's likely to be some, close measurements taken. That sort of thing can be, well, uncomfortable. You mustn't confuse that for feelings. After all, Aldwin is a commoner, and you are a noble. It wouldn't do to have-"

"I know what's right, Father," she interrupted. "Aldwin is a friend, nothing more. Naturally, he has to be...intimate to take my measurements, but that's normal under the circumstances. I don't have feelings for Aldwin. He's my armourer, that's all."

Her father nodded his head wisely, "Very well, I think we've said all that's needed on this subject."

Beverly smiled and nodded but felt guilty. She hadn't been entirely honest with him or with herself, for that matter.

Sir Harold's training continued throughout the summer, and by late autumn Aldwin had completed her chainmail shirt. It required a few adjustments, but the fit was as close to perfect as was practical, under the circumstances. Beneath the chainmail, she wore a padded shirt that was made by the local seamstress. Beverly found it too constricting and insisted on cutting away the material under the arms to allow for freer movement. Sir Harold gave some suggestions which Aldwin duly made a note of, for future reference.

Beverly insisted that any damage to her mail be fixed immediately, so after every practise she would make her way down to the smithy, where Aldwin would pour over the armour looking for rents, dents or cuts. It became a ritual, and the day her practise was cancelled due to Sir Harold feeling ill, she was disappointed. She meandered about the Keep like a lost puppy, out of sorts. She finally resolved to go to the smithy to see Aldwin anyway, perhaps the poor lad was starving, as Old man Grady was notoriously cheap when it came to feeding his apprentice.

They ended up talking into the wee hours of the night, for Aldwin had decided she should have plate over her mail. He was already learning how to work metal and felt he could make her some leg greaves without too much trouble.

She finally made her way back to the Keep to find servants scurrying around. The fact that it was such a late hour was worrying to her, and she sought out her father in the great hall. He was talking with Gerald in a quiet voice.

He saw her enter the room and turned to face her. "I'm sorry, my dear, but I have some bad news," he said. "I'm afraid Sir Harold has passed away in his sleep. He was very old."

She looked at her father, feeling tears come to her eyes. "It's all right, Father It was always his wish to die peacefully in bed."

"Beverly," he said, "I know this might not be the best time to bring this up, but Sir Harold believed that your training was complete. Yesterday, he suggested that you were ready to assume the duties of a warrior, that the best way to continue your training would be to accompany Gerald on patrols. "

"Truly, Father?"

"I believe you're ready to take up arms to protect the people of Bodden. Are you prepared to assume that mantle?"

"I am, Father," she vowed solemnly, "I most definitely am."

ELEVEN

First Blood

SUMMER 950 MC

The burial ceremony for Sir Harold was a solemn occasion held in the Bodden Chapel. Holy Father Baldrim had a great many words of praise for the fallen hero, before the body was ready to be lain to rest. Beverly, along with her father, Gerald, and three other knights, bore the casket to the place of internment, slowly walking by all the soldiers of the garrison who stood to attention. It was proclaimed a day of mourning, with festivities limited to celebrations in honour of the great knight.

Beverly felt abandoned. In his short time at Bodden, Sir Harold had taught her so much, things that she didn't even think about until he mentioned them. She had always thought of knights as heroic warriors, defending the helpless, protecting the weak, sacrificing themselves nobly. He taught her that no victory was complete without survival. Yes, a knight must sometimes sacrifice himself, but only if there was no other choice. There was no such thing as a fight of honour, for there was no honour in killing.

These words she took to heart, and she observed the other knights carefully from that day forth. She knew her father hated killing, knew he would do all in his power to prevent a fight, but sometimes there was no choice. This she understood. Other knights lived for combat, loved to engage the enemy and prove their mettle. These knights often overextended themselves or left many dead on the battlefield.

She sought out books on the subject, but authors were seldom knights, and the virtues they extolled bore little resemblance to the real world. From her research, Beverly came to understand there were two types of knights. First, were the noble knights, the knights of legend. These knights were idolized by the population, but were forced to live to an impossible standard. Noble knights were perfect, could do no wrong, were glorious in battle and humble in defeat. The second kind of knight was what the kingdom had now, spoiled rich sons with expensive armour and servants who looked after their horses and cleaned their weapons. Drinking and whoring were their pastimes, while they lorded their status above all they could. They would often take what they wanted, making them unpleasant to be around. With a thirst for blood, they were uncontrollable on the battlefield, rarely following orders in their quest for personal glory, only stopping when there was no one left to slaughter.

For years, Beverly had made excuses for the behaviour of the Bodden knights. She thought they were sent here to learn to be real knights, for her father followed the old code. She saw how being at Bodden moulded them, made them more like the knights of lore, the kind of knight she aspired to be, but all that had changed with the death of Sir Harold. Beverly now saw the knights as they truly were, pale imitations of the great knights of yesteryear, with only their own interests at heart. What she learned crushed her, but she was determined to be a noble knight, to follow the code of old.

She finally had a chance to observe the knights in action when she was asked to join a patrol. The patrol of horsemen Gerald was leading was comprised solely of knights. He called Beverly to his side, and they rode out of the Keep, followed by four pairs of knights. The day was warm, even though it was still relatively early. It was common to ride without a helmet. The better to hear the surroundings and so each rider dangled their helmet from their saddle, ready should they need it. The breeze was fresh on her face, and her hair tried desperately to escape the braids that ran down her back.

She looked over to Gerald, who was scanning the horizon. "I'm surprised we didn't head out earlier. We could have been miles away by now."

He glanced over at her and frowned. "You haven't been on patrols with knights before," he scowled, looking back over his shoulder. The patrol was already scattered in a long line behind them, having lost their tight grouping. "They're why we're starting late. If the enemy ever decided to march past the Keep in the morning, this lot would be too lazy to attack." The disgust in his voice was quite evident.

She decided she would not let his mood dampen her spirit. This was her first patrol, she intended to make the most of it.

"How's the armour doing?" asked Gerald, changing the subject.

"It's not bad," she admitted, "but I have to get Aldwin to make a few more adjustments, it pinches here and there."

"I suppose that's to be expected," Gerald said. "No one around here's ever made armour for a woman before. You're lucky Aldwin was able to craft it."

"Yes, thank Saxnor for Aldwin," she blushed slightly, looking away to hide her embarrassment. "I think he's learning as much as I am. Does it always feel so heavy?"

"You get used to it once you've worn it for a while. Let me tell you though, the weight feels like nothing once it's saved your skin. After you've been in battle, you'll learn to appreciate it. You almost feel naked going without it." He was staring straight ahead as he spoke, and then suddenly looked at her, "Sorry," he said hurriedly, "I didn't mean that, Lady Beverly. I just meant you get used to it."

Beverly was amused by his embarrassment, for he wasn't used to having a girl on patrol with him.

They rode west, past the copse of trees where Gerald had slain the band of raiders all those years ago and turned northwest. He showed her where they had rescued Aldwin and then they turned north. The plan was to make a circuit of the barony. They would keep turning every so often, and then eventually they would be able to turn south and return to the Keep.

They topped a rise and Gerald halted. He pointed northward and leaned closer to Beverly. "Do you see that?" he said.

"Yes," she replied. "Smoke just beyond that hill?"

"Yes, it could just be hunters, but I'll wager it's a group of raiders stopping to eat." He looked at her. "What would you do?"

She took in the surrounding countryside. "I'd take the men to the south end of that ridge. We'd be able to attack downhill and then drive them northward."

He nodded in appreciation. "Very good, you've learned well. When we attack, assuming they're raiders, of course, remember to stay close. Each pair of soldiers has to watch their partner's backs, got it?"

"Yes, Sergeant," she said, donning her helmet.

They trotted forward, the knights finally closing up their formation. They rode across the shallow depression, angling to climb up the south side of the rise. Just before making the ridge-line, Gerald stopped the troop and dismounted. Beverly followed suit, and the two half-crawled up to the top of the hill to look down. Below them, there must have been almost two dozen raiders moving about their camp

"What do you make of it?" asked Gerald.

She scanned the camp a second time, making a note of the details. "I see the horses picketed to the west. They've set up a firepit, and they look like they've just started roasting a deer." She glanced around some more, "I don't think they've set a watch at all."

"Norland raiders are mostly just brigands and thieves looking to make quick coins, not trained warriors. These are not the same lot that sieged Bodden years ago, just opportunists."

"What's the plan?" she asked, starting to feel nervous.

"We'll continue with your plan. We'll form up at the ridge-line and push them north. If they go for their horses, so much the better, but don't let them form up, we have to keep them running."

She nodded her assent, and they returned to their mounts. Gerald ordered the knights to form a line, and then they topped the hill. It must have been quite the sight, a line of glittering armour suddenly appearing on the ridge.

Gerald gave the command, and the horses began walking down the hill, keeping their line intact. Beverly watched as one of the raiders noticed their approach and yelled a warning. Suddenly the place looked like an anthill with men running everywhere.

A shout erupted from the end of the line as one of the knights unexpectedly spurred forward. She heard Gerald curse under his breath, and then it was as if the gates to the Underworld had opened. The knights broke their ranks, streaming down the hill at full charge. She witnessed Sir Leyland's horse break its leg as it hit a rabbit hole, tumbling them both to the ground, with the knight crushed beneath his mount's body. Sir Malcolm was holding his sword up high, yelling, then without warning, she caught sight of a crossbow bolt protruding from the back of his neck.

"What do we do now?" she yelled above the noise.

"No hope for it now, we must join the charge," Gerald responded.

They urged their horses forward, Beverly having to keep Lightning in check to match Gerald's pace. Bolts were whizzing past as the defenders starting organizing themselves. Gerald steered them slightly westward to cut off a group that was sprinting for their horses. He drove his horse onward, and Beverly relaxed her restraint on Lightning's reins, giving him his head, and then she surged ahead to match the sergeant's burst of speed.

A group of men had formed up in front of them, trying to set their shields to receive the impending charge. Gerald rode up first, and turned, slicing down with a vicious cut from his sword. At the same moment, Beverly pulled back on her reins, commanding Lightning to rear up and kick with his massive front hooves, sending two shielded men to the ground with the force. Her mount dropped back down, and she urged him forward, swinging her sword. It jarred as it struck the metal of a shield, and the bull of a man behind it grabbed her arm, trying to yank her from her saddle. Releasing the weapon, she pulled her arm back abruptly, breaking her foe's hold upon it. He retaliated by stabbing at her with a short sword, and she felt the blade graze her mail covered thigh. Reaching to the side of her saddle, she grabbed the hammer that hung there, swinging out with a backhand blow that landed squarely on the side of his head, barely landing her strike before the brute stabbed at her again. An explosion of blood signalled the crushing of the raider's skull, just before he fell to the ground, lifeless.

She gripped her horse with her legs and urged him forward, but she was quickly surrounded by raiders. She used her shield to block a stab from the left, then turned in the saddle and sent her hammer crashing down onto a man's head with an overhead swing. She felt the helmet crush under the impact, but had no time to reflect upon it. Twisting back to the right, she brought the hammer over Lightning's head with a lateral swing, but the intended victim ducked, thinking himself safe. The look of surprise on his face as she looped the hammer over her head and brought it crashing down on his head was priceless.

She felt strangely calm and realized, in an almost detached manner, that her body was doing the work. So hard had she trained all these years that the movements came without thinking; a shield bash to the one on the left, a kick with her right foot as someone tried to grab her leg. She felt a slight stab in the left leg, and her leg was suddenly wet with blood, but there was no pain. It was almost as if the entire fight was in slow motion. She struck to the right again, but no one was there. The raiders were running away, but she was so charged up with adrenaline that she almost ran after them, and then her sense of duty held her back.

Scanning the battlefield, she spied Gerald fighting with a mounted raider, watching as he drove his sword through the man's stomach. She witnessed his victim fall to the ground, before spurring her horse over to the sergeant.

"Let them go," he was yelling, "they're broken."

Beverly observed the raiders running in every direction to escape the carnage. One foolish knight didn't want to end the bloodshed and charged blindly after a group. They turned on him with a fury, impaling his horse with a spear. The doomed knight was thrown from his saddle, swarmed by men with axes and swords who hacked away at him. It was a grisly sight, reminding Beverly that this was war.

It didn't take long for the surviving enemies to flee, leaving the troop from Bodden alone, save for the dead and dying warriors strewn about the battlefield.

Beverly saw how the death and destruction affected Gerald, by the grim look he wore. She stared at the dead bodies, the wounded that were bleeding to death with no hope of recovery, the lifeless knights and raiders. This was grim, she realized, not splendid or honourable.

Sir Bentley rode over and flipped up his visor. "Is it not a glorious victory, Sergeant?"

Gerald removed his helmet slowly, glowering at the knight. Beverly noticed he was clenching his jaw, and knew he was about to explode.

"Glorious?" he said, maintaining a calm exterior. "What's so glorious about it Sir Bentley?"

"Why, we have defeated the enemy, covered ourselves in glory! I got two, myself," the man said, obviously pleased with his performance.

"Call the men in," Gerald said, a defeated sound to his voice. "We've got work to do."

Sir Bentley looked surprised, "Work?"

"These men won't bury themselves, and we don't want to encourage wolves," he said. "We need to take a tally. How many did we lose?"

"Three, I think," said Beverly, "I saw Sir Leyland pitched from his horse and Sir Malcolm took a bolt to the neck. Someone else charged forward and was taken down, but I couldn't see who it was."

Gerald regarded her in surprise at how much she had managed to take in, while engaged in her own combat. "I saw you fighting today, you did a good job," he commented. "Now, let's get to work."

They had been scant words, but the simple statement delighted Beverly. She had done a good job, that's all anyone could ask.

They stood for a moment longer and then Gerald turned, holding out his hand to stop her when she started to walk away. "Are you wounded?" he asked.

She looked down to see blood on her left leg and remembered the fight. She knelt down to get a better look. She had received a vicious slash on her leg which had bruised the skin and broken some links in her mail. The chain had saved her leg, for only the surface of the skin was cut, but several broken links dug into the wound. "It's nothing, just a surface wound," she said, and then called over Lightning. The great horse obeyed instantly, coming over and nuzzling up to her. She reached into her saddlebag, pulling out a handkerchief, and then pulled the mail from her wound before using the handkerchief as a bandage to cover it up.

Gerald inspected her handiwork before letting her continue. "Best be careful, lest it starts bleeding again," he said. "We'll get someone to look at it as soon as we're back. In future, if you get wounded, you must tell someone, understand?"

"Yes, Sergeant," she replied.

Now they had to carry out the most distasteful part of the battle, seeing to the wounded. Without healers, there was little hope for the more seriously wounded. She knew of just one healer in the kingdom, and he only worked for the king. Little else could be done for most of the wounds, and those that were suffering had to be put out of their misery. No prisoners were taken for the remaining walking wounded were given some food, had their weapons removed, and then were told to head north, back to their own land.

It was almost nightfall by the time the dead were buried. Gerald was standing over the graves, lost in thought when Beverly approached him.

He turned to her, "There's only one thing worse than a battle lost," he said, "and that's a battle won."

She nodded her agreement and stood silently.

"How would you rate the battle today?" he asked, unexpectedly.

She thought carefully about it before answering. "It was a victory, but a shallow one," she said at last.

"Why?" he prompted.

"We lost three men against fourteen of the enemy. If we continue to lose people at this rate, we'll run out of knights."

"Exactly," Gerald replied. "What do you think went wrong?"

"That's easy," she replied passionately, then thought better of it, and made her voice sound more neutral. "The knights disobeyed orders and bungled the attack. If we'd stayed in formation, we wouldn't have lost anyone."

"Well," mused Gerald, "we might still have lost some, but chances are we'd be in better shape."

"So what do we do about it?" Beverly asked.

"Do? We don't do anything. You can't control knights, Beverly, it's just the way they are. We report to the baron and tell him what happened, that's all we can do."

The trip back to Bodden was not long, but by the time the Keep was in sight, her leg was painfully throbbing. It wasn't the cut so much, but the bruising had swollen her leg, and now the chainmail was starting to cut off the circulation.

She tried to ignore the pain while she saw to her horse, then made her way to the smithy.

Aldwin was pounding away on a shin guard when she entered, glancing up to see her stagger to a chair, her composure finally failing.

"What's wrong, m'lady?" he said as he ran over with a look of concern on his face.

She grimaced, pointing to her leg. He ran back to the workbench, returning with a pair of tongs and began gingerly prying apart the metal links.

"We have to get you out of these leggings," he said, removing her armour.

She was in too much pain to complain, and soon her bare leg was exposed as Aldwin held it, examining the wound.

"It's all right, there's no metal left in the wound," he pronounced.

"Thank you, Aldwin," she said, the pain finally subsiding. With a tingle in her thigh, the blood flow resumed, and she took a deep breath, relaxing as she leaned back in the chair, her leg still held by Aldwin. The tender touch of his hands as he redressed her wounds made her feel so safe and comfortable, she closed her eyes. Awakening with a start, she gathered that she must have fallen asleep, for she was being gently shaken.

"M'lady?" Aldwin sounded alarmed. "Are you all right?"

"Yes," she said, opening her eyes to see him standing over her, a look of concern on his face. "I'm fine Aldwin, thank you."

"Stay here while I go and get help, m'lady," Aldwin said, leaving her to return shortly with servants who took her to her room. It had been a long day, but she would recover.

TWELVE

The Smith

SPRING 951 MC

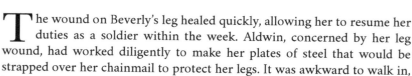

The wound on Beverly's leg healed quickly, allowing her to resume her duties as a soldier within the week. Aldwin, concerned by her leg wound, had worked diligently to make her plates of steel that would be strapped over her chainmail to protect her legs. It was awkward to walk in, but worked well on horseback. By the time she turned sixteen, she was properly outfitted with leg, and arm plates. Aldwin, not yet satisfied she was safe enough, was busy at work making her a solid breastplate.

Aldwin had become a very adept smith, though still serving as Grady's apprentice. He was the go-to person for that excellent sword, or to repair the grip on a battle axe. He had gained the reputation as someone who could fashion the most marvellous armour, but he was always too busy. Only Beverly benefited from his armouring skills, though she never knew she was the only one. He devoted hours to working metal, forging and then reforming bits of armour to get it 'just right'. The first plate he attached to her chainmail had been effective but crude. He had since replaced it with work that was more ornate, having in-laid scrollwork along the edges. Beverly was stunned by the skill that he displayed as he replaced each piece.

She spent all her off-duty hours in the smithy, watching him work. He toiled over the details, and she saw the dedication, the look of enjoyment, as he laboured. He talked worked, and she was fascinated by the increasing knowledge of his craft.

. . .

Insisting that a knight needed to dress themselves, she had asked the smith's apprentice to move the straps forward, so that she might be able to fasten them by herself. It was ungainly at first but slowly, through a process of trial and error, they arrived at a design that worked. Gerald was so impressed by their handiwork, that he recommended it to all the knights, but they wouldn't listen. Why would a knight need to dress himself, that's what servants were for.

Though technically not a knight, she was armed and armoured as one, and she certainly had the skill of one. It was not an unusual occurrence for her to lead a patrol, having earned the respect of the common soldiers through her constant concern over their safety, and her obvious ability in the role. The knights followed her orders, for she was the baron's daughter, but they did not respect her. They saw her as an interloper, someone who threatened their way of life. She heard rumours that they spread about her, but chose to ignore them. She gave up wishing to be a knight, for only the king could knight someone, and that was very unlikely. She strove, instead, to be the best warrior she could, to guard the lives of everyone in Bodden, and keep them safe.

Now a seasoned patrol leader, Beverly took out troops on a regular basis. The knights were left for Gerald to deal with and so Beverly commanded the Bodden Horse, a collection of mounted warriors with field experience. It was on a particularly quiet day in the middle of a warm spell when Beverly led her patrol back through the outer gate to Bodden. They rode through the town, the commoners stopping to wave, as they made their way to the inner courtyard. Sergeant Blackwood was her second-in-command, and when she dismissed the men, he made sure they looked to their own horses, a touch she insisted on. She joined them in the stables, seeing to Lightning herself, listening to the banter. It had become a ritual, after each patrol, to talk about the day's activities while they brushed down the horses. She was accepted by these men, and here, there were no knights to belittle her accomplishments.

After finishing tending to Lightning, she made her way to the smithy. She was looking forward to talking to Aldwin, for the new adjustments to her armour had gone very well. So deep in thought was she, imagining his smile that she almost walked right into the door. She stepped back in amazement. The door to the smithy was closed, but it was never closed! Now this was most strange indeed.

She grasped the iron ring and pulled, but to her dismay, the door would not budge. She rattled the door some more, but it seemed determined not to open. Someone had locked the smithy up, and she suddenly felt dread in her heart.

Intrigued to discover what had happened, she made her way to the map room where, doubtless, her father was dealing with this very problem. As she entered, she saw him speaking with Gerald and Sir Walter, the most senior knight.

"I suppose we'll have to send to Wincaster," the baron was saying.

Gerald saw her enter and nodded his head, causing the baron to look towards the door.

"Ah, Beverly, my dear, good to see you. I'm afraid we've some bad news."

"What is it, Father?" she asked, apprehension in her voice.

"The old smith, Grady, has passed away. He collapsed in the smithy and was dead almost instantly."

"That's terrible," she said, somewhat relieved.

"Well," he continued, "it wasn't exactly a surprise. He was, after all, an old man."

"We were just saying," added Sir Walter, "that we'll need to send to Wincaster for a new smith."

"Aldwin should be the new smith," she burst out. "He's more than capable. I've seen his work."

"I'm afraid, my lady," continued the knight, "that Aldwin is far too young. He can't possibly take on the mantle of a master smith."

"It's true he's young," said Beverly, "but his work is superior. He's by far the best smith in Bodden, and he's been doing most of the work for months."

Her father looked at her with an intense gaze. "And how would you know that?" he asked.

"I've seen him. He's a very hard worker and spends hours every day working at the forge."

"I'm not convinced," said her father, after a brief pause. "He's still quite young, as Sir Walter indicated."

"Go and look at his work, Father," she pleaded. "See the quality for yourself."

"Very well," he said at last, "let us go and examine his work. Gentlemen, if you'll join us?"

They made their way down to the smithy. The baron produced a key ring, handing it to Gerald, who then opened the door. The smithy was empty, and Beverly was shocked by the solitude found within. No forge warmed the room, no glow from hot coals, nor any light streamed in through the windows, which were shuttered.

Gerald opened the shutters to let in some light, while the baron and Sir Walter wandered about the room, viewing the works in progress.

Beverly walked over to a work table. "Over here is where he keeps the items he's working on, look at this," she said, producing a half-finished sword.

The baron lifted the sword carefully and held it to the light. The weapon was not yet complete, but already he saw the fine edge that was being developed.

"And over here," she said, continuing their tour of the room, "is where he finishes the weapons, polishing them and wrapping the handles."

Once again they followed her, Sir Walter lifting a fine dagger to examine it. He nodded in appreciation, then placed it back on the workbench.

"He even works on armour, here's an example of greaves he's been working on, look at the detail."

It was Gerald's turn to look on with appreciation, for the greave was embossed with delicate scrollwork, making it look like a piece of art.

"He's a dedicated worker, Father. I've watched him work for hours on a single blade."

Baron Fitzwilliam regarded his daughter with an intense stare. Suddenly, she realized she had said too much.

"She's right," he said, "Aldwin is perhaps the best smith I've seen in Bodden." He turned to Gerald, "Tell Aldwin that he's the new master smith. Oh, and he'll need a family name."

"Aldwin has no family, Father," Beverly dared to add.

He looked at Sir Walter, "We can't just call him Aldwin, he's not a boy anymore."

"Strong something?" the knight suggested.

"How about Strongarm?" Gerald offered. "He certainly has the muscles."

"Very well, tell Master Aldwin Strongarm that the smithy is his."

Gerald nodded in acknowledgement and left.

Baron Fitzwilliam turned to his senior knight, "Sir Walter," he said, "would you give us the room, please?"

The knight bowed, "Certainly, my lord," and left them.

There was an awkward silence between them, and Beverly suspected what was about to happen.

"Father, I-"

"Don't," he interrupted. "Don't say a thing."

She struggled to say something, but he forestalled her with his hand.

"I know," he said, "that you have feelings for Aldwin. I can hear it in your voice, and I see it in your face."

She couldn't stand it anymore, "Father, I lo-"

She was immediately cut off. "Don't say it," he warned, "or you will tread down a dark path."

Beverly loved her father, but for the first time in her life, she saw the lines that crossed his face. He was getting older, and the strain of being in charge was wearing on him.

"My dear," he continued, "I am sympathetic to your cause, but it simply cannot happen. You and I are nobles, and Aldwin is a commoner."

"I know, Father, but-"

"Let me continue, please. I know this isn't easy. Nobles are as restricted in this society as commoners. Oh, we have the wealth, and the nice clothes, but we are as much prisoners of this life as they are. In some ways, we have less freedom. As a noble, your life is in the hands of the king. In times past a noble would marry for love, and if the king approved, the marriage would go ahead, but these are different times, my dear. I know what it is like to give one's heart to someone else. I was fortunate enough to find your mother, but I fear you will not be so lucky. You are the daughter of the Baron of Bodden. One day I will die, and you must marry. If you are lucky, you will marry someone who you can learn to love, but if not, you must do your duty."

As he looked at her, she noticed the sadness in his eyes. "And I know you think you could run away together," he continued, "but how would that work? You would be hunted down and brought back, that's how. The king would not allow a single noble to destroy a system that has worked for hundreds of years. Even if you did manage to get away, how would you earn a living? No one in Merceria would hire Aldwin, and he would be an outcast. And without a sponsor, you could not even afford to look after your own armour. And what would be the other option? To keep Aldwin on the side? As soon as you marry, your husband would be rid of him, and then you've have taken away his livelihood."

Tears were forming in her eyes, "It's not fair, Father. All I wanted was to be with him, he's my friend."

He walked over to her, and embraced her, while she sobbed in his arms. "I know, my dear, life is cruel, but we must make the most of it."

He held her for a few more moments, then released her, placing her at arm's length, to study her. "See here, now," he said, "you must do right by Aldwin. I know how you feel about him, yet fate would deny your heart. You will still need to visit him for weapons and armour, of course, but from now on you will be supervised at all times when in his presence. Your friendship may continue, but nothing more."

With tears still streaming down her face, she nodded.

"Let me hear you say it, Beverly," he said gently.

"I agree," her voice breaking as she whispered the fateful words.

"Might I ask for one favour, Father?"

He smiled at her, "Of course, my dear."

"May I be the one to tell Aldwin?"

"Of course, but someone must be present, you understand?"

She nodded her assent, too grief-stricken to speak.

"Who would you like to be present?"

"Gerald will do," she said in resignation.

"Excellent choice, my dear. He will keep your secret, so you needn't worry about word getting out. Now, let's go and get you sorted out. You don't want to talk to him looking like you are now, do you?"

She shook her head, and her father led her away from the smithy.

It was sometime later when Beverly returned to the workshop, her escort, Gerald, in tow. She had been present when her father had given instructions to the Sergeant-At-Arms. He had been firm about giving them some privacy, but also that they should always be in sight. She entered the smithy while Gerald stood by the door.

Aldwin was just heating up the forge, and while the coals were warming, he was rearranging some of the tools. She saw him turn to face her upon her approach, and then he noticed the guard by the door. His face fell momentarily, followed by the clenching of his jaw. He looked at her and smiled, but there was a sadness behind his eyes. He knew what was coming, she thought, and she steeled herself.

"Aldwin, I..." she took a breath, "I can't spend so much time down here anymore." She glanced over at Gerald by the door. It was so hard meeting Aldwin's eyes, but she forced herself to turn back to see his tears forming. "It just, well, it just can't be. We're from two different worlds. I wish I weren't Lady Fitzwilliam, that I was just a commoner."

"Shh," he said, his voice breaking as he spoke, "I know."

She stared deeply into his eyes, wanting desperately to tell him how she felt, but part of her knew she would fall to pieces.

He cleared his throat and leaned in close to speak quietly. "I have always loved you, Beverly, and I always will. I know that there can never be anymore between us, but I'm all right with that. So I will make your armour, and when you wear it, it will be as if my arms are holding you. When you use your sword, you will know that I have crafted it to keep you safe. One day you will wed, and I will not lie, on that day I will shed my tears. But I will be happy for you and I will serve you all my remaining years. I give you my word." He looked over at Gerald, but Gerald turned away, and Aldwin planted a soft kiss on her forehead. "Now go," he said, "I have work to do."

She watched him turn away and walk towards the forge. She stared at him for just a moment longer, then turned to Gerald. "I'm done," she said, tears flowing freely down her face. They walked back to the Keep in silence.

THIRTEEN

The Long Winter

WINTER 951/952 MC

∿

Beverly's eyes flew open when the carriage jolted her awake. It took her only a moment to remember where she was, and why. She had left Bodden several days ago, several days of listening to Lady Constance Braddock, wife to Sir Walter, the woman her father had appointed as her chaperone. She had endured her company for far too many hours to not be able to perceive the stern look she was being given.

"I don't know why you have to wear that thing," her new 'best friend' said in disgust.

Beverly looked down at the sword strapped to her waist. "This?" she asked innocently.

"Yes, it's not very ladylike. Why do you insist on wearing it?"

"Because my war hammer is too awkward in the carriage," she said, smiling.

"Humph," uttered Lady Constance.

Beverly looked again at the red-faced woman sitting across from her. She was trying to be civil, but the constant lectures about not being ladylike were wearing thin. Her father was sending her to Hawksburg, ostensibly to visit her cousins, but she knew the real reason, he wanted her away from Aldwin. Of course, Lady Constance knew no such thing. From her point of view, it just looked like a visit to see Beverly's cousins. She had nothing against her cousins, of course, but she didn't really know them. She had met her uncle, for he had visited Bodden before when he delivered Lightning to her. Thinking of her horse tethered behind the carriage, she decided the cabin was too stuffy and slid the window down, eliciting a cry from her chaperone as a blast of cool air entered the carriage. She whistled loudly, and Lightning, the faithful beast that he was, trotted up beside them.

Standing, she hiked up her dress and then opened the carriage door. Lady Braddock cried out in dismay, but Beverly moved quickly, leaping onto Lightning, pulling herself deftly into the saddle, then urging her steed on, easily out-pacing the carriage. Watching her two escorts trying to keep up, their smaller horses straining with the effort, she laughed. The wind blew her hair out behind her as if she was flying, making her feel alive. She slowed the pace and surveyed the countryside, taking in her surroundings. They had only travelled three days of the much longer trip from Bodden to Hawksburg. The land here was open, hedged in on one side by the great forest known as the Whitewood, to the north, in all its majesty. Above her, a hawk drifted in the wind, and she watched it with interest as it circled around and then flew northward.

A recent drizzle had left the air feeling damp. Beverly sensed the moisture in the air, mixed with the scent of pine trees. The unpaved road they travelled on was little more than ruts in the ground. Generations of wagons had passed this way along with countless feet and horses hooves. The roadway was just a path, a well-worn path, and she wondered what it had been like centuries ago. Who had been the first to travel this route? She circled back to the carriage, feeling sorry for her guards, and picked a more sedate pace. Lightning appeared content and almost pranced, perhaps sensing her need for freedom.

Two hours later they stopped to water the horses. Lady Braddock had to answer the call of nature, leaving poor Richardson to escort her to a bush, holding up a sheet for her privacy. Beverly led Lightning down to the small stream where the carriage horses were watering and let him drink. She was rubbing his neck, scanning the area, when she observed the same hawk as earlier. It was sitting on a nearby tree, looking directly at her. She walked towards it, resting her hand on the hilt of her sword.

The hawk flew off at her approach, landing further back in the trees. Behind her, the rest of her group tended to the needs of the horses. Confident she was not going very far, she continued towards the bird. It remained where it was. It was then that she noticed eyes staring at her from the woods, many eyes. A moment later, she saw a wolf step out of the tree line. Several more followed suit, but she didn't feel threatened. None of these beasts were snarling or growling, and she suspected something else was about to make its presence known.

Sure enough, when the wolves parted, a woman stepped out of the woods. At first, Beverly thought it was an Elf, for she was tall and thin, but she lacked the drawn face and pointed ears of the elder race. She had long black hair that was tied in a braid down her back. The multi-coloured green and brown dress she wore made it difficult to distinguish her clearly against the backdrop of the forest.

"Greetings, Beverly," the woman said.

Beverly was astonished to hear her own name. "How do you know who I am?" she asked.

"Come now," the woman said, smiling, "how many red headed women wearing swords live in this area?"

"You have the advantage of me," Beverly countered, "for I know not who you are."

"My apologies," the woman said, "I am Albreda, the Woman of the Whitewood."

"And what do you want of me?"

She walked up to Beverly, examining her with great interest. "Years ago, your father did me a favour, and I have come to repay it."

"My father? He never mentioned it to me."

"Surely you wondered why the men of Bodden never hunt in the Whitewood?"

Beverly levelled her gaze at her. "You're a Druid," she announced, "and the Whitewood is your domain."

"Very good, Beverly, I can see you have your father's intellect.

"So his favour," Beverly continued, "was to grant you the Whitewood as your own?"

"Precisely," she said, smiling, "and I vowed to return the favour one day."

"I don't understand. How precisely would you do that, and what does it have to do with me?"

"I practice the magic of the earth," Albreda said, "and as such I see things. There is a great change coming to the land, a shadow growing over it, though I cannot see the details. Three times your father's Keep has been sieged, and three times he has driven off the invaders. But I see dark clouds in the future. One day you will return to Bodden to find it under its final siege. When that happens, you must call to the woods, and I will fulfill my vow."

"I don't understand," she said. "Is Bodden in danger?"

"It will be," the woman said mysteriously, "though I cannot tell you when, or how. But I must go now for I have other tasks, which call to me. You are on the cusp, Beverly, of events that you cannot imagine. Go with the grace of the woods and remember my words." She stepped into the woods, blending within its greenery. The wolves turned and followed, along with the hawk, leaving Beverly the only soul remaining. She stood still for a moment, seeking to understand the meaning of the woman's words, but none of it made sense. Making her way back to the stream, she glanced around at her travelling companions, none the wiser to her encounter.

Lady Constance had given up her nagging, so the rest of the trip to Hawksburg was quiet, giving her time to contemplate the meeting with the woman of the woods. The encounter had her worried. She tried to recall anything she had heard about Albreda, but nothing came to mind. Perhaps she might find some answers in Hawksburg.

They passed through the city of Tewsbury the day before their planned arrival, but didn't stop to visit, staying only long enough for a quick rest for the horses, and then they were on their way again. She had no idea if the Earl of Tewsbury was home or not, but her father had warned her about keeping her distance from him, so she carried out his wish.

They reached Hawksburg late in the evening. It was a thriving town, very spread out, with only a small keep to guard it. It was deep within Mercerian territory, and she could tell the town had never had to fight off attackers, for there were no walls to guard it. Once through the town proper, they were soon travelling up the laneway to her uncle's sprawling country estate. The servants were scurrying about, as they had seen the approaching carriage.

She recognized her Uncle Robert coming out the front door with what she assumed was her aunt, and their children tagging along behind. Her uncle introduced his wife, Lady Mary, whom she had never met before. They were joined by their eldest son, Tristan who was nine years old. Aubrey, their second child, looked on, with all her seven years of experience, greatly interested in meeting her cousin. The youngest was Samuel, though he was only five and spent most of the time hiding behind his mother's skirts.

Once Beverly introduced her travelling companions, they were escorted into the manor house where a meal had been prepared. The Brandon's were most welcoming, and young Aubrey seemed to delight in following her around everywhere.

Whilst they began eating their meal, Tristan immediately monopolized the conversation with questions for Beverly.

"What kind of armour do you wear?"

"What weapons do you use?"

"How many men have you killed?"

She politely answered all the questions she could before her Aunt Mary stepped in and hushed him.

Next up was Aubrey, who wanted to know all about Lightning.

"How is he?" the inquisitive young girl asked. "I haven't seen him since Father gave him to you for your birthday."

"Have you taught him any new tricks?"

"Is he a good horse in battle?"

It appeared that visitors at the manor were few, as her attention was constantly requested by the two eldest Brandon children. She didn't mind, the atmosphere was friendly, and she warmed to them rather quickly. They wanted news of all sorts; how was the barony going, how was her father, the usual type of thing she might expect. She asked about Albreda, but no one remembered the name. She resolved to talk to her father about it upon her return.

As the evening wore on Lady Constance succumbed to fatigue and retired for the evening, taking young Samuel with her. Soon to follow was Tristan, whom his father reminded him, had an early start to the morning with his tutor, leaving only her uncle and little Aubrey still awake. The inquisitive girl was sitting on her father's lap, enraptured by her cousin's stories. Beverly, noticing the child was doing something with her hands while she listened, bent her head and looked closer.

Aubrey was stitching a fine pattern onto a handkerchief, using delicate movements. The needlework was exquisite, and her hands moved as if they were enhanced by magic. Beverly was surprised to see such dexterity from one so young.

"Where did you learn such fine stitching, Aubrey?" she asked.

It was Lord Brandon who answered, "She takes after her mother. She's always using her hands, and you should see her penmanship, I'm afraid it's far better than mine. She uses more ink practicing than the entire barony, I think."

Aubrey smiled, "Shall I make you one? I could put your name on it, or a rose or something. No, wait, even better, how about a sword. I bet you'd be the only lady in the kingdom with a sword on her handkerchief."

Beverly laughed, "I would like that," she said. "Thank you."

Lord Brandon shifted Aubrey slightly on his lap, "You were asking about someone named Albreda earlier?"

"Do you know of her?" said Beverly.

"The name isn't familiar, but I wonder if she might be the person known as the Lady of the Whitewood?"

"Yes," she replied. "She said she was also called the Woman of the Whitewood. What do you know of her?"

"Well, I don't know how much you remember about your father's history. You know he wasn't originally the baron?"

"Yes, my Uncle Edward was the baron, but he died during a siege."

"That's right. For a time, under your uncle, the land had been plagued by wild animals. Mostly wolves, but there were other creatures too, bears, great cats, and such. It became a dangerous place. Your uncle tried to eradicate them, hunt them all down. Many men were lost in those days trying to tame the wild lands."

"But Bodden's been in the family for generations, had it always been a problem?"

"I can't speak for past generations," Lord Robert continued, "but I know the Norland raids were devastating the crops. Your uncle thought it best to supplement the food with hunting, but the more they went into the Whitewood, the more the animals attacked. It was getting to the point where only very large groups of soldiers could go into the forest."

"What happened?" said Aubrey, suddenly taking an interest.

"Just before the siege of '33, Lord Richard took a ranger into the Whitewood. They went there to track down whatever was organizing the animals, and that's when they came into conflict with the White Witch."

"White Witch? Another name? How many names does this woman have?" asked Beverly.

"Many," he answered. "Your father captured her. He could have had her killed and put an end to it once and for all, but he didn't, he's always been a man of conscience. He talked to her, resolved the situation diplomatically by striking a deal; if she kept her creatures out of his lands, he would stop his people from entering the Whitewood."

"Is she a witch? I didn't think such things existed?"

"Well, the term 'witch' is just used to describe a mage. Most of them are Earth Mages."

"Druids, actually," Beverly said, "I called her one, and she agreed."

It was Aubrey who spoke up next, "Druids are Earth Mages too. There are eight schools of magic, Earth is but one."

They both looked at her in surprise.

"The four elements make up the main schools," she continued as if reciting from a book, "Earth, Air, Fire and Water."

"What are the other four?" asked Beverly.

"Oh, that's easy," she replied, "Life, Enchantments, Death and Hexes. Death and Hexes are generally frowned upon. They're illegal in most realms."

"How do you know all this?" said Beverly.

"I found an old book about magic and mother purchased it for me."

"So, what exactly is a hex?" Beverly prompted.

"It's the opposite of an enchantment. Enchantments enhance a person's natural abilities, such as making them stronger or faster. Hexes do the reverse, making people weaker or slowing them down. Every school has its opposite; Life and Death, Enchantments and Hexes, Fire and Water, and Earth and Air."

"Fascinating," mused Beverly. She turned to look at Lord Brandon, "I think you have a budding mage in the family."

Her uncle laughed, "Unlikely, there's no one she could apprentice under. But it doesn't hurt her to learn as much as she can about it. All education is valuable in my mind."

"Her reading skill must be exceptional," Beverly observed

"She takes after her mother in that, as well. Mary's always been the reader in the family, looking after all the accounts at Hawksburg. Aubrey will take them over when she's older, it's a good skill for her to have. Now, it's getting late, and little Miss Aubrey needs to get to bed."

Aubrey groaned and complained, so her father picked her up like a sack and threw her over his shoulder. "Off to bed, Missy," he said to laughter, and they disappeared up the staircase.

Beverly sat alone for a few moments enjoying the solitude. It was nice here, and she imagined how much she had missed out on by not having a mother or siblings around. No, she corrected herself, my father did everything he could to raise me, I shouldn't complain. She forced herself to rise from the chair and reluctantly made her way to bed. She fell asleep imagining a happy house filled with children and a loving husband with steel grey eyes.

Her uncle kept up a hectic pace at Hawksburg, and Beverly did her best to help wherever she could. She assisted with the construction of the new church and the reorganization of the town militia. At first, the townsfolk looked strangely at Beverly for wearing a sword, but they soon began to ignore what they saw as her idiosyncrasies and accepted her as she became known for her dedication to their needs.

Aubrey followed her around constantly, and she found it rather entertaining. She grew quite fond of her cousin, and on the few times she was not otherwise occupied, she would take her riding. Placing Aubrey in front of her, they would race Lightning across the rich countryside which surrounded the town. Her cousin was a blessing, for the outings kept Beverly's mind engaged on those rare times she could have dwelt on what might have been.

Late in the autumn, she volunteered to teach Aubrey how to ride, and they developed the habit of early morning outings, her on Lightning, and Aubrey on her pony Lucius. It was quite enjoyable, for the townsfolk would greet them with a 'good morning', and the farmers with a wave. When the cold weather finally came, their time outside diminished slightly, but they kept up the rides as long as the weather permitted.

Truth be told, she found little time to think of Aldwin, so busy was her schedule. It was only during those social times, like the Autumn and Winter Festivals, when she saw other couples, that she wished Aldwin were here with her. She would often leave these events early, usually to wander alone with her thoughts.

Just as spring was blossoming, a messenger arrived from Bodden with the news that the king intended a visit to the barony. Her father wished her to return, for the king had never visited before, at least as far as she knew.

A few days later, she departed Hawksburg to return to her home. She bid farewell to her uncle's family, promising to write to Aubrey, and then set out. Aubrey insisted on escorting them for a few hours, giving them a chance for a last ride together until the time came for their final goodbyes.

She returned to Bodden a changed woman. She still loved Aldwin, perhaps more than ever. She understood that they could never be together, that she must marry someone else, but she knew that no one else would have her heart. This, she had accepted.

FOURTEEN

The Reward

SPRING 952 MC

~

U pon learning that King Andred IV would be coming for a visit, the
entire barony was put to work preparing. There would be feasts,
celebrations, speeches, and lots of visitors, for the king never travelled
alone. The Royal Entourage was famous for being large, which meant extra
horses, soldiers, knights, servants and most of all, food. The current king
had never visited Bodden having only assumed the throne some six years
ago, upon the death of his father. His preference ran more to cities that had
good hunting and sumptuous lodgings, than the barren locale of the frontier. No one thought to ask why the king was visiting, that was the royal
prerogative, but once it was announced, everything must be done to make
the visit perfect.

Beverly was needed here more than ever, and her time in Hawksburg
had helped her refine her organizational skills. Her father had given her the
responsibility of preparing for the numerous soldiers that would accompany the king. This meant building a new stable, albeit a temporary one,
along with finding places to billet the men. Bodden Keep was made to be a
strong, defensible fortress, it was not designed to hold large numbers of
guests. The normal garrison of Bodden numbered 200. This was usually
broken down by type; there were 100 archers, 50 footmen, and 50 horsemen, of which usually about twenty were knights. The king always travelled with a contingent of at least 50 Royal Guards, all knights from the
richest and most influential families. In addition, there would be two

companies of heavy foot and their attendants, smiths, suppliers and such camp followers that the king's entourage allowed. On top of that were the usual freeloaders, other nobles taking advantage of the host and currying favour with the king.

Although the queen would not be in attendance, the king's mistress, Lady Penelope Cromwell, would accompany him, requiring her own chambers, near to the king. Beverly's father had given up his quarters for the king but was annoyed that a place needed to be made available to the mistress of the king. Beverly solved the problem by giving up her room for the duration of the visit.

They spent six weeks preparing for the royal visit, and when the day finally came, they felt they had done everything they could to be ready. The first sign of the Royal Entourage was the appearance of the outriders. The royal party had sent two King's Rangers in advance to scout the road for safety, and to announce the imminent arrival of the king. Baron Fitzwilliam assured them all was ready and offered to billet them, but the oldest, a man called Falcon, refused. It was not the place of a King's Ranger, he said, to sleep in a soft bed, he had other duties to attend to. The baron bid them farewell, waiting for his regal guest to make his appearance. This gave Beverly the time she needed to change out of her warrior's garb, and much to her chagrin, attire herself in a courtly dress. Looking in the mirror, she came to the realization that she would have to leave her sword behind, for there was no way possible to wear both the dress and her blade.

The king's herald soon rode up to the gates and blasted out notes to announce the arrival. The entourage rode through the town of Bodden, led by members of the Royal Guard. Beverly and Gerald stood beside the baron as the group entered the inner courtyard. The knights were splendid in their gleaming armour, mounted on Mercerian Chargers, the largest war horses in the three kingdoms. The Royal Carriage drew up behind them and servants rushed to open the door. The remainder of the entourage waited in the village proper, for there was not enough space within the Keep's walls for them all.

His Royal Majesty, King Andred, stepped down from the carriage. His red cape fluttered in the wind as his ceremonial armour, embossed with the Royal Coat of Arms, glinted in the sun. He held out his hand, the fingers bedecked with expensive rings, awaiting his subjects to do their duty. Baron Fitzwilliam stepped forward, knelt and kissed the Royal Signet Ring, as did Beverly. Gerald, as a common soldier, knelt with his head down, as was the custom. The king called the baron to him, and they talked amiably as they entered the Keep, with the remainder of the entourage arriving once the Royal Carriage had departed.

Beverly took a deep breath, "I'm glad that's over," she said, looking at Gerald.

"Oh, I don't think it's over for some time yet," he said. "There's no telling how long his majesty will stay. I suppose we better see to all these men."

Gerald, as the Sergeant-At-Arms had the responsibility of looking after all the troops in the Keep, including visitors. Now that the king had arrived, Beverly had been assigned more domestic duties. She had to deal with Lady Penelope, the king's mistress, as well as any other ladies that were in attendance. Lady Penelope, fortunately, was easy to accommodate, for once she was escorted to her room, her servants took over, freeing up Beverly for more important duties.

The remaining ladies, on the other hand, proved to be a nightmare. It was always the wives of the nobles that caused the most problems. The Earl of Tewsbury's wife was exceptionally picky, with a long list of demands that Beverly found infuriating. Before she was even half-way through seeing to the Countess Tewsbury's seemingly endless needs, the Duke of Colbridge's wife appeared with a similar list of demands. The two were obviously fast friends. Beverly solved the problem by finally saying no to everyone. They all had to deal with what they were given, or they could take it up with the baron. It apparently settled the problem, for she received no more personal requests. No doubt they were bothering their respective husbands with their demands, but no one wanted to come to the king's attention about such trivial matters.

Every night there was an elaborate dinner for the king and his entourage. These feasts went well into the evening, with some guests lingering around till the next morning. Throughout all this, patrols needed to be carried out. Both Gerald and Beverly were pulling double duty, with patrols during the day, and Royal Entourage handholding in the evenings.

In the three days since the king arrived, the incessant needs of the guests were enough to provoke Beverly into actions not befitting the lady of the house. She had been groped on more than one occasion and had even broken the nose of a drunken Royal Guardsman after he propositioned her. She had tried to be diplomatic, and when he didn't get the hint, she drove the palm of her hand into the bridge of his nose. The man gave a yell, and others came running, whereupon she explained that he had walked into the wall. The matter never came up again, and she was left alone from that point forward.

It was early in the morning of the fourth day, the sun was up, but the vast majority of the guests were not. The king, always an early riser, wished to see the barony and had asked the baron for a tour of the lands. Lord Fitzwilliam had quickly assembled a troop, under Gerald's command, to accompany the king and his usual dozen knights. Beverly, eager to get out of the Keep, and her role as lady of the manor, armoured up and joined the men in Gerald's group.

They rode out of the gate to a sunny day, the sky exceptionally clear, and it was looking like it would be nice and warm with a gentle breeze. The baron rode with the king to the west, the Royal Knights keeping close behind them, and the Bodden soldiers taking up the rear guard. Beverly remained silent. She was so sick of the Royal Guard and didn't want any reason to have to interact with them. Riding past the farms, she saw her father describing the great efforts they had gone to move the farms closer to the Keep. The king appeared bored with the conversation, but looked to be enjoying the scenery, at least. Turning north, they entered the wild lands, where there was little in the way of civilization. Beverly always liked this part of her patrols, for the land was wild, feral even, and she found it reassuring that the presence of man had not destroyed the land.

They continued on until noon, and then the procession stopped by a stream to water the horses. A servant brought food to the king, who sat down on the ground to eat, more relaxed than Beverly had seen him since his arrival. He was quite jovial, chatting with her father, laughing at a joke. She watched them and wondered about the responsibility that must rest on the king's shoulders. She thought of her father's words, being trapped by their position in society. Was the king as much a prisoner as they were?

Once the king was finished, the expedition set off, this time travelling east for a while, then turning south, which would have them returning to the Keep in time for dinner. Off to the east Beverly caught sight of the edge of the Whitewood and she remembered her encounter with Albreda. Was she watching them now, from the trees, or did she use her hawk to observe them at a distance?

Her thoughts were interrupted by a cry from Gerald, "To the north, raiders!"

Hearing this, Baron Fitzwilliam rode up beside the king, "Your Majesty," he said, "I fear we must prematurely end the tour. Will you permit me to return you to the Keep?"

"By all means," the king said, rather nonchalantly.

The column picked up the pace, and Gerald brought up the rear, signalling Beverly to stay with him. As the others marched he leaned in close, "Take a look, Beverly, your eyes are better than mine. What do you see?"

She strained, trying to make out the details, but as the raiders drew closer, she swore.

"Damn, there must be almost two hundred of them. We have to tell Father."

"Maintain your position," Gerald said, "and keep the back of the line moving, I'll go tell the baron. The enemy won't catch up to us for quite a while."

Gerald rode ahead. Beverly lost sight of him amongst the knights in front who were slowing the whole procession down. The fancy horses of the Royal Guard were poor cross-country travellers. They were large beasts, used to pomp and circumstance, not countryside patrols. She cursed at them under her breath as their pace began to visibly decrease.

Far to the south, the outline of Bodden Keep was growing steadily larger. If they could just make the gates, all would be well. She glanced back at the raiders and noted there weren't enough for a siege, but they were a real threat to the king's safety. Horns suddenly sounded, and she turned back to see the enemy surging forward. It would be a race to the gate, but they had a significant lead, all they had to do was maintain their course.

One of the Royal Guard must have glanced back, and seeing the cloud of dust being raised, panicked. There was no other word for it. One moment the expedition was a carefully maintained line of horsemen, two riders wide, and the next it was a chaotic mess, with each rider pushing his steed to the maximum to get to Bodden Keep as quickly as possible. Beverly didn't panic. She kept her pace even, for there was plenty of time, she had run this race before. They were about to top the last rise before Bodden. The mob in front of her continued to rush onward, the panic spreading as riders were suddenly overcome with fear when a different horn sounded from the west.

A second group of raiders emerged, and it appeared they would cut the king's guards off from the haven of Bodden Keep. Her eyes went wide, something must be done, or there would be a slaughter. She saw Gerald and his men break off, heading west to intercept the new group. She urged Lightning forward to join them, then reconsidered, Gerald was more than capable of dealing with this new threat. The fight was brief, but it was effective in drawing the men away in pursuit, wasting valuable time. She turned, looking back towards the king, to observe a catastrophic development.

Unnoticed, a third group of raiders had snuck up from the east and were thundering down on the king. The royal party would have been safe, but the king's horse suddenly stumbled. She couldn't see what happened, perhaps the horse had hit a rabbit hole, or maybe it had tripped on a rock, she couldn't be sure, but the king went down unobserved, while the rest of his guard carried on in the direction of the Keep. Gerald was returning from the west, but wouldn't make it in time. The king's survival was in her hands alone. Instinctively, she charged into this new enemy, drawing her sword as she closed the distance. She struck the enemy cavalry head on. Lightning sideswiped the lead rider, while she swung her sword high, decapitating the man. As she passed by, she bashed the rider on the left with her shield and then swerved behind him to engage the next horse, who was approaching from her right side. She drove her sword down onto the horse's head, felling it instantly, sending the rider flying, the enemy horses' rears colliding with each other in the fray.

She advanced towards the king, swinging again only to be blocked by a shield, so she drew back and viciously thrust, penetrating her attacker's stomach, and he fell forward, trapped in the saddle by the blade. She let go of the sword and grabbed her hammer which hung from her saddle. She whirled it around to see the next rider flinch back. Seizing the opening, she struck him in the chest, knocking him from his mount. She was surrounded by mounted raiders, lost in a maelstrom of combat. She blocked a sword strike, using the hammer like a hook to pull the sword from the enemy's grip. Twisting in her saddle, she drove the hammer in a backhand blow against another opponent to her right. Abruptly, they were all gone, there was no one left in front of her to strike. The enemy was running. She glanced over to where she had seen the king's horse go down. The king was trying to stand, but it appeared as if his leg was injured. More raiders were bearing down on him, and she looked at Gerald for help. The sergeant had his own troubles, for no sooner had he turned from his pursuit than raiders from the north had come surging down on him. He disappeared in a whirl-wind of horses, but she had no time to worry, she must protect the king.

King Andred could not stand and sank to the ground, in obvious agony. The other members of the party had reached the gate before noticing he was missing, and were only now turning their horses about. Thundering towards the king, Beverly's charge was blocked as two raiders cut across in front of her in their own pursuit of the king. She let out a blood-curdling scream, grabbing their attention as she bore down on them. They rotated their horses around to meet her charge. As they pulled even, she ducked unexpectedly, and the first man's swing went over her head. She brought the hammer up from the ground into his face, feeling the impact as steel met bone, the helmet flying through the air. The raider on the left landed a savage blow to her shoulder, but the metal plate held, the sword sliding off easily. Her shield was positioned low, enabling her to ram the edge into her foe's face, sending him tumbling off his horse. She didn't stay to see the outcome, for she knew the king was still in mortal danger. Riding to his side and dismounting, she decided to throw him onto Lightning, but the enemy had other ideas.

Four riders approached as she was trying to help him up, and then they surrounded her, striking her from all directions. She pushed the king to the ground and stood over him, yelling for Lightning. A man groaned as a savage kick from her steed hit him. Her shield buckled from a heavy strike, and she looked to see yet another adversary wielding a massive mace. Again and again, he struck, and she struggled to keep her balance. Had she the room, she could have easily stepped back and recovered quickly, but the king must be her priority, so she held her position. A final blow landed, and she discarded the ruined shield, swinging her hammer in a wide arc to gain some manoeuvring space. Her left hand sought out her dagger, and she stood, waiting. The riders were around her, four of them and one of them came forward. This time, as he swung, she bent at the waist and used her hammer to snag the mace, pulling him off balance. He went down, and she drove the dagger into the back of his head. She felt a sword strike her back and once again her armour saved her. She twisted on her heels and smashed the hammer into the next one's arms, causing him to cry out in pain as he dropped his weapon.

There were only two men left, and they must have concluded who she was protecting, for they came on in a fury of blows. She took the first hit to the back of her forearm then struck with the dagger. She missed, but her attacker pulled back, fearful of the blade. She turned again to see her final opponent, now on foot, about to defeat her with a two-handed overhead strike. She let the blow come, shifting slightly at the last moment to see the blade strike the ground harmlessly. She stepped forward head-butting him, and as he fell, she drove the dagger into his chest.

The one she disarmed came back again and tried to run her down, but Lightning smashed into his horse, knocking it sideways. The man swung in a desperate last attack, and the blow hit her helmet. All she could hear was a large ringing sound, and she shook her head trying to focus her eyes. She swung her hammer wildly but missed. Without warning, she was once again encircled, men were yelling, and then she shook her head, finally aware of her surroundings. The Royal Guard had arrived!

The king's captain, Valmar, was pulling the king onto his horse. She looked for Lightning and finding the great beast waiting, hauled herself into the saddle. The next thing she was aware of was the thunder of horse's hooves, and she realized they were riding over cobblestones. They had reached the gates of the Keep. The entrance was crowded with knights and soldiers. She saw her father, looking on with concern at the warriors who had just made it to the safety.

She dismounted, trying to catch her breath, too spent even to remove her helmet. She bent over at the waist, taking deep breaths, while she felt somebody patting her on the back. She slowly became aware that the courtyard was quiet, and then her arm was gripped, and she was pulled upright.

The king stood before her, staring intensely.

"You are brave, sir, braver, it seems, than my entire guard." He turned to face the assembled people. "Be it known that this soldier, this exceptional warrior, has earned the king's gratitude and shall this day forth be considered a Knight of the Realm." He turned back to Beverly, "Kneel," he said.

Beverly dropped to one knee, her head still reeling. The king drew his blade and placed it on her left shoulder. "In the name of the king," he said, and then moved the blade to the right shoulder, "and in the name of the throne, I now knight thee, Sir..."

He paused a moment, with a look of dismay on his face. "Remove your helmet and tell us your name that we might celebrate your achievements," he commanded.

Beverly removed her helmet and her red hair, which had been tied up in a bun, cascaded down her shoulders. "Lady Beverly Fitzwilliam, Your Majesty."

There was a collective gasp from the crowd, and the king smiled. "Very well," he said, "I now pronounce thee Knight of the Realm. Arise, Sir... Dame Beverly Fitzwilliam."

She had done it! She had accomplished the impossible, had achieved her life's ambition. Her head swam, and she felt faint. The crowd roared with applause, and she struggled to stand, felt hands helping her, and then she was being borne along by the crowd. They carried her over to her father who was smiling widely. She thought of Aldwin and looked for him, but couldn't find him in the crowd. They deposited her beside her father, and he embraced her, beaming with pride as he congratulated her. The whole situation was somehow surreal. She was smiling from ear to ear and turned to talk to Gerald and then remembered he had gone down.

She glanced about frantically, "Gerald?" she asked, desperate to know his fate.

"He's here, my dear," said her father, "but he's wounded, they've taken him to the surgeon."

She hugged her father again, and as the crowd cheered, she turned, grasped her father's hand, and then raised it into the air. There was a great change coming, Albreda had said, and Beverly suddenly understood that the great change had already begun.

FIFTEEN

Interim

SPRING/SUMMER 952 MC

The king left Bodden the day after the assault, escorted by the small army he had brought with him. Baron Fitzwilliam believed that the raiders had somehow known of the royal visit, but without proof, there was little that could be done. Life at the Keep reverted to the way it was before the king had graced them with his presence. Beverly, just returning from her first patrol since being knighted, was called to the map room. Leaving Lightning in capable hands, she quickly made her way there, for it was an uncommon thing for her to be summoned like this.

She arrived to see her father talking with Sir Walter, while they scanned over the map.

"Ah, my dear," her father said, "come in, come in, we were just going over a few things, nothing that might concern you."

"You called for me, Father?" she enquired.

"Yes, sit down. Let me pour you some wine."

Her father's behaviour alarmed her more than any enemy army. He usually got straight to the point, and now he looked to be overly concerned with frivolities. She sat down at the table and waited while he poured her some wine. He wandered over to the window and looked out, surveying the land.

"Well?" she prompted.

"Well what?" he replied.

"You didn't summon me here to pour me wine. What is it, Father?"

He turned to face her, then wandered back over to the table. "It's Gerald," he said at last.

"What about him?" she said with a sense of rising panic.

"I'm afraid his leg wound is worse than we thought."

"Surely they're not going to amputate?"

"No, but the wound is giving him pain, and I'm afraid he's not able to fulfill his duties anymore."

"Maybe not as a warrior, but he's still your most trusted advisor, Father."

"Oh, I know, my dear, I know. But I think I have a better idea. I wanted to run it by you."

"Go ahead," she said cautiously.

"I'm going to send him to Wincaster."

"Wincaster?" she said incredulously. "Why Wincaster?"

"That's where the King's Healer lives."

"But surely our healer here-"

"No, you don't understand, my dear, the King's Healer is a Life Mage. He can use magic to cure Gerald's leg."

"But," she said, thinking it over, "the king only lets the healer work on him or his family."

"True enough," said the baron, "but we may have someone who could influence him otherwise."

She thought about this carefully. She knew the king was very selfish. Who could convince him to share his mage's services? The queen? Unlikely, those two were only seen together on rare public occasions. The king's mistress? Also unlikely, as she was as possessive as he was. She gave up trying to figure it out. "Who?" she finally asked.

"What do you remember about the battle?" he asked.

"It was all rather confusing, but I think I remember most of the details," she said.

"At the end of the fight," he continued, "after you defeated that last raider, Captain Valmar led a group of knights out to rescue the king."

"I remember," she said, still not sure where he was going with this.

"Well," he paused for dramatic effect, "the king decided to make him his new marshal-general."

"Marshal-General? In charge of the whole army? But, Father, you're more qualified than Valmar, he's just a guard captain!"

"Let's not argue over the king's decision, he is the king, after all. Besides, I'm needed here in Bodden more than they need me in the capital."

Beverly put down her drink. There was wisdom in what he said, and she marvelled at how calmly he appeared to take it. "So you think that Valmar, pardon me, Marshal-General Valmar, might put in a good word and get Gerald healed?"

"It is my hope. Then he can return to us here in Bodden, his home."

"And if he isn't healed?"

"Then we'll find something for him to do, he's a warrior at heart. I can't imagine he would like being a glorified clerk."

"When is he to be shipped off?" she asked.

"Four of our knights are due to be returned to Wincaster at the end of the month. That'll give him time enough to heal up for the journey. I also have to talk to you about something else."

"Go on," she prompted, warily.

"Well, as we were saying goodbye to the king, he mentioned that he wants to formally knight you in Wincaster, you know, in front of an adoring crowd. Doubtless, he wants to milk it for all the goodwill he can. He's not popular with the people these days."

"You're saying I have to go to Wincaster?"

"Not immediately. He suggested the middle of summer, that'll give you time to fix your armour. It took quite a beating, as you know. I'll be accompanying you to Wincaster. We'll leave Bodden in Sir Walter's capable hands while I'm away. You'd best get down to the smithy and see to that armour. I suspect it will take some time to fix."

She stood to leave, "Who is to be my chaperone in the smithy now that Gerald is unavailable?"

"I think you're mature enough to see that nothing untoward happens, don't you?"

She grinned, "Yes, Father," she said, then ran up to him and kissed him on the cheek, "Thank you, Father."

She left the room, and the baron turned to Sir Walter. "That went better than I expected," he said.

Sir Walter smiled, "And what of the smithy? Is it going to become a problem?"

"I trust her to do the right thing. Soon, she will be away from Bodden, and I doubt she'll be back for many years." There was a hint of sadness in his eyes, and he downed the last of his wine. "But we have more important things to worry about. What do you think of Blackwood as our new Sergeant-at-Arms?"

Beverly made her way down to the smithy, collecting her shield to bring it along. It was badly damaged, and she wondered if Aldwin could even repair it. Perhaps it was time for a new one? She was deep in thought as she reached the bottom of the stairs and turned towards the smithy.

Expecting a workshop bare of people save for Aldwin, she was instead shocked to be met by a bevy of women vying for his attention. There were five of them, and they were crowded around the workbench asking questions. A bare-chested Aldwin, covered in sweat from the effort of using the forge, stood behind the counter, answering them. She stopped and watched, trying to decipher what was happening. The women all looked to be of a similar age as her. They were asking him to fashion daggers or knives for them. She knew that Aldwin's skills were sought after by many, but it only just dawned on her that others might find his physical appearance to be pleasing. She had grown up with him, had fallen in love with his mind, his personality and those steel grey eyes, but now she looked on as an observer might, and she had to agree, he was a fine physical specimen. Hours at the forge had given him a strong, chiselled body and suddenly she had the urge to interrupt this gaggle and free him from its clutches.

"Master Aldwin," she said in a voice that was perhaps a little too loud, "I have work here for you if you've finished with your...socializing."

The women all turned at once. She knew them, they were kind people, but just at this moment, they infuriated her. She was feeling possessive, hurt, and sad, all at once. "If you girls will excuse us," she finally said, taking control of her emotions, "I need my armour repaired." She looked at the assembled women. "Unless one of you knows how to fix this?" she said, holding up her battered shield. They bowed and left the room, giggling as they looked back over their shoulders on the way out.

She dropped the shield on the workbench and starred at Aldwin. He stood, looking back, no trace of guilt or anger, and she almost melted in his eyes.

"I, ahh," she mumbled, suddenly at a loss for words.

He cleared his throat, "I see, m'lady, that your shield needs some repairs. How fairs the rest of your armour?"

"It, ah, needs some work too," she said, at last, finally finding her voice. She was cursing herself. Why did she have to feel so nervous around him? Then it hit her, this was the first time she was here without a chaperone in more than a year.

"Let me see," he said, coming around to the front of the workbench. "Stand still," he requested, and then moved around her, examining her armour.

She blushed heavily and found her breathing becoming shallow. She forced herself to take deep breaths.

"Doesn't look too bad, I'll have to reforge part of the helmet, and there's some dents to straighten out. I'm afraid your shields had it, though. I'll have to make a new one for you. Do you want to undress now?" he said.

Her mind was suddenly awakened by his words. "What?" she said in a near panic.

"You have to remove your armour if I'm going to repair it."

"Oh, yes, of course," she said.

"Shall I help you, m'lady?" he offered.

She felt too nervous to speak and simply nodded her head.

He moved around her carefully undoing the buckles and straps and removed the armour plating one piece at a time. To Beverly, this was like a dream, and she found herself blushing with her thoughts. Finally, he was finished, leaving her in the chainmail shirt and leggings.

He had dropped the armour onto the workbench and now walked around the other side of the table.

"When do you need the repairs by?" he asked.

"I have to go to Wincaster by mid-summer," she answered.

Aldwin's eyes snapped up, "You're leaving Bodden again?" he asked. "How long will you be gone this time?"

She hated to see the sadness in those eyes yet again, and felt anguished.

"I'm afraid I don't know Aldwin. I might not be back for years." She saw the look of disappointment on his face before he tried to cover it up by examining the helmet he grasped. "I have to go to Wincaster for the knighting ceremony."

"I thought the king knighted you in the courtyard," he said bitterly.

"He did, but there's to be an official ceremony, the king demands it."

"Then I shall do all I can to make you the best armour that a knight could have," he said, a determined look taking hold of him.

"Thank you, Aldwin, I shall not forget this," or you, she thought to herself.

The weeks seemed to drag on for an eternity. They sent Gerald off with a celebration in his honour, but it was a melancholy event, for everyone suspected he would not be back. Her father tried to keep his spirits up, but she knew he was losing a good friend. Gerald had been his right-hand man, loyal and true to a fault. He had handpicked his successor, but Sergeant Blackwood was no Gerald. He followed orders well, but lacked the instincts that Gerald had honed over the years.

As the day for her to leave drew closer, Beverly made her last trip to the smithy to pick up her armour. She had been in for trial fittings over the intervening weeks, and Aldwin had done a magnificent job on the repairs.

He brought out the final pieces and dressed her in her new armour. Several plates were brand new, and he had gone to extraordinary lengths to decorate them with delicate scrollwork. He had arranged for a full-length mirror to be brought to the smithy, and now she stood looking at her reflection. How she had grown, she thought. The woman in the mirror was almost unrecognizable from the little girl that had long since first walked into this smithy.

Her thoughts were interrupted by Aldwin, who coughed. She looked up to see him carrying something large, covered with a cloth. It could only be her shield. He carefully removed the covering, and she saw the final product that he had spent so much labour creating. The shield was made of metal, and inlaid with the coat of arms of the Fitzwilliams. There was something different about the coat of arms though, and she moved closer to examine it in more detail. Above the coat of arms was a rose, embossed, into the shield as a delicate set of inlaid silver. She looked at Aldwin with surprise.

"Your father," he said, "suggested we give you your own version of the sigil. I understand that the rose would have special meaning to you."

"Yes," she said, deeply touched, "it was my mother's favourite."

Tears welled up in her eyes, and she moved towards Aldwin, touching his face gently with her fingertips. "You will forever be in my heart," she said softly.

She might never see him again, but she would always remember the face, the smile, and the piercing grey eyes. She gathered up her things and left the smithy, afraid to look back. She was leaving a large part of her life behind her now, and though she didn't know what the future would bring, she knew that she loved and was loved, and that would have to carry her through whatever might come her way.

They rode out sometime later with a detachment of guards who would escort them to Tewsbury, and from there they would continue on to the capital without guards. A carriage was accompanying them, but they chose to ride their horses for the first part of the trip. As they topped the rise leading away from Bodden, Beverly halted her horse, taking one last look at the place she had called home, and thought only of the smith she left behind.

Her father rode ahead, stopped and waited, understanding perhaps, the complex emotions that ran through her head and heart. Then, she turned, nodded at her father, and they rode off towards Wincaster.

SIXTEEN

Wincaster

SUMMER 952 MC

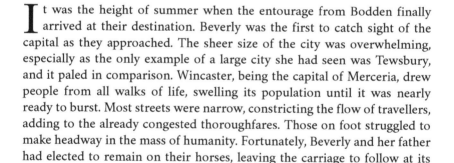

I t was the height of summer when the entourage from Bodden finally arrived at their destination. Beverly was the first to catch sight of the capital as they approached. The sheer size of the city was overwhelming, especially as the only example of a large city she had seen was Tewsbury, and it paled in comparison. Wincaster, being the capital of Merceria, drew people from all walks of life, swelling its population until it was nearly ready to burst. Most streets were narrow, constricting the flow of travellers, adding to the already congested thoroughfares. Those on foot struggled to make headway in the mass of humanity. Fortunately, Beverly and her father had elected to remain on their horses, leaving the carriage to follow at its own pace, to meet up with them later.

As befitted the Baron of Bodden, Lord Fitzwilliam possessed a manor house in Wincaster. He hadn't been back to it since the death of his beloved Evelyn, for the city no longer held any interest for him. From his point of view, it had become a place filled with intrigue and corruption, and he shared these insights with Beverly. She, on the other hand, was thrilled to see, at long last, the city that the Bodden knights always carried on about. From overhearing their conversations, she had built an image of a mythical place in her mind. It only took a few moments of trotting down the street for her to perceive that the reality did not live up to the fantasy she had fabricated. It was the stench that penetrated her illusion first. Had she not been more alert, a bucket of slop tossed from a second storey window would have covered her with the smell of the city.

Beverly had chosen to enter in full knightly regalia, save the helmet, raising a few eyebrows as they rode through the streets. The sight of such a large horse was rare enough, but carrying a woman was inconceivable to nearly everyone. Numerous people stood by, awestruck, speculating who this strange person might be. More than one onlooker remarked, "Must be a foreigner."

Having entered the capital through the West Gate, they continued along the main thoroughfare for some time, fortunately turning north to the richer area of the city, bypassing the slums. With the smell here so unpleasant, Beverly did not want to imagine what odours would waft her way had they headed south instead. Almost immediately upon turning onto Royal Avenue, the quality of the buildings improved, leading to the Royal Palace, in all its glory. The Palace was huge, and Beverly realized that it was bigger than the entire Keep at Bodden. Surrounding the Royal Residence were the capital's largest houses, with well-cut lawns, while upon the street, the ornate carriages traversed slowly, seemingly without a care in the world. This was the first time that Beverly glimpsed the town guards patrolling, chasing away merchants that should not be hawking their wares in this part of town. In the midst of all this affluence was a noticeably derelict house. Her father explained that it belonged to the Royal Life Mage, a man of unusual habits.

Finally, they reached the manor house, where the waiting staff greeted them. Beverly insisted on seeing to Lightning herself, creating quite a stir with the servants. While she was busy in the stables, their carriage arrived, and the servants began to unload their trunks, giving her the time she needed to finish with her steed. Upon entering the house, her father suggested they change and make their way through the town on a little sightseeing tour. She readily agreed, and in less time than it had taken her to tend to her mount, they were walking towards the Palace. She had changed into a walking dress but still carried her sword. Her father, knowing better, didn't say anything, but many people on the streets gawked at them.

As they neared the Palace, her father stopped her, "Beverly, we need to go in here. They used to make the best cheese I have ever tasted. Let's find out if they still do," he said, ushering her into a local tavern called the Queen's Arms.

They walked into a large open room, with tables strewn about in a rather haphazard manner. There were clients of all types here ranging from nobles, like themselves, down to middle-income commoners. She saw an

Elf sipping wine at one table while a Dwarf, sitting across from her, noisily gulped down an ale from a massive tankard. Her father went directly to the right side of the room, where he could sit with his back to the wall. Many different discussions floated about, but none loud enough to impede her father's conversation with the server.

Much to his delight, they still served Hawksburg Gold, the elusive cheese from his youth. As the platter was walked by Beverly, on the way to her father, she sniffed the foulest smell she could imagine. She fought back the urge to gag and ordered a hot cider which she kept as close to her nose as possible to cover the stench, but her father kept talking.

"Father, honestly, your breath is enough to kill a donkey," she interrupted him.

He merely laughed, and she swore he purposefully exhaled into her face. Surprisingly, she smiled to see her father in such high spirits. Bodden was his job, his responsibility, but here he began to relax. As he ate the cheese, she looked at him and realized how much he had aged in the past few years.

"Must you eat so much of that, Father?" she asked.

"Oh, my dear," he said, "you have no idea. We have to go and talk to the bureaucrats at the Palace. I want my breath to be as bad as possible."

She looked at him, trying to determine if he was joking.

"It's simple," he said. "No one wants to keep someone around if their breath is so foul, and until I have the answers I need, I'll be sticking around." He smiled as if his reasoning was obvious.

She wasn't sure of her father's tactic, but chose not to say anything for the moment. Leaving, they made their way to the Palace, where she had her first encounter with bureaucrats in the capital. Beverly thought that she would simply have to check in to find out the details of the ceremony. After being sent to clerk after clerk, she realized that this would be anything but easy.

Each clerk needed to confirm the date of Beverly's investiture before speaking with her. After repeating herself so many times she was just about ready to give up, the last clerk finally told her that she needed to be assigned to a duty roster. She was a knight now, and officially under the command of the king. Typically this meant someone would assign her duties, as the king seldom intervened, and so the clerk dispatched runners to determine if she had any current assignments waiting for her. The entire experience felt like a colossal waste of time. Beverly said as much to her father, but he just laughed.

It was not just all the unnecessary paperwork that she disliked at the Palace, it was the knights who were everywhere, leering at young women, herself included. These knights were all young men, in their prime, with highly polished armour that had never seen a battle. She did her best to ignore them but quickly grew tired of their lecherous stares and scurrilous remarks. Had her father not been there to keep her in check, she was sure she would have challenged the lot of them to a duel, even though she thought the practice a waste of time, she would have at least put a dent in their perfect armour!

In the end, they got what they needed without bloodshed. The investiture was one week away, and until then, Beverly would stay at the manor, moving into the barracks after the ceremony. For most knights, if there was not an assignment for them in the capital, they, or their family would find a sponsor, who would then request the knight from the king. This had been the custom for years, but she was a woman, and that presented all new challenges to the Royal Court. The clerk agreed to send word when the arrangements were made, and with their objective complete, they returned to their Wincaster home, to find an unexpected surprise.

A carriage was standing in front, unloading her Uncle Robert and his family, including Aubrey, who, upon seeing her, ran over to say hello. It was a warm welcome, and she felt more at home now. Lord Robert had come down from Hawksburg to watch the investiture, and the whole family had insisted on accompanying him.

Later in the evening, after consuming a delicious meal and talking about family matters, she sat with her father and uncle as they sipped their wine. Aubrey, as was her usual habit, was in her father's lap when the conversation took a particularly interesting turn.

"Did I ever tell you how your parents met?" asked Lord Robert.

"Oh, don't tell that story, Robert, I beg of you," said her father.

"You must tell me everything, Uncle. Never mind what he says."

Her uncle looked mischievously at his brother-in-law. "Well, you know your Uncle Edward used to be the Baron of Bodden before your father, but before your grandfather died, both brothers were just knights, and your grandfather sent them to Wincaster to season them."

"What were they like back then?" she asked, her curiosity peaked.

"Well, your Uncle Edward was always the wild one, but your father had his moments too."

She found that hard to believe. She had never met her uncle, as he had died years before she had been born, but she always saw her father as a man who controlled himself.

"Evelyn was, of course, my older-"

"And better looking," Fitz interrupted.

"Yes, I'll give you that, old man, she was better looking. Anyway, she was my older sister, and she was visiting the Capital with our mother. I was younger at the time, so I was likely learning to ride or slaying dragons or some such thing." Aubrey giggled at her father's explanation of his younger self's whereabouts.

"Anyway, your uncle decides he wants to woo this lady of the court, and so he has a few drinks to steady his nerves and then makes his way to her estate."

Beverly looked at her father to see him hiding his face in his hands.

"Once he arrives at the estate, he makes his way underneath the balcony and then decides he needs a flower or something to profess his love. Now you need to know, he's dragged your father there along with him, and both of them are drunk, remember. So he starts crawling about on his hands and knees in the garden looking for a flower to pick. Of course, he's completely destroying the garden as he does this."

"Oh no," Beverly said. "What was my father doing?"

"Your father was embarrassed by the whole spectacle, just like he is now, and starts yelling at his brother to stop. 'Get out of the plants, Edward' he says, but of course, he's also soused. They're making so much noise that someone comes out on the balcony to see what the ruckus is all about. Edward catches a glimpse of the figure and pulls himself to his feet, professing his love to the woman and telling her that he wants to elope with her. Your father tries to stop him, but Edward won't have any of it. He steps into the clearing, and that's when he realizes he's talking to the girl's mother. Well, all he can think to do is say 'run', and they both try to escape. Of course, they're so drunk, they don't know which way is which, and they end up crashing through the hedge, into the neighbouring estate. Your Uncle Edward stops as he exits the other side of the hedge, but your father rushes out, straight into a fountain."

"Oh no, that's terrible," Beverly said, chuckling.

"Wait, that's not the best part. The other side of the hedge was our back-yard, you see, and it just so happened that our family was entertaining guests at the time. As your father staggers through the hedge and hits the edge of the fountain, he desperately tries to grab something to steady himself, and manages to take hold of my sister's cloak, dragging them both into the fountain." Robert was barely able to get this last sentence out, for he was laughing hysterically. Soon, they were all laughing so hard they couldn't breathe. Even her father finally joined in.

"And that," Lord Brandon finally said, catching his breath, "is how Lord Richard Fitzwilliam met Lady Evelyn Brandon." He rose and bowed, and everyone clapped.

Aubrey piped up, "How did you meet Mummy, Father?" she asked.

"Well, I'm afraid that story isn't nearly as funny. We were introduced by your Uncle Matthew, and I'm pleased to say, I didn't get her soaking wet the first time I met her." He smiled at his daughter. "Now," he continued, "it's long past somebody's bedtime."

"Wait," said Aubrey, "can cousin Beverly put me to bed?"

Lord Robert looked at Beverly, "If it's all right with her?"

"I'd be happy to," she said. "Come along you, off to bed." She chased her cousin up the stairs.

As she tucked her into bed, Aubrey spoke, "Do you have a story of how you met your husband, Beverly?"

Beverly was stunned. "I don't have a husband," she reminded the young lady.

"No, not yet," the little girl persisted, "but you've already met him, haven't you."

She smiled at Aubrey, "Never you mind, missy. Now get to sleep."

She turned to leave, but Aubrey called out, "Wait, you have to tell me a bedtime story."

"Really, at this hour?"

"Please," she pleaded, "it helps me sleep."

"All right, what story do you want to hear."

"Tell me the story of how you met Aldwin." Beverly's eyes opened wide, and Aubrey just smiled.

SEVENTEEN

Investiture

SUMMER 952 MC

～

On the morning of her investiture, Beverly started the day very early to ensure she was at the Palace long before the ceremony commenced. There were six initiates, including herself, who had arrived shortly before sun up. Each one had a sponsor to help them prepare, and she was glad her father was there to lend her a hand and keep her company.

"Are you nervous?" asked her father.

"Only restless, Father," she said.

"I remember my investiture, I found it all quite overwhelming. Let's go over it one more time, to make sure you're ready."

"Very well," Beverly sighed. They had been going over this for days, and she was sure she remembered everything. She was starting to wonder if this was more for his benefit than hers, but she decided to humour him this one last time. "We go into the Palace Chapel to receive a small blessing. Then we go to the great hall where we will be served a simple breakfast. The Holy Father will give another blessing, then we move to the courtyard. You'll be there with Lightning, and so I will go and stand by you. The Knight Commander will order us to mount, and then I leap into the saddle."

"You know you don't actually have to leap, you just climb up."

"Quiet, Father, you're interrupting my chain of thought. Once we're mounted, we follow the Knight Commander. He leads us out of the Palace and down the Royal Promenade. There'll be lots of people lining the street, and we're allowed to wave if we want to."

"What happens when you reach the Cathedral?" he prompted.

"We dismount, and I pass the reins to you because you and the others have been following along behind. We follow the Knight Commander inside where we are told to stand at the front. Then, each initiate will be struck by the Knight Commander to demonstrate we can take a blow. He will then turn and say we are worthy. The Holy Father says a long boring speech, then the king comes forward, and we all kneel. He smacks us on the shoulders with a sword, and we swear fealty. Then he says we're knights and the celebration begins."

Her father gave her a stern look. "More or less correct, though I don't think the king will be 'smacking' you on the shoulder." He took out a handkerchief and rubbed away an imaginary smudge on her armour. "We're all very proud of you, my dear. Your mother, were she here, would be proud of you, too."

"Thank you, Father, that means a lot to me."

A thin man, a royal courtier, stepped into the room, announcing it was time to begin and the other initiates lined up in front of her. Taking the lead was Sir Balton, the oldest. She had learned that he had been wounded in the battle that had seen him knighted, and it had taken more than a year for him to heal. Second in line was Sir Malcolm, with his finely styled blond hair. He was dressed immaculately, and Beverly wondered just how many coins his armour had cost, for it was inlaid with what appeared to be gold. Following Sir Malcolm was Sir Graham, who was the tallest of the bunch, but what he had in height he looked to lack in wit. She wondered how well he could fight, for had to be constantly reminded of where he was supposed to go. Sir Preston came next, and he appeared to be an ordinary type, a little rough around the edges, but carried himself well. When he was a captain in Mattingly, he had helped repel a Norland raid. Beverly wondered if the man ever shaved, for during all their practise runs, his face was perpetually in need of a shave, and today was no exception. Lastly, in front of Beverly, was Sir Neville, the son of the Earl of Eastwood. He had tried to insist during practise that he be given the lead position, but was told the order was based on the dates they were originally knighted, and Beverly, being the most recent, came last.

The group made their way to the chapel where the Holy Father, a small bald man in a robe, sprinkled water over them while he intoned a blessing. Beverly bent her head, as did the others, but spent her time thinking about the ceremony, not thanking Saxnor. She was sure he would not care one way or the other, for he was, after all, a God that valued deeds not words. The blessing complete, the next stop on the ceremony tour was the great hall where the traditional meal was ready for them; bread that they might be sustained and red wine that symbolized their blood that would be spilt in service to the crown.

She bit into the bread and finding it stale, reached for the wine while glancing up at Sir Graham, who had decided to gulp his down. His eyes bulged, and he spat it out. "Saxnor give me strength, that's horrid stuff," the knight exclaimed through a coughing fit.

Beverly, thankful for Sir Graham's well-timed warning, re-thought her actions and took a small sip. The wine was coarse and burned her throat, definitely not a superior vintage! Perchance someone was being mischievous, she thought, but choose not to voice her opinion. Poor Sir Graham, his cup was refilled, and he was told he had to drink it all. Beverly decided that sipping her own wine little by little would alleviate the chances of her having to imbibe a second glass. Looking around, she noticed Sir Neville had finished his in one large gulp and merely made a face. Sir Preston seemed to enjoy his, and he drank it heartily, then asked for more. She wondered if they all had the same wine and was about to break her silence when the doors were opened, and they were ushered out of the room.

The Holy Father, who had been mumbling something during the meal, now led them to the courtyard where the horses were waiting. Beverly took her place by her father. The Knight Commander strode to the beginning of the line, and looking towards the first candidate, yelled in a clear voice, "Who sponsors this knight?"

The elderly man beside Sir Balton replied in a thin, but steady voice, "I, Sir Albert, do sponsor this knight."

The ritual was repeated down the line until it was Beverly's turn.

"Who sponsors this knight?" the Knight Commander called out for the final time today.

"I, Lord Richard Fitzwilliam, Baron of Bodden do sponsor this gallant knight," her father pronounced.

The Knight Commander took a step back and in a clear voice commanded, "Knights, mount."

Beverly put her foot in the stirrup and leaped into the saddle in one smooth motion. Sir Preston, who had been looking around as he was preparing to mount, was surprised by the swiftness of her actions, and misplacing his foot, completely missed his stirrup. It threw him off balance, and he fell to the ground with a loud groan escaping. Laughter burst from the assembled audience while he stood up, red-faced, and tried again. This time he succeeded, and finally, all the initiates were ready to proceed.

The Knight Commander, now mounted, lined up in front of the initiates and gave the order to advance. The knights fell in behind him, forming two lines, three deep. Sir Preston appeared uncomfortable on his horse and was slow to respond, so Sir Neville, eager to show off, took his place in the line. Beverly brought up the rear, with Sir Preston forced to ride by her side.

Their path took them through the archway to the promenade and then south through the city. Hundreds, perhaps thousands of spectators lined the streets, cheering. Merchants were dashing back and forth selling all manner of items. Children would watch the knights pass and then run ahead to watch them again. The pace of the march was agonizingly slow, and she found it difficult to rein Lightning in at times, his long legs were unused to the slow gait, but she managed to maintain control over her steed.

The noise of the crowd was overwhelming, and she turned to Sir Preston to comment on this, only to notice the uncomfortable position he was in. "Shift your bottom forward, Sir Preston," she leaned in to suggest, "you're too far back in the saddle."

Moving up slightly, he nodded his thanks.

"And stop gripping so tightly with your legs, you're making your horse nervous."

Sir Preston was pale, and sweat trickled down the sides of his face. He looks terrified, Beverly thought to herself. Suddenly, his problem dawned on her, he couldn't ride. How could an accomplished knight be such an abysmal horseman?

Turning back to the front, she witnessed Sir Malcolm in all his glory. He was smiling at the crowd, waving, flashing his bright white teeth at all the ladies. One woman ran from the side of the street and threw him a rose. He caught it with a flourish, smelled it and then tucked in into his sword belt. The crowd cheered, and he continued in his display of theatrics, obviously relishing the attention, but this slowed their pace down even more, something she had not thought was possible.

Turning towards the west gate, they sped up for some unknown reason. Beverly was grateful but wondered why, until she spotted a grand procession ahead of them. It must have been waiting, for when they arrived, trumpets blared, then unexpectedly, there was an army of soldiers, Holy Fathers, and courtiers ahead of them. The new procession moved forward to the tempo of the trumpets, and their small group matched the cadence. It was a marvellous feeling, and Beverly couldn't help but smile. Caught up in the pageantry herself, she waved to the crowd and saw faces smiling back at her. Little girls were waving wooden swords, and it struck her, she had become a symbol for them. Turning to share her observations with Sir Preston, who was facing the other side of the street and trying to wave, she watched as he lost his balance. Beverly grabbed his cape and held on, preventing him from sliding off his horse. The hapless knight leaned heavily in the opposite direction due to his overbalance, and she tugged harder, pulling him back into his saddle. He smiled his thanks and kept both hands on the reins for the rest of the trip.

The Cathedral finally came into view as they made their last turn. It was a magnificent building, with pure white stone and a large dome on the top. The roadway leading to the building had been cleared of spectators, leaving room for the knights in front of them to dismount and form a guard. Once reaching the rendezvous point, each of the six initiates dismounted in turn, passing the reins to their sponsors. The other knights formed a line to either side of them, creating a path that led into the Cathedral. Once again, Sir Neville took advantage of someone's tardiness and was now the third person in line. He had snatched Sir Graham's spot and said knight stared daggers at Sir Neville, stepping forward as if to strike the arrogant man, but Beverly grabbed his arm. "Not here, Sir Graham," she said in a pleasant voice, "your family is watching."

The angry man looked at her before nodding his thanks, finally falling back in line behind the usurper. They proceeded into the Cathedral and walked through the atrium then halted. Individually, they would walk down the nave, each waiting until the one before them had completed the long walk. Sir Bertram went first, and Beverly watched as he proudly strode along, his footsteps echoing in the high ceilinged structure. He was only one-third of the way towards the Holy Father at the far end when a chorus of young voices began to sing. The assembled guests, who filled the seats on either side of the nave, stood as the choir began, watching Sir Bertram as he strode by. The sound echoed through the majestic structure as if the Gods themselves had unleashed their blessings.

Once Sir Bertram reached the end, he was directed by a Holy Father to take up a position near the altar. Sir Malcolm went next, repeating the process, forming up beside Sir Bertram. Sir Neville tried to push forward, to be the third in line, but a rough hand grabbed his arm. He turned with a snarl to complain and saw Marshal-General Valmar holding him. The man shook his head and pointed to his correct position. Sir Neville sulkily moved in front of Beverly, looked around and gave her a look of disgust. And so it went on, each initiate having their moment of glory, each standing in line before the altar.

Finally, it was Beverly's turn, and she strode forward with confidence. She kept her eyes looking straight ahead, but could make out the distinctive blue of her aunt's dress out of the corner of her eye, and then she heard Aubrey's distinct voice, "There she is, Mama!"

Murmurs came from the crowd. A woman had not been knighted in the cathedral in living history, and some people thought it was most improper. Others were cheering her on, with a number of female voices drowning out the men who were complaining. She kept her eyes on the altar and took up her position alongside Sir Neville.

Now a hush fell over the crowd as the Knight Commander entered the Cathedral. Everyone knew what was about to happen. He quickly strode down the nave to stand in front of the knights, facing the altar, waiting. The Holy Father blessed the assemblage, and then the Knight Commander turned, calling forward Sir Bertram.

Sir Bertram walked over and stood to face the man. Beverly knew what was coming next, but the suddenness of the blow startled her, for the Knight Commander had struck him forcibly on the left arm. Sir Bertram swayed with the power of the blow but made no noise. The Knight Commander turned back to the Holy Father and announced the knight was worthy. Sir Bertram returned to his previous position, and Sir Malcolm was called forth. When he was struck he staggered back a step, and the assembled crowd uttered a collective gasp. This pattern was repeated with each knight being struck, and then pronounced worthy. Beverly, the last one called, stood in front of the Knight Commander and waited. The man hesitated, and then suddenly struck her a heavier blow than she had previously witnessed this day. She was ready, and leaned into it slightly as he swung. She noticed him wince when his hand struck her armour. Serves him right, she thought, for being tougher on me because I'm a woman.

The man turned and announced she was worthy, but she detected less enthusiasm than he had for the others, almost as if he had been hoping she would succumb to the blow.

Beverly returned to her position. As the Commander knelt, so too did the initiates. The Holy Father now gave a long speech, and Beverly's knees began to ache in this uncomfortable position. Finally, the devout man ceased his incessant droning, and the trumpets blared. King Andred approached with Marshal-General Valmar following behind him, carrying a sword upon a plush cushion. The king grasped the sword and held it high in the air, instantly hushing the entire Cathedral.

"Since the time of our ancestors," he said, in a strong, clear voice, "men have come forth to serve this kingdom. We stand here today to welcome our brothers to the Order of the Sword," he said, then paused, "and our sister," he added quite unexpectedly.

He strode over to a kneeling Sir Bertram and laid the sword on his left shoulder. He began speaking, and Beverly was reminded of a story she had heard. The tradition had always been right shoulder then left, but King Andred, in his first ceremony as king, had made a mistake and done it in reverse. It was now the tradition to do it thus, and she wondered at the ego of a king who could not admit his error.

The king shifted to the next knight, and she berated herself for not paying attention. He performed the same ritual, chanting the words in a monotonous tone, first laying the sword on the left shoulder, then the right. He made his way down the line repeating the gestures until he came to Beverly.

He smiled down at her and placed the sword upon her left shoulder. "The Order of the Sword was created years ago to recognize the skill and honour of those who proved themselves worthy. Do you claim this honour?"

"Yes," she replied in a loud voice.

He placed the sword upon her right shoulder. "Recite the oath," he said.

"I do hereby swear to place the safety of my sovereign above my own, to faithfully serve the crown in all its majesty, to the end of my days," she proclaimed.

It was only after she completed the litany that she realized she had made a mistake, she was supposed to serve the king, not the crown.

The king ignored the mistake or didn't notice it.

He walked back to his original position, turned, and faced the crowd. "Be it known," he said, "that these men and women have been inducted into the Order of the Sword, and that from this day forward, they should be shown all the courtesy and respect that is their due. Arise, Knights of the Sword."

The knights struggled to stand, for they had been kneeling in armour for some time. Finally upright, Beverly felt the blood begin flowing back into her lower legs.

The choir sang as the king was escorted out of the Cathedral. The knights followed out in single file, back down the nave to the atrium, where they could relax. It was done, the ceremony was complete, and now she was officially Dame Beverly Fitzwilliam, Knight of the Sword.

EIGHTEEN

Life at Court

SUMMER/AUTUMN 952 MC

~

The king spared no expense in entertaining his guests with the elaborate celebration that followed the investiture. All the new knights, and many of the guests drank to excess and gorged themselves, save Beverly, who was more modest with what she drank and the food that she ate. It was astounding the amount of drink the knights could imbibe, and she politely refused when 'dared' to drink a large tankard of ale. It was tradition, the other knights insisted, but she would have none of it. There were stories told of battlefield prowess, but Beverly was sure that most of them were made-up. The details didn't seem to fit the stories, and her experiences were quite different.

Most of the nobles presently residing in the capital were in attendance, including her father and the Brandons. She sat at the table of honour for some of the evening, but as it wore on, she moved to sit with her family, beside little Aubrey. Not long after joining them, Aubrey indicated she needed to visit the garderobe. Lady Mary was about to take her, but Beverly insisted, so the two of them made their way from the room on their mission. Stepping into the hallway, they were directed up a set of stairs, where a small room had been set aside for the guests. At the top of the stairs, as they neared the second floor, they heard talking. The stairs opened into a hallway where they saw a richly clothed man pushing a woman up against the wall. The lady was struggling to stop him, but he was ignoring her complaints, with his hand already under her dress.

Beverly quickly assessed the situation. Telling Aubrey to stay where she was, she moved forward and grabbed the violator by the back of his neck, her other hand clutching his belt. She hurled him against the far wall, and the mongrel sank to the floor in a drunken stupor. She knelt over him to see if he was still breathing, and then turned to his prey, who nodded her thanks as she fled down the hallway. Aubrey left her spot of safety with her hand out for Beverly to lead her away. The two of them continued on their way, ignoring the man dozing in the hallway, silently agreeing not to talk about this.

They returned to the festivities a little while later to overhear her father and uncle talking.

"...they're not sure who did it, but the man's going to have a massive headache," her father was saying.

"What was that, Father?" she asked.

He turned to face her, "Oh, you missed some excitement, my dear. Sir Jeremy over there, was attacked by someone. They laid a beating on the poor fellow. He's very upset about it."

Beverly looked over to see the man she had thrown against the wall. "How terrible," she said in a neutral tone. "Do they know who's responsible?"

Her uncle piped up, "No, but he swears it was a bear of a man, very large and very strong. Aubrey, you were up that way, did you see anything?"

Beverly looked at Aubrey, putting her finger to her lips. "No, Father," her cousin responded, "we didn't see anything."

The table turned to a different subject, and no more was said on the matter.

Beverly awoke early the next morning, ready for the start of her new life. She went to report to the administration office but found nobody there. It soon became quite apparent that not many knights were awake after the previous evening's debauchery. She was used to the discipline of the Keep where patrols had to be mounted, soldiers posted to lookouts and such. She was sorely disappointed to see the lackadaisical manner of the Order of the Sword. Technically, the order formed the Royal Bodyguard, but many of its knights were assigned elsewhere. The king did this to defer the cost. Knights under service to a noble were paid and supplied by that noble, rather than the crown, so it was in the crown's best interest to farm them out whenever possible. In years gone by, a knight swore fealty to a noble who, in turn, was sworn to the king, but the current king's grandfather had changed all that. He had insisted that all knights swear direct obedience to the king. It was part of a gradual tightening of rules that drew more power into the hands of the sovereign.

She was musing over this very fact when she noticed a fellow new knight. "Sir Preston," she called out.

The young man turned at the sound of her voice. "Oh, Lady Beverly," he replied.

"Dame Beverly, now," she corrected.

"Sorry, Dame Beverly. I suppose I must get used to that now."

"Where is everybody?" she asked.

"Most of the knights are still in barracks, though I saw a couple out in the practise yard."

The practise yard sounded like an excellent idea, so she nodded her thanks and headed in that direction.

The barracks were located at the back of the Palace and formed a square around the practise yard. It was quite sizable, and Beverly appreciated the extra space compared to the cramped yard at Bodden. She was walking through the archway looking at the cobblestone flooring when she passed two knights off to the side. One was leaning with his back against the wall, while the other stood just in front of him. They were deep in conversation, so Beverly paid them no heed. Just as she passed, the second man stuck out his foot, and she stumbled over it. Hearing the men laugh, she turned angrily to face them.

The knights both looked at her with smiles on their faces, and the one who wasn't leaning puckered his lips in a kissing motion. She stepped forward and struck with the flat of her palms against his chest. He fell backwards, into his companion, knocking them both to the ground. She stood, glaring at them, enjoying the sudden look of fear on their faces. Good, she thought, if they fear me, they'll leave me alone.

"Problem, gentlemen?" she said in a polite tone.

"No, not at all," one of them said, "my mistake."

Beverly turned and continued to the yard. She started her normal practise movements, carefully testing her footing, pivoting, swinging the sword. She soon got into her rhythm. Her motions were graceful, though it was not something that crossed her mind. Other knights began to watch, but she ignored them. She found the yard large enough that she could practise her drills in a circular pattern, rather than having to constantly back up as she did in Bodden. Her day's training complete, she strolled over to the well to draw some water. Nearby, a large knight stood, moving to intercept her. Arriving before her, he leaned against the well, blocking her access. She had no choice but to halt.

"So you're the new knight, I presume?" he stated more than asked.

"I'm Dame Beverly, yes," she answered, in a neutral tone.

"Well, Dame Beverly, we have certain traditions here. You don't want us to treat you differently, do you?"

She crossed her arms. "No, of course not. All right, I'll bite, what's the tradition."

"Well," the sizable knight said, a sly smile crossing his face, "women who come to the well have to pay the toll."

Beverly frowned, but knew she had to go through with this. "What, might I ask, is the toll?"

"Well," he said, standing up straighter, "you can give us a kiss or touch us."

A smile crossed her face. She knew where this was going, and she had the perfect solution. "So let me get this straight," she said in her most innocent voice, "I can either kiss you or I can touch you?"

"Yes, my dear."

"And where do I touch you?" she asked.

The knight pointed at his groin, "Right here, my dear."

She looked at his groin and smiled, "You're going to uncover it, aren't you?" she asked sweetly.

The knight's eyes lit up, he obviously had not expected this to go so well. He dropped his pants revealing a modest set of family jewels. "Ready when you are, my dear."

"All right," she said, "close your eyes. Here it comes."

She drove her armour-plated knee into the man's groin, and he collapsed like a sack of potatoes. He was writhing on the ground in agony, and those who were watching were suddenly holding themselves as if they shared the big man's pain.

"That's what I think of your tradition," she said, "and only my father calls me dear."

She leaned down close to the squirming man's face, "Do we understand each other?"

The man squeaked out his capitulation.

"I'm sorry," she said, feeling vindictive, "I don't think the others can hear you."

"Yes," he yelled out through gritted teeth.

She stepped over him and drew some water, while two other knights rushed over to carry the casualty away. Serves him right, she thought, the man was an arse.

The barracks were two-story structures with a common area on the ground floor. At one end was a set of stairs that led to the men's sleeping quarters while at the other end were stairs leading to the captain's office.

The second floor was three-quarters bunks and one quarter for the officer, but there was no door adjoining the two. The Barracks weren't set up to house women, so one of the captain's offices had been set aside to offer her some semblance of privacy. Beverly found this arrangement satisfactory, and she settled in without too much trouble. The others were most accommodating since the encounter at the well, and though she despised the necessity of it, she was pleased with the results.

Over the next few days she came to understand there were no official duties for her to attend to, but while searching through the captain's office, she discovered a number of interesting books she recognized as ledgers. Upon further inspection, she discerned that each knight was supposed to contribute to a common fund, which would then be used to pay for 'entitlements'. These could include paying for entertainment, extra food or wine, or even man servants. The records indicated that nothing had been collected in months, and after making some enquiries, she discovered why. The previous captain had been Valmar, and after his promotion to marshal-general, nobody had taken his place. She resolved to fix this discrepancy and approached the other knights directly. She didn't seek command over them, merely to have them pay their dues and make some arrangements.

Most of the knights were young, arrogant men, full of desire for food, women and drink, and not necessarily in that order. There were a handful of decent chaps in the mix, but they were often the ones to pull the guard duty. She was not sure how that worked, but came to the conclusion that coins in the marshal-general's pocket could get anyone out of their responsibilities. She approached these dedicated men first, and after getting a positive response, starting in on the rest. Within two weeks almost everyone was on board, and when they used the new funds to purchase some fine wine, the final holdouts joined in.

Keeping track of the funds was the easy part, for she kept meticulous accounts. The biggest problem was collecting from the more spendthrift individuals. She resolved to fix this situation permanently in the third week. She hired a cook to cater a special meal for the knights, but those who were not paid up in full had to watch their companions eating an elaborate dinner. After that, all the knights in the company kept their dues paid.

The summer grew into autumn, and things settled down into a regular routine, boring, but predictable. A few of the knights, perhaps shamed by her constant training, had begun practicing on their own, and they asked her to teach them. There was only a few, but it gave her something to do, and she found the work enjoyable, yet she yearned for something more worthy of her skills.

As the cooler weather approached, she was asked by a small group of rather embarrassed knights if the fund might be used to bring in women. Beverly was shocked by this request, but after careful thought concluded that it might curb their lecherous tendencies towards the women of the Palace. Uncharacteristically, she found herself planning on going into town to hire prostitutes, an act that she didn't have a clue about, nor had ever thought she would ever need to know anything about. Realizing that she was out of her depth on this, she sought out help from some of the more discreet knights, and then made the arrangements. It proved a success, but she didn't get much sleep. So noisy were they beyond the thin wooden wall that she choose to stay at the Bodden Manor for the night, to gain some privacy. Lying in her comfortable bed, she reflected on the life she was leading and decided there must be something better. She resolved to see Marshal-General Valmar in the morning to find out how her talents might be put to better use.

Her first task of the day saw her at the Palace, making enquiries on where she would find Marshal-General Valmar. As luck would have it, his office was just a small distance from her barracks. She didn't have an appointment, so she had to sit and wait for an opening. The marshal's aid hinted that a small donation could speed things up a little, but she refused. She hated to think that the man in charge of the army was such a scoundrel, but the evidence kept piling up. Valmar had saved the king's life, well, actually she had saved his life. Valmar had just used his horse to collect the king. Since then, he had been made a marshal-general and was now one of the king's closest confidants, some even said, his closest friend. There was a lot of resentment amongst the aristocracy, for Valmar was not born a noble. Not to say you had to be a noble to be competent, for Saxnor knew Gerald Matheson was not one, and he was very competent. Valmar, on the other hand, couldn't, it seemed, even organize his own clothes.

For half a day Beverly sat in the hallway until Valmar happened to come out, probably to go and eat. She followed him and spoke up.

"Marshal-General, sir, might I have a word?"

Valmar turned around, irritation showing on his face. "What is it?" he demanded, not appearing to recognize her.

He was notoriously bad at remembering faces, and she wondered if this was some sort of mental weakness or if he just didn't care to take the time.

"I was wondering if you might have an assignment for me?" she asked.

"No," he said, and stormed off, annoyed with the interruption to his day.

Beverly fumed, this was no way to run an army. She sat down and thought it through, coming up with a simple solution. It would take some time, but she was sure it would work. For the next two weeks she researched Valmar's schedule, then she started showing up everywhere he went, always with the same question. The result was inevitable. After only two and a half weeks of constant interruptions, he gave in. She would report to his office in the morning to receive her orders.

NINETEEN

Royal Bodyguard

She reported to Marshal-General Valmar's office in her full armour. The aide escorted her in while Valmar sat behind his desk, nursing a tankard of ale, glancing up at her approach.

"Dame Beverly," he directed, "do have a seat."

She was surprised by his civility for he was known as a difficult and obstinate man. She sat down, waiting for him to speak.

"I've been trying to decide what to do with you," he said, pausing to take a sip. "I think it might be wise to use your talents to protect the princess."

She smiled, "Thank you, Marshal-General."

"How much do you know about her?" he asked.

"She's nine years old?" she offered hesitantly.

"Yes, that's correct. She only comes to the capital in the company of the queen, and as you probably already know, the king and queen are rarely in the capital at the same time."

Beverly nodded. She was very familiar with the habits of the king and queen, and with the influence of the king's mistress. It would be disastrous if she and the queen were to meet, so they were rarely in the same place at the same time.

"What are to be my precise duties?" she asked.

"You are to remain in the company of the princess whenever the queen desires it. That means you may only see her once or twice a week or, if the queen likes you, you might be utilized more often. You'll be commanded by the queen, so your precise orders will depend on her."

"Yes, Marshal-General," she said.

"Oh, and one more thing," he said, as she was about to stand. "You won't need to wear that armour."

"I beg your pardon, Marshal-General?" she responded, not sure if she had heard properly.

"You'll need to wear attire appropriate to the court," he explained. "It would be unladylike to wear armour or carry a sword, and Princess Margaret is not to be confused about how a proper lady is to behave. You do know how a lady behaves, don't you?"

"Of course, Marshal-General," she said, "I AM a baron's daughter."

"Well, see to it that you remember that."

"But sir," she objected, "how am I to protect the princess if I'm not to carry a sword or wear armour?"

"Frankly," he replied, "I don't care. You were only knighted because the king didn't know you were a woman, but what's done is done, and we can't undo it, or the king will lose face. Of course, if you don't like it, you can always leave the Order of the Sword, and return to Bodden to resume your life there. Is that what you'd like to do?"

"No sir," she replied.

"Pity, it would have made things so much easier." He stared into his tankard for a moment before continuing, "The queen is hosting a Midwinter Gala next week. You'll need to be in attendance. You should take a few days to acquire a suitable wardrobe, at the expense of the crown, of course. Report to the queen on the seventeenth, that's the day before the gala. Do you understand?"

She felt like telling him she was not an idiot but thought it was better if she didn't. She simply replied, "Yes, Marshal-General," nodded, and left the room.

Thankfully, nobody was waiting outside the office to witness her, as she stormed away, seething with anger. After weeks of trying to procure a real assignment, she finally secured what should have been a prime position, only to have it hurled in her face. She would be a glorified babysitter, a job that could easily have been done by a lady-in-waiting or a maid.

She spent a considerable amount of time trying to ascertain what type of dress was most appropriate for her new role at court. It was difficult to determine, for the position had never existed before. The objective was not to overshadow the royals, but to at least display the importance of the position. In the end, she opted for a plainer dress, made of superior material. She located a capable seamstress in town that had some additional suggestions, and by the time the date arrived, she had three new dresses in her wardrobe. She ended up wearing the green dress with a gold belt, which circled her waist, hanging down the front. She completed the ensemble with a dagger, a popular accessory at court that could also be used at mealtimes.

Reporting to the queen on the seventeenth of the month, Beverly found her to be stern of countenance. The queen smiled little, seemingly unimpressed by having a new member assigned to her entourage.

The Midwinter Festival was a popular celebration marking the middle of the season and reminding people that spring would be coming before long. Bodden had always hosted a feast, and part of the celebration would be her father and others visiting the poor with gifts of food and coin. Here in Wincaster, the tradition was much different. The Midwinter Gala was a party for the influential members of society. Only the titled and important people were invited to attend. The king spent the winter in the south, usually Shrewesdale, and the prominent men of the kingdom would follow him there, the better to represent their interests. Their wives, on the other hand, would come to Wincaster to socialize with the queen. Beverly had seen the guest list and was astonished at the number of unaccompanied women that were due to attend. It was easier to track who would not be gathering than who would. Of course, she knew her father would not be present, he was far too busy on the frontier. She recognized many names, but she knew them only by reputation. There were few in attendance that she had ever met, and both her aunt and uncle were noticeably absent from the list.

With the festivities starting just after midday, she arrived early at the Palace, as per the queen's request and was surprised when the guests began arriving shortly thereafter. With no actual orders, she chose to spend the first few hours helping nobles from their coaches. It was amusing to watch each trying to outdo the others with their grand entrances.

Upon arriving, guests were escorted into the great hall, which had been decorated with bright ribbons to celebrate the season. Many of the nobles had brought their children along, and they ran about the hall, mostly unsupervised. There were many knights in attendance, and Beverly was annoyed to see that they were all in their best armour, although bereft of helmets. She recognized them of course, for they were all billeted together in the barracks. Noticing that only a few were here, she wondered how they had been chosen for this duty, for they varied from veterans to newly knighted. She put the thought from her mind as she made her way into the

hall escorting the Duchess of Colbridge to be introduced to the queen, and
then left to make her way around the festivities.

The Gala was not a feast in the traditional sense. Instead of a great table
heaped with food and chairs all around, they had adopted the new style of
celebration with tables to the side of the room and people standing around
eating off plates. The centre was left open for dancing later in the evening.
This intrigued Beverly, for the only dancing she had ever witnessed was
that of the commoners in Bodden. She had heard that the dances in
Wincaster were highly organized affairs requiring careful study and
practise.

Someone rapped a staff on the floor to get everyone's attention just as
she had made her way over to the food table to sample the delights heaped
upon it. The guests were instructed to take their places on the dance floor.
She watched in interest as they lined themselves up in two rows. One row
was all women, and the other, facing them, were men, including some
knights. Beverly wondered how on earth they would dance in armour, but
as she watched she realized it would not be difficult, for the dance consisted
of carefully planned walking while holding their partner's hand. It was
perhaps the strangest thing she had ever seen, and she wondered where this
idea had come from.

Most of the afternoon and evening consisted of her snacking on food
and watching the dancing. She was even asked to dance by a young noble
but politely declined, as she was on duty. The man was gracious and
commented that perhaps she might take up his offer at a later date. She was
flattered and didn't want to offend him, so she replied, "Perhaps."

She spied Princess Margaret sitting with a group of like-aged children.
They were eating small cakes and pastries while drinking some sort of pale
cider.

As the evening wore on it became readily apparent that there was no
threat here to either the princess or the queen. She found the entire gala to
be a surreal event. It was a different world here in the capital, a world that
she just couldn't quite grasp.

She left the room briefly to use the garderobe and ran across the
Duchess of Colbridge. The woman was chatting with a knight. On her
return she saw them head out of the room, climb the stairs, with the
Duchess leading, holding the young knight's hand. Beverly shook her head,
mistrusting what her eyes beheld. The Duchess was not a young woman, in
fact, she was old enough to be the knight's mother, if truth be told.

It was upon her return to the gala that the reality of the situation hit her.
She looked around the room to observe that most of the knights were
paired up with the noble ladies. All of them were young and handsome,

prime examples of manhood. Her discovery shocked and disgusted her. Here were the wives of the most powerful men of the kingdom, and they were carrying on scandalously. She thought of Valmar's words to her and realized the irony in them. He was worried about her being a bad influence, but in truth, the nobles were far worse.

Eventually, she was summoned by the queen. Princess Margaret was getting tired, she was told, and needed to be escorted to bed. Beverly was tasked with the job, in the company of a maidservant.

She escorted them to the princess's chambers, where the maid changed her and put her to bed. Margaret was lying in bed being tucked in when she suddenly spoke to Beverly.

"You're that lady knight, aren't you?" she enquired.

"Yes, Your Highness," Beverly replied.

"Can I ask you a question?" the little girl asked.

"Certainly," she responded.

She was expecting questions about knighthood but was surprised by the young child's question.

"Are you a noble?"

"Yes, my father's the Baron of Bodden."

"Can you tell me how marriages are arranged?" she asked bluntly.

"I beg your pardon?" Beverly was unsure how to respond to such a question.

"Well, I suspect that noble marriages and royal marriages must work the same way. How was your marriage arranged?"

"My marriage?" she asked, with a look of shock on her face.

"Well, aren't you married? You look old enough. Surely your father had to have arranged one by now. I was wondering how that's done."

Beverly blushed and immediately thought of Aldwin. Of course, she could never marry Aldwin, but she had decided that if she couldn't have Aldwin, then no one else would do. She had no intention of explaining that to the princess.

She must have mulled this over longer than she thought for suddenly the princess spoke again.

"Well? Are you promised?"

"No, Your Highness," she replied, thinking fast. "Bodden, where I come from, is on the frontier and we were kept far too busy to deal with such matters."

"Oh well, I was hoping to learn how it all works. Never mind, you can go now."

"Yes, Your Highness," she bowed and left the room, leaving her in the capable hands of her maidservant.

. . .

The Gala proved to be the high point of her royal assignment, for the queen had little use for her afterwards. Although she was always on call, she was seldom required and found herself with lots of free time. Left to her own devices, she practised with her weapons every day, even finding some new ones in the Palace Armoury. Soon, she was proficient with every weapon there but had no cause to use them.

Spring eventually arrived and with it came warmer weather allowing for casual riding, and the queen again requested her services. It was conveyed to her that armour was not necessary, and she was forbidden to ride Lightning, lest the great horse scare the princess. Instead, she was given a much smaller horse, a well behaved, docile creature which looked ridiculously easy to handle.

The queen and her entourage arrived at the stables as Beverly was checking her mount's tackle. Beverly looked up, noticing the princess was not in attendance and wondered why. The queen beckoned her over.

"I need you to go and collect the princess," she said. "She'll be at her afternoon lessons. Make sure you tell the tutor she'll be back at dinner time. He is to continue her lessons upon her return. Have you got that, girl?"

The queen always treated her like an idiot, but she had come to expect that from everyone at the Palace. "Yes, Your Majesty," she replied, making her way to the sun room where the princess traditionally took her lessons.

She knocked on the door and was granted leave to enter. Inside, the princess was sitting on a chair and the tutor, a man named William Renfrew, was drawing on a chalk slate that was sitting on an easel.

As she opened the door, the tutor glanced over at her with a slight look of distaste. "Is there something I can do for you?" he said with a sneer.

"Her Majesty, the queen, has requested the presence of the princess at the stables. They are to go riding today."

The princess jumped out of her chair with a smile. "Thank you," she said, "I shall be glad to head to the stables as soon as I change."

She headed straight for the door, two ladies-in-waiting accompanying her, leaving Beverly in the room with the tutor.

"I am also instructed to inform you that the queen would like you to continue the lesson upon the princess's return."

Renfrew looked up from the slate that he was erasing and stared at her for a moment. "Very well," he finally said.

She turned to leave, but he spoke again, "Hold on a moment," he said, "you're that knight, aren't you?"

"Yes," she said, turning, "Dame Beverly Fitzwilliam."

"Fitzwilliam, I know that name. You must be from the frontier."

"Yes," she replied.

He walked up to her, and she felt his eyes roaming over her body. "How are you finding life at the Palace, my dear?" he said.

Beverly was immediately on the defensive. She hated being called 'dear' by anyone other than her father, but chose not to show her displeasure.

"It's...interesting," she said at last.

"You know Wincaster is a very large city, I'd be happy to show you around if you like."

"That's very kind of you," she said, "but unnecessary. I've become quite familiar with the layout of the city."

"You know, I could also show you around the Palace. There are many rooms we could investigate together."

She watched him move his head, this time he eyed her up and down. Finishing his inspection, he settled his eyes on her breasts, and let out a little sigh.

"That dress looks a little tight, perhaps we should loosen it."

She was about to respond when he reached up and pulled the string that held the top of her dress closed. She pushed his hand away, and he suddenly grabbed her by the dress and tried to pull her into him.

"Come on, you little tart," he said, "I know what you want."

She pushed him back with more force than she expected, causing him to stumble, but he kept his footing. He laughed and moved towards her again.

"Oh, playing hard to get," the tutor sneered. "I love a challenge."

"Challenge this," she said and slapped him hard across the face.

Renfrew spun around and fell, grabbing his face with his hand as his body impacted with the floor. He squirmed on the ground, and then rolled over on to his back, looking up at her.

She stepped towards him, and his eyes went wild with fear. He shuffled backwards, and she heard a small cry of despair coming from his mouth. She raised her hands in the air as if in surrender, and turned to leave the room. As the door closed behind her, she heard him yelling.

"You bitch," he was yelling, "you'll pay for this."

The next morning she received a summons to report to Marshal-General Valmar. She entered the room to see him sitting behind his desk. His face looked plump and red, and she made out the movement of his jaw, as if he was biting down hard.

Even before she sat down, he was in action. "Are you pleased with yourself?" he asked venomously.

"I beg your pardon?" she said, not sure what this was about.

"I have it on good authority that you have been acting in a most un-ladylike manner," he said, "and setting a bad example for Princess Margaret." His voice was rising both in volume and in pitch. "And I specifically told you that you had to behave like a lady. Now I hear you've been putting all sorts of strange ideas into the princess's head."

Beverly's mouth hung open, unsure of how to respond. "Who has made these accusations?" she finally requested.

"They have been made by the Royal Tutor, a man with great integrity."

She looked appalled. The tutor, Renfrew, was the one responsible. It appeared her humiliation of the man had come back to haunt her.

"I have been informed by the queen that your services as bodyguard are no longer required. Congratulations 'Dame Beverly', you've just managed to disgrace both your name and the order."

"I must protest," she said at last. "This is completely unfair-"

"Unfair?" he interrupted. "I'll tell you what's unfair. Being stuck with you is unfair. Do what is right, renounce the order, leave this city and return to the pigsty that is Bodden."

"I will not leave the order!" she declared obstinately.

"Then I have little left to offer you."

He looked down at papers scattered across his desk.

"I am hereby reassigning you. I may be forced to tolerate you in Wincaster, but I'll be damned if I have to have you at the Palace. You are ordered to the barracks of the Wincaster Light Horse. There, you'll assume the temporary command of the company, and stay until further notice."

She knew what the posting meant. The light horse was used for picket duties and for running messages, it wasn't a company in the real sense of the word, merely a collection of runners and messengers. Putting a knight in charge of such a unit was an insult, and could be seen as nothing more, but she had to bear it. She was about to open her mouth when he interrupted her.

"Say anymore, and I will reconsider laying charges against you. You are dismissed. Don't let me see you in this office again."

She turned and left, tears welling in her eyes, but was determined not to let him see her cry. Upon entering the waiting room, the aide handed her the official transfer orders. Damn Valmar, he had planned this all along. Orders in hand, she left, her anger overcoming her previous urge to cry.

TWENTY

Summer in Wincaster

SUMMER 953 MC

The barracks of the Wincaster Light Horse were located halfway across the city from the Palace, and Beverly immediately understood why. It was a ramshackle building with a stable that looked like it would fall over in a mild wind. The barracks themselves were not much better, consisting of a plain wooden structure with little in the way of amenities.

Sergeant Hugh Gardner greeted her upon entry, and together, they inspected the facilities. From the moment she walked in, she realized that the interior was in as bad of shape as the exterior. She knew that she should not have been surprised, for this was more of a punishment than a true duty, but she was sorely disappointed by the state of the barracks. Frustrated with the situation she found herself in, she realized that it would not do to take it out on the men of the company. She was determined to familiarize herself with them, but it proved difficult. Whenever the army needed to send a message of any type, they would send for a rider and the light horse would provide one from their numbers, sending him on his way. This meant that the barracks were perpetually half empty, and those that were present remained here for only a short time.

On paper, the company numbered fifty men, but with many off on courier duties across the kingdom, and some residing in the town, there was simply no method in place to tell how many were available at any time. The next step was to address the men directly, but for that, she would have to have them assembled. She detailed Sergeant Gardner to collect the men for morning inspection on the morrow. She would then check those present against the payroll and find out who was missing. Following roll call would be an inspection of the quarters and the stables with the men in tow, perhaps between them all, they might figure out a way to improve their situation. It was going to be a lot of work, but she was determined to make a difference. Let Valmar think that he was punishing her. She would show him that she could make a positive change to this company.

The next morning revealed what she was dealing with when the men lined up on parade. They were a sorry looking lot, mostly older warriors who were invalided out of their regular units due to minor injuries or just plain old age. Their equipment varied remarkably, such that no two men had the same armour and weapon combination. She talked to each man in turn, learning their names and their past service. They were decent enough soldiers, thrown into this company as a last ditch effort to wrench some further service out of them. They were old and tired, and their morale was non-existent. Beverly was sure that with the right kind of support, they would make a fine company, but there was a considerable amount of work to be done.

Next, they did a walk-through of the barracks. She encouraged the men to talk honestly, and she found they all complained about the same things. The walls were drafty and the roof leaked. The stables were little better, and the horses billeted here were in a sad state, poorly groomed and badly fed.

With the inspection complete, they made their way to the yard, the small enclosed area that formed the parade ground. She organized the men into several groups based on their backgrounds. Some were handy with wood and these she tasked with repairs to the buildings. Others were more skilled with horses and these she detailed off with specific orders for the stables. The issue of equipment was another matter entirely, for a few of the men had their own weapons, but the company itself had very little to offer. She would have to come up with a way to make up the shortfall.

The easiest change to make was to create a duty roster. Beverly called each soldier into the office and recorded which cities they had been to in the past, in the service of their duties. She then made a list for each city, of riders that were familiar with the area. From now on, when a rider returned with a dispatch that was to go outside the city, they would report back to the barracks first, and a soldier familiar with the area would be tasked with the delivery. In this way, the messages would be routed more efficiently. She also ensured the men received their back pay, which was somewhat in arrears, due to the old captain leaving the company, and it being leaderless for a brief period of time.

Once she had the men settled, she needed to get to work on acquiring supplies. She dispatched Sergeant Gardner to Army Headquarters at the Palace with a request, a long list of items ranging from swords and light armour to wood and thatch. She didn't expect much to come of it, but it was worth a try. Sergeant Gardner returned from the Palace with bad news, the army would not provide what they needed.

Determining that most of her men did not have basic horse care skills, she took it upon herself to personally organize the clean out of the stables. She created a rotating duty to make sure all the horses were groomed and fed regularly. Feeding this many horses proved to be difficult, due to food shortages from the poor harvest the previous year. The company had funds to buy grain, but it was scarce and expensive in the city, so she sent men out to the outlying farms to buy up any hay that might be available. Word soon got around and farmers starting bringing the hay to the barracks in return for easy coin.

One of the advantages of having old soldiers is that they know lots of people. She armed them with coins and sent them around to taverns near the other companies. They soon learned the truth, it was only the light horse that was being denied supplies. Marshal-General Valmar's hand was behind this slight, but she hit upon a solution. One of her men had served with the Wincaster Foot, a unit of infantry billeted in the capital. It was a simple matter for him to obtain a copy of the captain's signature, which she practised until she could duplicate it. A requisition was then written out with the good captain's signature and sent to the Palace along with some imposters. Sure enough, they returned with the wood they needed and some decent new swords.

With the repairs soon underway, the buildings were looking much better. The soldiers were learning their horse craft, and within a fortnight, the horses showed a marked improvement. Once the repairs were complete, Beverly started training the men. Since their primary task was carrying dispatches, she began by improving their riding skills. Some were already quite proficient, and these she put to work helping the others. While this was going on, other riders returned from their trips to be introduced and interviewed. By the end of her first month with the light horse, she was making progress. The men were happier and began feeling a certain pride in their captain, the only woman to command a company in the kingdom.

. . .

It was on a particularly hot summer day that Beverly was standing in the centre of the yard, while six men rode in circles around her. She was watching their technique, making corrections when her attention was distracted by a horseman riding up to the barracks through the north entrance. She was about to reprimand the interloper when she recognized the rider.

"Father!" she said in delight.

"My dear," he said, "so good to see you again. I dare say, you've been busy."

"I've had to make the most of it," she said with a smile. "Valmar won't give me the time of day. How is everyone in Bodden?"

"They're well. They send their kindest regards. Tell me what you've been up to," he insisted.

She looked around at the barracks and smiled, "Tell you what," she said, "let me show you."

She led him around, introducing the men, giving him a tour of the work they had done. She was generous in her praise, and they responded in a heartfelt manner. They joked with her and her father and spoke highly of all the good she had done. Eventually, they made their way back to her office and sat down.

"Well," he said, "I see you've done well for yourself despite your…strange assignment."

"I'm not going to let Valmar dampen my spirits," she said, "and besides, these men deserve better. But enough about me. Tell me, what brings you to Wincaster? Shouldn't you be in Bodden?"

"I must confess I came here to see you, my dear. I've missed you terribly. With you and Gerald both gone, I've had to spend a lot of time training up new patrol leaders."

"What happened to Gerald?" she asked. "He was supposed to be healed by the Royal Life Mage."

"I'm sorry to say that never happened. It appears the king is too possessive of his wizard to let others use his services. Once Valmar got his hands on Gerald, we couldn't get him back."

"So where is he now?" she asked.

"It appears he's been assigned to the Wincaster Foot."

It was Beverly's turn to blush slightly. "Oh dear," she said, "I'm afraid we might have stolen some of his supplies, I hope it doesn't land him in trouble."

Her father laughed, "I'm sure there's no harm done. I've been up to the Palace, and I haven't heard anything bad. I'm sure if Valmar figured it out, he'd be all over you. Don't give it another thought." He laughed and poured a drink, passing it to her over the table. "I hear there's a food shortage."

"Yes," she agreed, "and there's likely to be trouble in town because of it. The king has been hoarding food, and of course, he's feeding the soldiers so they can put down any trouble. I'm afraid it might blow into something bigger if the crown isn't careful."

"Let's hope it doesn't come to that," he said, sipping his wine. "I wouldn't like to think about the slaughter that would occur if the king set the soldiers on the townsfolk, it could get nasty very quickly."

"Agreed," she said, "but let's hope the king has more sense than that."

They ended up talking well into the night, and she realized how much she missed her father. He left with a promise to return later in the week, and she retired for the evening.

Two days later, riots broke out in multiple areas in the city. The army was called in, with units dispatched to block the rioters off from the richer sections of town. The light horse was running dispatches throughout the city, and with the increased number of messages, Beverly knew that something was about to happen. She soon heard the reports, and it was not good news. A mass of rioters had ransacked businesses along Walpole Street, and a troop of infantry had been sent to block their way. Fighting had erupted between the two sides, resulting in a general slaughter. The captain of the company was killed in the fighting, and the Palace was on the verge of recalling all their companies home to suppress the rebellion. The whole city held their breath, but thank Saxnor, the riots subsided. Perhaps the slaughter had been enough, or perhaps the threat of the army had convinced them of the futility of their actions. After three more days passed without riots, the populace breathed a collective sigh of relief.

The messages grew less frequent, and life began to return to normal. She was back to watching the men drill with their swords when her father next visited, this time on foot.

"Have you got time to spare?" he enquired.

"Of course, Father. I'll get Sergeant Gardner to carry on with the training." She made the necessary arrangements and then walked towards her office, her father in tow.

"What is it?" she said, once they were out of earshot.

"I was wondering if you might be available for something tomorrow?"

"I can be," she offered. "What is it you need me for?"

"I've arranged a special meeting with some important people, and I'd like you to be there."

"This sounds awfully mysterious," she observed.

"Oh, it's very important. I'd like you there in your armour if it's not too much trouble."

Her face turned serious, "Of course, Father. When will you need me?"

"I'll meet you here just after lunch, and we'll walk over to the Palace together."

"You're meeting them at the Palace rather than the manor house? How important are these people?"

"I'd rather not say more at this time, I'll explain it to you tomorrow."

"Very well, I'll be ready," she said.

He left her deep in thought. She couldn't help but wonder what her father was getting her into, but knew he was a man who planned things very carefully. She would have to wait to see who these mysterious men were.

Her father had impressed on her the importance of the meeting, so she spent the morning cleaning her armour. She would leave her helmet behind, for it was the custom at the Palace not to wear them. They met at the barracks, walking in silence most of the way. Her father was rubbing his beard, his habit when deep in thought and she didn't want to disturb him.

Upon arriving at the Palace, they went into the west wing where the army offices were located. He had arranged for a private room to be made available, with drinks and cups waiting inside.

"I'm not sure how long it will be before my visitors arrive," he said at last. "Will you take up a position in the hallway and let me know when they make their appearance? I have to think over a few things before they get here."

"Certainly, Father," she said, taking up a guard position outside the door.

She was only waiting a few moments before the door opened and her father was standing in the doorway.

"Beverly," he said, "Come inside a moment, I need to talk to you."

"Yes, Father," she replied, stepping into the room. "What is it?"

She noticed his face had a faraway look, he was carefully framing his words. She had seen this before.

"I am about to have a meeting with Lord Barrington and Lord Montrose," he said. "You know of them?"

"Yes," she replied. "Barrington is one of the king's advisor's and Montrose is the Earl of Shrewesdale, one of the king's strongest supporters."

"No doubt by now you would have heard of the massacre at Walpole Street?" he enquired.

"Yes, though I don't know all the details."

"Tell me what you know," he gently prompted.

"Lord Walters lost his head and let the troops massacre the townsfolk. If he had not died in the assault, they would have dismissed him!" Her disgust was evident.

"Well, that's true, but it looks like his family wants a scapegoat, someone to blame for the blunder."

She knew the captain was killed and wondered who might shoulder the blame.

He paused for a moment as if trying to find the right words. Finally, he sighed and spoke, "They want to blame his sergeant, Gerald Matheson."

Beverly was shocked. "No, that can't be!" she said. "You know he would never condone such a thing!"

"You and I both know that Gerald Matheson would never support such action," he said, "but I'm afraid that they want a scapegoat. This meeting, I hope, will avoid any public humiliation for him, but I fear his military days are over."

"But that's not fair! He served you for years, for Saxnor's sake! He trained me, taught me to use a sword! He's been a mentor to me!"

"I know that, and believe me when I say I will do everything I can for him. I owe him much. Save for his wound, I would have kept him on at Bodden. The King's Life Mage could have been more cooperative and healed him. Then he could have returned to us, but you know how the king is, wants to keep all the magic to himself. I sent him here to recuperate, with letters to Marshal-General Valmar to ask for his intervention, but to no avail. Instead, he assigned him to this local company, and now we have to deal with the results."

She sneered at the name Valmar, and it didn't escape the notice of her father.

"You must learn to hide your emotions, my dear. Valmar is a powerful friend of the king."

"Valmar is incompetent," she interjected. "We both know that you should have been made marshal-general."

"Be thankful I was not," he replied, "or Bodden would be someone else's responsibility, and the north would have surely fallen by now."

She knew he spoke the truth, but still felt he had been overlooked. "So what is it you want me to do?"

"I want you to be present for the meeting, stand inside the door, just observe and listen. One day you will succeed me, and you need to be able to handle yourself diplomatically."

She scoffed at the thought. "I cannot inherit the title, Father. You know that!"

"True," he replied, "but when you marry, your husband will inherit the title. Everyone at Bodden respects you, and they'll do as you say. Marry a weak-minded man, and you will control the barony!"

She smiled. Her father always had a nice way of wording things.

"Now," he continued, "take your position outside the door. When they arrive, show them in and remain inside the room rather than returning to the hallway. They will probably ignore you, but it will keep them on their best behaviour."

"Because I'm a woman?" she asked, already starting to bristle.

"No, because you're a witness!"

She returned to her station in the hall and stood silent. In her mind there was a lot at stake here and she didn't want to see Gerald suffer because of an inept captain. The thought made her analyze her own position, was she a capable captain? A year ago she wouldn't have doubted it for a moment, but now, with recent events still in her mind, she wasn't so sure of herself.

She saw two people approaching the room. They were dressed richly and could only be the expected guests. Before she could say anything, they announced themselves.

"The Earl of Shrewesdale and Lord Barrington to see the baron," the older of the two proclaimed.

"If you'll allow me, Your Grace," she said, opening the door.

Her father turned to greet his visitors. "Your Grace," he said, facing the Earl of Shrewesdale.

"Good to see you, Fitz," said the earl, "You know Lord Barrington, of course?"

The men continued with their conversation, and Beverly listened intently while remaining in the background. Her father was trying to save Gerald, while the other two wanted someone to punish for the failure at Walpole Street. Her father was a persuasive man and could be forceful when needed. In the end, the Earl of Shrewesdale agreed to her father's plan, and Lord Barrington followed along reluctantly.

The conversation finished, the earl turned to leave, placing his glass on the table.

She saw Lord Barrington down his drink in a rush and hurry to catch up. He placed his glass absently on the table as he passed, and she saw it precariously balanced on the edge. She stepped forward just in time, catching it as it fell towards the floor. She placed it back on the table and closed the door, the distant sound of their footsteps echoing in the hallway.

"That was neatly done, Father!" she exclaimed.

"I wish I could have done more, but these are dangerous times and it's best not to push the king's confidence these days."

"What now?" she asked.

"We'll have to wait a few days to see what develops. I think everything should go as planned, but sometimes these people get strange ideas in their heads. Let's meet in, say, three days? I'll buy you lunch at the Queen's Arms."

"Yes, I can meet with you then, but surely there is another tavern we can get together at, Father?

"Excellent, I'll see you there then. Now, if you'll excuse me, I have some arrangements to attend to."

He kissed her on the forehead and walked out the door, completely ignoring her request for a different rendezvous spot. Damn, he would eat that stinky cheese again, she just knew it!

"Feel free to take what's left of the wine," he said on the way out.

She walked over to the table and looked at the bottle, recognizing it to be an expensive vintage from her uncle's winery. She took the bottle and poured herself a glass, then wandered over to the window. Her father spent a lot of time looking out windows. It reminded her of the map room back in Bodden, and she could picture him with his hands absently stroking his beard. How she missed Bodden.

Three days later Beverly found herself in the Queen's Arms, her father sitting outside as she approached. He had a tankard of dark ale beside him, and the serving wench had just placed a plate down beside him on the table.

"You look pleased with yourself!" she remarked.

"Ahh, Beverly, my dear, so pleasant to see you. Come and try some of this delicious cheese." He placed a piece of the horrid stuff into his mouth, proclaiming, "A most excellent Hawksburg gold!"

She sat down, and catching the girl's eye, indicated she wanted an ale. "I don't know how you can stand that, it smells awful!" she said, the smell of this cheese no better than the first time he brought her here.

"I must admit that the taste far exceeds its smell!" His grin said he knew how bad it truly smelled, and he didn't care one whit.

She waited patiently while the waitress brought the ale and then turned to him.

"What news?" she prompted. "Has everything been arranged?"

"Yes. Even as we speak, Gerald is en-route to the Royal Estate at Uxley, where he will take up the position of groundskeeper. We have kept him safe!"

Beverly breathed a sigh of relief. She was worried that the constant plotting in the Palace would spell disaster for Gerald, but it looked like, for once, that it had turned out in their favour. She was just starting to relax when her father spoke again.

"Now we just need to get you a position at court!" he said.

"I had a position at court, and it didn't turn out very well," she said defensively.

"I don't mean a position 'in' the court, I mean we need to find you a sponsor, someone you can serve."

"Have fun with that," she said. "I'm not exactly popular at court right now."

"Don't be so negative, my dear," he said with a smile. "There's bound to be someone looking for a knight of your calibre. Let me do some asking around on your behalf, discreetly of course."

"I'm sure that the marshal-general hates me enough to have poisoned the whole court against me," she said bitterly.

"Then we'll look outside of court. There's bound to be an earl or duke that is looking for knights," he said. "The kingdom doesn't exactly have a surplus of them. We'll find you something worthwhile, something that gets you out of Wincaster."

TWENTY-ONE

Shrewesdale

SPRING 954 MC

~

Beverly was outside in the sun rubbing down Lightning, enjoying the fresh spring air when she heard someone approaching. She looked up to see a man wearing a chainmail shirt, striding into the yard with a scroll of some type gripped in his hand. He stopped momentarily to talk to one of her men who pointed towards her. Beverly put down her brush as the newcomer walked across the yard.

"Are you Captain Fitzwilliam?" the man asked.

"I am," she replied, smiling, "and who might you be, if I may ask?"

"I am Captain Harlon Eldridge, the new commander of this company."

She was stunned. She knew the assignment was temporary but had expected more notice of her dismissal.

"My orders," the captain said, handing her the scroll.

She untied the message and read through it. It was pretty standard stuff, and she saw Marshal-General Valmar's seal at the bottom. The orders were clear, Captain Eldridge was to assume immediate command of the company.

She took a breath to calm herself, "Congratulations, Captain," she said, "you're getting a fine company. Shall I introduce you to everyone?"

Eldridge was taken aback, as if the concept of meeting the men was distasteful. "No, that won't be necessary," he said somewhat stiffly. "I can go over all that later."

"Shall I have someone gather your belongings? I assume you'll want to move in right away?" she offered.

Harlon's eyes widened, "Why on earth would I want to do that? I'll be staying at my townhouse, not here. You can have the men carry your things if you'd like, I shouldn't like to be seen as ungracious."

She was taken aback by the man's tone. What had Valmar told him, she pondered?

Captain Eldridge spoke again, "I understand you are to report to the knight's barracks at the Palace immediately."

"Very well, I'll be on my way. I'll just get Sergeant Gardner organized to deliver my belongings. Will you want to address the men at all?"

"No, I'll worry about all that later, I have a rather important meeting to attend. I trust your things will be removed promptly?"

"I'm sure that by the time your meeting is over, my presence here will be completely erased," she declared.

"Then, good day to you, Captain Fitzwilliam."

Packing did not take long, for she really didn't have a lot. The sergeant arranged for her belongings to be taken to the knight's barracks immediately. It was a sad occasion for her. All the men came to say goodbye, and despite their rough and tumble nature, she had grown fond of them. The feeling was mutual, as evidenced by the lack of dry eyes when she departed.

She rode out of the yard on Lightning, wearing her armour. She was damned if Valmar was going to tell her not to wear it again. This time the trip down the Royal Promenade was certainly not as auspicious as her first, during her investiture. Perhaps, she thought, it was time to give up the order and return to Bodden. Father could find a position for her with the local garrison, of this she was sure.

Arriving at the Palace, intending on continuing around the back to the barracks, she spied a carriage halted there. It bore the coat of arms of the Earl of Shrewesdale, and she watched with interest as she rode closer. The earl was evidently inside the Palace, based upon how relaxed the attendants were standing about. She had to move past them to go under the covered arch leading to the training yard in back. As she was about to ride by, the attendants all stood to attention, and there was a commotion in the doorway.

The door opened and the Countess of Shrewesdale, Lady Catherine Montrose exited the building, followed by two ladies-in-waiting. Beverly paused, giving her the right of way. As the lady approached her carriage, she noticed the knight astride the massive horse.

"Come here," she beckoned, and Beverly dismounted, her horse standing still on her command.

"My Lady," she said, bowing.

Lady Catherine was an imposing woman, although she was not overly tall, her grey hair and wrinkled countenance betrayed a lifetime of commanding respect. Rumour was that the earl had only married her for her title for her father had been the previous earl, and her older brother had died without issue. Her husband was a few years her junior and was notoriously free with the ladies.

"You are Lady Beverly Fitzwilliam, are you not?" the woman enquired.

"I am, my lady," Beverly answered.

"Am I to understand," she continued, "that you are currently not, how should I put it, in service to a lord?"

"That is correct, my lady. I have just left my last assignment."

"How would you feel about coming to Shrewesdale?" she asked.

Beverly's eyes went wide. This was most unexpected.

"Shrewesdale, my lady?"

"Yes, I have need of your services. Come to my city estate this afternoon," she said, "and we'll discuss it in more detail. I think you'll find it to your liking. Feel free to wear the armour if you wish, I shouldn't mind at all. In fact, it might prove to be useful. Shall we say at three?"

"Yes, my lady, I shall be there promptly at three bells."

"Excellent, Hobson here will give you the address, I shall see you then."

With that, the Countess entered the carriage. Hobson handed her a note with the address on it, and then hopped up to the back of the carriage, which drove off quickly, leaving Beverly in a mild state of confusion. It appeared the day was about to get a lot more interesting.

She arrived promptly as the bells struck three and was escorted into a well-appointed room. Lady Catherine was sitting on a comfortable looking chair as a servant poured her some wine.

"Come in, come in. Have a seat."

Beverly chose the large couch, careful that her armour did not damage it.

"I suppose you're wondering why I wanted to see you?"

"The thought had crossed my mind, my lady," Beverly said.

"Let's get straight to the point, shall we? As you are no doubt aware, I am an old woman. Being the Countess of Shrewesdale, I have the...distinction of being married to Lord George Montrose who, due to his marriage to me, became the Earl of Shrewesdale, following in my father's footsteps."

"Yes ma'am, I was aware of that," said Beverly guardedly.

"Well, what you are probably not aware of is the fact that my husband is a notorious womanizer and spendthrift. I daresay he's gone through the family coffers in record time and wasted most of the funds that my father left to me."

"I see, my lady, but how does this concern me?"

The countess smiled, "As the lady of the household, it is my prerogative to hire and fire staff, including guards. I have had it with my husband's abuse of the serving girls in the household. I want you to be in my service, sworn to serve me. Your duty will be to make sure that the women of the house are not, how shall we put it, corrupted by my husband's actions. Since you will be in my service and not his, he will have no jurisdiction over you. You shall have complete freedom to operate however you see fit, providing you can meet my conditions."

"I beg your pardon," she said, "but won't he just go outside of the household to obtain what he wants?"

"Of course, my dear, but at least I shan't have to be witness to his indiscretions. I am no fool, I know that he married me for my wealth, but I did my duty by my father and carried out his wishes. Isn't that what a daughter is supposed to do?"

"I suppose so," Beverly agreed.

"Tell me," continued Lady Catherine, "have you been spoken for?"

Beverly blushed, "I'm afraid my father has not made any arrangements for me, as of yet," she said.

The countess laughed, "That's not what I meant. I meant have you taken service to another noble? I can't take you into service if you're already committed elsewhere."

"No ma'am, I'm afraid I'm out of favour at the moment."

"Excellent, then you'll fit right in at Shrewesdale. I will be leaving Wincaster in a week's time, and I should like you to accompany us as our escort. Is that to your satisfaction?"

"Yes, my lady," said Beverly, smiling, "it will be my honour."

Lady Catherine insisted that she remain for a light meal, and they talked for more than an hour. She found that Lady Catherine was, despite her reputation to the contrary, a very warm and friendly person. By the time Beverly returned to the Palace, she was feeling much more positive about things. Perhaps, she thought, her luck was changing. A new city promised a new start, and she looked forward to serving her first noble sponsor.

The trip to Shrewesdale was lengthy, with more than two hundred miles to traverse to their destination. It took even longer than expected due to the Countess, who insisted on stopping at Burrstoke to admire the view of the Glowan Hills. They stayed for three days, during which their host, the Baronet of Burrstoke, Sir Walter Herbert, gave her ladyship a tour of the area. It was a most pleasant visit, and Beverly noted a hint of sadness in the Lady Catherine's eyes upon their departure. They continued on the road until Haverston, a town situated at the crossroads on the way to Shrewesdale. It was mainly a farming community, but with the many visitors who now stayed here on their way south, the number of inns was impressive. The stopover here was quick, for while there were lodgings to be had, there was nothing of interest in Haverston for a traveller. The road forked north, but they continued south, entering the Shrewesdale Hills which took their name from the fabled city. Shrewesdale was old, some said older than even Wincaster, and at one time it had been the cultural capital of the kingdom. In recent years, however, the great southern swamp, which extended for hundreds of miles to the sea, had been creeping ever closer, and now the city was only saved by the very hills they had just entered.

The carriage jolted along the uneven road, with Beverly sitting inside, while Lightning trotted behind. The first sign that they were approaching the city was a strange smell that she detected. She wrinkled her nose and looked out the window to see the cause.

The countess smiled, "Don't worry," she said, "after a while, you won't even notice it anymore."

Beverly looked back at her. "What is it?" she asked.

"It's the miasma, as they like to call it. It comes from the Great Swamp."

"It smells like something is rotting," she said.

"Yes, but after a few hours, you'll learn to ignore it. We use a lot of scents in the manor house."

The carriage rounded a corner, and they got a glimpse of the great city itself.

"Have you ever been to Shrewesdale?" the Countess asked.

"No, but I've heard a lot about it."

"Most of it is probably true," said Lady Catherine, "it is a very old city. I think you'll find the architecture particularly unique."

Beverly could make out the city gate looming large before them as she looked out the window. It was flanked by the massive towers that dwarfed the carriage in comparison. The Countess was evidently recognized, for they passed through the gate without delay. The city reminded her of Wincaster, but the stonework here was rather ornate, with more brick and less wood than the capital. People waved as they made their way through the town. The Countess, it seemed, was held in high esteem here.

The estate was located in the very middle of the city, surrounded by rich gardens. It was smaller than the Palace, but the grounds around it were far more grandiose. The carriage pulled up in front of the entrance, where an army of servants descended upon them. Beverly insisted on taking care of Lightning herself. The stable master guided her to the estate's stables, which she found to be in excellent shape. She introduced herself to the friendly stable hands while tending to her horse's needs, and then she made her way to the manor house itself.

The countess arranged for Grenville, the estate steward, to give her a tour of the house, and the sheer size of it was overwhelming. The rooms here were larger than the Palace, though there were not as many. Her quarters were on the third floor of the manor house, not in the barracks, which surprised and delighted her. In the morning she would meet with the Countess to learn what her duties would be, giving her the rest of the day to unpack and learn the layout of the house. At the end of the tour, Grenville asked her if she could read a map. She almost laughed out loud and then realized the poor man was serious. "Yes," she replied, "I know how to read a map."

He provided her with a floor plan so that she could find her way about the estate, freeing him up for other duties. Returning to her room, she walked around it, enjoying the sheer size, for it was even larger than her room in Bodden. She knew she should feel a little guilty taking pleasure in it, but after living in barracks for so long, she resolved to appreciate the change. It was opulently decorated with the finest of furnishings and felt more like a house than a room. Her belongings, such as they were, had been delivered and she took time to unpack them herself, despite the offer from a housemaid to assist.

Wearing her armour might be a bit too much inside the manor house, so she changed into a simple dress and made her way down to the kitchen. She decided to take a private tour to familiarize herself with her new surroundings and hoped that the less formal clothing she had chosen would help her to blend in. The kitchen was the logical place to start, and upon entering, she saw a full staff, perhaps two dozen people, hard at work. A young man was standing to one side watching, a knight judging by his superior clothing, and he delighted in pinching the women as they moved past him. She resolved not to say anything but made a careful note of his features while avoiding his direct gaze. One of the pinched maids walked near her, and she stopped the girl with her upheld hand.

"Who's that man?" Beverly asked.

The girl looked over her shoulder, "That's Sir Remington, one of the earl's knights," she said.

"Does he always act like that?"

"Aye, and sometimes worse."

Beverly's eyes narrowed, "Worse? How so?"

The girl blushed, "He's been known to be free with his hands when coming across a person in the hallways. Young Maggy had his fingers thrust up into her, if you know what I mean."

Beverly's calm resolve instantly evaporated. "Really? You're not just making this up?"

"No, I would never make up such a story," the girl responded. "It's true, I swear it."

Beverly put her hand down and let the girl go. She stared at Sir Remington for a few moments more, then walked over to him.

He noticed her approaching and not recognizing her, took her for a new servant, leering at her as she drew closer.

"Well, what do we have-"

Her vicious slap to his face cut off his words mid-sentence, leaving him speechless.

"How dare you treat these women in such a callous manner," she exploded.

The room came to a complete standstill, the only noise was a bubbling pot.

Sir Remington rubbed his face, "Saxnor's balls, who do you think you are?" he yelled at her.

"I am Dame Beverly Fitzwilliam of Bodden, and under the authority of the Countess, I'm here to tell you that your behaviour will no longer be tolerated."

The man's jaw dropped, causing him to look completely lost. She saw him take a breath, ready to argue the point and interrupted him again.

"Get out, now. Immediately!" Beverly demanded, and when the knight didn't move, she struck him on the chest with the flat of her palm. He staggered back against the wall, clutching his chest. A bruise would be there tomorrow, she was sure of it.

Pointing at the back door to the kitchen, she gave him his marching orders, "That's the way out, and if I ever hear a word that you are back here, I will come and hunt you down, is that clear?"

Sir Remington recognized the look of determination in her eyes and left. As soon as he had exited, the room exploded in a spontaneous cheer, and all the workers came forward to thank her. She introduced herself to all of them and remained in the kitchen to get to know them a little better. She was particularly interested in hearing any more complaints they may have had concerning other knights and what their names might be. She had a feeling that this was only the tip of the sword. There were likely to be more problems throughout the place.

That evening, after learning the layout of the manor house, she chose to take a walk in the extensive gardens. There, before she had even gone twenty paces, she saw two men approaching determinedly. One she instantly recognized as Sir Remington, while the other was unknown to her. She stopped to watch their approach. The unknown man stepped forward slightly while Sir Remington kept his distance.

"I understand you are Dame Beverly of Bodden?" he asked politely.

"Yes, and you are?"

"Sir Vincent Tarville," he said slightly bowing.

"And what can I do for you?"

"I am here representing Sir Remington, whom you slighted today. He demands satisfaction."

"Pardon me?" Beverly responded.

"Sir Remington demands satisfaction. He would have taught you a lesson himself, but you are technically a knight and so deserve the formalities."

Beverly looked into the man's eyes and ascertained he was serious. "I see, so we are to fight then?"

"Correct. He demands you present yourself for the satisfaction of his honour."

"Very well, where and when?" she enquired.

"Shall we say tomorrow morning? At the front gate to the estate?" They were obviously hoping to humiliate her in front of as many people as possible.

"That is agreeable," she assented very formally. "What about weapons?"

Sir Vincent looked surprised, "Weapons?"

"Yes, what weapons would he like to use?"

Sir Vincent looked at Sir Remington, who shrugged.

"I mean," said Beverly, "do you want to use great swords, long swords, daggers, warhammers, perhaps tridents, spears or will bare hands do? I'm familiar with all those weapons and more."

Sir Remington turned slightly pale, and so Sir Vincent spoke up quickly, "Swords will do nicely, not great swords though, this is an affair of honour, to first blood, not death."

"Very well," she acquiesced, "make sure your armour's in good shape for mine's battle-hardened."

The man's eyes went even wider if that was possible, and they turned and left hurriedly. Typical, she thought to herself, always trying to back up their actions with force.

. . .

The next morning Beverly showed up at the gate to the estate. Word had gotten around, and there was a large crowd assembled. She saw members of the town watch present, but they assured her they were only to keep pick-pockets at bay; the affair of honour was none of their concern. A large circle had been chalked out on the cobblestones with the crowd gathered around it. Beverly stepped forward, noticing a fair number of women who had come to witness the event. She wondered how common duels were in Shrewesdale but decided it didn't matter, this would be her one and only. She would have to make a good show if it to ensure it didn't become a common occurrence. The last thing she needed was to be constantly fighting other knights.

She strode into the circle and waited. The crowd parted to let Sir Remington come forward with Sir Vincent at his side.

"We are gathered here today," said Sir Vincent in a dramatic fashion, "to see to an affair of honour."

The crowd roared their appreciation.

"Make your statement," he said, pointing at Sir Remington.

Sir Remington confidently stepped forward to stand in front of Beverly. "I hereby charge," he announced loudly, "that this…woman did treat me with disrespect and failed to show me the common courtesy due to one of my station."

The crowd made a collective gasp.

Sir Vincent turned to Beverly, "How do you answer these charges?"

The crowd hushed waiting to hear her words.

"I charge that Sir Remington has treated the servants abominably and that he got what he deserves."

The crowd cheered enthusiastically, forcing Sir Vincent to use his hands to quiet them.

"Sir Remington, what would you have?"

"I would have an apology before these witnesses," he responded forcefully.

"And Dame Beverly, how do you respond," Sir Vincent prompted.

"I refuse, nay, I insist that he apologize to all the women of the manor." The women all cheered, but the men started murmuring.

"Sir Remington, what say you?" Sir Vincent was enjoying his role as ringmaster of this circus.

Sir Remington stepped back slightly, "I say we fight!" The crowd erupted into a cacophony.

"Sir Remington, Dame Beverly," Sir Vincent said gravely, "prepare yourselves."

They each went to opposite ends of the circle. Beverly drew her sword and firmly grasped her shield while she swung her arms a little to loosen up. Opposite, her opponent did likewise

Sir Vincent drew his sword, holding it point down on the ground. The crowd hushed as he held it high up into the air. "Let the fight begin," he yelled, swinging his sword for emphasis. The throng of spectators resumed their cheering.

Beverly took a small step forward, waiting. Sir Remington was bouncing on his feet, trying to dance around. Beverly had fought Norlanders, anyone who didn't plant their feet firmly was asking for trouble. She stepped forward quickly and deliberately. Remington's sword swung first and was easily blocked by hers. She countered with a simple thrust, more to judge his response than to actually hit him. He swung again, and then she took one step forward and shield bashed him. It was one of the techniques that Gerald had taught her back in Bodden. She thrust her shield forward using her body mass to add more power. The shields connected with a loud bang and the knight fell backwards, clattering onto the cobblestones. She stepped back slightly, allowing him to stand.

He looked flustered but shook it off. In he came, with an overhead swing aimed at her head. She blocked with her sword, easily deflecting the blade to the side. She waited again, and he tried a thrust, which she side-stepped. His attack was unplanned, and she could tell he had little experience, but she just waited. He came at her in a wild series of slashes and swings, and she backed up, deflecting the blows one after the other. Sir Remington backed up and then mounted another attack using the exact same manoeuvre. This time she waited until he was at the end of his advance, then she stepped into the attack. She slashed viciously from the side, and he blocked the attack, his shield ringing out with the strength of her blow. She continued with a sword thrust, then, without warning, suddenly rendered a backhand slash across his arm, causing him to lose his grip on his shield. Seeing this, she swung her shield, using it to knock his flying from his hand to land at the edge of the circle. She stomped forward, striking him in the centre of the chest with the edge of her shield. He tumbled to the ground. She moved to stand over him, the tip of her sword suddenly at his throat, held there in an iron grasp.

Sir Remington looked up, real fear finally showing in his eyes. "I submit," he choked out.

The crowd becamequiet, and Beverly held her sword in place. "I believe you owe an apology to the women of the manor," she said, her face displaying a calm demeanour.

"I apologize to all the women of the manor," Sir Remington proclaimed. "I'm so sorry," he said, starting to choke up, tears pouring down his face, and it dawned on her that she had, perhaps, taken things too far. She stepped back and sheathed her sword.

"On behalf of the women of the manor, I accept your apology," she said.

"What is this?" a voice boomed out. "Who dares to mock the Knights of Shrewesdale!"

The crowd parted to reveal a giant of a man. He was more than six feet high, with huge muscles bursting out from his sleeves. Aldwin was heavily muscled after years of working the forge and anvil, but this man was even larger. He stepped into the circle and levelled a steely glare at Beverly.

"I cannot let this pass," he proclaimed, drawing a large battle axe from his back.

Beverly prepared to fight again. This time, it was going to be a much tougher fight. This man looked seasoned, and as he strode about swinging his axe, she knew he had seen battle before.

She stepped back into the ring. They circled, probing each other for weaknesses with light swings. He was gauging her, she thought, learning what he could of her technique. The knights' champion was big but sure-footed. She could not overpower him the way she had Sir Remington. She watched him carefully, and as he swung the axe, she blocked it. It was an easy block, but it sent a shudder up her entire arm. By Saxnor's balls, the man had power. Having trained with axes before, she knew their weaknesses, they were slow. She waited for the next strike, dodged, then as he was carrying through with the swing, she struck, her sword coming down on his arm. His chainmail deflected the blow, but she heard a grunt of pain. He had definitely felt the shock of the strike.

She tuned out the crowd, concentrating solely on her attacker. He swung again, this time with an overhead blow. She slipped sideways and thrust with the sword into the man's gut. Once again the chainmail stopped the blade from penetrating. She felt a wash of pain as the big man bashed her with side blow from his shield, then she staggered to the side to get her footing secured. The knight came on in a sudden burst of speed, striking with his axe while driving her back with another shield blow.

The impact was jarring, and she had to shake her head to clear it. They had neared the edge of the circle, and her opponent backed up into the fighting area. The expression on his face was serious, but she glimpsed something else, something that said he was hurt. She observed him carefully and noticed he was not swinging his arm quite as freely as when he started. Perhaps her early bash was causing him some pain? The knight swung his axe behind him as if to strike with an overhead swing and Beverly made her move. She stepped forward rapidly, slightly to her left, placing her on his right-hand side, and even as he swung the axe over his head, she drove the edge of her shield into his leg. As he suddenly crouched to protect his leg, his dropped his arm down, and she struck again, this time with her sword to his injured arm. He let out a bellow of pain as the axe dropped from his grip. Holding the tip of her blade to his face, the strain showing as it wobbled slightly, she asked for his surrender. He dropped the shield and stepped back, announcing, "I yield."

Beverly lowered her blade, thankful that the fight was over. Unexpectedly, she was struck from behind, and staggered forward, barely able to stay on her feet. Another blow hit her arm, stopped from penetrating by her arm bracers. She dove to the right and rolled, coming up on her feet a moment later. Quickly gathering her wits, she beheld two knights, both armed, determined to have it out with her. This was insane, she thought, how many of them must I fight to prove myself?

The first stabbed with his sword, while the second delivered a backhanded strike. Beverly blocked one with her shield, using her sword to ward off the other, all the while backing up to keep them in front of her. The crowd retreated as the combatants neared the edge of the circle. This fight was beyond a simple duel now, someone was going to get hurt. Again they struck, and as she was blocking the first, the second man smashed her with the edge of his shield. She staggered back, pain lancing down her side where the shield had impacted. Over and over the two assailed her, relentless in their attempts. Suddenly, she crouched just as the pair both undertook overhead blows. With her shield protecting her once more, she sliced forward, her blade cutting into the leg of the assailant on the left, who tumbled to the ground. Wheeling on the foe to her right, she smashed her shield into his chest, pushing him backwards. She swung her blade overhead and saw him raise his shield to block it, so she quickly changed tactics and stopped mid-air, circling the blade to cut from the side instead. The blade bit into the man's arm, where he had no armour, and he staggered. With both her opponents defeated, she withdrew, only to see three more men were facing her, with another joining the group. They were about to charge forward when a booming voice stilled them.

"Enough!" the giant axe wielder yelled as he stepped forward. "This duel is over. Go home, there's nothing more to see here. She has fought valiantly, and we must respect the rules."

Her adversaries retreated, and the giant moved closer to Beverly. "You have fought well, Dame Beverly. You have proven yourself, go in peace."

"Thank you," she replied, out of breath.

The man turned to leave, "Wait," she asked, "who are you?"

He turned back to face her, "I am Sir Heward," he answered, "but most people just call me The Axe."

"Thank you, Sir Heward, you have proven yourself to be an honourable man."

He bowed slightly, and she saw a slight smile crease his lips. "And you are an honourable woman. Peace be with you."

TWENTY-TWO

Olivia

SUMMER 954 MC

Beverly sat on the back step, her sword resting on her knees, enjoying the first of the warm summer days. She reached into her bag to retrieve the oil rag she always used to wipe down her blade. Examining it, she determined it was too worn, so she pulled out a fresh rag, then retrieved the small vial of oil. She gently removed the stopper, tipping the contents over the rag only to be rewarded by...nothing. She held the small container to the light and observed, with some frustration, that it was empty. Staring at it for a few moments, she tried to will more oil out of the thing, but finally gave up. She could, of course, have just used the old rag one more time, but she was always particular about the care of her weapons. No, the only solution was to get more oil. She packed the now useless container back into the satchel, along with the rags and returned them to her room.

Questioning the other knights, she learned who they felt was the best smith. She changed into a dress, making her way into town. Things had been quiet of late, her reputation had done wonders to restore morale at the manor, and the townsfolk soon learned of what had transpired. She was a respectable woman, and her red hair made her easily identifiable to those that saw her.

She made her way through the trade district and soon spotted the wooden sign that denoted the presence of a smith. The smithy was quite different than her experience in Bodden. Here the smith worked outdoors with a fresh breeze to keep the heat away. A man, in his early thirties, had his bare back turned to her while hammering away at a steel rod on an anvil. He was heavily muscled, and it made her think of Aldwin, though this man lacked the fine sculpturing that her favourite smith displayed.

She must have been reminiscing longer than she thought, for a voice broke through her reverie.

"Like the view?"

"Sorry?" she responded, startled by the intrusion.

A brown haired woman smiled up at her from her seat nearby. "I was wondering if you liked the view?" she repeated.

Beverly was confused, "I'm not sure what you mean."

The woman stood and walked over to her, "I was referring to the heavily muscled man sweating in front of you."

"Oh," said Beverly, blushing, "I didn't mean to stare, I was lost in thought."

"I bet," the woman said. "My brother has that effect on lots of women."

"No, that's not what I meant," she replied hastily, "only he reminds me of someone else, someone…special to me."

"He must be special if he makes you ignore what's in front of you. What's his name?"

Beverly stared at her. Who was this person who was so forward? Was she trying to bait her or just being friendly? She peered at the woman's face, but couldn't detect any sign of deception. She took a deep breath, "His name's Aldwin," she provided. Beverly was suddenly hit with a feeling of guilt. Was she right to admit her feelings out loud?

"Nice name," the woman acknowledged. "I'm guessing he's not from around here though, never heard of a smith named Aldwin in these parts."

"He lives in Bodden," Beverly explained.

"Oh, you must be Dame Beverly, the whole town's been discussing you. Don't worry, it's all good talk. I'm Olivia, by the way, and that hunk of manhood is my brother, Colin. He's pretty much deaf from all the hammering, so I take care of the business side of things. Other than ogling my brother, did you have some business here today?"

Beverly blushed again and cleared her throat, "Yes, actually I'm looking for some oil, for my weapons."

Olivia laughed, bringing a smile to Beverly's face. "Most knights looking to oil their weapon visit the whorehouse down the street."

Beverly looked at the woman as if she was crazy. What was this woman prattling on about?

Olivia gazed back, "You know, oil their weapons? Men with their weapons?"

"I'm sorry, I don't know what you mean."

Olivia walked over and put her hand on Beverly's shoulder. "Well aren't you the naive one. You see men have these things they like to put inside of women."

"I know that, I'm not an idiot."

"Well, around here, they often refer to their manhood as a weapon."

"Oh, I see," said Beverly not really sure what she was inferring, until she suddenly understood, and blushed.

"You aren't from around here, are you?" the older woman asked.

"No, I'm from-"

"Bodden, yes I got that from our conversation earlier. Look, I'm not trying to make fun of you, I just think you need a guiding hand. Shrewesdale can be a very dangerous city for some. You should find someone to show you around, acclimatize you before you get taken advantage of."

Beverly smiled, "Know anyone that's available?"

"As a matter of fact," Olivia replied, "I finish work soon. I could give you a tour."

"And what would that cost me?" asked Beverly.

"Merely a pint or two at the Crow's Foot, a good deal if I may say so myself."

"Very well, I'll take you up on it, but I still need that oil."

"No problem," Olivia replied, rummaging behind the serving counter. "I have a small vial here, we only use the highest quality ingredients." She handed the vial over to Beverly.

"Thank you," Beverly replied. "How much?"

Olivia looked over at her brother, whose back was still to them, "Let's say this one's on the house," she said with a wink. "Now you come back here when the bell strikes three and I'll be ready to give you the grand tour."

Beverly laughed. This woman impressed her, though she was not sure why. "All right then, I'll see you at three bells."

The tour ended up being much more interesting than she thought. Shrewesdale was an old city, dating back to the early days of Merceria, over 700 years ago. The buildings were stylish, with carved stonework being very popular. The city boasted an impressive array of theatres, and it was said that the first one in the land was built here. It was home to the great poets and playwrights of the realm. Olivia knew everything about the city, and it was clear that she loved the place. The famous Library of Kendros housed the largest collection of knowledge in the land, some even said the known world. The city boasted a stadium where, long in the past, prisoners fought to the death. That had ceased more than 500 years ago, but the stadium was still home to competitions, mainly of horsemanship, with everything from racing to obstacle courses, usually with knights competing to show off their abilities.

The Great Stables of Archon were another attraction. Centuries ago the ruler of the city had bred a special breed of horse, more nimble and quick, favoured by runners and scouts. Today the Archon Lights were a favourite breed of the King's Rangers. Much smaller than the great Mercerian Chargers, of which Lightning was a member, the Lights were several hands smaller. They were clever animals, very sure-footed, and able to pick their way through difficult terrain. They also had a keen sense of hearing, which was of immense interest to the rangers, who operated in the wild lands. The two women spent several hours looking over the horseflesh, for this was a particular passion of Beverly, and as she soon found out, of Olivia's as well.

"How is it," said Beverly, "that a smith's assistant knows so much about horses?"

Olivia laughed. She had a light-hearted way about her that put everyone around her at ease. "I wasn't always a smith's assistant. I used to be a knight."

Beverly stopped brushing the horse and looked at her. "You were a knight? What happened?"

"I left the order a long time ago."

"Why?"

"That's a long story," Olivia replied, "and one which requires an ample supply of ale."

"Then we should be off to the Crow's Foot," urged Beverly. "This is a tale which I would very much like to hear."

They made their way to the tavern and took up seats at a table in the corner. Beverly ordered two ales and after a deep draught, looked at Olivia.

"So," she said, "you were going to tell me about life as a knight?"

"It's a long story, so I'll give you the short version," said Olivia. "You were born a noble, but I have always been a commoner. I was married to a wonderful man named Wendel Jacobson. He was a foot soldier, and we lived together in the barracks. When the northern wars kept raging on and on the king called on the nobles to send troops to aid in the fight. Wendel's company was sent, and I followed along with them."

"From my experience, that's very common when an army marches," said Beverly. "Whenever a new company came to Bodden, we'd have to accommodate all the extra camp followers."

"It was a rough life, but I loved it, thrived on it, actually. I would organize the other wives, look after the camp, all that sort of thing. I was about your age, just shy of twenty. Seeing the country we marched through, meeting others, it was all thrilling for someone who had grown up here in Shrewesdale."

Beverly saw the faraway look in Olivia's eye, and she began to smile as she reminisced.

"Anyway," she continued, "we marched to a place called Wickfield, right on the border with Norland."

"Yes, I've heard of it, just north of Hawksburg," said Beverly.

"We were there for a few months and then the worst winter in years decided to descend on us. The company was sent upriver to guard a ford. Of course, the water was frozen so the enemy raiders could cross pretty much anywhere they liked. We had a watchtower there at the time, and the men took turns manning it. They built up some makeshift defences around the base, creating a small fortified encampment. I still remember the day they crossed the border. It wasn't a small force. I learned later that more than 300 Norlanders invaded, and we only had a company to stop them. Counting all the able-bodied men, we might have had forty in total. They came across the river in what looked like a swarm. We all ran to the barricades, but we didn't have much warning for the blowing snow had stopped the sentries from seeing their approach. They were on us before we could even grab weapons. A group of men, including my Wen, managed to organize a defence. We pushed them back across our makeshift wall and for the moment, they retreated, but the cost had been high."

She took a draft of her ale, and Beverly sat quietly as the tears formed in Olivia's eyes. "Wen had taken a wound to the stomach," she said after taking a deep breath. "It was so bad, but he insisted on standing at the wall. I bound him as best I could, but the bandages were leaking dreadfully, I knew his time was up. They made another rush, and he went down almost immediately, an arrow to the head. I grabbed his sword and began hacking away. Anger filled me, anger at these northerners who had taken my Wendel away from me. I fought like Saxnor himself, blood was everywhere. I don't remember anything but stabbing and slashing and blood, so much blood. When I was done, the enemy had retreated, leaving bodies everywhere. The attack had been brutal, and only nine of us survived out of the whole company, but we stopped the invasion. Reinforcements arrived later the next day from the Earl of Eastwood, who had been commanding the northern army and decided to strengthen the defences."

"And so they knighted you for holding off the enemy," Beverly clarified.

"Yes, but it was all a blur to me. I was more concerned with burying my

Wen. The earl heard everyone's version of the story, and there were even some prisoners that corroborated it. I didn't know till later, but I was the only one left on the wall. I had held them off all by myself, for a short while. The king knighted me on the earl's recommendation. I was stunned by the news, but I would have gladly traded that title for the return of my husband's life."

She took another long pull of her ale. "After that, I took up the life of a warrior woman, using my husband's armour and weapons. I stayed in the north for a while, but the return to Shrewesdale was...troublesome."

"How so?"

"On the frontier, any fighter is valued, as I'm sure you're aware, but back in 'civilization', they like their knights to be men. I had a hard time fitting in and they made my life difficult."

"I know what you mean," Beverly commiserated, "I had to go through the same thing in Wincaster. How did you handle it?"

"I didn't. I renounced the order, gave up my knighthood. My brother has always been a smith, it runs in the family, and he took me in. I do leather work for him. It's a skill I picked up with the army."

"And you never remarried?"

"No. Oh don't get me wrong, I may dabble with the odd man now and again, but my heart belongs to my Wen. That will never change."

Olivia placed her mug down on the table, looking inside it. "Appears to be empty," she pointed out.

Beverly called the server to bring two more ales, then looked across at her new friend, and smiled. "You should be careful of odd men," she began, "you never know what they'll be like. Better to stick with even men."

Olivia looked her straight in the eyes. "By Saxnor's beard, Beverly, did you just try to tell a joke? There's hope for you yet!"

Beverly found herself visiting Olivia often, and the two soon became fast friends. They went riding, watched plays, but mostly just talked. They spent much of their time at the Crow's Foot, and it became a ritual. Twice a week they would meet up, enjoy a meal, and chat till the wee hours of the morning, usually with plenty of ale. Beverly drank little, her father's influence, but Olivia could consume large amounts of alcohol with little obvious effect. The woman had an unquenchable thirst, but Beverly didn't mind. The conversation was pleasant and illuminating. For her part she talked about Bodden, her father, even Aldwin once Olivia pressed for details. She found it easy to open up to this woman. It was like having a mother, or perhaps a sister, considering her age.

One night, late in the summer, they had returned to the tavern after watching a notoriously bad play. It was called 'The woman who had a bad knight', and it had been as bad as the title. It was meant to be a comedy, playing around with the idea that a woman poses as a man to become a knight. She is mistaken for a man, and the duke's wife takes a fancy to him. It had its moments, but they both agreed their time would have been better spent staring at water evaporating in the sun.

They were sitting at their normal table as Maureen, their regular server, brought over their usual drinks along with some food.

Beverly was nibbling on some cheese when Olivia spoke. "I wonder if the other women ever have that problem?" she mused.

"Other women?" said Beverly.

"Yes, the other women knights."

"There aren't any other women knights," corrected Beverly, "I'm the only one."

Olivia set her tankard down on the table. "Is that what you think? Nothing could be further from the truth."

Beverly was astounded. "You're saying there are other Lady Knights?"

Olivia scoffed, "Lady Knights, no, you're probably the only noble, but yes, there are other women knights."

"Like who?"

"Well, let me think, there's Dame Abigail Thompson, Celia Blackburn, her brother is also a knight. Then there's Levina Charleston, then what's her name."

She stopped for a moment, looking upward as if Saxnor might supply the information she needed. "Oh yes, Dame Juliet something, I forget her last name. There's one more, let me think, Aelwyth I think her name is. Strange name."

"Common enough in the north," said Beverly. "So all these women are knights? Tell me you're not making this up."

"It's the honest truth. Mind you, I don't know much about them. I think most of them are in smaller towns, so they probably don't attract much attention. I doubt you'd ever see them at court."

Beverly was dumbfounded, "And all of these women were knighted by the king?"

"Well yes, of course they were. It's not like in the past when the nobility could knight people themselves, but they were all recommended for knighthood for different reasons. Some, like Dame Levina, took over the duties of her husband when he was killed, others just did something extraordinary."

Beverly's eyes lit up. "I must try to find these women," she announced

Olivia looked at her with a suddenly sober expression. "To what end? Are you going to start your own order?"

"No, but I'm sure we've had similar experiences, it would be good to have someone to commiserate with," she smiled. "I'm lucky, I have you as a friend, but I'm sure some of them are having a hard time adjusting."

"Fair enough," said Olivia, "let's see what we can do about it."

TWENTY-THREE

Disgrace

SUMMER 956 MC

The Countess of Shrewesdale was dead. The woman had been old when Beverly met her, and now, two years later, she had succumbed to the ravages of age. Her trusted entourage gathered about her deathbed, openly weeping, both for the loss of their patron, but also of their safety. It was only a matter of time before the hammer fell, for the Earl of Shrewesdale was not inclined to follow the same rules as his wife.

Her passing was not unexpected, having been ill for some time, but the shock of her actual death cast a pall over the entire household. Everyone dreaded the earl and his retinue, and upon their return, it wasn't long before their fears came to life. Within the hour, the orders arrived, and most of the staff were dismissed, with Beverly assigned to the knight's barracks.

The move didn't take her long, for expecting it, she had packed her things beforehand. She dropped her belongings in her new room and then headed down to the smithy to share the news with Olivia. The woman was working on a fancy scabbard, her chisel working the leather carefully as she carved the fine scroll work into it.

She looked up at Beverly's approach. "Beverly, what are you doing here?" she asked.

"The countess passed away this morning," she answered, solemnly.

"That's terrible news," said Olivia. "What are you going to do now?"

"I've been ordered back to the barracks. I may return to Wincaster now that my service is officially over. I was just wondering if you wanted to head down to the Crow?"

"I can't, I have to finish this scabbard for a customer. Tell you what, I'll drop by the barracks when I'm done. I'll bring a strong bottle of wine to drown our sorrows in. That reminds me, I've got that dagger you wanted for your cousin around here somewhere. My brother did some exquisite work on the handle. I'll bring it with me when I see you."

Beverly half-smiled, "Great, I'll meet you later then. I suppose I should really sort out my new lodgings."

She left the smithy and meandered back to the barracks, trying to delay her ordeal as much as possible. Entering the training yard, all eyes were on her. Evidently, the news had travelled quickly, for it appeared all the knights knew of her loss of her benefactor. She had been given her own room as a courtesy, and now she made her way there quietly. It was late in the afternoon, and she stripped off her armour to get more comfortable. Sitting alone eating the food she had grabbed on her way back to the barracks, she thought more about her future than the taste of the food. She should go back to Wincaster. Perhaps by now, Marshal-General Valmar had forgotten about her. She could always go back to Bodden, she supposed, but didn't want to admit failure. Her time in Shrewesdale had been wonderful. She had been given the respect and authority to do her job, and she thought, she had done it well. It was true that she had made some enemies in the beginning, but things had been peaceful for such a long time now, surely they had forgotten or forgiven her? It started to get dark outside, and she poured herself some more wine, perhaps a little too much, if the truth be told. She wished Olivia were here, but finally gave up waiting. The day had been long, and the wine was beginning to have a soporific effect, so she crawled into her bed, quickly falling into a sound sleep.

Abruptly awoken by a crashing sound, she heard the splintering of wood a second before a hand was pressed over her mouth. Her eyes shot wide open, but she saw nothing, the room was dark, lit only by the moonlight outside. Without warning, her arms were pinned in place. She started struggling, kicking out with her legs, before they, too, were held fast. With her eyes adjusting to the lack of light, she could just make out shapes in the dark. It looked like four or five people blocking out the light. Held fast, they ripped her dress from her, baring her breasts to the night air. She struggled to breathe, tried to shake her head, but the hand over her mouth held her in a vice-like grip. There was laughter, a dark, twisted sound that penetrated to her soul.

"Now the bitch'll get what she deserves," said a voice that sounded familiar. "Bring her over here, I want to take her over the table."

The rough hands dragged her up off the bed, pulling her forward, while another set pulled what remained of her clothes from her body, leaving her naked. The right side of her face was thrust down onto the table, smashing the earthen bottle on it, small pieces of it cutting her. She struggled for breath and tried to fight, but the iron hands that held her were tempered with steel. Her eyes were adjusting to the dark, and she recognized one of the men. It was Sir Vincent, and he was looking behind her, laughing. "Come on, Remy," he was saying, "we all want a turn, don't take all night."

"I'm just about ready," said Sir Remington, and then Beverly felt hands on her backside. He slapped her hard, announcing, "This is going to be fun, and I've waited a long time for this."

The horror of the attack burst upon her. She knew what was coming, but could do nothing to stop it. For the first time in her life, she felt unquenchable fear. Panic seized her, and she began shaking uncontrollably

She tried to prepare herself for the impending pain, but it was impossible. They would each rape her and then they would kill her. They could not spare her, for if she lived, they would forfeit their lives for assaulting a noble.

A primal scream erupted from behind her, and she braced herself the best that she could, but then Sir Remington bellowed in pain. Sir Vincent's face took on an aspect of fear as he released her arm. She tried to act, tried to move, but she was frozen in place by her fear. The other hands gripping her vanished, and she slipped to the floor without their force to hold her upright. Figures were struggling in the dark, but she couldn't make anything out in all the confusion until blood splattered her face, and then she saw Remington on the floor, crawling towards the door.

"Get out, all of you," yelled a voice she instantly recognized as Olivia's, "or I'll gut you too!"

The attackers fled, carrying Sir Remington by the arms, the man crying out in pain as they left. Olivia moved over to Beverly, "Saxnor give me strength, are you all right, Bev? Let's get you over to the bed."

Olivia held her arms gently, guiding her. She sat her on the side, wrapping a blanket around her nakedness.

"Those bastards," her friend said, "they'll pay for this."

Beverly was in shock, her body still completely out of her control, shaking. The world took on an unreal aspect as if she was out of her body.

Olivia brought over a cup, "Drink this," she said. "It'll help."

Beverly gulped down the drink in a daze, not noticing the strength of the brew.

"I saw them," Olivia said, "I know exactly who they are. They won't get away with this."

Even wrapped up in the blanket, Beverly continued to shake, so Olivia wrapped her arms around her, and Beverly buried her head into her shoulder and wept.

Time seemed strange to Beverly, as if she were stuck in some unending nightmare. It felt like only a moment had passed when all of a sudden the room was ablaze with lantern light, and angry voices once again pierced her mind.

"There she is, my lord," said Sir Vincent. "The bitch is consorting in an unholy manner." He stepped to the side, and the earl stepped forward. "See? She's not even wearing any clothes."

"It's true," said another voice from behind him. "We came across this other woman having carnal knowledge of her, and then she went berserk and stabbed Sir Remington. The woman's mad, they both are."

"That's not true," said Olivia, her voice rising.

The earl stepped forward and slapped Olivia across the face. "I can see exactly what went on here," he said. "You attacked a knight, and the penalty for that is death. Take her away, men."

Two of the knights moved forward and pried Beverly from Olivia's arms.

"And you," the earl said, looking at Beverly, "you are a harlot and not fit to serve the king. If it were up to me, you'd be punished for this, but you're a noble and nobles have rights."

"What about Olivia?" screamed Beverly, "You've no right to arrest her."

"Oh, I have every right. I am the law here and don't you forget it. You'll be taken to the dungeons for now, for your own protection. Tomorrow you'll leave Shrewesdale, never to return, and I'll make sure that everyone knows about your indiscretions. Take her away, and throw some clothes on her."

The men leered, touching her as they threw a dress over her head, and then she was walked, barefoot, to the dungeons.

All night long she sat in darkness, listening to the rats scurry across the floor. Morning came, and with it, a sliver of light penetrated her gloom. A guard came to the door to escort her to the earl who awaited her in the great hall.

She was cold and clothed in a ripped and dirtied dress, bereft of any footwear, but she held her head high. She would not succumb to this humiliation and miscarriage of justice. They roughly dragged her before the earl, who was sitting at a table, eating.

"I have come to the conclusion that you have been misguided," he said in a conciliatory tone. "Led astray by the wicked acts of a woman of loose and questionable morals. She will pay for her crimes with her life, but you I shall spare. You will be taken to the gates of the city and set on the road with no more than the clothes on your back."

Beverly knew speaking would do no good, for only his knights were witnesses, so she held her tongue.

"Untie her gentlemen," he said. "I'm sure the Lady Fitzwilliam can walk by herself."

The guards took up station beside her, and she knew what was going to happen. They would escort her through the streets to the gate for all to witness her disgrace.

The earl could be heard laughing as she left, with the voices of the knights soon joining in.

Walking with purpose, she kept her head high, ignoring the crowds that came and gawked. She expected to be taunted, to have things hurled at her but the crowd was quiet. They were all standing with their faces downcast. They would not watch her disgrace, they were saying, but they would pay her the respect she deserved. Tears came to her eyes, but she kept them in check as best she could. She focused on walking, on the road ahead, and soon they were at the great gate, the doors open for her. The guards stopped as she did.

"This is it, bitch," the guard said quietly, "good luck surviving out there." To lend an aura of power, he pinched her behind, and she cringed at the memory of the previous night. She moved forward a step and then turned her head to look at the gathered crowd. There were nods among the people, and she nodded back in acknowledgement. Taking a deep breath, she walked out of Shrewesdale on the road to Haverston. It was a long road ahead, more than forty miles, and she had nothing, but she was determined to make it.

She kept moving, to get away from this place as fast as she could, and then stopped short. There, just in outside of the gate, at the side of the road stood a hanging cage, and inside it was a person bruised and bloody. It was Olivia.

"Olivia," she cried, grabbing the cage with her hands.

The wreck that was Olivia looked back at her. Through battered lips, she tried to speak. "Beverly," she said, struggling with the pain.

"What have they done to you?" she cried.

"What haven't they done? They beat me black and blue, broke my limbs, degraded every part of me and then put me here to die." She coughed, blood oozing from her mouth.

"I'll get you out of here," said Beverly.

"No," coughed Olivia, "I'm dead already, you must live. Promise me you'll get the bastards one day."

"I promise," Beverly said through tear-filled eyes.

"Good, I can die in peace, but you must take me out of my misery."

"I can't Olivia, you're my friend!"

"You must, Beverly. The agony is unbearable, and I might not die for hours or even days. I'm suffering."

"I would, but I have no weapons," she said looking around for anything that might be of use.

"Perhaps this will help," said a voice from behind her.

She turned to see Sir Heward The Axe standing behind her, holding Lightning's reins. He held her sword out to her.

"Sir Heward?" she said, disbelieving her own eyes.

"I shall be forever sorry for what has happened to you," he said, "though I know it does no good. When I heard what was to become of you, I retrieved your things. You are an honourable knight, Beverly Fitzwilliam, and nothing will change that. You have suffered a tremendous amount since the death of the Countess. Go in peace that you might one day punish those responsible."

Beverly took the sword, "Thank you, Heward," she said. "I shall not forget your kindness."

She turned back to Olivia to see the pleading in her eyes. "Goodbye, Olivia. May you find eternal peace."

She stabbed, killing her friend instantly, and the body slumped, lifeless, against the cage. One of the guards from the gate came running towards her, and Sir Heward turned and growled at the man. The guard stopped abruptly and then backed up towards the gate.

She took Lightning's reins and mounted her faithful steed. Sir Heward had bundled up her armour, laying it across the horse's back in a cloth bag. She turned back to Sir Heward, saluting him by placing the sword in front of her face. Without a final look, she quit this horrible chapter of her life. Her time at Shrewesdale was done.

TWENTY-FOUR

Return to Wincaster

AUTUMN 957 MC

~

S he returned to Wincaster with no fanfare, not even an
acknowledgement of her situation. She was assigned a billet and given
the captain's quarters again for privacy, but the other knights shunned her.
The days passed slowly, and she found it easier to endure them by adopting
a routine. She would go out riding early each morning, then practise with
weapons until lunch. The afternoons were usually busy doing paperwork,
for she was still one of the few knights who could understand the accounts.
She had already found numerous cases of corruption. It appeared every
supplier of equipment overcharged, and it hadn't taken long to find out
why for the suppliers were all associates of Marshal-General Valmar or the
king. It looked as if the king's favour extended to making a considerable
profit. She had put an end to some of it rather quickly, by conducting the
sale herself. She would travel to the supplier and negotiate prices, without
indicating who she was buying for. She had already managed to save more
than she had spent, and she was just warming up.

She had been back for almost a month and was poring over the knight's
books in her room. She was sure the suppliers were shorting her on grain
for the horses, so she was meticulously examining the ledger for any signs
of tampering when there was a knock at her door.

"Come in," she said absently.

The door opened, and a man entered. She looked up to see who the
intruder was.

"Father!" she exclaimed. "I didn't know you were back in Wincaster. How have you been?"

"Very well, my dear," he answered, and she relaxed for the first time in a long while. She felt the warm glow of her father's love and smiled. Knowing she couldn't tell him about Shrewesdale, she tried to deflect the conversation.

Of course, he wanted to know all about how she was doing, what she up to, all the usual topics of conversation. It only took a few moments for him to make her feel good about herself again.

Finally, he came around to the true purpose of his visit. "Tell me, you had to guard Princess Margaret a few years ago, do you remember the name of the tutor she had?"

"Hard to forget," she answered. "His name was Renfrew." She remembered the trouble she had caused by slapping him. Would she change her actions if she could? No, the man got what he deserved, even if she had to pay the price.

Her father was being mysterious and wouldn't say why this was so important.

"Meet me tomorrow for a luncheon, and I'll explain it all to you," he said. "Agreed."

He walked over to her and hugged her as if sensing it was what she needed. Had he heard of her disgrace? She swallowed her tears. She didn't want to burden him with it.

"I'm very proud of you, Beverly, and your mother would have been as well. Tomorrow then, the usual place?"

"Of course, Father, but perhaps I'll wait till you've had time to finish that smelly cheese."

He laughed as he left and Beverly smiled. It took her back to Bodden, to a life she loved. He disappeared around the corner, and she turned back to her books. Time to track down the missing grain.

Looking once more at her notes, she read she was to meet the blacksmith later today. She meant to check around town to see if she could find an alternative at a lower price before the meeting, so she was in a better bargaining position. The city bells pealed noon, snatching her from her musings. She was supposed to meet her father, and now she would be late. Hurriedly, she closed the book and grabbed her sword, she never went anywhere without it.

It didn't take long to travel to her father's favourite haunt, and she was relieved to see that he had already finished eating his cheese. He was sitting at a table out front, watching people as they passed by. She smiled and waved, enjoying seeing him break into a grin when he caught sight of her. It was hard to be in a bad mood around her father, he was always so cheerful.

"Well, my dear, you're looking quite pleased with yourself today. How are things going? It's been so long since I saw you last."

"It was only yesterday, Father," she said, and then noticed the grin on his face. "So tell me, what's all this mystery, and why did you want to know about Renfrew?"

Her father looked around to make sure no one was listening, and then leaned forward to talk in a lower voice. "There's something strange going on at Uxley. I'm going to go down there and have a look around."

"What do you mean, 'something strange'?"

"I can't quite put my finger on it, my dear. Gerald's mixed up in it somehow."

"You don't think he's in any danger do you?"

"No, he's quite capable of looking after himself. I think perhaps it's more of a mystery than something dangerous."

"You just can't ignore a mystery, can you?" she said.

"Not when my friends are involved," he replied, "and I want to make sure Gerald is safe. That man Renfrew has shown up in Uxley."

"Renfrew? In Uxley? Why would he go there?"

"I'm not entirely sure, but I have the beginnings of an idea." He leaned in even closer. "You know there have always been rumours of another royal child."

"That's just Palace gossip, Father. You, of all people, should know better than to listen to that kind of talk."

"But gossip has to start somewhere, and there may be a kernel of truth to it."

Beverly was intrigued, "So you think this child is at Uxley?"

Fitz looked around again to confirm they were alone, "Yes, I've been looking into things. After the king took up with his mistress, the queen secluded herself. She stayed at the Royal Estate near Hawksburg. She wasn't seen back in Wincaster for over a year, more than enough time to have a child."

"But if that's true," said Beverly, "then why take the child to Uxley. Surely Hawksburg is further away from the capital?"

"True, but travellers go past that Royal Estate all the time, it's much more public. Uxley is miles away from the village, and very secluded. What better place to raise a hidden disgrace."

"So you think the child was illegitimate?" she asked.

"Actually, I suspect the child probably suffered from some sort of deformity, and the queen was blamed. That might explain why the king took up with Lady Penelope."

Beverly thought this over carefully. It was all so plausible, she didn't know all the facts, but knew her father well. He would have looked into this in some detail before bringing it to her.

"This could be dangerous, Father. Who else knows?"

"I've only told you, my dear. If anything should happen to me, you'll find a letter in the townhouse. Take it to your uncle, he'll know what to do. I'm afraid these are dangerous times. If I need your help, and I very well might, I shall send someone you trust to talk to you directly. Nothing is to be written down. If the king were to hear of this, he would think someone was conspiring against him."

"Isn't that what we're doing?" she pointed out.

"No, my dear, we are merely trying to protect Gerald. Somehow, he's stumbled onto the king's best-kept secret. I fear that if the king learns what we know, he would kill any witnesses. I want to make certain that doesn't happen, but I have to be sure of what's going on first, that's why I'm travelling there in person."

"What can I do in the meantime? I want to help, Father," she offered.

He smiled, "Well, on that matter I have some good news. I've arranged for you to serve on the staff of a noble."

Beverly rolled her eyes, "Here we go again."

"Don't worry, I'm sending you to Hawksburg. Robert's stuck here in the capital for a while, and he needs someone to take charge up there. You'll report to your aunt. If I have any further news for you, I'll send word."

He reached into his tunic and pulled forth a neatly folded paper, complete with wax seal. "These are your official orders, I had your uncle whip them up. It's amazing what you can do with the proper connections. Do you think anyone in Wincaster will be upset with you leaving?"

"Relieved is the word I would use, I'm not very popular right now." She felt bitter, and it must have reflected in her voice.

"My dear," he said, placing his hand upon hers, "I know that things have been bad of late, but I promise you I will do all I can to rectify the situation. Enjoy your time in Hawksburg for I fear the future will be...tumultuous. We must be strong for what is coming."

"And what, exactly, do you think is coming?"

"I should think it's war of some sort. The king is a tyrant, and the nobles are becoming increasingly concerned with his erratic behaviour. Either someone will snap and challenge him, or some outside force will try to take advantage of our internal strife."

"Invasion or rebellion, is it that bad?"

"I'm afraid it is. I shall do what I can, but I have few resources. Can I count on you to do your part when the time comes?"

"Of course, Father, I shall do whatever needs to be done."

"Good," he said at last, "in that case let's not be maudlin about it. Server, another round of cheese!"

"And that's my signal to leave," said Beverly. "Take care, Father, and please be careful."

She stood, leaning forward to kiss her father on the forehead. She was not sure what would happen, but events appeared to be spinning out of control. She almost wished she didn't know, but felt a sudden rush, perhaps she had a purpose after all.

TWENTY-FIVE

Hawksburg

SUMMER 958 MC

They struggled to put the heavy wooden beam into place. The job was made harder by the waist-deep water and the sticky mud which sat at the bottom of the stream. When an ox had put its hoof through one of the rotting old bridge's planks, they knew it was time to replace it. Lord Robert was in Wincaster again, looking after the Royal Estates, so it had fallen to Lady Mary to organize the work, but it was Aubrey who dug up a book with the plans for rebuilding the bridge. At fourteen, Aubrey was an insatiable reader, a trait which she inherited from her mother. She now watched from the bank while Beverly and some townsfolk all pitched in. Pulling down the old bridge had been easy for it was quite literally falling apart. They had sunk the new pillars as deeply as they could, and now they were connecting the horizontal beams that would support the planking. It was a heavy, wet chore on a hot day, with all workers all in trousers and shirts, along with a liberal coating of mud, including Beverly, who had forgone both armour and a dress for practicality's sake. She had brought along her sword, for she never left her room without it, even here, but had left it at Aubrey's side on the bank, while she laboured alongside the townsfolk.

It was hard work, but rewarding. She had adjusted to life in Hawksburg easily, and her hands-on approach was remembered by the townsfolk. She would always be the 'strange lady knight' who wore a sword, even when dressed for dinner, but they respected her for her work ethic was strong, and she was always eager to lend a hand.

With a final one, two, three count, they heaved the massive beam up onto its rightful place. Two workers on the frame used their mallets to tap the beam down, its notch lining up perfectly with the rest of the structure. The workers bent over to catch their breath after giving a rousing cheer.

Beverly made her way to the bank with the others, rubbing her sore arm. The beam had slipped, causing her to fall and catch the beam on her shoulder as she went. Other than a dunking and a few bruises, she would recover. Stepping up onto the bank, Aubrey handed her a tankard with some sweet cider in it. She downed the icy cold liquid quickly and then wiped her mouth with her forearm. Aubrey laughed. Beverly looked down to see just how muddy she was, and that was when she realized she must have wiped mud all over her face. She grinned back, "Let me give you a hug, cousin!" she yelled and chased after the girl. They ran up towards the road, but Aubrey suddenly stopped. Beverly was about to say something when she noticed a rider. He was sitting on his horse watching the activity. Beverly's eyes went wide, it was Aldwin!

Her heart skipped a beat when she recognized him, but then panic set in. She had not seen him in such a long time, did he still feel the same? She felt unworthy, the events of Shrewesdale still buried deep within her.

"Excuse me, sir," requested Aldwin, "could you direct me to Dame Beverly Fitzwilliam?"

She caught her breath for a moment, and then remembered she looked like a man, filthy with mud, dressed in pants, her hair tied up. He didn't know who she was!

"It's me, Aldwin," she explained and watched for recognition to dawn on his face. He dismounted clumsily and led his horse closer. "I see your horsemanship hasn't improved over the years," she joked, trying to lighten the atmosphere.

He grinned back, "I'm a smith, not a horseman, but it's good to see you, m'lady."

Aubrey, who was now standing beside Beverly, stared at the man. "You must be Aldwin," she said finally.

He looked down at the youngster, "I am, but I'm afraid you have the advantage of me," he said.

"I'm Lady Aubrey Brandon, daughter of Baron Brandon and cousin to Lady Beverly Fitzwilliam," Aubrey said, curtsying.

"Pleased to meet you, Lady Aubrey," he responded with a bow, "but I'm a commoner, you shouldn't curtsy to me."

"Nonsense," she said, "you're a guest here, and I should extend you the proper courtesy."

"Aldwin," said Beverly, interrupting, "what are you doing here?"

"Your father sent me to deliver a message to you."

She remembered her father's words the last time they had met. Someone she trusted would deliver a message. Who better than the smith that had stolen her heart!

"What's the message?" she said, still mulling over his presence.

"I'm afraid it must be delivered in private, away from prying ears," he said, glancing at Aubrey.

"Well," the young girl said, "I can tell when I'm not wanted. I'll take the workers over to the food, Mama must have it all set up by now. You're welcome to join us, Aldwin, after you've delivered your message."

"Thank you," he said, "perhaps I shall." He turned to Beverly, "Is there somewhere we can talk in private?"

"Yes, let's put your horse in the stables, and then I'll take you up to the manor house. It's so good to see you, Aldwin," she said, and then suddenly felt guilty. They walked to the manor house in silence, while Beverly wrestled with her conscience. She considered her reaction in her head from every angle. Why was she feeling this way? Had Shrewesdale ruined her? Was she incapable of loving someone because of what a handful of knights had done to her?

Still gripped in her self-imposed silence, she led Aldwin into the drawing room. Almost as soon as they entered, she turned to him, only to find he was much closer than she expected. Throwing caution to the wind, she threw her arms around him, hugging him tightly. Her fears disappeared as he enclosed her in his strong arms. Her body felt as though it was melting, melding with his. She looked up at him, and overwhelmed by emotion, kissed him passionately on the lips. They stayed that way for what felt like forever and yet not long enough. She was not sure who pulled back first, but then Aldwin pushed her back slightly.

"We cannot, m'lady. We are still of different worlds."

She straightened herself, trying to smooth the muddy shirt to make it look presentable. "Of course Aldwin, you're right. I'm sure my father didn't send you here for this." Her heart was soaring, she was not broken! Aldwin still felt the same as her, she knew it now with a certainty.

"He entrusted me with a message that, quite frankly, I find strange. Would you like to sit, it's quite lengthy."

She was about to sit when she suddenly remembered how muddy she was. Overcome with a desire to look clean and proper, she realized that it was because of Aldwin. It was a shock to the hardened warrior within her that she was now reduced to the vanity of a young girl.

"I should probably clean up first, I'm covered in mud."

"Why don't you go and change," he said, "and I'll stay here. It's nothing that can't wait a while."

She grinned at him. "Good idea, I'll just be a few moments." She was about to leave the room when she suddenly broke out into a fit of laughter.

"What's so funny?" he asked.

"Your face has mud on it," she said with a wicked grin. "I wonder how that got there?"

She left the room to change, her feet felt light on the floor as if she could fly. She tried to control her giddiness as she rushed to her room. What was wrong with her? She felt so…young. She proceeded to her room, stopping along the way to request a ladies maid. On a typical day, she would dress herself, but she wanted to look particularly nice.

She returned to the drawing room only to see Aldwin's eyes bulge when he beheld her cleaned up state. She had chosen to wear a low cut dress, while Constance had managed to quickly twist her hair up into a curled braid. As his eyes took her in, she felt a warmth spread across her heart. She smiled and curtsied then sat down on a chair, indicating with her hand for Aldwin to do likewise.

"Please," she requested, "tell me what my father had to say."

Aldwin cleared his throat. "He visited Uxley and confirmed what he had suspected. Her name is Anna, and she is healthy. Gerald is looking after her, but he has learned that the marshal-general is sending troops to the estate. He feels she may be in danger."

She nodded as she took it all in, for the possible repercussions were overwhelming. "Did my father have specific instructions for me?" she queried.

"Yes, m'lady, you are to make your way into the service of Prince Henry. He says not to go to Uxley directly, it may be seen as a power play. Instead, you must convince Prince Henry to send you to protect her. It must be the crown's idea."

"Interesting, I would have thought the king would be a better bet."

"The prince visited Uxley recently and was attacked, so he now has a vested interest in protecting her."

"My father's been busy. Did he say how soon I must proceed?"

"Events are moving slowly, but he suggested you leave within the week. No doubt you'll need some time to wrap things up here."

"Who else knows about this?" she asked.

"Just your father. He didn't tell me the whole story, said it was safer that way."

"Thank you, Aldwin, for everything."

"Everything? All I did was deliver a message from your father."

"Oh, you did much more than that Aldwin, much more than that."

Beverly started making preparations to leave for Wincaster. She was not sure where the prince was, but it was the place to start looking. Aldwin decided to stay for a few days. Her aunt made it a point to include him at the dinner table for some reason, and Beverly highly suspected her cousin of revealing her secret to her aunt.

Aldwin was captivating to watch. He was not used to eating at a dinner table and fumbled on occasion. Aunt Mary was polite, ignoring the errors, while Aubrey kept grinning at her cousin whenever their eyes met.

Aldwin came upon her the next morning while she practised, and was shocked to see the state of her armour. She had tried to keep it in good shape, but the smiths of Shrewesdale had not been skilled enough to get all the dents out from her duel. Aldwin insisted on fixing it himself, and so he took over the smithy for a few days. He smoothed out the dents, replaced some straps that were getting worn and worked out the nicks on her sword. She tried the armour on for him, and he made some final adjustments.

Before she felt ready, it was time for her to depart. She didn't know what the future might hold, but she knew that she fought for her family, and the man she loved. That, perhaps, was her most significant discovery, for she had finally admitted to herself that she loved Aldwin. Not just a childhood crush, but a love that would last her a lifetime. They choose to leave the haven of Hawksburg on the same day, he to return to Bodden, and she to travel south to search for a prince. Aldwin left first. Beverly rode with him to the outskirts of town where he turned briefly, his eyes drinking her in, perhaps for the last time. She was seized by the urge to run away with him, to ignore all that was expected of her, but instead held his eyes with hers. He kissed her hand, and turning, rode off down the road. She watched him go, saddened at his leaving, but pleased to know that with the coming storm, he would be safe in Bodden. She rode back to the Brandon estate, thinking of her future. Would it include Aldwin? She could only hope it would.

Finally, it was time for her to leave. She gathered her belongings and mounted Lightning. She would be away for some time, of that she was certain. What the future held for her she didn't know, but she remembered the words of Albreda who said she was on the cusp of events that she could not imagine. She now understood that something big was building and she had a role to play.

She turned in her saddle to wave one last time. Lady Aubrey and Lady Mary were standing at the estate entrance along with the servants. Several townsfolk had shown up to wish her well, and as she rode off to the south, she was once more filled with determination and purpose. It would be a long road, she suspected, but she would find Prince Henry, and she would do what she could to protect the princess.

TWENTY-SIX

The Prince

AUTUMN 959 MC

It had been a long search. It had taken months to finally track him down, for Prince Henry was a young man on the move. After learning in Wincaster that he had gone west, she crossed the kingdom, all the way to Kingsford, only to find him departed, his destination unknown. She wintered there and then traversed back to the capital, to be informed he had travelled south. This game of cat and mouse continued as she chased him over half the kingdom, finally catching up with him near Eastwood, locating him at the Royal Estate that lay near the great northern city.

She rode up to the estate with the looming shadow of the Deerwood to the west. Its thick underbrush made the terrain all but impassable. To the east was the indistinct shape of the great mountain range which formed the eastern border of the kingdom. Beneath the mountains lay the Artisan Hills, home to the savage Orc tribes, but that was miles away. Orcs had not troubled the region for many years and were unlikely to do so anytime soon, for the Earl of Eastwood maintained a large army which was ready at all times.

Passing through the town of Eastwood, she had asked directions, and now she was riding up the trail towards the estate. The trees here were thick, not quite the full brush of the Deerwood, but enough that they lined the road, their great boughs forming arches overhead. The trail wound back and forth until finally, the road opened up into a field of well-kept grass. She saw the manor house in the distance, a gleaming white two-floor structure, with a large awning on the front.

Sitting upon Lightning in her full armour, including her helmet, she braced herself for what was about to transpire. Being one of the very few female knights in the realm, she fully expected to have to prove her skill. When she was in Shrewesdale, she had written to a number of the other women knights, but only one had responded, Dame Levina Charleston, who had been full of helpful advice. She was serving in Colbridge and had invited Beverly to visit her, but then events had taken a tragic turn before she had to opportunity to make the trip. She had written to Levina when she was in Hawksburg, but now, having been on the road for so long, any chance of a reply finding her was remote. Dame Levina had reinforced the same point each time they corresponded, a Dame must keep proving herself, lest the men see them as inferior. Beverly knew it was true, through her own horrible experience, so now she was always prepared. Since Shrewesdale, she had taken greater steps to protect herself, sleeping with weapons handy and not dulling her senses with strong drink. She was ready, as prepared as she could be, but at the road to the front of the estate, she felt a mild moment of panic. No longer was she the self-assured young woman who wanted to take the world by storm. Now she was cautious, almost timid in her movements. She shook herself mentally. She must control herself, her father had tasked her with a critical mission.

A stable-hand greeted her as she entered the yard, and contrary to her usual habits, she handed Lightning off to him, leaving her helmet and shield with her mount with a promise to visit her horse later. A young lad led her through the manse, to where the prince and his entourage were sitting around behind, admiring the view. A large, well-groomed field behind the estate boasted a patio overlooking the greenery, where Prince Henry was sitting on a couch, his feet up on a footstool. A young woman, wearing a thin, see-through dress, sat beside him, feeding him while he absently gazed out at the trees in the distance.

"I should think," the prince was saying, "that the hunting will be good tomorrow, there's been a few sightings of deer this year."

Another man, of a similar age to the prince, agreed. She walked down the half steps and turned to look at Prince Henry.

"Your Highness," she said, bowing.

Prince Henry looked up, taking his feet off the stool. "Well, what have we here?" he leered.

He turned to his companion, "Is this your doing, Bernard? I must say I like it, does she have a name?"

Beverly resisted the urge to slap him, "I am Dame Beverly Fitzwilliam, Your Highness, come to Eastwood seeking to serve you."

Prince Henry flashed a smile. A smile, people said, that could charm the clothes off of any woman. Beverly thought it looked well practised, but it didn't impress her.

"Well if the prince doesn't want you, you can come over here and serve me," offered Bernard.

"Wait a moment," said the prince, "Dame Beverly, I know that name. Weren't you the one that got into that trouble in Shrewesdale?" the man grinned.

"Oh yes," agreed Bernard, "the one that tried to lie with all the earl's knights. Didn't know you'd gotten us all a present, Your Highness."

"I am here to protect you, Your Highness," she said, ignoring the jibes, "and I can outfight anyone here."

"A pretty bold statement, Dame Beverly. I've some pretty impressive fellows in my retinue."

"Let me prove myself," she said, "and then you decide if I'm valuable to have around."

"I see a wager coming," said Bernard, "shall I call the others?"

Prince Henry looked Beverly straight in the eyes, weighing her determination. "Yes, and assemble the knights. Let's see who's willing to take on this Lady Knight."

It only took a few moments to summon the knights. The prince's friends, however, took considerably longer, and from the looks of them, many were either hung over or still drunk.

Prince Henry lined his men up. He had twenty knights, all sons of influential or rich nobles, and they looked the part. Their armour was immaculate, their weapons obviously expensive, but Beverly sized them up quickly, not one had the look of an experienced fighter.

"Which one shall you fight?" the prince asked her.

"That is for Your Highness to decide," she responded. "You know them better than I. Who is your best?"

Henry looked at Bernard for the answer. "Sir Galliard, no doubt," said Bernard. "I mean, look at the size of the man, he's huge."

Beverly sighed. Nobles always thought big means better. Sir Heward had been large, but it was his experience which made him dangerous, not his size. These young men all looked pampered and spoiled.

"Very well, Your Highness, shall we begin?"

"Yes, by all means. Perhaps on the grass where we can all see you?" Prince Henry requested.

She walked down to the grass, drawing her weapon and swinging it to loosen up her shoulders. Sir Galliard took up a position opposite her, doing likewise. They both looked at the prince.

"As you may," he said.

Beverly shifted her feet slightly, acting as if she were nervous. Sir Galliard, immediately falling into her trap, lunged forward. She nimbly sidestepped and struck her opponent across the back with the flat of her blade. The gathered crowd responded with a collective gasp. She rotated as the knight turned around to confront her, his face growing redder by the moment.

He held his shield up and advanced slowly this time, more wary of her. If she had her shield, she would have played it differently, but she needed to finish this quickly and assert her position. Sir Galliard predictively used his shield to attempt to block her next attack. At the last moment, she pulled the swing short then jabbed at his exposed shins. The man yelped and jumped back. The crowd laughed and more than one noble jeered.

Sir Galliard approached once more, this time crouching to provide better shield protection. She stepped forward with her sword above her head as if to impart an overhand strike, and he raised his shield, blocking his own view. She grasped the top of the shield with her left hand and pulled it down to reveal the surprised look on the man's face as she placed the tip of her blade at his throat. Clapping erupted from the audience, but Beverly kept her eyes on her opponent.

"Impressive, Dame Beverly," said the prince. "Tell me, are all your victories so quick?"

She withdrew her blade and bowed to Sir Galliard, "No, Your Highness, sometimes I have to break a sweat."

There was a murmur in the ranks as the knights argued amongst themselves.

"Perhaps, Your Highness," said Bernard, "one of your other knights thinks they can defeat her?"

Henry looked at his men. "Very well, who among you dares face the wrath of Fitz the Younger here?"

Beverly smiled at the compliment, being compared to her father was an honour.

As the knights huddled together she saw some of them shaking their heads. Was not even one of them willing to face her?

Finally, one of the knights was pushed forward slightly. He bowed, "I shall defeat her, My Prince," he said.

"Very well, Sir Clifford, off you go, but before you start, Lady Beverly, did you bring a shield? I should very much like to see the quality of your shield work." He turned to Bernard. "I always like to see a shield in use, it's so valorous, don't you agree?"

"It is the true test of mettle," the man agreed.

"Yes, Your Highness, it's back with my horse."

"Let's have someone retrieve it for you." He pointed at a servant, who ran off to gather the shield.

"You have interesting armour," commented the prince pleasantly, "I don't believe I've seen its like before. Who made it?"

"The smith in Bodden, Your Highness," she replied.

"Really? I would have thought it made by a master smith. He must command a high price for such work."

"He is in service to my father, the baron."

"Well, he does you proud," said the prince.

The servant arrived, awkwardly carrying the shield. She took it from him, holding it in her left hand.

"Now," continued the prince, "let's be fair, no head strikes, we don't want any fatalities today. You may begin."

Sir Clifford advanced cautiously, swinging the sword lightly, testing her reflexes. She blocked the blow effortlessly then, as he stepped back slightly, she took a step forward, smashing her shield against his, with the full weight of her body behind it. Her opponent had not braced to absorb the blow, and she had instantly spotted it, taking advantage of his being off-balance to push him down to the ground, his shield falling to the side. She stepped over him, placing the blade at his throat.

"Yield," she said calmly.

"I yield," Sir Clifford pleaded.

The prince chuckled, "I see your reputation is well earned, Dame Beverly. Welcome to my guard."

Bernard turned to the prince, "Your Highness, is that wise, she's lain with women, she can't be trusted."

"I don't give a rat's arse who she's lain with, the woman can fight. Besides, if she likes women, we don't have to worry about the men diddling her, do we?"

Bernard shook his head, "I suppose not, Your Highness."

The prince turned back to Beverly, "I am most impressed Lady Fitz. I shall have the servants prepare a room for you. We'll settle you in, and you can start on your duties tomorrow. I understand you have some experience in battle. Saved my father, if I'm not mistaken?"

The other knights looked shocked by this news.

"Yes, Your Highness, I have that honour," she agreed.

"Good, then perhaps I'll have you see to the pickets tomorrow, I've a feeling that they're not very secure. In the meantime, you can unpack and get something to eat." He turned to one of the servants, "Sanders, see that Lady Fitz is looked after."

"Yes, Your Highness," the servant replied.

Beverly left the patio, pleased that the first part of her plan was now complete. She was not sure how things would unfold, but the first step had been accomplished The prince looked like a nice enough fellow, but she was not going to take chances. That night she slept with locked doors and weapons at hand, She had had far too many bad experiences with knights.

In addition to the knights, the prince travelled with a number of foot soldiers. These palace guards were numerous, but woefully under-trained for their duties. The placement of the pickets was a complete mess. You could march an army of men through them and not be noticed. She moved guards around to strategic locations, making sure they were always within sight of each other at all times. They were decent men but lacked proper training, so she resolved, with permission from the prince, to spend time drilling them each day.

With regular practise, their skills quickly improved, and within days they were doing their jobs without much supervision. Prince Henry was impressed and let her have free rein with the rest of the men. The knights were more aloof and went out of their way to insinuate that she preferred women. Knowing that any rebuttal on her behalf would just make them more insistent, she ignored them and soon the jibes stopped.

The prince kept himself occupied. During the day he would go hunting, and in the evenings, women from the town were brought to the estate. The women were quite willing, for the prince was a generous man, and much more refined than their usual clientele. Beverly tried to politely refuse the offer when the prince decided, in an admittedly drunken state, that she should also derive some pleasure from his generosity and sent a woman her way. Beverly had to awkwardly explain that she was not interested, and the woman laughed it off as she was still paid no matter what occurred, so the two of them shared a drink and chatted to pass the time. It was odd, she thought, how two women, from vastly different backgrounds, could converse in such a friendly manner. If only men were capable of discussing things without the need for intimate relations.

They stayed at the Eastwood estate for a few more weeks, until Prince Henry received a letter from his mother. He ordered them all to be ready to depart the next day to take the long trip to Burrstoke. Apparently, Her Majesty wanted to see her sons, and had written to the prince. He was to go to Haverston to pick up his younger brother, Prince Alfred, and then travel on to Burrstoke. Beverly didn't know why, but the soldiers told her that once a year the queen would summon her sons for a visit. No one thought it unusual, and as she learned, the queen loved Burrstoke, or, more specifically, the Glowan Hills where a Royal Estate was built to her own tastes. The trip would be a lengthy one, with the first stop in Wincaster, then west on the king's road, turning south at Stilldale, and ending up at Haverston. She wondered why they went so far out of their way, for it would have been a shorter route to go through Burrstoke, but she supposed that the queen might be insulted if they travelled through the town without visiting her.

The journey itself was without incident. Beverly rode with the troops and placed pickets at night. She made sure they screened the prince and his retinue as they travelled, with riders in front, behind and to the sides. They were to range far ahead and return if danger should threaten, but despite Henry's concern for his safety, no assassins appeared.

The route was more than 300 miles, and they managed to cover almost twenty most days. Including the stopover at Wincaster, the trip took just shy of three weeks. Their arrival in Haverston brought Beverly back to a darker time, as she had not been this way since her flight from Shrewesdale.

Both princes had additional titles, besides being that of being a prince. Alfred, the younger of the two, was also the Viscount of Haverston, awarded to him by his father, while Henry was the Duke of Wincaster, the traditional title of the heir to the throne. Alfred acted like he was disillusioned by being the spare to the throne, at least this was Beverly's opinion of the moody and opinionated young man. He cared little for his servants and ordered people about with no regard for their feelings.

Beverly kept out of the younger prince's way, busying herself with pickets and duty rosters. When she had started with the pickets, she found they were on duty for twelve hours at a stretch. She took it upon herself to make sure they had a proper duty roster which allowed for breaks. The foot guards responded with a fierce pride in her, their new captain. More than once she heard of fights breaking out in taverns, no doubt caused by her reputation being bandied about by others.

Late one evening, Beverly finished inspecting the pickets and headed over to the field kitchen to grab a bite to eat. The cook filled a wooden bowl with a meaty stew, along with some bread. She took it over to a table and sat down, grabbing a spoon on her way. She was halfway through her meal when Sergeant Phillips sat down, nodding at her.

"His Highness is in a terrible temper," he said.

Beverly looked up, "How so?"

"Apparently he asked for volunteers from his knights, and no one stepped up."

"Volunteers for what?" she asked.

"Some sort of bodyguard duty," replied the sergeant digging into his bowl of stew with gusto. He lookup up from his food to see Beverly was gone, her stew still sitting on the table. The sergeant shrugged, knights could be so strange sometimes. He looked around, and not seeing anyone, poured her stew into his bowl and continued eating.

She entered the great hall in the middle of a conversation. Alfred and Henry were sitting at the table facing the entranceway, the knights aligned along either wall, the entire setup forming a big U shape.

"She's still a royal, Alfred," Henry was saying, "and we can't have people attacking a royal."

"But she's illegitimate," Alfred replied "Who cares, she's not in line to the throne. Even if Father acknowledged her, she can't inherit, she's a girl."

"Don't you get it, you thick-headed twit. The death of any royal would be bad. We rule by divine right. If we can be killed the whole divine part goes out the window."

Alfred grumbled and muttered something under his breath.

"Your Highness," Beverly said, walking up to stand directly in front of the table. "I understand you were looking for a volunteer."

Prince Henry looked at her a moment. "Yes," he said, "I want to send someone to act as a bodyguard."

Beverly held her breath, this was what her father was hoping for. "May I ask for whom?"

"My sister. Well, my youngest sister, that is. Her name's Anna."

"I would like to volunteer, Your Highness."

"How do we know she's worthy?" grumbled Alfred.

"You haven't seen her fight," snapped Henry.

Alfred sat up, "She can fight? I thought she could only screw."

The knights laughed nervously while Beverly held her tongue.

"Don't be such a cur, Alfred, yes, she can fight. She bested two of my knights in a row."

"I'd like to see that," he said. "After all if she's going to protect this 'sister' of ours she'd have to be good."

"Very well," said Prince Henry. "Will you, Lady Fitz, be so good as to demonstrate your abilities?"

Some of the knights snickered, for Alfred's men did not know of her skill with weapons. She knew this was it, an all or nothing gamble that would secure the prize. She must not let her father down.

Beverly turned to Alfred, "Choose your three best men, I'll take them all on at the same time."

Alfred almost choked on his drink. "Three men! By Saxnor's beard, for a woman you've got some hefty balls!"

Henry smiled, obviously enjoying his brother's disbelief. "Let's move outside, Brother, we don't want to mess up the hall, and she'll need some room. Gather your men, any melee weapons they like, and have them meet up out front. Lady Fitz? If you would like to retrieve your gear?"

"Of course, Your Highness," she responded.

She went to retrieve her shield and decided to do something completely unexpected. She knew it was different, but she was facing multiple opponents, and she had trained for this.

A crowd had gathered, including some townsfolk, who, having heard the commotion, had come to investigate, and had joined in, forming a rough circle. Alfred's three best knights stood inside it, ready to fight. The crowd opened to allow Dame Beverly entrance. She stepped forward, a warhammer in her right hand and a longsword in her left. The three knights looked at each other, this was completely unexpected.

She knew the stakes. This was not the time to shy away from the challenge. She should expect no mercy from Alfred's champions, knowing how the younger prince felt about her. Each knight before her wore heavy chain and plate, with a full helmet. She eyed them carefully as they moved about, warming up. Their helmets drastically reduced their vision. Hers would also restrict vision, but Aldwin had seen fit to put vents on the side, and this helped immensely with her battle awareness.

She flipped the visor down and stepped forward, waiting for her opponents to make the first move. She didn't have long to wait. The first one rushed forward with a powerful overhead strike, which she easily blocked with her sword, at the same time swinging her hammer sideways, hitting him on the shield arm he had failed to raise properly. He dropped his weapon and clutched his injured arm, moving away from the fray.

The second two had delayed, waiting and watching the first attack, and as soon as the lead knight moved aside, they rushed in, stabbing furiously with their swords. She swept their blades aside with her hammer, its weighted end easily knocking the lighter blades away, then she thrust with her own sword, lightly sticking the second man in the chest. It was only a small wound, but it put him off his guard. The man yelled an obscenity and backed up. Her original foe was shouting instructions now, he wanted to encircle her. They all backed up and began repositioning themselves. She knew she couldn't stop them, so she didn't even try. She let them get into position, and then suddenly launched an all-out attack on the knight in front of her. She struck him first with her sword, which he blocked with his shield, and then she hooked the shield with her hammer and yanked it towards her. This manoeuvre threw him off balance, and he lurched forward, directly into the path of her sword. Beverly felt the tip injure the man just under the armpit. He gave a yelp and shouted, "I yield," in a panicked voice. She wheeled suddenly, ducking as a sword swung over her head, then rose from her crouch to drive her hammer into her rival's groin. It was not a forceful hit, but it impacted the man's codpiece, and he immediately dropped his sword and shield, crumpling to the ground, holding himself.

Feeling a sword glance off her back, she silently thanked Aldwin for her fine armour. She twisted, swinging her hammer wildly with all her might. The impact of it striking the final knight's shield reverberated up her arm. His shield crumpled in the middle, and he dropped it, shaking the arm that was now numb from the impact. She immediately stepped forward, thrusting with her sword. The knight clumsily tried to block it, so she twisted the blade at the moment it struck. His sword flew through the air leaving him defenceless.

"Yield," she demanded.

Defeated, the knight nodded. "I yield," he said, removing his helmet.

Two men had yielded, and the third was still rolling around in misery on the ground. She turned to face Prince Alfred.

"Your Highnesses," she said, bowing deeply at the waist.

Alfred's eyes were wide, while Henry looked quite pleased with himself. "Pay up, brother dear," said Henry. "I told you she was good."

"Fine," Alfred sulkily agreed. He beckoned to a servant, who brought over a pouch of coins. He carefully counted them out, while his brother looked on in interest. With the bag in hand, Henry passed the coins to his servant and then turned to face Beverly.

"I do command you," he said in a loud voice, "to travel to the Village of Uxley, where you will take up the duties of a knight in service to my sister, Princess Anna of Merceria. Do you accept these duties?"

It was, of course, a mere formality, for no one could refuse such an order, but her father's plan had worked wonderfully.

"I do so accept this duty," she said, bowing deeply.

"Then you leave for Uxley first thing in the morning. Take the road through Burrstoke, it's faster, and the cold weather is due soon."

"Yes, Your Highness," she said.

The crowd began to disperse. Beverly had done it. Her father would be proud. The soldiers congratulated her, their praise warm and heartfelt. Even the knights she had defeated grudgingly admitted she had done well, except for one, he was busy screaming as they applied a cold compress to his groin.

TWENTY-SEVEN

Uxley

WINTER/SPRING 960 MC

~

Beverly left early the next morning, before the sun was even up, and was well on her way when the first flakes of snow began to descend. Prince Henry had given her a second horse to speed her journey so she could alternate which one she was riding to make better time. She rode eastward, where the road meandered through the Forest of Mist. For much of the trip, the sky was camouflaged, blocked by the canopy of green that covered the woods. Here the snow was sporadic, only the occasional flake making its way down to earth. A couple of days later, she cleared the trees to witness just how much snow had fallen. Indeed, it was still falling, slowing her pace considerably. By noon the horses were having a difficult time of it. The snow was knee deep with no previous path, so they had to push their way through it. She had Lightning take the lead with the small palfrey following behind. By evening, even the great beast was tired from forcing his bulk through drift after drift. It was exhausting work, and she was glad to arrive at the small roadside inn that catered to travellers. She saw to the horses stabling, grabbed a hearty meal, and rested the night in a private room, still not comfortable sharing the common room. Burrstoke was only a day away, but looking out at the weather that was setting in, she thought it might take her twice that long to make the trip. She purchased some extra saddle blankets and fodder from the innkeeper before setting out.

The weather turned worse, and the relentless blowing snow blocked all sight of the countryside. Following the road was difficult, and on at least two occasions Beverly had to backtrack when she found herself going the wrong way. She built a shelter that afternoon in a small copse of trees as the blizzard did its worst. The wind had picked up considerably, and the poor horses were walking straight into it. She built a fire and fed the horses while she waited, unsure of how much progress she had made. It wasn't until it was almost dark that the storm abated. She saddled up and made her way back to the road, determined to get a few more miles in before nightfall. The sky was clear for the moment, and the Glowan Hills could be seen off in the distance. As night fell, she saw the glow of Burrstoke and pushed the horses to complete the journey. It was nearly midnight by the time they arrived, and more flakes of snow were beginning to fall. She decided to spend a day in town, hoping the weather would clear, but the thickly falling snow continued for two more days.

Eventually, it let up enough that she decided to carry on with her travels, but the accumulated snow and colder than usual temperatures slowed her progress immensely. She found every mile to be laborious and by the end of each day she had made less progress than she had hoped. The trip from Burrstoke to Wincaster was about seventy-five miles. In good weather, she could have easily covered this in less than a week, maybe even three or four days, but with winter bearing down on her, she was lucky to progress five miles a day. To make matters worse, she couldn't cover enough ground to reach the roadside inns that were evenly spaced for daily travel. As a result, she spent more time finding refuge from the cold, building a fire, rigging up some protection from the wind and cold than travelling. She came to the conclusion she couldn't travel much further for fear she might perish on the road. Her horses were spent, and she knew that once they went down, she would be doomed, for she could cover far less ground on foot. She must seek out shelter and settle down for the winter. Uxley would still be there in the spring, and she suspected that with the harshness of the weather, anyone intending harm to the princess would be just as hampered as she.

Beverly was four days past Burrstoke when she cleared the Glowan Hills and started heading across the vast plain that led to Wincaster. The wind here was particularly harsh for there were only sparse clumps of trees to protect her from the ceaseless buffeting. On the road ahead, she sighted a large farmhouse and decided she must stop. The horses were so tired from pushing their way through the virgin snow, blazing a trail, that would no doubt be covered by nightfall. She forced them off the road towards what she assumed was the barn. She opened the great door and led the horses in, closing it carefully behind her. Looking around the cold barn, she saw that it had a high roof, and bales of hay lined one wall, but there were no recent signs of animals. Perhaps the owners had fled the harsh weather and expected to return in the Spring?

She clapped her hands to warm them, and the numbness turned painful as the blood began to return to her fingers. Glancing around, she could find no obvious place to safely start a fire, which was not surprising, considering it was a barn. She opened the door a crack and looked at the farmhouse for signs of habitation, but there was no movement. No lit lanterns were visible, no smoke came from the chimney despite the stack of wood she spied piled beside the house, half covered in snow. Stomping around the barn trying to get her blood circulating, she decided to dash to the house itself and was temporarily blinded by a cold gust of wind that took her breath away as she stepped outside. She trod through the knee-deep snow to the closest door at the back of the house, noticing that a portion of the thatched roof had been burnt away as she drew closer. The back door had no resistance and swung open with little effort. The building had, at one time, had an upper floor which consisted of a raised section at one end of the house, likely the sleeping area, but it had collapsed, along with the entire northern end, probably due to the damage from the fire and the recent weight of the accumulated snow. The damaged front door across the room dangled from a single hinge while inside, what was not covered in snow was covered in soot, and any valuables had been taken by the owners or ransacked by thieves. She made her way over to the collapsed roof to see a skeletal foot protruding from underneath the fallen timbers. This must have been the work of thieves, for there were no survivors. Looking about the house, she located the fireplace, but it was behind a large pile of snow and debris and was not going to be of any use. If she were going to survive this weather, she would need to get a fire going, and soon.

Beverly made her way outside the building and looked around, finally spying a two-handed axe lodged in a tree stump. Retrieving it, she made her way to the barn, but the cold was taking its toll on her, her hands were losing their feeling. She removed her gloves and stuck her hands under her armpits to try to warm them. It helped, but made her body feel even colder. She had to go out one more time to retrieve some of the wood from the woodpile. Clearing an area in the centre of the barn, she used straw and wood to build a fire. Getting the fire started was the most difficult task, for though she had flint and steel, striking them with her numb hands proved almost impossible. After several curses and prayers to any deity she could come up with, she saw the sparks take hold and soon had a small fire which she nurtured into a larger flame. The warmth penetrated her limbs, and before long, she was sweating.

With circulation returning, she took stock of her situation. She was low on rations, perhaps two weeks if she stretched it very thin. Fortunately, water was plentiful, for she could melt snow with an old pot she had spied in the ruins. If she were going to be here for any length of time, she would need to find food. Having spent almost her whole life training for combat, she realized that she had very little in the way of survival skills. She would need to find a way to feed herself. She looked at the two horses, but couldn't bring herself to consider killing one of them for food. With two weeks of rations, she had time to come up with a different option, and perhaps by then, the weather would break. The horses were well taken care of, for there was an abundance of hay piled up. Without a solution for the lack of food, she decided to make her surroundings more comfortable by moving the straw into piles against each wall, the better to cover the cracks that let in cold air.

The storm lasted for two more days and when she finally woke the barn was quiet, save for the shuffling of the horses. The ever-present wind against the outer walls had ceased.

Beverly went outside, walking around the house to ascertain what was available to her. It was only upon her return that she noticed, buried beneath some of the collapsed north wall, a hatch. Evidently, there was a cellar, probably used to store food. She thought it unlikely that the thieves had emptied it, for that end of the house would have been on fire. She began the process of clearing away the debris to gain access. It was exhausting work, and after the first day, she was ready to give up. It was while she was back in the barn warming up that she noticed a harness hanging on the wall. The previous owners must have had a plough horse, and though no animals were left behind, she had a Mercerian Charger, one of the largest breeds of horses alive.

It took her some time to figure out how to attach the harness to the larger pieces of debris, but then she started pulling timbers out of the way. With an abundance of rope in the barn, once she started, the work progressed quickly. Lightning was a strong horse and so great was the rapport between them, that she didn't have to lead him with a rope, but could tell him verbally what to do.

The final obstacle came loose with a mighty heave, revealing the floor hatch. Beverly detached the last timber from Lightning's harness and walked over to see a recessed ring, and it only took a slight heave to swing it open. It revealed a ladder which led down to a dirt floor, a room perhaps five feet in depth. She climbed down, crouching to avoid hitting her head and waited for her eyes to adjust to the dim light. Rough wooden shelves were filled with food stocks. There were sacks of grain, clay jars of mead and wine, even some meat which hung on hooks dangling from the ceiling. The room was frigid and the meat looked completely frozen. She took careful stock of what was present. She could be here a very long time and must take precautions to make sure the food lasted.

The winter of 960 was the worst in living memory. The cold weather was bad enough, but the amount of snow that accumulated brought the entire kingdom to a standstill. Beverly kept herself busy, continuing to practise with her weapons every day. To keep herself from getting lonely she began to talk to the horses. Lightning turned out to be an excellent listener but Archibald, the palfrey, liked to ignore her. She talked about everything with them, secure in the knowledge that they wouldn't repeat any of it. She had a lot of time to talk, for she stayed inside for most of the time due to the weather.

Lightning seemed to think that if she couldn't marry Aldwin, she shouldn't marry at all and Beverly was compelled to consider the options. She didn't want to disobey her father, but she couldn't imagine being married to anyone else. By the time spring rolled around, she was forced to conclude that she would never marry, despite her father's wishes. It was a hard choice, but it gave her a renewed look at life. She would concentrate on her service as a knight. She would find the princess and serve her faithfully, putting all her energies into that.

By early spring, Beverly had matured considerably. She had been truly alone for the first time in her life, and it had forced her to understand herself better. She was no longer a young knight with an uncertain future. Her isolation had hardened her, had forged her into a woman of determination and grit.

The spring thaw allowed her to bury the bodies found in the ruins of the farmhouse. She didn't know who they were, but she wept as she stood over their graves, for they had been innocent victims of the violence of bandits. She swore on their graves that she would do whatever she could to protect people like them, who couldn't defend themselves from the brutality that life so often dealt out.

It was with a heavy heart that she left the farmhouse, for it had been her home for months. She turned onto the road and stopped to look once more at the farm. She patted Lightning's neck, he was such a good listener. She twisted around to look at Archibald, munching on a stray strand of grass that had poked through the remaining snow, he was not a great conversationalist. She turned back to face north and urged her mounts forward to Wincaster.

The capital was busy. The sudden blooming of spring had released the nearby villagers from the stupor of winter, and they poured into Wincaster to celebrate. It was often like this in the spring, some coming to buy new seed, visit blacksmiths to sharpen tools or to purchase a new horse. Spring brought a freshness that seemed to invigorate everyone. Everywhere Beverly rode, people were waving and smiling. She chose to stay at an out of the way inn called the Green Lady. Better to not involve the army in her travels. She could have stayed at the barracks, or the Fitzwilliam manor house, but she thought Valmar might hear of it and remembered her father's warning.

Uxley was two long days away, and she wanted to get started early, so she rose before the sun. The king's road ran directly west, anchored on either end by the great cities of Wincaster and Kingsford. It was the only paved road in the kingdom. It had been completed some fifty years ago by King Andred II, grandfather to the current king. People had scoffed at the wasted expense at the time, but the road had stimulated trade and become a tremendous source of commerce.

Heading out the western gate, she noticed an exhausted-looking rider galloping in on a lathered horse. Jumping off his mount, he passed a dispatch to one of the guards. "Take this to the king immediately. It is of the utmost importance."

"What is it?" said the guard. "What's the news?"

"We've been invaded," the man said, gasping for breath. "An army crossed the border north of Kingsford and was bearing down on the city when I left. The king must send troops."

The guard shook his head. "The king's not here," he said, "and there's no troops to send. Let's get you some food and water, we'll send the message to the marshal-general."

"Where is the king?" the messenger asked.

"In Shrewesdale, he's wintering there."

Beverly took it all in. The kingdom was in danger. She cursed herself for delaying her trip but then realized that without the delay she wouldn't have been privy to this information. "How many men crossed the border?" she asked.

"At least several hundred, but some reports say it could be almost a thousand."

She shook her head, this was dire news. She didn't know the strength of the garrison at Kingsford, but the duke there would never surrender. Perhaps the city could hold out until they were relieved. She spurred her horse forward, her mission was now more vital, for if the army bypassed Kingsford, they could march through the heart of Merceria. She must find the princess and get her to safety as quickly as possible.

The distance between Wincaster and Uxley was a good seventy or so miles by road, but if she cut cross country, she could slash the length to less than fifty. With some luck, she could cover that in a day, a very long day. She resolved to do so and left the city behind her as she travelled northwest.

It was quite dark by the time she glimpsed Uxley in the distance, the glow of the village guiding her the last few miles. She knew the Royal Estate was nearby but lacked directions. She entered the town looking for a tavern and soon found the Old Oak. The hustle and bustle of the place proclaimed it as the busiest business in town, and she stepped through the doors, leaving her horses just outside. The warmth of the area enveloped her, and with the rush of heat from the fire, she suddenly felt exhausted. She stepped up to the bar to talk to the bartender, and as she did so, a familiar voice cried out.

"Lady Beverly?"

She looked around to see Arthur Greenwald, one of her father's soldiers. "Arthur? What are you doing here?"

"It's not good news I'm afraid, an army has come down from the north and Bodden is under siege. The baron sent me with a request for help. I only just made it out before the army encircled the Keep. I've been riding almost non-stop for days now."

Her heart almost stopped at the news. Two armies were now marching on Merceria, and the king was far away in the south. She wondered if she should ride for Bodden, but knew her duty to the princess must come first.

"I'm riding off in the morning for Wincaster, the king will surely send help," said Arthur.

"No, ride to Shrewesdale. The king is there, there's no one in Wincaster to help you."

"But what about Marshal-General Valmar?" he asked.

"By now he's already on his way to Shrewesdale," she said.

Arthur looked downcast, his trip of two more days had now become weeks. "Aye," he said, "then I'd best get to bed, for I'll have to rise early to make up the miles. I'd advise you do the same."

She considered his words carefully for arriving at the estate at this late hour would accomplish little. Better to clean up and rest the night, visiting first thing in the morning.

. . .

Beverly arose later than she had intended the next morning, for fatigue had
taken its toll. She forced herself to awaken, eating a hasty breakfast and
then saw to her horses. The innkeeper was kind enough to provide directions, and so, a little while later she found herself riding up to the Uxley
Estate. She entered the grounds through the large open gate, glimpsing a
white stone building in the distance where a number of people stood out
front, watching her approach.

As she got closer, she recognized Gerald Matheson beside a young girl
with blond hair, obviously the princess. On the other side of the princess
was a younger bald man. A formidable dog sat next to the small group,
watching her every move.

Beverly increased her speed, dismounting mere feet from the dog,
hoping she didn't startle it. She drew her sword and knelt in front of the
girl, the point of her blade held against the ground.

"Your Highness, I pledge my life, my sword to your service," she spoke
the oath with all the feeling she had been holding in reserve for this
moment.

The young girl looked back with a blank expression. "I don't understand," she said.

It was Gerald that spoke, "She's pledging to serve you, offering to
become your knight, your protector."

"Why would she do that?" asked the young girl.

Beverly spoke quickly, felt the jumble of words tumble out of her
mouth, "Long have I sought someone worthy to serve, Your Highness."

The princess still looked confused, "What makes you sure I'm worthy,"
she innocently asked.

Beverly kept her eyes on the girl for a moment. Was she serious? She
glanced at Gerald's solemn face. "The fact that Gerald Matheson is here is
proof enough for me," she said. "He has always been a loyal servant of the
crown."

The princess focused her intense gaze back on Beverly. "But I'm not
looking for a knight, though I'm flattered of course."

Beverly's mind raced. How could this child not want protection? Could
her life here have been so secluded? Then it dawned on her, "Have you not
heard the news, Your Highness?" she asked.

"What news?" asked the girl.

"The kingdom has been invaded. An army from Westland has crossed
the border and a second, from Norland, has attacked Bodden. We're at
war!"

A strange look passed between Gerald and the girl before the princess spoke, "It is the obligation of the nobility to protect the people."

"Those are my father's words," Beverly pointed out, surprised.

"Interesting," said Anna, "I learned them from Gerald, he's quite the teacher."

"It appears we have something in common, Highness, he taught me as well."

The bald man coughed.

"Oh," said Gerald, "allow me to introduce Master Revi Bloom, the Royal Life Mage."

The wizard bowed slightly, "Pleased to make your acquaintance, Dame Beverly."

"And you, Master Bloom. Though I'm surprised to see you here. I would have thought you'd be with the king."

"Alas," he replied, "my skill is not sufficient to impress His Majesty, and so I have remained at Uxley in the company of the princess."

"Should we not make preparations, Your Highness?" asked Beverly. "Time is of the essence."

Gerald looked back at the princess, "I'll tell the captain, Your Highness, and have him assemble the men."

"Yes," she agreed. "Come inside, Dame Beverly, and we'll decide what we're going to do."

Beverly spoke up, "There's no room for discussion, Your Highness, we must get you to Wincaster as soon as possible."

The young girl turned on her suddenly, "We'll go to Wincaster if, and when I decide. I'm the royal here, and you have pledged your service to me, not the other way around."

Beverly felt her cheeks flush. She had overstepped in her zeal, and she cursed herself for her impetuousness. "Yes, Your Highness, sorry if I've caused any offense, I'm only concerned for your safety."

"It's all right," the princess said as she led them into the Hall. "I'm sure you didn't mean any offense. Gerald has told me a little about you. I'm lucky to have someone of your skill in my service. What do we know about the attackers?"

"Not much I'm afraid, there are rumoured to be close to a thousand or so men attacking Kingsford, and we can probably expect a similar number at Bodden."

"How do you know that?" the princess asked.

"My father wouldn't send for help for anything less. The Keep there will stand a siege for a considerable length of time."

"So our priority should be Kingsford," said the princess, musing to herself.

"Excuse me, Your Highness?" said Beverly. "What do you mean?"

"I mean," continued Princess Anna, "that any move to defeat the invaders would have to march to Kingsford first. Is the king in Wincaster?"

"No, Your Highness, he winters in Shrewesdale."

"And who commands in his absence?" she enquired.

"Marshal-General Valmar, but he's likely sent word to the king already."

"Will Valmar march to Kingsford, do you think?"

Beverly thought quickly. What she knew of Valmar was not encouraging. "No, I don't believe so, he is a cautious man."

"Have you spent much time in Wincaster?" asked the princess.

"A number of years, Highness. Why do you ask?"

"What kinds of troops are stationed in the Capital?"

She had to think this over carefully. As far as she knew, there were a couple of companies of archers, some foot soldiers and some heavy foot that made up the Royal Guard. "I should say about 300 foot, 100 of those are Royal Guards, there's also two companies of archers and two companies of light horse. Certainly not enough to take on an invading army of a thousand or so troops, and pulling them out would leave the capital defenceless."

They waited in the great hall until Gerald returned with another man. "This is Captain Arnim Caster," he said introducing the new arrival. "He commands the princess's bodyguard."

Beverly eyed the man suspiciously, "You were sent by Marshal-General Valmar, weren't you?" she asked.

"Yes," Caster replied, adding quickly, "but I serve the princess."

The two weighed each other carefully, neither one trusting the other. Had Valmar already inserted his control over the princess? Was Beverly too late?

"Gerald," said the princess, "Lady Beverly wants us to go to Wincaster. What do you think?"

Gerald looked at Beverly, then back to the princess. "I think it's the best option until we know more. We need to find out what's happening in the capital."

Anna nodded, "Then it's decided, we'll go to Wincaster. Once we're there, we can determine what to do next."

"Your Highness," said Beverly, "Marshal-General Valmar commands in Wincaster, he'll have control of the troops."

"Not when a royal is in residence," said Anna confidently. "Don't worry, Dame Beverly, I know how the law works."

Beverly was pleasantly surprised and relieved. This young girl appeared far wiser than her age would indicate.

TWENTY-EIGHT

The Temple

SPRING 960 MC

❦

C aptain Caster nervously paced back and forth in front of his assembled men. Appearing to have finished with his internal discussion, he walked over to the princess.

"What is it?" she asked him.

"One of my men is missing. I sent him out earlier to find you, and he hasn't returned."

Gerald, who was beside her, looked at Beverly. "We'll find the missing man and then catch up. You should get the princess to safety in Wincaster."

"No," said Beverly, "it would be better if we all travelled together."

"I agree," said the princess. "Let's get a search party out and find him. He might be injured."

They organized a search party and rode out across the grounds, determined that none should be left behind. Forming a long line, within hailing distance of each other, it didn't take long to locate him. As chance would have it, Beverly was the one who found him. As she was crossing the old crop field she came across a derelict well that was boarded up. Its walls were long since ruined and boards had been placed over what was now little more than a hole in the ground. A few of the boards were freshly broken and cracked. Dismounting, she called the others over, and then stared into the darkness, yelling into the shaft, only to be greeted by some moaning.

Revi Bloom knelt at the side of the hole, peering into the gloom. He uttered words foreign to Beverly while holding his hands in front of him, palms facing upwards. A small globe of light appeared, floating just above his hands. It was bright, as bright as a lantern, and as he stared at it, it began to move through the air, through the cracked wood and into the old well. Well, this was an interesting development, thought Beverly, but she didn't have time to investigate it further, they were here for a reason.

Beverly and Revi both looked down as the globe of light descended. It soon reached the bottom where they could make out the injured soldier. He was about twenty feet down and lying across roots which appeared to have broken both his fall and his leg, for it was twisted painfully beneath him.

By now the others had joined them and formed a circle around the well. "I'll get a rope," offered Gerald, making his way to his horse.

"It's my man," said Arnim, "I'll go down and get him."

"You'd better take Revi with you," added Anna. "It looks like he'll need some healing."

"What can I do to help?" Beverly offered.

"Stand by up here," said Gerald, returning with a rope. "We'll need some muscle to pull him up."

Arnim tied a loop in the rope, and then placed his foot inside it, while the rest lowered him down. Revi stood by, controlling the floating light. It didn't take long for Arnim to reach the injured man and a moment later he called up. "His leg is definitely broken, but I can get him loose. It might be best to heal him up there, where you can see him better."

They all agreed, and a moment later they were hauling the poor fellow up. Arnim remained below on the side of the well where it had partially collapsed, forming a small ledge for him.

Revi laid his patient out, and went to work, calling up arcane forces to repair the leg. Beverly was amazed as she watched. Moments later no blood or bruising remained, save for what had bled onto the guard's clothes.

A shout from the well grabbed their attention.

"I found something down here," yelled Arnim, "a flat surface. It's got runes or something on it."

Revi helped the wounded man to his feet and then passed him off to the other guards. "Take him back to the Hall, he'll need to rest for a time as he'll be a little weak." Revi made his way back over to the well. "Lower me down," he said, "and I'll take a look."

Once again Beverly helped lower the rope, watching from the top as the mage and the captain examined the runes.

"It looks like an ancient language," said Revi. "Hold on, I'm going to cast a spell."

They heard a faint noise as he called upon the arcane powers once again, and then he commanded the glowing light to come closer to the wall. "I was correct. It's an ancient language, Saurian to be exact, but I can't fully comprehend what it says."

The princess suddenly took an interest, then Beverly saw her turn to Gerald. "Gerald, we must go and get Lily, she might be able to read it."

Gerald nodded, "All right, but I don't know if she'll come for me, you'd better come as well."

Anna nodded, then peered down the well, "We're going to get some help. See if you can clear away the wall, maybe some of it's covered by dirt. Beverly, you come with us."

Beverly leaped onto the back of Lightning, and the sturdy horse, as if sensing something important, fidgeted as it strained to be let loose. Riding across a significant portion of the estate, she wondered where they were going. It was only after entering the wetlands that they finally slowed their pace.

"Wait here," commanded Anna, before she and Gerald dismounted and started moving down into a grotto.

"Let me go," yelled Beverly, "you've got a bad leg, it'll take too long."

Gerald looked back at her and patted his thigh. "Not anymore," he said, "the mage saw to that."

It was at that moment that Beverly noticed Gerald was walking without a limp. "When did he do that?"

"Years ago," he called back as he turned to follow the princess.

Beverly cursed her father, for he must have known about this ages ago. She wondered what else he was withholding from her as she waited patiently, still not understanding what was going on. A few moments later they emerged with a small being, about Anna's height, walking between them. The creature looked like a lizard, but walked upright, like a Human. It wore no clothes but had a cloth satchel slung across its shoulders. Anna stopped and then pointed at her, saying, "Beverly."

The creature looked up at her, "Bev - er -ly," she repeated in a sing-song voice.

"Beverly, this is Lily," she made the introductions as if seeing an upright lizard was an everyday occurrence. "She's a Saurian." Anna saw the look of bewilderment on Beverly's face and smiled. "Don't worry, it's a long story, and we'll fill you in on the way back to the well."

Anna mounted her horse, holding her hand out expectantly for Lily. The diminutive thing hesitated only a moment or two, and then grabbed the proffered hand, hauling herself up and placing her arms around the princess's waist.

The princess told Beverly all about the strange creature as they road back to the well. Lily, the name that Anna had given her, was one of oldest races in the land, at least according to Revi. It was thought that the Saurians had died out centuries ago, she explained, but she and Gerald had found Lily, and they had become friends. Now they wanted her help to unlock whatever was below the well.

They arrived back at the well with their new companion, but to Beverly's surprise, the guards took it all in stride. She must be the only one here who didn't know that Saurians still existed. The princess brought Lily over to the well and asked for them both to be lowered down.

"Your Highness," Beverly interrupted, "if you're going down, allow me to go first. It's my duty to keep you safe."

The princess looked at Gerald, who merely nodded. "Go ahead," she said, "but it's going to get crowded down there."

A shout came from the well. "We've opened a door," said the mage, "and it leads to a corridor of some length."

"Hold on," yelled Anna, "we need to get more people down before you go charging in."

They lowered Beverly first. Brick lined the side of the well, but as she got closer to the door, the brickwork changed and appeared to be more of a fitted stone. Arnim and Revi were standing in the doorway, with a door unlike any she had seen before. Rather than being hinged on one side, it pivoted in the centre so that one side swung out while the other swung in.

Beverly drew her sword as Revi floated the light into the corridor before them. The floor was constructed of stones fitted together, and the walls appeared to also be set with stone, but she could see no mortar in either design. The globe continued to levitate down the hall as Arnim and Revi entered behind her.

Soon, Anna and Lily were there, with Lily chattering excitedly. The mage incanted another spell, and Lily began conversing with Anna in a rapid dialogue.

"Lily thinks it's a temple," translated the princess.

"That would make sense," Revi concluded. "The Saurians traded all over Merceria, well before it was Merceria, of course."

Beverly looked at the young mage. "Your wisdom impresses me," she said. "You look so young for someone so knowledgeable."

"Andronicus kept me hard at the books for years," he replied. "I hated it at the time, but now I appreciate all the work."

"What else do you know about these people?" she asked, as they made their way down the corridor.

"The Saurians, that's our name for them, are thought to be the oldest race. They populated this land along with the other Elder races; the Elves,

Dwarves, Orcs and such before Merceria was formed. They were an advanced race who traded with everyone. It's said that they could travel unhindered, but I have no idea what that means. In those days they helped the other races advance their cultures, build cities and such. They were known as teachers and masters of knowledge."

"What happened to them?" she enquired.

"No one knows for sure, but by the time of the coming of man, they had withdrawn from the land. Perhaps they saw the advance of Humans and decided their time was waning or perhaps some calamity befell them, no one knows for sure. Until they found Lily, I would have said they were extinct."

They soon came to a corridor that led to their right. "What do we do now?" asked Anna.

"I say we split up," suggested Arnim. "We can cover the area quicker that way. We have no idea how big this place is."

"I can only control one light at a time," reminded Revi.

"That's all right," interrupted Anna, "I brought a lantern down with me. Give me a moment to light it." She knelt down and made a small pile of straw, then pulled out a flint and steel. A couple of strikes and she had some sparks.

Beverly watched the young princess with interest. It appeared she had learned some unusual skills, and was much more than she seemed to be.

Anna soon had the lantern lit. It was a hooded lantern, with a metal covering that would only expose light on one side, allowing her to point it down their corridor. "How shall we split up?" she asked.

Beverly had turned away as she lit the lantern and was now staring down the side passageway. "There looks to be something glowing down this corridor. Is there anything you know of that could cause that, Mage?"

Revi shook his head, "No, as far as I can remember there's nothing that would cast a glow like that. I suggest we proceed with caution."

"Well, we can't leave something behind us, they could cut us off," interjected Arnim. "We need to take a look down the main corridor first."

"Excellent advice," came a voice from behind them as Gerald arrived. "Sorry to startle you, I thought you might like some company."

Anna smiled, "You mean you didn't want to miss anything."

Gerald grinned back, and Beverly noticed the natural camaraderie between them. She had known Gerald all her life, and yet she had never seen him this way before. He had lost his family years before she was born, but now she saw...what precisely?

Gerald's voice interrupted her thoughts. "How about Arnim and Revi stay here to keep an eye on the side corridor while the rest move forward? If we find another passage or anything else of interest, we'll give a holler."

"Good idea," said Anna. "Dame Beverly, will you take the lead?"

"Yes, Your Highness," she replied. Taking the lantern in her left hand, while keeping her sword at the ready in her right, she moved slowly down the hallway. The structure looked very old, its bricks placed with incredible artistry. Each stone seemed to fit perfectly in the complex arrangement that made up the walls.

They didn't have to go far before they found a small chamber and a dead end. The room was small, no more than a foot's length wider than the corridor, with rings set into the wall. Beverly's first inclination was to think of a jail cell, but she quickly dismissed that thought. The rings were wooden and would be easy to break, plus there were no bars to restrict a prisoner. She swung the lantern around the room, noticing a stone-tipped spear hanging from a ring. Obviously this was not a jail. The shaft of the spear was made of wood, with reeds used to attach the head. Where the two parts joined, a peg extended and this was used to hook the weapon to the ring. It had been here many years, and the wood that made up the pole was dried and warped. Never one to pass up an opportunity to inspect a new weapon, she moved to the back of the room.

She had always been fascinated by weapons. Initially, just in their use, but as her friendship with Aldwin had blossomed, so too had her interest in the making of them. She scabbarded her blade and took down the spear, examining it as she brought it up to the lantern.

"Fascinating," she mused out loud, "the construction shows some skill, this isn't just an Orc spear."

Gerald came forward to see for himself. "The stone on the tip still looks very sharp."

"Yes," she agreed, "much sharper than I would have imagined. How do you get a stone that sharp?"

"Magic, perhaps?" offered Gerald.

She nodded in agreement. "Probably, if what Revi said was true, it would make sense that they had magic."

"In that case," said Anna, "we'd better be extra careful, there might be magic traps down here. What do you think this room was for?"

Beverly looked at Gerald, who nodded his agreement. "It must have been a guard room. I suppose they would be here to watch for intruders."

Lily was fascinated by the spear, despite its warped handle. Beverly handed it to the small creature and then drew her blade as she made her way back to the side corridor. "I suggest we get moving. There's still an army out there trying to invade the kingdom. We can't afford to take forever searching out this place."

They rejoined Arnim and Revi and started down the side corridor. The glowing from further away gave off a greenish hue, and as they walked, she saw Revi Bloom, the mage, stroking his chin absently. She chuckled, for it reminded her so much of her father, but where her father had a beard, Revi had none. It was indeed strange to see someone so young acting so old.

They soon encountered another problem, for they had not gone far before they came to a four-way intersection. The party stopped, almost at the same time. "What do you suggest now?" asked Arnim.

Revi was looking down the corridor staring at the flickering green light. "This way," he indicated. "That's no ordinary light, it's magical."

Lily chattered, and Anna spoke up, "Lily says it's an eternal flame. This structure must be a temple of some type."

"A temple?" said Beverly. "What do we know about their religion?"

"Nothing," said Revi, "but perhaps the word Temple is lost in translation. I believe this may have been an outpost."

They continued, with Arnim watching warily behind them, passing through another chamber. There were no doors that they could see, only openings. This chamber held rush mats on the floor, though they looked far from comfortable.

"Beds," said Anna, "just like Lily has in her cave."

"Yes," said Gerald, "but these look far older for they've accumulated lots of dust."

"There's a side passage here," said Beverly, "it looks as if part of the wall has collapsed part way down it though."

"Never mind that," said the mage, "here is the real treasure."

He stepped through an archway and Beverly watched as the green light glowed around him. She followed him through, making sure the way was safe for the others. It was a chamber about the size of the previous one, perhaps twenty feet per side. She saw other openings to the left and right, but the structure in the middle held her attention. The ceiling was higher here, arched, and in the centre of the room was a stone structure, a small stepped pyramid with a flat top. At the top of it, green flames flickered, creating the eerie glow that had drawn them in.

Gerald looked at the base of the flame. "There's no fuel here. How is that flame sustained?"

"Magic," said Revi, "notice the green colour? It's powered by magical energies."

"You mean the whole pedestal is magical?" asked a wonderstruck Anna.

Revi scrutinized the flame before answering, "No, although there is some magic to it. I suspect the flame is kept alive by the ley lines."

"What's a ley line?" asked Arnim.

"Magical forces crisscross the land," Revi explained, "they concentrate in certain areas. Ley lines cross roughly North South and East West. If I'm not mistaken, the lines cross right here. That makes this place unique. It can't be a coincidence."

Lily chattered while Anna moved to inspect the pedestal. "There's writing on these stones."

Revi moved closer, floating his light until it was almost touching the stone. "These are magical letters," he said absently, deep in thought.

Beverly had no idea what they were talking about. She thought of her cousin Aubrey, she would probably understand. "Could someone explain this to us ordinary folk?"

Anna stood up and faced her. "Magic uses symbols to represent the Arcane Powers. Language varies from culture to culture, but the Arcane Letters are consistent. It's their shape that gives them power, as far as I can understand. Lots of people can read the Arcane Letters, but few can use them."

"That's correct," said Revi. "It takes a person with magical potential to unlock the runes. There's very few of us these days, but this proves the Saurians had magical ability, or at least some of them did."

Beverly looked at the flame again. It began to draw her in, to captivate her. "I can see something in the flames," she said after a moment.

The others stopped their examination of the stones to look again at the flame.

"Yes, I can see something," said Anna. "It looks like…trees?"

"Yes, I can see that too," said Beverly. "It looks like we're looking over the tops of trees."

Lily chattered excitedly.

"She says it's home," said Anna. "We must be seeing a picture of the Saurians home. Is that possible?"

"I suspect it's more than possible," said Revi, "I think we are scrying, remotely viewing it as it truly is."

"Like a portal?" said Arnim.

"Yes, like a portal, or a window."

"Lily says there's a term she's familiar with, 'step through the flame'. Does that mean anything?"

"It means you can transport through the flame, like a dimensional doorway or a gate."

Everybody looked at Revi, who blushed slightly. "Sorry, I don't want to sound like I'm bragging, but we've just discovered the most amazing thing in more than five hundred years!"

"So we can travel through this thing?" asked Beverly, a little skeptical.

"Yes, but we'd need to learn the words first," the mage replied.

"Words?" she asked.

"Yes, the correct combination of Arcane Letters that would unlock the transport spell."

"How long would that take?"

"Months, maybe even years, though I suspect that Lily here would be a big help if we could communicate better."

"But I can talk to her, so can you, using your spell," said Anna.

"Yes, but only at a basic level. This would require a much higher level of language."

"If I were to learn her language, would your spell improve it?" she asked.

Revi looked at the young princess. "Yes, the spell enhances your own ability. It can grant you basic communication skills or enhance what you already have."

"Good," she said, "then for the next little while you can keep casting that spell on me and I'll endeavour to learn her language."

"I admire your determination, Your Highness," Revi replied, "but I think you're underestimating the difficulty."

"Don't tell her how hard it is," said Gerald. "It only makes her more determined."

"We need to keep moving," reminded Beverly. "Remember the invaders?"

"Yes," agreed Gerald, "we need to wrap this up. I know you'd like to stay here Master Revi, but we really do have to keep moving."

"Fine, fine, let's complete this search quickly then. The flame is fascinating, but there may be more to see."

"There's another chamber over here," said Beverly, pointing with the lantern. "There are shelves and what looks like a workbench."

She stepped further into the left-hand chamber. The racks reminded her of bookshelves, but instead of books, there were slabs of slate, each less than half a fingers size in thickness and slightly larger than a splayed hand. There were more runes and other scratches which were undecipherable.

Gerald looked over her shoulder, "That's Saurian," he said. "We found similar scratchings in Lily's cave."

"I can read this one!" said Anna in surprise. "How is that possible?"

"It's the spell," said Revi. "It allows you to read as well as speak."

"You mean I'm reading magic?" she asked in amazement.

Revi looked at the slate she was holding. "No, that's not magic, it's probably a recipe rather than a spell."

"Recipe for what?" she asked.

"I don't know, what does it describe?"

The princess looked over the slate carefully, conferring with Lily. "It sounds like a recipe for something, I recognize some of the ingredients. They use Lily's names for them, but I don't know what they are in our language."

"Likely a potion," he said, "not magical in nature, but with magic-like effects."

"I thought potions were the stuff of legends," said Beverly, not quite believing her ears.

"Oh, potions are real," explained Revi. "They just take time and careful work to produce. My parents can brew some potions. Almost every village has someone who can brew a tea to help the sick, or a poultice to help a wound recover."

"Fascinating," said Anna, "I'm going to take this one with me."

Revi had stopped what he was doing. He was staring at a slate, all the while his eyes were growing larger.

"Something interesting, Master Revi?" asked Beverly.

"This slate, it's a spell recipe," he said quietly.

"Is that important? Don't you already know spells?"

"You don't understand," he explained. "Magic has been passed down from master to apprentice for generations. There hasn't been a new spell in centuries. This spell can do miraculous things."

"Like what?" she asked, once again feeling a little lost in all this magical chatter.

"Like heal people," he said with a reverent tone to his voice.

"I don't understand. Can't you already heal people?"

"Not like this. I can fix broken bones and mend tissue damage, but this would allow me to do so much more."

"I don't understand," she shook her head in consternation. This was far beyond her comprehension.

"This will enable a caster to regenerate something that was lost, a hand or foot that was cut off, for example."

"You mean you could replace lost limbs? That's incredible." Beverly saw so many possibilities for this magic.

"Oh, it's a ritual, a spell that's cast over a long period of time, but it would work."

"We'd best gather up all these slates," said Gerald. "You can examine them when we get to Wincaster."

"Listen up, everyone," Anna interjected unexpectedly. "What we've found here is a major discovery, but enemy troops are traipsing around the kingdom. We need to keep this information to ourselves. Only the group of us here knows about this, I suspect we should keep it that way. We don't want word of this getting to the enemy."

"Agreed," said Revi, "we'll just tell those above that we found some old ruins, don't mention the flame or the tablets."

Beverly watched Arnim, was he planning to tell Marshal-General Valmar? She suspected he was a spy, but kept her thoughts to herself. She nodded along with the others. She would have to keep a tight eye on Captain Arnim Caster.

TWENTY-NINE

The Capital

THE CAPITAL

The trip to Wincaster, once they had gotten underway, had taken them two days. For most of the journey, Revi had travelled in the carriage along with Gerald, the princess and Lily. Beverly preferred to escort astride Lightning, and rode beside the carriage whenever possible. The group had commandeered a wagon from the estate, with Arnim's guard travelling aboard it while the captain rode on the other side of the carriage.

She spied Revi inside, studying the tablets he had retrieved. Anna and Lily were continually talking, the young princess following through on her decision to learn the language. Gerald slept. It was hard to imagine him in this situation. She had watched him lead out patrols on a regular basis in Bodden, but as she looked at him now, asleep in the carriage, she noticed how old he had grown. He appeared at peace with himself, and she wondered how he had dealt with his situation after being dismissed from the army. Was it anything like her experiences, she wondered? The carriage slowed unexpectedly, interrupting her daydreaming, and she looked back to the road. The city was in sight, but there was a commotion at the gates. Surely the enemy could not have reached Wincaster already?

She rode forward, only to see it was a press of commoners, trying to gain entrance. The city gate had its portcullis down and was refusing entry. She spurred ahead to investigate and soon found herself facing the guards at the gate.

"What's going on here?" she demanded.

"Sorry, we have our orders. No one is to be admitted to the city."

"On whose authority?" she barked.

"Marshal-General Valmar," the guard replied with a shrug.

She wheeled Lightning around, galloping back to the carriage.

"Your Highness," she said, "Marshal-General Valmar has ordered the gates of the city closed."

Anna leaned out of the carriage to look down the road. "What about all these people? What are they supposed to do?"

"The guards won't open the gate. They've been left to fend for themselves."

"This won't do," she said. "You and the captain clear a way through the crowd, and we'll get the gates open."

"How do you intend to do that, Your Highness?" Beverly asked.

Anna smiled, "I'm sure a mere gate guard is not going to refuse an order from a Princess of Merceria."

Beverly made her way forward, using Lightning's bulk to part the crowd once more, Captain Caster following suit. The captain's horse was much smaller than her Mercerian Charger, but people still moved out of the way. Soon, they were before the gate.

"Open in the name of Princess Anna of Merceria," shouted Beverly.

The guard gathered some men to help, and they pushed the crowd back to allow the carriage through. It had rolled forward no more than ten feet when Anna ordered it to stop.

"Sergeant," she directed the guard, "come here."

The sergeant dutifully came as beckoned, taking up a position of attention in front of the window.

"Do you know who I am?" she asked politely.

The man looked at the Royal Coat of Arms that decorated the door to the carriage. "Aye, Your Highness," he said.

"I order you to open the gate and let these people in. This is a royal command. Do you understand?"

"Yes, Your Highness," the man responded with a look of relief on his face.

He yelled out the orders, and they raised the portcullis. Anna had the carriage wait while the crowd rushed to get into the great city.

"That was a noble act, Your Highness," commented Beverly.

"They're just scared," she replied. "Valmar should be protecting these people, not shutting them out. When we get to the Palace, I want you to go and find Valmar and bring him to me. Can you do that?"

"With pleasure, Highness," Beverly replied.

Once the crowd began to ease their struggles, the carriage continued on its path, with the farmers cheering them as they passed by. Soon, they were moving through the massive gates of Wincaster and entering the city proper. It was funny, thought Beverly, how I keep ending up back in the capital.

They arrived at the Palace with little fanfare. The Royal Standard was not flying, indicating no royal was in residence, and it soon became apparent why. The king was still in Shrewesdale, along with his sons, leaving the city without any leadership. Even Marshal-General Valmar was gone. Apparently, upon hearing of the invasion, he took it upon himself to travel to Shrewesdale to alert the king in person. His audience with the princess would have to wait.

The princess began issuing orders as soon as they arrived. She wanted all the capital's troop captains summoned to the Palace. Plans for the defence of the realm needed to be made immediately, so messengers were sent even as Anna, along with her dog Tempus, made their way into the Palace. The rest of her group trailed behind, last being Arnim, as he issued orders to the guards.

They met in a drawing room where Anna sat down in a large chair, her loyal hound lying beneath her feet.

"We must act quickly," she said. "Ideas, anyone?"

It was Gerald that spoke first, "We have little to work with Your Highness. The quality of troops here is not very high."

"Agreed," Beverly said, drawing upon her time in the capital. "They're not battle-hardened."

"Then I shall make it the job of you two to do what you can to make them ready. Gerald, you've worked with foot soldiers before, I'm making you my commander. You will take control of the footmen. Beverly, you will command whatever cavalry we can muster. Arnim, you will remain in command of the Royal Bodyguard, they'll form the headquarters' detachment. We're going to be marching an army and we need to organize our supply lines. Who can do that?"

"I can sort that out with Gerald, Your Highness," offered Beverly. "We've done long patrols in the past, this will just be a bit more complicated."

"Excellent," the princess continued, "it's important that we take all our food with us, we can't stop to forage. We're running out of time."

"Just what is the plan, Your Highness?" Beverly had hesitated to ask but felt compelled to find how they were going to proceed.

"We will march to Kingsford as soon as we can muster an army, then we move to help Bodden."

There was a stunned silence in the room as everyone looked around.

"Will Bodden be able to hold out?" The princess directed this question at her new knight.

"Yes," said Beverly, "my father is well equipped to handle a prolonged siege."

"Excellent, then what's the problem?"

"We don't have enough troops, Princess," said Armin, "We can't leave the city defenceless."

"Tell me, Beverly, how fast does an army move?"

"How large, Your Highness?" she countered.

"Say, a thousand men."

"It would move slowly, Your Highness, especially if they have to live off the land."

"I'm betting the invasion force has a tenuous supply line at best. They need to take Kingsford if they want to move supplies in, and that means a siege. From what I've read about Kingsford, it would require a large army to take the city so, short of some kind of magic or miracle, our invaders are probably digging siege lines, and that will take weeks, so we have some breathing space."

"Gerald," she continued, "do you remember the dressmaker?"

"The one you ordered the green cloak from?" he asked.

"She was an Elf, wasn't she?" The princess was going somewhere with this, but Beverly had no idea where.

"What of it? There are many Elves in the city," Gerald replied.

"Yes, but where do Elves come from?"

Everyone in the room looked confused, they weren't following the logic, but Beverly began to see where she was going with it.

"From the Darkwood," she supplied, "that's where Elves come from, isn't it?" She looked at Revi for confirmation, but the mage was silent.

"Yes, we're going to go the Darkwood and ask the Elves for help."

"Is that wise, Highness," asked Arnim. "How do we know we can trust them?"

"Don't you think, Captain, that if they were going to attack us, they would have done so years ago? Besides, we are going to offer them something in return."

"That being?" asked Arnim.

"I haven't quite figured that part out yet. The Darkwood is a day and a half to the east of Wincaster, down the old east road. I propose that we take only a small group, leaving the main garrison here. Gerald, you and Beverly will lay out some training plans for the troops, but I want you with me when we go east. The captains will be arriving shortly. I want you two to brief them, I have other matters to attend to. Remember, I have placed you two in command so don't let the captains bully you. You're appointed by the crown. If you have to replace someone, you have the full authority to do so."

She rose from her seat and left the room, the hound Tempus following along behind her.

Beverly looked at Gerald, "It looks like we have a full day ahead of us. How do you want to proceed?"

Gerald returned her look. "Let's meet the captains first. Once we have a handle on them, we can inspect the companies. I suggest we do it quickly, catch them by surprise before they expect it."

Beverly smiled, "Devious, I like it. Is that how you kept the soldiers at Bodden in top shape?"

He smiled back, "Now now, I can't go revealing all my secrets."

They met with the company commanders, and the news was not good. The garrison at Wincaster was small, only 500 men to defend the largest city in the kingdom. The quality of the troops was little better. There were some good archers, and the footmen had a smattering of veterans, but, by and large, they were untried in combat and lacking any real training.

There were two companies of heavy foot, the highly armoured infantry that was so effective in combat, but their heavy armour precluded them from marching quickly. They would have to remain in the capital or slow down the entire army. They both agreed the bowmen were essential, but they couldn't leave the city without archers, so unless others could be recruited, it slimmed down their numbers considerably. Beverly hoped the princess was right, if the Elves could be convinced to send even a small force of archers, it might be enough.

The training began with Gerald concentrating on teaching the infantry how to stand in a shield wall, while Beverly started working with the cavalry. Being woefully under-trained, she focused on fighting from the saddle rather than worrying about formations. It was not perfect, but it would have to do.

Arnim did what he could with his Royal Bodyguard. He obtained better armour and weapons for them from the Palace Armoury and then worked on their individual combat skills. They would not be expected to stand in a line of battle, but they must be able to guard the princess.

Revi was trying to crack the riddle of the Saurian tablets. It was two days before the princess called them together again. They all gathered in the drawing room, what appeared to be her favourite meeting place. Once again, Tempus acted as her footstool, lying obediently while she absently rubbed him with her feet.

"I've made some enquiries," she began, "and I think I know how to contact the Elves."

"I thought we were just going to march to the Darkwood?" stated Captain Arnim.

"That would do no good. The Elves don't come out of the woods unless they want to, and no good ever came from entering that place uninvited."

"Then how do we contact them?" he continued probing.

"There's an inn called the Last Hope, and it sits on the road just at the edge of the Darkwood. It's run by a man called Falcon."

"I've heard that name before," announced Beverly. "Is this Falcon a King's Ranger?"

"He used to be, but he left the service a few years ago and disappeared. Rumour has it he now runs the Last Hope, and he is the person to see when someone wants to get hold of Elven goods."

"That's great, that means he has contacts with the Elves," chimed in Revi.

"Yes," agreed Arnim, "but does that mean he'll help us?"

"We don't know for sure," said Anna, "but he was a King's Ranger. Hopefully, he'll have some respect left for the crown. I've gone over the books here, and I'm ready to offer him a sizable bounty if he can accommodate our request. This will be important for us, for without their help, we don't have any chance of success. Even with a few Elves helping us we'll have to defeat two armies. The odds are not in our favour. Anyone is free to back out now if they want."

She looked around the room. No one moved. Beverly looked at Captain Caster, but he was silent.

"I'm in," she said, "to the end, one way or another."

"Me too," agreed Gerald.

"It goes without saying," said Captain Caster, "that I'm in."

"I suppose it's a golden opportunity to try out some new magic," said Revi. "I've deciphered a lot of those tablets."

"Good," said Anna, "then it's decided. We depart first thing tomorrow morning. Leave instructions for the troops to continue training. Captain Caster, I want your guard to remain here and train, between Beverly, Gerald and yourself, I'll have enough protection."

Arnim opened his mouth to protest, but the princess cut him off.

"It's not open for negotiation, Captain. If you wish to object you may complain to the marshal-general, after all this is over, assuming we survive."

"I would like to accompany you, Your Highness," said Revi, "I think I may be of use to you."

"Agreed. Everybody, see to your duties. We leave at first light. Beverly, stay a moment, I want to talk to you."

The rest of the group filed out to make their preparations. When the door closed behind the last person, Beverly turned to face the princess, "Your Highness?"

She had no idea where this was going, and it was a feeling she was starting to have regularly around this young princess who was nothing like her sister, Margaret.

"Gerald tells me you know a lot about horses, is that true?"

"Yes, Your Highness," Beverly warily responded.

"Good, because I need you to do me a favour," said Anna, somewhat timidly.

"A favour, Highness? Don't you mean a command?"

"No, well maybe, I'm not sure."

"What is it, Highness, what's troubling you?"

"Well," the young girl responded, "I need a horse."

"There are plenty in the Royal Stable, that shouldn't be a problem." Beverly was still waiting for the real reason for this line of questioning, for it had to be going somewhere.

"It's not that, it's just that I...I'm not very good at riding, and I need a horse that's going to behave. Usually, I travel by carriage or by wagon, but I know that would slow us down."

Beverly smiled, seeing the little girl still inside the princess. "I shall find you the perfect mount, Your Highness, quick of foot and even of temper. I will look into it immediately."

"Thank you, Dame Beverly," said Anna, "and please, don't mention it to the others."

Beverly smiled again, "It will be our secret, Your Highness."

It did not take long to find a suitable mount and Beverly made her way back to the Palace to inform the princess. She knocked on the door to the study and hearing a quiet, "Enter," she opened the door.

Princess Anna was sitting at a large desk with a massive tome in front of her. The pages were illuminated with colourful script, and Beverly strained to see what the volume held. "Light reading, Highness?" she asked.

"It's the charter of nobility, a list of all the nobles of Merceria. You're in here, along with your father of course. There's also an entry when you were knighted."

"Looking for something in particular, Your Highness?" asked Beverly.

"Yes, I'm looking for some clues, but I haven't found any yet."

"To what, if I might ask?"

Anna suddenly looked up, and Beverly could swear she was embarrassed for some reason, for her face had turned red. "Oh, nothing important, I was merely looking up the family tree. How did you make out with the horse?"

"I've found the perfect animal for Your Highness. I'll make sure it's saddled and ready to go tomorrow. What kind of saddle will you want?"

The princess showed a blank look. "What kind of saddle?"

"Yes, Your Highness, what kind of saddle do you want?"

"One that you sit on?" she answered hesitantly.

Beverly saw the lack of understanding written all over the young face, "I'm sorry, Highness, I meant to ask if you wanted to ride side-saddle or upright?"

"Oh," said the princess, "I'll ride the same as you."

"Very well, Your Highness, I'll see to all the arrangements."

"Thank you. Oh, and Lily will be riding with me, will that change anything?"

"No, Ma'am, you're both light, the horse shouldn't have any problems. Is there anything else?"

"Yes, actually. You're a lady, that is to say, you're the daughter of a baron, correct?"

"Yes, Ma'am," Beverly replied cautiously. Speaking with the princess was like walking a rabbit infested field, she never knew when she would stumble into a hole.

"Well, I was wondering if you might help me," continued a now shy Anna.

"Of course. In what way?"

"I've sort of made a mistake, you see. I left Sophie in Uxley, and now I can't dress myself properly."

Beverly looked at her blankly. "What do you mean?" she asked.

"I mean, I need someone to tie up my corset and help braid my hair. I have to act like a royal now, especially leading an army."

"Then I shall be your lady-in-waiting until you get your maid back," Beverly almost breathed a sigh of relief with how simple the request was. "I braid my hair all the time. Besides, you're only a little younger than my cousin, and I've braided her hair lots of times."

"Thank you," responded a grateful Anna.

"You're welcome, Highness," she replied.

THIRTY

The Last Hope

SPRING 960 MC

~

The early morning mist was still blanketing the land as they set out on their mission. They would have left before sun up, but they had to wait for Revi. The mage finally arrived looking dishevelled.

"You look tired, Master Bloom," said Beverly. "Did your apprentice not look after you?"

"What apprentice?" snarled Revi. "I don't have one."

"Well," muttered Beverly, "I guess he's not a morning person." She raised her voice slightly, "Perhaps you might consider training one to look after you. Remember, you're the master now."

"I haven't the time for an apprentice. It takes years just to teach them to read and write. Besides, it's hard to find someone who has the potential. Not anyone can be a mage, you know."

"So how do you know if someone has the potential?" she asked, trying to make conversation with the prickly mage.

Revi brought his horse up alongside Beverly, "That's a good question. Normally, we would look for magic in the family, but it's rare to have that kind of information these days. The ideal candidate would be dexterous and possess an inquisitive nature. They would typically always be busy with their hands and would love learning and solving riddles and such."

Beverly almost stopped her horse. "Wait, you say they would be good with their hands, even at a young age?"

"Yes," he agreed, warming to their conversation. "They often exhibit symptoms or knowledge of the primary schools of magic."

"Let me see, that would be earth, fire, water and air along with life, death, enchantments and hexes, is that right?"

Revi looked gobsmacked. "For a knight, you show an uncanny knowledge of the schools of magic. How do you come by this information, if I might ask?"

"I have a cousin, Aubrey Brandon, who fits that description perfectly. Do you think she might have magical potential?"

"I think it would be worth investigating at some point in the future. How old is she?"

"Let me see, I think she's sixteen now. She's a voracious reader and remembers everything. She even figured out how to rebuild a bridge."

"Impressive for someone so young. I'll have to pay her a visit once we've finished with all this business."

"All this business?" she said, teasing him.

"Yes, all this invasion nonsense. I have research to do, much more important than gallivanting around the countryside stopping a rebellion. That Saurian Temple we found could change the way we look at magic. If I can decipher the runes, it would mean instantaneous travel across great distances, just think of it."

She couldn't make up her mind if the mage were inspired or insane, and decided not to push it. "Well," she said at last, "this business won't end happily if we don't find the Elves, so we'd best get moving."

The small column headed east, out of the city, Beverly leading the way. The princess followed, with Lily on the same horse, while Gerald rode along beside her. Arnim and Revi brought up the rear, chatting together amicably. The mage seemed to talk for most of the time, and she was thankful that he remained at the back of their column.

It was just past noon of the second day when the Last Hope came into view. Beverly dropped back to inform the princess that they were close. Anna rode forward to examine their destination before they made their appearance.

"A fitting name, don't you think?" asked Beverly. "This truly may be our last hope."

"More fitting than you might think," said Anna, "it's from a poem. It refers to the Elves last hope to live alongside mankind."

Beverly once again found herself looking in fascination at the princess. Was she making this up? This small girl appeared so intense that she must be telling the truth, she decided. How could one so young know so much? She immediately knew the answer, like her cousin, this girl read, a lot. Beverly had always thrown herself into fighting, horses, things with a military connection, but this girl threw all her energies into learning, and why not? She had lived a life of isolation, by all accounts, what else was she to do?

"Let's hope the Elves are familiar with the poem as well, Your Highness. Maybe it will help swing them to our cause."

They resumed their journey and were soon pulling up in front of the inn. The innkeeper, an older man with slightly greying hair, came out to greet them, alerted by the sounds of the hooves. Beverly recognized him immediately, for the ranger had escorted the king to Bodden on that fateful trip years ago.

"We're looking for a man named Falcon," said the princess. "Is that you?"

"There's no one here by that name," the man said simply, "but I've rooms available. You're welcome to rent one or two."

Anna stared at the man, "How many rooms do you have?"

"Only two, I'm afraid we don't get many visitors here."

"And yet you chose to build an inn here?"

"What can I say? I'm not a very good innkeeper." The man turned and re-entered the inn, leaving the party to fend for themselves.

"It appears we have wasted our time," said Revi.

"No, we haven't," said Beverly, "that man is Falcon, and he's lying."

Anna turned to her, "How do you know that?"

"I met him, years ago. He was one of the rangers that brought the king to Bodden."

"Interesting," Anna mused. "We should keep an eye on him. Gerald, go and pay for the rooms. Beverly, you and Arnim set up a schedule to keep an eye on our new friend. I suspect he's up to something."

Beverly and Arnim walked the horses to the stables, while the rest entered the inn with Lily chattering excitedly and Anna answering back in a similar tone. Beverly didn't remember Revi casting the spell of tongues today, and thought it strange, but decided not to say anything.

Taking the horses into the stable, they removed their tack and harness. Beverly rubbed down the horses while Arnim filled the water trough from the well outside. They worked in silence while they saw to their mounts. Beverly watched him carefully, still not trusting him, wondering if he had a secret agenda from Marshal-General Valmar. Was she seeing too much? Was she trying to find conspiracies where none existed? She doubted it. She trusted her father implicitly and knew he had good reason to suspect

Valmar was up to something. She must continue to be wary of Caster's loyalties until she knew more about him.

They finished their chores and made their way to the inn. "I'll take the night watch," said Arnim, unexpectedly, "and you can watch him during the day."

"I think it would be better," she said, "if we split the watch at midnight. That way we'll both get some sleep and be alert for the morning."

Arnim looked at the ground as they walked. He waited a moment before he spoke, "All right, I'll take over at midnight. I'll turn in early to get some sleep."

Beverly was about to argue. She didn't want Caster skulking around in the wee hours of the morning, but decided she could better protect the princess by being in the room with her.

The others were sitting in the common room around a table, drinks in hand. Lily was staring into the mug, occasionally sniffing it but not drinking. Gerald took a mouthful and grimaced.

"This has to be the worst ale I've ever had," he complained

"I'm surprised they're still in business with grog like this," said Revi.

The common room was empty save for their little group. The innkeeper brought over a large platter of bread and cheese with some sort of sausage that gave off a strong smell. Gerald smiled and cut into the sausage with a knife, "Now, that's more like it," he said sliding the slice into his mouth. He chewed the meat, then chewed it some more. It went on for far too long, and then finally, with some effort he swallowed it.

"How was the meat?" asked Revi.

Anna was about to pop a slice into her mouth, and he gently touched her hand, indicating she should put it down. "It's wonderful, Master Revi, try some."

The mage took the bait and tossed a slice into his mouth. He only bit into it once or twice, and then a terrible look came over his face as he got the full taste of it. He sat there, his mouth half open, looking for somewhere to spit the food out. Finally, he turned to the side and spat towards the roaring fireplace. The slightly chewed meat landed just short of the fire and Revi turned to Gerald.

Everyone laughed, while Revi blushed slightly. "Not funny, trying to poison me like that!"

"Come on," said Gerald, "I've had worse. You should see what the army gives you."

"Hey, now," said Beverly, "my father always provided the best food he could."

"That's true," he replied, "but when we were sieged back in '32 we were reduced to eating rats and let me tell you, they are not a taste you can get used to."

Revi grimaced, "I'd open a gate to the Underworld for some decent food."

Everybody stopped and looked at him. He flushed a little then spoke. "I'm kidding, I can't really open a gate, that would be necromancy. I'm a healer, remember?"

He surveyed the group, hoping the see them all smiling at his little jest. Beverly was delighted to see him starting to sweat at the hairline.

"Seriously though," declared Revi, "isn't anyone else hungry?"

"Well this cheese isn't so bad," offered Gerald, "though the bread could be fresher."

Beverly reached for a piece of cheese, grabbing a knife to cut some off.

"It reminds me of Hawksburg Gold, you ever had that?" he said, grinning, looking at Arnim.

Beverly immediately stopped what she was doing. It would just be bread and ale for her tonight.

Beverly, Lily and the princess were sharing a room, the men in another. Arnim, as planned, had gone to bed early and Beverly had remained in the common area to keep an eye on Falcon. For the most part, he was puttering around the inn, with no one else present. He had no staff and no customers as far as she could tell. She had plenty of time to think, and she put her mind to work. She kept returning to the problem of the enemy invasion. No matter how she looked at it, she couldn't imagine defeating an army of a thousand or so and still having enough men left to march to Bodden. Her mind went in circles, and she soon found herself getting drowsy. Rising from the table she stepped outside, the fresh night air would sharpen her mind. She decided to walk around the inn and was just turning the corner when she saw movement. She flattened herself against the side of the inn, making out light off in the distance. Someone was using a covered lantern to flash a signal from the edge of the trees. She looked towards the back of the house and saw a man standing there. Edging around the corner, trying to be as quiet as possible, she unexpectedly stepped on a piece of bark making a noise. She had looked down when she stepped on it, and when she looked up, Arnim Caster was advancing on her with a drawn blade. She stepped out from beside the inn to free up space and pulled her sword. Now she would settle this problem once and for all.

Arnim ran up to her and placed a finger to his lips, pointing ahead of her. She shook her head in disbelieve as he moved past. Turning, she saw what he was referring to. A man, presumably Falcon, had left the inn and was walking towards the light. She swallowed her questions for now and followed.

Falcon cut across the field, no doubt thinking that he was alone. He carried no light but made his way sure-footed across the open area. Soon, he was at the tree line and then they heard the low murmur of conversation.

They moved closer to listen, remaining silent. Beverly fought to control her breath, to slow her heartbeat, this was not the kind of fight she was used to. She concentrated on the voices and finally began to hear distinct words.

"I don't know how long they're going to stay, they said they were looking for Falcon," said the innkeeper.

The other man had a slightly higher voice, which had almost a melodic quality to it. "What of it, it's no concern of ours. Who are these people? What do you know of them?"

"One of them's a lady knight, I've seen her before, but I don't think she recognized me. The young girl is someone important, the rest look like guards. I think one of them's a Holy Father, they keep calling him Revi, strange name I thought. Oh, and there's a strange lizard creature."

"A lizard creature? Tell me more."

"Like a person, but looks more like a lizard, you know, long snout, beady eyes, that sort of thing, and a tail, of course," Falcon responded.

The stranger turned suddenly in Beverly's direction. "It appears we have company," he said calmly as he made a hand signal.

Beverly's eyes went wild, they'd been discovered! She rose from her crouch and stopped for three shadowy figures were pointing bows at them. Arnim rose beside her, and the stranger moved into the moonlight to reveal his pointed ears and elongated face.

"What do we have here?" he said, advancing towards them.

She spotted Arnim beside her, out of the corner of her eye. He was gripping his sword's hilt tightly and looked ready to spring into action.

"I am Dame Beverly Fitzwilliam, daughter of the Baron of Bodden, and I serve the Crown," she announced, trying to distract them.

The Elf waved at his men absently, and they lowered their bows. "Greetings, Dame Beverly, I am Lord Arandil Greycloak, and I am Ruler of the Darkwood. What, may I ask, is the reason for your visit to the Last Hope, and why do you seek the man named Falcon?"

"We came seeking Falcon here," she said, looking directly at Falcon, "to find you, Your Grace. We have come seeking the help of the Elves."

"And who," Lord Greycloak continued, "is 'we'?"

She looked at Arnim, who nodded. "Princess Anna of Merceria, Your Grace, along with her advisors."

"Ah," he said, nodding in understanding, "you are her protectors. The man in the robes, is that Revi Bloom by chance?"

It was Beverly's turn to be surprised, "Yes, how did you know?"

"I keep an ear out in Merceria. I like to keep tabs on mages, you never know when it might come in useful to meet a fellow Arcanus. But perhaps now that we've met, it might be better to step inside. I'm sure your mistress would like to be informed of my arrival? We shall join you directly. I just have to inform my archers that they won't be needed."

The archers disappeared into the woods. Falcon looked at Beverly and Arnim, "This way then," he said, "his lordship will be along shortly."

They made their way back to the inn, and Beverly quickly informed Anna and the rest of the developments. Shortly, they were sitting at a table with Lord Greycloak. An Elf woman accompanied him, but stood behind, her swords crossed on her back. She looked alert and likely was his body-guard, for she scanned the group constantly, always looking at their eyes.

"Now, Princess," said Lord Greycloak, "I understand you've been looking for me?"

"Yes, Your Grace," she said. "Merceria has been invaded, and we need your help."

"I see, and why would this be of interest to the Elves?"

Anna looked back at him for a moment before replying, "Merceria has left the Elves alone for hundreds of years, and during that time there has been no trouble between our two peoples. If there was unexpectedly a new ruler, that could change in a moment."

"True," said the Elven Lord, "but kings die all the time. I have lived through dozens of Mercerian Kings, why would it bother us now?"

Beverly was surprised to see Anna biting her lip, "There must be something you want, Your Grace, something that would better the lives of your people?"

Lord Arandil smiled, "I see you've become an expert negotiator for someone so young. Yes, there is something. I want a trade agreement with Merceria, to have a Royal Charter to be able to sell Elven goods in your land."

Anna nodded slowly and glanced around the room, everyone looked confused. "Elven goods are highly taxed," she explained. "What Lord Grey-cloak is asking for is for the import tax to be removed, or reduced. Tell me Lord Greycloak, what would you offer in return?"

"I will send you two hundred Elven archers and a hundred Dwarven arbalesters. That should suffice to keep your precious capital safe."

Anna was taken aback, "Dwarves?"

"Yes, we have allies to the east, the Dwarves of Stonecastle. I'm sure the Lord of the Stone would like a similar deal, I can assure you I can speak on his behalf."

Anna paused then spoke, "I cannot guarantee what the king will do when he returns, but I will promise to do all I can to make this happen. I will sign a charter as soon as I return to the capital, and I will send a copy here, to the Last Hope."

Lord Arandil smiled, "Then it is agreed, I shall await the charter and march the troops to Wincaster as soon as I can muster them. The Dwarves will take a little longer. I suggest you leave them to defend the city walls. As for my own troops, a hundred will remain in Wincaster while the rest will march with your army. That is what you wanted, isn't it?"

"Your Grace is correct," said the princess. "I agree to the terms."

"Excellent, then I bid you a good night, Your Highness, and wish you well on your journey. I shall see you soon."

"You'll see me?" she asked, somewhat bewildered.

"Oh yes, I will command the Elves that accompany your army. You don't speak Elvish do you?"

"No," said the princess, but Beverly saw something in her stance that made her think that was just a temporary problem for the young royal.

"So I'll have to issue their orders as my troops don't speak your language," he smiled and left, his bodyguard following behind.

Beverly looked at the others. They had accomplished their objective, but nobody knew if it would be enough. The future of the kingdom was now in the hands of this small band of people who sat before her. Only time would tell if they were up to the task.

THIRTY-ONE

The Battle of Kingsford

SPRING 960 MC

The princess created and stamped the charter the moment they returned to Wincaster. Not knowing if the king would support it, the princess was hopeful that saving the kingdom would convince him of the wisdom of her decision. Three days later, Lord Greycloak, true to his word, brought two hundred Elven archers into the city. He left half of them in Wincaster, along with the heavy foot from the city garrison, while all the other troops marched that day for Kingsford. Gerald had organized a supply system that almost doubled the army in size with its complement of carts, wagons and camp followers.

Lord Greycloak was an intriguing enigma. He talked little but received the unconditional loyalty of his troops. They took the lead, just behind the light cavalry, marching quickly, never seeming to tire nor complain. Each Elf carried their own food, and when it was time to set up camp, they always chose a spot some distance away from the rest.

They needed to travel over two weeks to meet the enemy in battle, and every evening the princess insisted the cavalry practise their special manoeuvre. It would only work once, she had said, and Beverly hadn't questioned the need for training. Each night her troops collapsed, exhausted, into their billets.

The cavalry scouts finally came upon the invaders stretched out across the king's road late on the fifteenth day. Everyone knew the morning would bring the battle of a lifetime.

The princess called together her war council that evening before the battle. It was the same group that had travelled from Uxley; Revi, Arnim, Gerald, Beverly, even Lily was present. Lord Greycloak was unexpectedly there as well, to advise them how best to utilize the Elves.

"What is the plan, Your Highness," Beverly asked. "How are we to fight an enemy that outnumbers us?"

"We must do the unexpected," she replied. "Gerald, you will form a line across the road, place your shortbows between the foot and be ready to form a shield wall if needed. No matter what happens they must hold the line, understand?"

"Yes, Your Highness," he replied, "my men will hold the line at all costs."

It was a bold statement, but Beverly knew that if they didn't hold, an absolute slaughter would occur.

"We are outnumbered, Your Highness," Arnim said, "They have twice our cavalry, and it's armoured."

"True," the princess replied, "but only half is armoured, the other half is much like ours, in fact, if you put theirs and ours side by side you wouldn't be able to tell the difference."

"That's why we have standards, Your Highness," Arnim said defensively, "to tell them apart."

Anna, ignoring the comment, continued, "Lord Greycloak will be placing the Elves in the woods to our left. That's the way the enemy will attack with their cavalry."

"How can you be so sure?" Arnim asked.

"The Elves sent some scouts forward just after dusk and discovered that the enemy cavalry is picketed on their right flank. I doubt they would move them by morning. When the sun comes up, all they will see is a pitifully small group of infantry strung out across the road. They won't be able to resist the target."

"Isn't that a bad thing?" the captain persisted.

"On the contrary, it's exactly what we want them to do. When the enemy gets within range of the Elves, they will open up with their Elvish Bows. Lord Greycloak assures me they are devastating against armoured opponents."

"So we take out their cavalry quickly," said Arnim, nodding approvingly. "That still leaves a lot of infantry to deal with, including their archers."

"That's where Beverly comes in," Anna said cryptically. "I've kept everyone in the dark. Only Gerald and Beverly know the details, and to be honest, Beverly only knows half the plan."

Beverly looked shocked at the announcement. This young girl was going to get them all killed with her outrageous scheming!

Gerald spoke next, "It's a good plan, but it relies on some good luck, as well as careful timing. The princess has examined our assets and reasoned out the best way to utilize each one. Remember, after this battle, we'll still need to travel north, to help Bodden. We must defeat the enemy here with a minimum of bloodshed. When we break them and trust me, we will break them, we must harry them all the way back to the river. Prisoners will be locked up in Kingsford, to be paroled back to Westland as soon as possible."

"Shouldn't we just execute them?" asked Arnim. "A survivor can return to fight again."

"No," Anna interrupted, "these people are merely pawns. There's something much bigger going on here."

"What do you mean?" asked Revi, finally appearing to take an interest.

"Think about it. An army of, what did the scouts estimate, Your Grace?"

"We estimate twelve hundred, Your Highness," said the Elf.

"Yes, twelve hundred. Tell me, Captain Caster, could you take Kingsford with only twelve hundred troops?"

"No," he said, "you'd need at least twice that on a good day."

"Precisely," she continued. "I believe this whole situation was orchestrated to pull our troops here."

"You mean a trap?" Beverly asked.

"Yes, I think while they are drawing us away from the capital, another force will appear from somewhere to attack Wincaster."

"Then we should have stayed in Wincaster," said Arnim glumly.

"No, we still need to deal with this force, before it can link up with the army from Bodden. We stand and fight tomorrow, and whatever comes at us, we must prevail, or the whole kingdom will be at risk. Get a good night's sleep. It will be a long day tomorrow and may fortune favour us in the battle ahead."

The advisors dispersed quickly, leaving Gerald and Beverly at the makeshift table.

"Sleep before a battle, that's the funniest thing I ever heard," Gerald said. "We'll be lucky if any of us sleep tonight."

"This plan, you came up with it?" Beverly enquired.

"Oh no, that was entirely Anna's idea, Her Highness's, I mean."

"She means a lot to you, doesn't she?" Beverly was still surprised to see how much Gerald had changed from the man she knew from her younger days.

Gerald looked her directly in the eye, "You grew up with a family, a loving father and a roof over your head, while mine was ripped from my arms by invaders. I've known you a long time, Lady Beverly, but Anna is like my daughter, and I'll do whatever I have to do to protect her and keep her safe."

"As will I, Gerald," said Beverly, astounded by the depth of Gerald's words. "I meant it when I pledged to serve her, but are we wise to follow the tactics of a young girl?"

"That young girl has read more books on battles than you, and I combined. Trust me when I say she knows what she's doing."

She left him to return to the troops. She had to get into position before morning, and the orders were explicit, no campfires for the cavalry, or the whole plan would fall apart.

The sun was not yet up, but Beverly was ready to go with the light cavalry arraigned behind her. It was a risky plan, and it all depended on her. Here she was, waiting, hoping the enemy would take the bait. She sat, anticipating the rising sun, a dark grey cloak keeping the morning chill from her. Her armour wrapped her body in its protective cocoon while she closed her eyes and imagined it was Aldwin's strong arms holding her, keeping her safe. She was a little perplexed. She had fought before, more times than she cared to remember, but today, here, she was nervous. This was no ordinary battle, for it relied so heavily on timing and a bold gamble, using men's lives as pawns in a game of chance.

The sun finally broke through the early morning mist as an Elvish runner came scrambling towards her. The enemy cavalry had started to move. They were doing exactly what the princess predicted they would, advancing against the left flank. She looked over to the edge of the wood to see Lily there, watching her intently, a spear in her hand. There was a period of silence, while each horseman said their private prayers, some more vocal than others. In the distance, the sound of horses moving, the rhythmic jangle of their tack was almost mesmerizing until the sound increased its tempo and the horses hastened their pace. This was the hardest part of the plan, for she couldn't see the enemy. The trees blocked the view of any approaching force, and when she moved, it would have to be quick and sudden. She watched as a flaming arrow struck the ground. The signal from the scouts to proceed.

Lily also noted the arrow and took up her position at the edge of the wood. Beverly raised her sword high and swept it down, the signal to begin the advance. They had practised this many times over the last few days, but still, problems arose. The twang of the Elven bows was heard as they sought out their targets, shot after shot whistling through the air. The light cavalry advanced at a trot, heading roughly north where they would round the edge of the wood and move towards the enemy. Her hidden horsemen rode closer to the corner, and then Lily carried out her part, a thick mist suddenly engulfing them. Now all their training was put to the test.

The horses didn't panic or stumble in the mist. With the verbal command given, the group began to curl around the edge of the wood. Cries of pain and fear reverberated through the mist as they broke through trees. Men were groaning on the ground, horses were whimpering, and the walking wounded were milling around in the thick fog, clutching at arrows that protruded from their bodies.

"Retreat," echoed a lone voice from the fog, and then added, "to me, to me, this way!"

The enemy cry was a beacon that stirred the cavalry into a faster trot. "Back to our line," she yelled, the sign for the men to carry out their ruse.

Soon, her small troop of riders merged with the retreating cavalry, blending in. The enemy was intent on returning to the safety of their lines and had little time to take stock of the new riders amongst them. Beverly's horsemen continued the ruse, not attacking, merely riding with the retreating forces.

Back the invaders went, back to the enemy line, never aware of the infiltrators amongst them, past their infantry that lined the road. Now was Beverly's opportunity, the moment she had been preparing for. She roared the command at the top of her lungs, surging Lightning forward. They were behind the enemy lines, with one hundred Mercerian horsemen bearing down on the enemy rear.

She was among the enemy foot troops in an instant, her sword swinging down in a vicious overhead slash. Lightning pushed his way through the line, knocking down three men and trampling a fourth. Beside her, the soldiers of the light cavalry attacked the enemy with a relentless vengeance. Swords glinted in the air, the clash of steel deafening. Beverly was halfway through the enemy line, and surrounded, when a roar of panic erupted from the enemy troops.

She felt a spear glance off her shield and twisted in the saddle to swing her sword to her left, ducking just as another spear glanced off of her helmet. She kicked with her foot and sent a man sprawling to the ground, and then she turned Lightning, using her legs to guide him. The mighty horse caved in the prone foe's head with a hoof and moved to fill the gap. A forceful blow to her right shin sent a wave of pain up her leg, and she twisted again, stabbing down at the perpetrator, an enemy with a massive mace, who took her blade in the chest, staggering back. A fountain of blood showered her when she pulled her sword free. All around, her men were fighting the enemy, but the invaders held their ground. She blocked another swing and then responded with a lateral cut over her horse's head, striking a spear that tried to impale her. Lightning pushed forward, and she drove the edge of her shield into the face of yet another adversary. The man staggered back, giving her a momentary glimpse of an armoured warrior directing the troops behind him. The enemy footmen were still holding the line despite Beverly's surprise attack. The fight was becoming more desperate by the moment. She needed to cut the head from the snake as quickly as possible.

One of her men went down, impaled by the long spears the enemy were using. The man had been lifted from his saddle, and now the horse ran off without its rider, blood streaming from half a dozen wounds. The enemy swarmed around her, forcing her to dedicate all her efforts to deflect the blows, her sword and shield becoming tools to block rather than attack.

The shield buckled as a powerful blow hit it, sending a shock up her left arm. Lightning sidestepped to give her a bit of space. She dropped her shield to the ground and shifted her sword to her left hand, freeing up her right hand to grasp the handle of the hammer that hung from her saddle. This was time for her to go on the offensive.

The attacker on the left stepped forward to fill the space, but as he swung his massive club, Beverly deflected the great weapon with her sword, leaving her open to crash his head in with her warhammer. With a sickening sound like a melon breaking open, the man dropped to the ground. Twisting suddenly to the right, she employed a backhanded hammer strike to knock another spear to the side, repeating the same movement, only this time the sword crashed down. The blade glanced off a helmet and dug into the victim's shoulder, nearly severing his arm. Lightning screamed, a spear was sticking out of his flank. The great beast was kicking and biting at anything that was near him. The group of men around her had backed up, clearing the area directly in front of her horse and that was when her opportunity materialized. She urged her mount forward through the opening in the retreating crowd to the armoured warrior she had spied earlier, who was stabbing at a dismounted rider. When she was within feet of the leader, she had her horse sidestep.

Turning to face her, he was met by the full fury of her hammer crashing down upon him. He desperately tried to protect himself, raising his shield in an attempt to block the attack. Beverly stood in her stirrups, and now the full weight of her was behind her attack. The head of her warhammer punctured his shield, sinking into the flesh of his arm, eliciting a scream of agony as he staggered back. Beverly launched herself from the saddle, bearing down on him, forcing him to the ground. Over and over again she swung with hammer and sword, driving the steel into the man, hearing the crunch each time the hammer struck his armour. She was on top of him when he pulled out a wicked looking knife. Dropping the sword, she held the warhammer on either end and pushed down on the knave's neck. His legs kicked at her in a vain attempt to dislodge her, but they soon stopped, his eyes rolling up into his head.

She moved off of him and stood, wildly swinging in case anyone else was nearby. The hammer struck a man on the back as he was running by, felling him. Scanning the area, her eyes beheld a macabre scene, straight from the tales of the Underworld. All around her was a giant free-for-all as individuals fought it out to the death. Seeing one of her men struggling, she stepped forward, striking the attacker on the shoulder with her hammer. The man fell, clutching his arm.

"To me!" she yelled, and slowly her men moved towards her through the mass of humanity.

Onward, the enemy came at them with what appeared to be a continuous display of opposition. The Mercerians formed a small ring, with the wounded placed safely in the middle. Strike, block, strike again, the struggle seemed endless. Her legs were shaking, her arms growing heavier by the moment, but she kept up the fight. If this is my final battle, she thought, then let them taste the metal of a Fitzwilliam! This thought was interrupted as she blocked an incoming strike, and then counter-struck, driving the hammer into her attacker's arm. Another of her attacks broke a spear, and she almost lost her balance as the weight of the weapon tipped her slightly forward. She stepped back into the line, and calmness overtook her as Aldwin's mark on her warhammer's handle stared back at her. His voice echoed in her head, "I will make your armour, and when you wear it, it will be as if my arms are holding you," and she knew she would survive.

The enemy was attacking in waves now, striking forward in a rush, but then backing up when they encountered the ferocity of the defence. Four times the enemy rushed, and four times they were repulsed. As the invaders moved back this last time, Beverly, roaring a battle cry born of desperation, charged, her men following their leader without hesitation. The enemy presented a thin line of resistance, and then, suddenly, they broke. Weapons were dropped in fear or exhaustion, while others merely ran to get away from the impending slaughter. Beverly halted, trying to catch her breath, her lungs aching with the effort. The enemy was running, streaming back towards Kingsford, and hopefully certain imprisonment. Surveying the area, searching for the cause of their fear, her eyes observed a welcome sight. Gerald had led the infantry forward and engaged the enemy from the front while she had led the charge from behind, just as the princess had planned.

Seeing Lightning, pierced by spears, laying on his side amongst the wounded, she staggered over, barely able to stand and tried to comfort him, the tears streaming down her face nearly blinding her. She grabbed the spears, one by one and pulled them free to let the poor beast die in peace. She wrapped her arms around his neck and burrowed her face into him, closing her eyes, only to hear his laboured breathing. She knew what she needed to do, to stop his suffering. She released him and pulled her dagger from her belt. She was about to drive the blade into his ear to ease his suffering when she heard a voice.

"You sure you want to do that?"

She turned, too stunned to speak.

Revi Bloom was looking at her curiously. "I was about to heal him, but if you would rather finish him off, that's up to you."

She looked at him blankly, too overcome even to speak. The mage smiled and knelt by Lightning, placing his hands on the horse's wounds. He began muttering an incantation, and Beverly watched in awe, as the flesh knitted itself back together, the injuries disappearing as Lightning's breathing eased and became more regular. Revi finished his spell, stood, then stepped back as his patient rose.

"He'll be a little weak from blood loss, but he should make a full recovery. Now, how about you?"

"What?" she replied, half deaf from the sounds of battle.

"You look like you've taken a few blows yourself. Let me have a look at you."

Beverly took a step towards him, but her leg gave out, felling her as a great pain shot up her shin.

"That looks nasty," said Revi. "It appears your shin's broken. Stay down while I cast."

Again the mage began to invoke the words of magic, and the pain subsided. She looked at her leg and saw it bend backwards, the shin splintered. This time she felt the skin knitting, but the pain returned.

"I can mend the flesh, but the bone needs resetting first, or else the fragments will continue to pierce the skin. We need to straighten the leg before I cast again."

Beverly's head swam, barely able to comprehend what the mage was telling her. It had been a desperate fight, and now her energy was expended, leaving her spent.

Revi called two men over, and they grasped her leg, ready to set the bone. She struggled to focus, to understand what was happening. One of the men was Arnim, and he was looking at her with concern on his face.

"This is going to hurt. A lot," he said. "Are you ready?"

She nodded, and he placed the handle of a dagger in her mouth to bite on.

"One, two," he counted out, and then suddenly an excruciating pain shot up her leg, nearly knocking her unconscious. Revi got to work quickly, and soon the pain subsided.

She looked down to see Revi had removed her shin guard. He held it in front of him to show her the massive dent in it. "You're lucky this withstood the blow, or you would've lost your leg, it was the only thing holding you up."

Arnim looked at him, "I thought you found a way to regenerate?"

Revi looked insulted, "I haven't exactly had the opportunity to learn that yet. It takes time to learn these things. It's not like a recipe you can just whip up."

They were still bantering back and forth when Beverly finally succumbed to her exhaustion.

THIRTY-TWO

Kingsford

SPRING 960 MC

~

B everly was kept busy with all that needed to be done before the army
moved on to Bodden. The prisoners needed to be escorted to Kingsford, where the garrison locked them up. The plan was to parole them back
to Westland, but that would take time. Their leaders must first be interro-
gated to find out who was behind the invasion.

It was evening, the second day after the battle and Beverly, tired from a
long day, decided to clear her head. She took a walk down by the river
where the fresh air would do her good. Standing by the old bridge looking
over the water, she watched as the moon cast its glow on its smooth
surface.

"Nice, isn't it," said a voice and Beverly turned to see Princess Anna.

"Yes, Your Highness, it's very relaxing."

"You don't have to call me 'Your Highness' when we're alone. Please call
me Anna."

"I don't think that would be proper, you're a princess of the Royal
House."

"I suppose so, whatever that means," said Anna.

Beverly turned, surprised at the tone of voice.

"I spent my whole life isolated from the court," the princess continued, "I
must be the most un-royal princess ever."

"But the king provided for you, didn't he?"

"Not really. Oh, it was his coin that was used to have me looked after, but he only ever visited once. My mother used to visit once a year, but that stopped a long time ago."

"I'm sorry, Your Highness, I didn't know. I can't imagine what it would be like to not have a family nearby."

"I have a family," said Anna, "and I don't mean the king and queen. Gerald is like a father to me, he raised me."

"Then we have something in common, he taught me how to fight."

Anna smiled, "I guess that kind of makes us like sisters then."

Beverly returned the smile, "He was more like an uncle to me, I had a father, but I never knew my mother, she died in childbirth." Clouds rolled over, temporarily covering the moon and Beverly could just make out Anna's face. She looked to be wrestling with something, biting her lip.

"Can I tell you something, Beverly?" she asked finally. "Something you can't tell anyone else?"

"Of course," she replied, "I swear not to repeat your words."

"The king is not my father. I believe the queen had me by another man."

"I beg your pardon, Highness, but I think anyone who sees your blond hair realizes that."

"Yes, but I think I've discovered who my real father is."

The clouds parted, and the moonlight returned to reveal her features. She was staring at the water as it glistened. Beverly waited patiently. It was evident that Anna was struggling to come to grips with something.

"I believe," Anna said at last, "that my real father was the queen's confessor."

"Might I ask how you came to this conclusion?" Beverly prompted.

"Remember when you came in and I was looking for something in my family tree? I was going through the records in Wincaster for the king likes to track everything. All the expenses from when royals travel are listed. I know the date of my birth, so I looked for any records before that date for a year."

"And what did the records tell you?" Beverly pressed.

"The queen had a small entourage, mostly women. I did find references to guards and such, and I compiled a list. I then researched each one to find which had hair the same colour as me. It's rare in Merceria, you know, to have such light hair. Anyway, the only name that came up was someone named Father Baldrim. He was the queen's confessor for that period of time."

"Baldrim? A Holy Father in Bodden had that name, I wonder if it's the same person? Was this before or after the king took up a mistress?" asked Beverly.

"After. Lady Penelope came to court about eighteen months before I was born."

"So your father drove her to it?"

"Well, the king did. Remember, he's not my father. He's never recognized me as an heir, so I'm just a prisoner of my situation."

"But your brother, Henry, cares for you. He sent me to protect you."

"Yes, I suppose. Perhaps someday the king will recognize me, and I'll be accepted at court."

"Is that what you wish for?" Beverly asked.

The princess stood quietly for a few moments before answering. "I suppose so. Isn't that what everyone wants? Acceptance?"

Now it was Beverly's turn to think. Was it true? What was it that she wanted? She wasn't so sure anymore.

As if in answer to her thoughts, the princess spoke again. "What is it you want out of life, Beverly? To be accepted as a knight? To find someone to live your life with? A nice rich husband?"

"It's a question I wouldn't have felt comfortable with even a year ago. I've come to accept my situation in life. I've found my purpose, to serve you."

"But surely you must have more you want?" It was Anna's turn to prompt for a confession.

"Perhaps someday I'll consider that, but we must think in the here and now. There are things that need to be done, and we are in a position to make a difference."

"Well spoken, Beverly," she said, "but tell me, do you ever dream of marrying?"

Beverly smiled, "I don't have time to consider that right now."

Anna stared at her, looking for any telltale clues to her answer.

"I suspect there's something you're not telling me. When I mentioned marriage, you avoided the answer and had a faraway look in your eyes. I'm betting there's someone in your heart, but you don't want to reveal it. It's all right, I won't tell anyone, your secret is safe with me."

Beverly's eyes went wide, was this child a mind reader, or was her love for Aldwin so obvious. Young Aubrey had also detected her secret long ago. She must strive to keep better control of herself.

"On another note," continued Anna, "Gerald tells me that your father has some experience in siege environments."

"Yes," said Beverly, happy to change the subject. "He's held the Keep many times. He's built up the defences over the years and always keeps a good stock of food for such eventualities."

"Good, he'll need to hold on for a while longer. I'd hate to arrive and have to take the Keep back by force, we aren't equipped for that."

"You can be sure my father won't yield Bodden, Your Highness. He would rather die than surrender."

"Well, let's hope it doesn't come to that. Now, I've called a war council for midnight, but I have to go and visit the Duke of Kingsford first. Care to come along?"

"Of course, Highness. Whenever you're ready."

"Come along, then," said Anna, reverting to her little girl persona, "It's just a few blocks from here."

They made their way through the city to the duke's residence, an opulent house with ornate marble pillars out front.

A servant conducted them into the large waiting room, while someone ran to fetch the duke. A few moments later an elderly man with shoulder-length grey hair and an immaculately trimmed beard entered the room and immediately bowed deeply.

"Your Highness," he said, "let me say how honoured I am that you would grace us with your presence."

"Please, Lord Somerset, get up, have a seat, I have things we must discuss."

"Of course, Your Highness," he said. "How may I be of service?"

"We've taken a number of prisoners, as I'm sure you've been informed. I would like you to take the responsibility of shipping them back across the river to Westland so that they might return home. Each man must take an oath to never fight against the crown of Merceria again."

"Are you sure that's wise, Highness? These men are criminals, invaders. Should they not be punished?"

"They are common people who were hired by tarnished gold. We are striving to determine who hired them, but they are not evil, merely ill-advised."

"And if they should not give their word?" he prompted.

"Then they shall remain prisoners, but I doubt many will choose that option."

"What of their leaders, Ma'am?"

"The senior leaders fled, unfortunately, but we do have some names for you. If they show up in the city, you are to arrest them immediately, though I suspect they are long gone by now. May I ask what the strength of your garrison is?"

"Only a few hundred men, I'm afraid. It's a good thing they didn't assault the walls of the city, we scarcely had enough soldiers to man them. Might I ask why?"

"I must consider my options, and I can't leave Kingsford undefended. I'm holding a meeting with my advisors later tonight, Lord Somerset, and I wonder if you might be present to give your thoughts."

"I would be honoured, Your Highness, and may I add that if you should ever need a favour, of any kind, I would be happy to be of service."

"Thank you, Lord Somerset," she replied earnestly, "that means a lot to me."

They chatted amiably for some time while Beverly sat quietly, going over their options in her head. She knew the supplies were getting low, and there was a very long march ahead, but if they left troops in Kingsford, it would make the relief of Bodden more difficult.

She was awoken from her reverie by the princess.

"Come along, Dame Beverly," she said. "We've taken up enough of the duke's time. We shall see you at midnight, Your Grace?"

"Of course, Your Highness," the duke replied, bowing deeply.

They arrived back at their temporary headquarters sometime before midnight. Anna sent her out to rustle them both up some food, and by the time she returned, the princess was standing at a table with lists of numbers in front of her, reports from all parts of her army.

She placed the plate down on the table, careful not to disturb the dozing Tempus.

"Your Highness," she said, "you should eat."

"Oh, yes, thank you, Beverly," said Anna, absently grabbing a chicken leg. "What do you make of these numbers?" she asked.

Beverly looked at the sheets of parchment on the table. "Are these the supply numbers?"

"Yes," said Anna.

"I thought so. I recognized Gerald's writing. It looks like we've almost run out of food."

"Indeed, and the march to Bodden will be longer than it was to get here. The road is not the king's road, in fact, it's little more than a dirt track."

"In that case," Beverly pointed out, "we'd be lucky to make ten miles a day with a wagon train."

"Precisely what I was thinking. Tell me, if you were marching troops across the country, how much food would one man carry?"

Beverly thought carefully, "In Bodden, we would often send out long-range patrols carrying five days of food per man."

"Could they carry more if it was, say preserved?"

"I would think so, the main problem would be water. A man can only carry so much water, and the longer you march, the more you'll need."

"A good point," said Anna, pulling a paper out from beneath the pile. "This is a map of the area. You can see the road I mean to travel on takes us through Redridge. The only other option would be to backtrack on the king's road more than a hundred and fifty miles, which would cost us too much time. We need to cover the distance to Bodden as quickly as possible."

"How do we do that?" asked Beverly.

"That's the golden question," pondered Anna.

They spent some time going over the reports, with Beverly helping her find what she was looking for. It was Gerald's arrival with Lord Greycloak that signalled the meeting was due to start. Arnim and Revi showed up together, and Lily came out of a back room where she had been sleeping. They gathered around the table as a servant brought them something to drink. The arrival of the duke signalled the start of the war council.

"Gentlemen and ladies," Anna said, "we face a difficult decision. I've gone over the numbers, and we cannot march the entire army to Bodden."

There were objections all around, but Anna raised her hand to halt them. "I know, I know, but these are the facts. We can't transport enough food to supply the complete army through the long march to Bodden. We've used almost all our food stocks marching here, and there is little to spare in the city."

Arnim threw up his hands, "Then what are we supposed to do, Princess? Let them take Bodden?"

"No, of course not Arnim. I have an idea, but I'd like to hear everyone's thoughts first. Gerald?"

Gerald looked at the map before speaking, "It's true the road is rough, and the more men we march through, the worse it will get. I'm afraid many of the wagons wouldn't survive the harsh terrain."

"Will the men be able to handle the march?" asked Anna.

"As long as they're fed and watered? Yes. We've won a victory, Your Highness, they would follow you to the gates of the Underworld, if you asked them."

"Captain Caster, your thoughts?"

"I say we strip the city of everything we can and march overland, avoiding the road entirely. We'll take all the food we can carry."

"That wouldn't work," interrupted Beverly, "we'd have a hard time navigating in the wilderness, and it's likely to be even harder travelling."

"Revi?" said Anna. "You've been quiet, your thoughts?"

The mage was staring at the map with a faraway look in his eyes. "Cured fish," he offered.

"I beg your pardon?" said Arnim.

"The city fishes the river, then the fish is cured and stored for winter time. There's a surplus as they stockpiled it when they heard an army was coming, in case of a siege. Each man could carry a sufficient amount of perhaps a week or more. It probably wouldn't taste the best, but it would keep them fed."

Anna smiled, "An excellent idea and one I hadn't thought of. Your thoughts, Lady Beverly?"

Beverly looked around the table, "I say we send a smaller force than we brought here."

Again, there were objections all around.

"Why do you say that?" urged Anna.

"A smaller force can move more rapidly and can respond quickly to threats."

"I had been thinking along similar lines," said Anna. "Lord Somerset, how much food do you have stockpiled?"

"I'm afraid you have me at a slight disadvantage, Your Highness. I was not informed I would need that information for the meeting, but I will send someone to find out if you like?"

"Don't bother," said Revi, pulling out a rolled parchment, "I have the numbers here."

Anna took the parchment and unrolled it carefully, laying it flat on the table. She bent over and examined it in some detail while the others quietly watched.

"Gerald, what are our numbers like?" she asked.

"We're pretty much at full strength, Highness. We took only light casualties, but we can replace losses from the garrison if we need. Revi has been working to heal the injured, and so we're only down about fifty men in total."

"So that leaves us with, say, four hundred and fifty or so?" asked Anna.

"Yes," confirmed Gerald.

Anna nodded her head as she looked back at the numbers. "I think I've come to a decision," she said. "We will take a reduced number north. The rest will remain in Kingsford to garrison the city. We can't rule out the possibility that another force may invade from the west. It's risky, but it's imperative that we get to Bodden in time."

"What troops are we taking, Highness?" asked Beverly.

"I would like to take the Elves and the footmen. We'll leave all the bowmen here in Kingsford, along with half the cavalry."

Consternation was evident on most of the faces, "I know," she continued, "that would reduce us to only three hundred and fifty men, but it's better to arrive on time with a few men than arrive too late."

"What's the plan when we arrive?" asked Gerald.

"That," she said, "will depend on what we find. We shall have to rely on Beverly's cavalry to screen us and warn us of any danger. Would anyone care to offer suggestions?"

"I can have the foot set out as soon as they get their provisions," volunteered Gerald.

"Excellent," she said. "Revi, I'll put you in charge of the provisioning, as you already have a handle on it. You can coordinate with His Grace, the duke. See that the infantry is supplied first, they'll be the slowest movers. Lord Greycloak, will your troops eat the fish?"

"I'm afraid not, Your Highness, but my troops have their own supplies, you needn't worry about us. They have enough food for two more weeks of travel."

"Excellent. Gerald, make sure everyone tops off their canteens before leaving. Beverly, since one of your companies is remaining here, I want you to use some of them to make up for casualties, as yours was the hardest hit in the battle."

"Yes, Your Highness," Beverly agreed.

"I shall want your cavalry to form a screen once we're on the way, but that won't be necessary until we turn north in two days' time. Your troops will leave the city last as I'm sure they'll have no problem catching up. Captain Caster, your guard will march with the infantry. We leave as soon as we can. I intend to have the foot outside the city by sun up."

Everyone nodded their agreement with the plan before being dismissed by the princess. They trailed off, each set on their missions. Beverly waited until only Anna, Lily and herself remained.

She saw the strain of command on the princess, who looked haggard with dark lines under her eyes. "You should get some sleep, Highness. It will be a long march tomorrow."

Lily chattered something, as if in agreement. "I shall try," Anna said, "but the future weighs heavily upon me, and I have more to do before we depart."

Beverly moved around the table and put her hand on Anna's arm. "You're no good to us if you can't stay awake," she said, "even Tempus knows he needs to sleep."

"I will, I will, but I must finish this first."

"Nonsense," Beverly insisted, "everything is in our hands now. You're going to sleep, or I'll fetch Gerald. If you don't sleep, the army won't march."

Anna looked at Beverly and smiled, "Is this mutiny?"

"No, just common sense."

Anna knew she was defeated. "All right, I'll go off to bed."

"Good," said Beverly, "I'll tuck you in and tell you a story, that way I know when you've fallen asleep."

"That's hardly fair," said Anna.

"You haven't heard my story yet," Beverly replied with a grin.

She escorted the princess into her room and put her to bed. Her story didn't last long, for Anna was asleep almost as soon as her head hit the pillow. Beverly sent orders to the cavalry and then grabbed some sleep herself, it would be a long day tomorrow, and she, too, needed to rest.

Beverly led the cavalry from Kingsford just as the sun was coming up. Princess Anna had left with them. She would catch up to the guard once they were underway. They were clear of the city by the time the morning mist had burned off. It looked like it would be a warm day, the sun was out, with very few clouds visible. As they rode along Beverly caught sight of Tempus, the sturdy dog seeming full of energy, bounding ahead, only to lie in the sun and wait for the troops to catch up. By noon her contingent had met up with the main group of infantry. They had stopped by a stream to water themselves and to refill their canteens. Beverly rested the horses while she escorted Anna to her guards. Captain Arnim had a dour expression on his face, apparently not pleased at being ordered to march without his charge, but he didn't complain. The guard soon took up their positions around the princess to keep her from harm.

Beverly, seeing Gerald, rode over to speak to him. The footmen had kept up a brisk pace and more than a few of them, after filling their canteens, chose to take off their boots and dip their feet in the stream. Gerald stood watching them with a trained eye.

"How was the march?" she enquired, as she approached.

He turned to look in her direction. "Good, we set a decent pace. Glad to know my legs still work. I thought after marching to Kingsford I might have worn them out."

"They look to be in fine form," she said and watched him blush. It was too easy to tease the man, he was humble to a fault.

"How is the cavalry?" he asked, changing the subject.

"Better than I expected. We lost almost half in the battle, so the two companies were merged, with not too many left behind."

"You should have just brought all of them. A few extra men would have been useful."

"I thought of that, but we lost too many horses. As it is, the remainder will be serving as footmen in Kingsford until they can train replacements. How far do you reckon we've come?"

"Probably close to ten miles already," he said, "though I suspect they'll slow down a bit this afternoon. With luck, we'll be able to make twenty miles today, mainly because we won't have to set up and cook dinner."

Beverly rummaged around in her pack and brought out the salted fish. It looked like a piece of bark and gave off a rather pungent odour. She broke it in half and handed some to Gerald. "I hope this stuff tastes better than it smells," she said. She took a bite and made a face. It reminded her of her father's stinky cheese.

Gerald laughed and then took a large bite of his own, "You should get used to army food, I suspect they'll be lots of it in our future."

Beverly wanted to spit it out, but took courage from Gerald's example, the man could eat anything. She chewed it until it felt like paper in her mouth, and then used a long drink of water to wash it down.

"Don' worry," said Gerald, "you'll adjust to it over time, though I have to say I miss the old days back in Bodden. Your father always made sure we had decent food."

"Yes," said Beverly, "I only hope we'll get there in time to help him."

"Oh, we will," said Gerald, "you forget, I've been there during a siege. It would take a lot to breach the walls of Bodden."

"Didn't the northerners breach the wall when you were younger?" she reminded him.

"Yes, but your father's improved the wall since then, not to mention the ditches he's built around the Keep. I imagine he's up in his map room surveying the enemy force right now."

"I can imagine," remembered Beverly. "He always did like the view from up there. How many enemy soldiers do you think surround Bodden?"

"I suspect rather a large number, or your father would sally out and make short work of them. I would think there might be, say, two thousand?"

"Why so many?" she asked.

"Anything less and they wouldn't be able to encircle the Keep. They're probably trying to keep him bottled up, so his troops can't be put to use. They must know he has knights and no one wants those unleashed on their soldiers."

Gerald was right. The heavy armour of the knights made them almost impervious to bows, save for the Elven type. It made her think of their new allies. "I haven't seen Lord Greycloak yet today, have you?"

"Oh, aye, I saw them earlier this morning. They left before we did. Those beggars move fast, I bet they're halfway to Bodden by now."

Beverly frowned, "Halfway? Really?"

"No, of course not, but they must be a mile or two up the road. They march in thin lines instead of a column, and they move very fast. I'm glad they're on our side."

Beverly choked down the rest of the fish and refilled her canteen. "Well, we've got more marching to do, old man, I'd best be on my way. I'll see you later when we make camp."

"Of course," he replied, "I'll have dinner waiting for you, something special."

"Special? You've peaked my interest.

"Yes, salted fish, followed by a dessert of salted fish. Not only that but if you're lucky, you can have salted fish for breakfast."

"You're enjoying this far too much!"

"Yes. Yes, I am," he grinned.

THIRTY-THREE

Bodden

SPRING 960 MC

The push to Bodden was the most arduous march that Gerald or Beverly had ever participated in. The nearly non-existent road was often washed out or was so covered with debris that they had to bypass it. Luckily, the streams that ran off the Margel Hills provided plenty of fresh water. Despite the sorry state of the roads, the army made good progress, and within a week they had reached the northern road that ran west towards Bodden and east towards Tewsbury. Off to the north was the looming shadow of the Whitewood, named for the birch trees that were found there in abundance. This was the road that Beverly had taken when she left Bodden all those years ago, and as she thought back, she remembered her encounter with Albreda.

She realized with a start that events had unfolded just as the druid had predicted, for once again, Bodden was under siege. What was it she had said? Call to the woods, and she would fulfill her vow. Her heart raced, might this be the answer they needed? She left her men under the sergeant's care and rode off in the direction of the woods. If she found Albreda, they might stand a chance.

She paralleled the army's advance, riding along the edge of the woods, keeping the troops in sight. She called out Albreda's name several times but had no idea where the White Witch might be. Finally, as the sun started to go down, she resolved to re-join the army. She turned from the woods and spotted a hawk circling in the air. She stopped and watched as the bird flew towards her, settling on the branch of a nearby tree. Beverly dismounted and walked towards it, leaving Lightning standing nearby. Sure enough, eyes stared out of the woods at her, and a group of wolves emerged from the trees to encircle her. This time she stood still and remained calm. A moment later the Lady of the Woods appeared out of the shadows, wearing the same green and brown dress.

"Greetings, Beverly Fitzwilliam," she said.

Beverly bowed, "Lady Albreda, you honour me with your presence."

Albreda laughed, the sound like ripples on a lake. "I am no lady, Beverly, though I am flattered you address me so."

"Still," Beverly persisted, "you are a woman of considerable power and deserving of respect."

She bowed her head slightly, "I am glad you think so," she said finally. "I assume you have come to ask for my help."

"Yes, you once told me that when Bodden was in danger, I should come to you."

"I have been expecting you," the woman said. "I have much to share, but first you must tell me who you travel with, for despite my powers, I did not foresee this eventuality."

It took some time to relate the story, and Albreda listened patiently. She appeared both surprised and intrigued at the mention of the princess. Beverly told of the trip to the Elves, the journey to Kingsford, the battle, and the recent march to Bodden. The mage took it all in, asking for details at various points. Soon, her tale told, Beverly halted.

"You must take me to your princess, Beverly Fitzwilliam, and I will inform her how I might help."

Beverly led her to Lightning, but she declined to ride, instead walking beside the great horse, a lone wolf following them closely.

As they neared the camp, the sentinels raised the alarm, but at the sight of Beverly, they relaxed. Even so, there were wary eyes that watched as the strange woman and the overgrown wolf accompanied her to the princess's campfire.

Anna was sitting on a log, absently stroking Tempus' head when they approached. The other leaders were present reporting on their progress for the day. Tempus barked once and sat up, and suddenly all eyes turned towards the new arrivals.

"Who have you brought to see us, Dame Beverly?" asked the princess.

She handed off the reigns of Lightning to a cavalryman and stepped forward, bowing. "This is the Lady Albreda, Mistress of the Whitewood, Your Highness. She is here to help us."

There was a murmur from the others, this was news indeed!

Anna beckoned her forward, and Albreda strode towards the fire. The large wolf followed behind, sitting on his haunches by her side.

"Greetings, Your Highness," said the witch, "I have come to repay an old debt to the Fitzwilliams."

"Indeed? And how, may I ask," said the princess, "is this debt to be repaid?"

"I have news of Bodden, Highness," the woman explained. "It is surrounded by some two thousand invading troops who have dug in."

A look of consternation crossed the face of some of the commanders present.

"It is worse than we thought," said Arnim grimly. "We have no hope of defeating that many."

"Nonsense, Captain," said Gerald, "it's precisely what we expected."

Albreda turned to Beverly, "Do you know the large elm tree that sits to the east of Bodden, where the road turns?"

"Yes, I've ridden past it many times, why?"

"Choose your attack force, Your Highness, and have them prepare to march. Form them up to the east of The Elm, ready to move on Bodden. They must be in place the morning after tomorrow. With the rising of the dawn's mist, you shall hear a thunderous noise, do not panic. Also, tell your men not to hunt near these woods, nor take the life of any animal that dwells there."

"When shall they march?" asked Anna.

"You will know when the time is right," she replied cryptically, "but do not act until then."

"And you will help us defeat the invaders?" implied the princess.

"I owe a lot to the Fitzwilliams," said Albreda, "and I am a woman of my word. You must succeed in this, for there is more to accomplish. There are powers at work that threaten the world as we know it."

Albreda moved to return to the woods, then turned back. "Now I must go, for I have much to prepare. Remember, the morning after tomorrow, near the great elm." She walked away, leaving the group in silence, the wolf following her. Beverly thought it best to escort her back through the sentries.

They walked past the guards, to the waiting circle of wolves. As she drew closer to them, Albreda spoke, "Will your friends follow through?"

"I hope so, Your Grace," said Beverly, "but I fear they may not understand what is to happen."

Albreda stopped suddenly and turned to face her, "Then you must convince them. It is vitally important."

"I'm not sure I can, I am but one of many," replied Beverly.

"Your words carry more weight than you realize. If you believe, then so will they. Do you doubt my abilities?"

Beverly thought for a moment. She had no proof of Albreda's powers, yet her father had believed her despite the trouble with her uncle. She trusted her father without reservation, so she must trust this woman the same way. "I trust you completely," she said at last.

"Good, then talk to your people, convince them that I can help. I will carry out my part regardless, but if you are not there to take advantage of what I offer, the opportunity will slip away."

"I will heed your words, Your Grace."

Albreda smiled. "Good, that's all I ask, now stop calling me 'Your Grace' and just call me Albreda."

Beverly smiled, the White Witch putting her at ease, "Yes, Albreda."

"I shall see you the morning after tomorrow," she said, as she walked into the woods. One moment she was there, and then suddenly she seemed to blend into the foliage and was gone.

Beverly returned to the camp to find a vigorous discussion in progress.

"We know nothing about this woman," Arnim was saying. "How can we trust her? It might be a trap."

"A valid point," Anna confirmed. "Lord Greycloak, you've been silent. What are your thoughts?"

The Elf had been staring into the fire, and now turned his eyes up to look at the princess. "I cannot speak on behalf of this Albreda, for I have never heard of her. She appears to be a mage of some sort. Perhaps Master Revi can shed some light on her?"

"I've never met her," said Revi in response, "but I've heard her name. She's an Earth Mage."

"What does that mean exactly?" asked Arnim warily.

"It means she has learned the way of the living world. She can likely manipulate animals and plants or move earth. I've heard her described as a druid, which usually means talking to animals."

"She did say that no animals were to be harmed," piped in Gerald.

"Yes," said Revi, "that supports my argument."

Gerald looked at Anna, and something passed between them, a look. Beverly knew they were hiding something but didn't press for details.

"What do you favour, Highness?" prompted Gerald.

"I say we follow Albreda's request. I have some experience with her."

The assembled group looked stunned, and even Beverly was shocked into silence.

"The truth is," said Anna, "I've been in correspondence with Albreda for a few years. Her name was given to me by Andronicus when we were investigating the existence of Lily. I trust her completely. Beverly, do you feel the same about her?"

"Yes, Your Highness, she has always lived in peace with my father's barony."

"Good, then I thank all of you for your input, but I've made my decision. We'll have the men form up to the east of the Elm the morning after tomorrow. Dame Beverly will show the men exactly where that is. Gerald, I'll have you see to the troops. You will have to decide how to line them up. Beverly, you'll lead the cavalry into battle when you deem it best."

"What are the orders for the troops, Your Highness," asked Arnim.

"Why, to do what they always do, follow their leader's orders."

"And what are the leader's orders?" he prompted.

"To use their initiative. We don't know for certain what will transpire so you'll need to improvise."

Eyes went wild. It was not a typical command a soldier would expect from their leader.

"You'll have to tell your men to be prepared and remember, no hunting. No animals are to be harmed, or we risk losing everything."

The group began to break up, returning to their commands. The princess gave some final directions to Gerald and then settled down on a blanket beside her dog for some sleep.

Gerald issued orders to some nearby soldiers, then returned to the fire, warming his hands, for the night was turning colder.

"What do you make of it?" he asked Beverly.

"Improvise? I like it," she replied.

"I thought you might, we've been improvising in Bodden for years, but I doubt these city folk have any idea what that means."

"The princess surprised me. She knew all along whom Albreda was, but didn't say anything," she challenged.

Gerald grinned, "Aye, that's true enough. She's learned a valuable lesson. She listens to everyone before she makes a decision. If she'd said that at the beginning, she'd have gotten no suggestions from anyone."

"Did you teach her that?"

"No, but I've noticed that she loves to plan things. She'll be thinking this thing over all day tomorrow. I expect by tomorrow night she'll have additional orders for us. That reminds me, I'll need some of your men tonight, those you can trust."

"What for?"

"We need to make sure no one sneaks out of camp to hunt. It would be bad to anger the White Witch."

"I'll take care of it myself," said Beverly, "you get some sleep, you're not as young as you used to be, old man."

Gerald made a face and was about to complain until he saw the grin on Beverly's face. "Very funny," he said as he left.

The troops were lined up behind the Giant Elm tree before dawn. It had been difficult, moving them in the dark. They had lined the way with torches, but even so, constant supervision was required to get the men into position. Bodden was out of sight, just beyond a slight rise and sentinels had kept a watchful eye on the town all night long. Beverly had arraigned the cavalry in front, followed by the companies of foot. The Elves had placed their troops to either side, careful not to let any past The Elm tree.

The early morning mist didn't help settle the nerves of the soldiers, nor the leaders for that matter. Everyone was restless for no one knew what to expect.

It started in the distance, a low rumble that rapidly grew in volume. Beverly didn't recognize the sound at first, but as it drew closer, it reminded her of the noise that cavalry made when it was charging. It grew in intensity, along with the nervousness of the horses. Behind her, she heard Gerald's clear voice shouting at the men to hold their position. The fog was still thick, and while the sun was just starting to rise, the darkness of the night was gradually being replaced by the white of the fog as the noise grew to a tremendous roar. Beverly strained her eyes and soon saw dark shadows in the fog. Whatever it was, it was approaching The Elm, and it looked like it would run directly past them.

Out of the fog leaped a deer, a wild look in its eyes. It raced by the troops, past The Elm and down towards Bodden Keep, disappearing back into the mist. Another deer appeared out of the fog, then another and another. Soon, an entire herd went streaming by, and then she understood why. The wolves were herding the animals, guiding them down towards the enemy troops that surrounded the Keep. She drew her sword and raised it high, "Prepare to advance," she commanded. She held her breath, counting to herself as a smaller group of deer streamed past followed by three wolves. When she had counted to ten, and when no more ran past, she gave the order, "Advance!"

The cavalry began to move as they had practised. They started at a slow walk and then gradually gathered speed to a trot. They would keep this pace until the fog lifted, and then break into a charge. The sun was rising rapidly, and she knew it would burn off the fog shortly for years of living in Bodden had gotten her used to it. She could feel the descent as the horses topped the hill and began entering the slight depression where the Keep kept the town safe.

She heard Gerald's voice behind them, and then it was lost as the sound of the horses intensified. Now they were creating their own thunder, the very ground trembling beneath them. The distant yelling ahead of them had her guessing that the stampede had reached the invader's camp.

"Draw your weapons!" she commanded, and the rasp of steel as blades were pulled from their sheaths could almost be heard over the thunder of the hooves.

The mist was burning off rapidly, and now the riders were above the fog while a thin layer remained below them. It gave them a sense of strangeness, as if they floated upon the mist. The walls of Bodden were straight ahead, with defenders manning the barricades, no doubt drawn to them by the sound of the stampede. She nodded to the man beside her, and he lifted a horn to his lips, blowing three times.

The horses spurred on, and instantly the mist disappeared, revealing the carnage in front of them. The earth had been trodden down by hundreds of deer and it looked as if a giant brush had painted a swath, directly over the enemy lines. The cavalry broke into a charge and added their own sound of thunder to the attack.

The enemy had encircled the Keep, with catapults still under construction. The first area that had been hit by the flight of the deer was the workshops, were the invaders laboured away at constructing the giant siege engines. Red smears on the ground denoted where the workers had been trampled. Two of the catapults were broken by the force of the stampede, and Beverly noticed numerous deer, impaled by bits of wood or other obstacles that they had run into in the crush.

She led the cavalry through the devastation, looking about quickly. The stampede had carved a path through the troops to the east of the Keep and then circled around to the south. For the second time in this campaign, she felt like she had been thrust into the Underworld where pandemonium reigned. As she watched, wolves tore at men's flesh, and she gave an involuntary shudder. Wheeling the cavalry north, she drove them into the enemy's lines. The horns of Bodden sounded, and she knew her father was getting ready to lead the knights out of the main gate.

The enemy was still sleeping, with few even formed up as the charge drove through their camp. Those that were awake, wandered about, stunned by the ferocity of the surprise attack. One man was organizing a defence, gathering a group of perhaps twenty men and attempting to form a line. She spurred Lightning forward, and as he leaped, he struck a man down as he landed on top of him. Beverly heard a sickening crunch as the beast landed, but ignored it. She jabbed down with her sword, connecting with a target, and then raised the sword to strike again. The enemy troops around her scrambled in a blind panic, looking for safety that could not be found. Her own soldiers were chasing down small groups of men before they could form. The enemy soldiers about her broke, some throwing down their weapons, while others tried to run. She held Lightning in check while she surveyed her position. The Mercerian Cavalry was operating in pairs as she had trained them, watching their partner's backs while they fought. The northern line was broken, but the greatest mass of troops still lay to the west, opposite the main gate, and even as she looked, she heard the sound of horns again. Bodden had unleashed the knights!

~

Horns sounded from the walls as the knights rode forward, Baron Fitzwilliam at their head. He had studied their lines carefully from his map room and knew where to strike. They charged straight through the enemy lines, directly for the ornate tent that held the enemy command. The knights drove their mounts mercilessly, the great beasts surging forward at full speed. They ate up the distance to the enemy lines quickly, and Fitz realized that the enemy soldiers were trying to form a wall, but the jarring impact of the armoured horses of the Bodden Knights shattered it like a mighty hammer. Fitz stabbed down with his sword, neatly skewering a man in the throat. He pulled the blade out, and with great precision, slashed at the next one in line. The unlucky man fell back howling in pain, a cut to his face. All around Fitz, his knights were raining down swords and axes on the enemy. He pivoted his horse slightly as two men rushed him with spears, deflecting one with his shield while his sword broke the shaft of the other. His horse kicked out, striking a man in the chest, forcing him to the ground in agony. Collectively, the knights delivered their vengeance upon the enemy that had held them prisoners in the Keep for so long.

The top of the command tent was plainly in view, but as he drove the charge closer, a resistance was being organized. A swarm of men stood behind the thin line, moving to mount a defence, and he knew the objective was now out of reach. They chipped away at the defenders, striking down the enemy as they came closer, forcing them back with the mass of their horses. The first line broke, and suddenly the knights were unopposed, surrounded by little more than stragglers, but the enemy's sacrifice had bought the time the second line needed to form a shield wall, long spears now set to receive them. Sir Charles charged boldly forward only to impale himself on a long spear while others tried hacking away uselessly with their swords, helpless to do more.

~

Gerald brought the infantry in as fast as he could. They followed the path of the stampede, around the south end of the Keep. He was able to pick up the pace on this flatter land, making better time than expected. There was no resistance. The enemy was fleeing west, hoping to form up with the remainder of their troops. The stampede had spent itself, running off to the southwest, now the battle was up to them.

They rounded the Keep, to witness the Knights of Bodden surrounded in a sea of enemy soldiers. Fitz the Elder hacked away with his calm, efficient strokes, then the enemy troops broke revealing a second line. Gerald called to his captains, and they formed a line of their own, intending on approaching the enemy from the south, forcing their foes to turn from the cavalry to face his new threat

He looked at his troops and used the hilt of his sword to hammer away at his shield like a drum. The action was taken up by the men, and suddenly, all across the valley, the sound echoed like the drums of doom, calling them to the Afterlife. The soldiers, previously exhausted, were invigorated by the pounding, cheered and began their slow, steady advance towards the enemy.

~

Fitz the Elder, hearing the rhythmic thumping, saw the men forming to the south and instantly knew what it meant. He called to his knights to have them form up. Spent by the effort they had already given they still obeyed his command. This was the final stroke, the final blow to ruin the enemy, he thought, and it must be perfectly executed.

The invader's line watched the cavalry withdraw, while they heard the drumbeats coming from the south. The enemy commander did the only thing he could and tried to turn half his line to face the new threat. It was a complicated manoeuvre. The men on the right flank would have to back up, all the while trying to keep the line intact. His soldiers were not trained for this, and as the line began to move, it grew less distinct, wavering as soldiers tried to coordinate a drill they had never practised.

Fitz saw the opportunity and committed his forces. He led a handful of knights southward, just out of reach of the spears. They suddenly turned north, straight into the enemy line. The spears were out, but not evenly, and it was a simple matter to knock the tips aside to get past them. The foot soldiers were all looking at the ground as they tried to stay in formation while they backed up.

The enemy realized what was happening too late and their line disintegrated under the onslaught of the cavalry. They dropped their weapons and fled, while a cheer went up from the Knights of Bodden.

Fitz spied the enemy commander. He was mounted and turning to flee. The baron drove his horse forward, but the Mercerian warhorse was no match for the enemy's fleet mount. The leader rode north, past the lines, while Fitz looked on with regret.

~

Beverly brought her cavalry around the north of the Keep to see the fighting in the west. She halted her men, allowing the horses to catch their breath. The enemy line began to pivot, and then a small group of Bodden Knights struck, sending the enemy fleeing in all directions. A cheer broke out amongst her men and then, just as she was starting to relax, she spied a lone horseman sprinting north.

She broke Lightning into a gallop, calling for her men to follow. Her horse was a Mercerian Charger, a large horse built to carry weight, but he did not wear the traditional horse armour that the Bodden Knights carried. He leaped forward with pent-up energy, and she changed their course to intercept the rider by the drainage ditch that ran away from the Keep. She was part way there when she saw Captain Caster. He, too, had seen the enemy commander fleeing, and was almost upon him. She watched as he skillfully directed his horse in front of the man, causing him to veer off to the side. As the horses came together, she saw swords flash, and then the enemy commander fell from his horse. Arnim dismounted to stand over the commander, who was clutching his side with his hands.

Beverly rode over, accompanied by some of her men, "What in the name of Saxnor are you doing way over here?" she asked.

"The princess sent me to check on the battle. She can't see the western side of the Keep from her vantage point. I noticed this man trying to get away, thought he might be someone important."

"Impressive," she said, "and here I thought you were just a bodyguard."

Arnim didn't reply. Instead, he reached down and helped the injured man to his feet. "Do you surrender?" he asked.

The enemy commander nodded, "Yes, I surrender, and I offer my parole."

"There's no parole for rebels," Arnim replied, a grim look on his face.

The man looked defeated but had no other option. Arnim tied his prisoner's hands behind his back, and then two soldiers helped lift him back onto his horse. Arnim took the reins and started to lead it back towards Bodden.

"Beverly, my dear," cried a familiar voice, "it's so good to see you!"

She turned in the saddle, "Father! I'm glad you made it. I was beginning to think we'd have to do this all by ourselves."

The baron smiled, "Quite the battle. Who organized the stampede? It was absolutely incredible."

"That," she replied, "was Lady Albreda. She told me she owed you a debt of honour."

Her father looked stunned and just sat, staring at her.

"How about," she continued, "we go inside Bodden and prepare to receive the princess. I'm sure she'll want to talk to you."

"The princess is here?"

"Yes, we just marched from Kingsford where we defeated a small army."

"An army? Is the whole realm at war?"

"It's a long story. Let's head in, and I'll tell you all about it, but no cheese!"

THIRTY-FOUR

After the Battle

SPRING 960 MC

~

They all met that evening in the map room. The princess had insisted that all her commanders be present, including Baron Fitzwilliam. The Lady Albreda chose to grace them with her presence. Anna was sitting at the huge map table, dwarfed by its size, and as always, Tempus lay at her feet. The scene reminded Beverly of her own experience as a child, fascinated by the maps her father had collected.

Revi, being the last of her advisors to arrive, entered the room apologizing for his tardiness and then stopped suddenly, looking at Beverly.

"You're wearing a dress," he declared out loud.

Beverly looked back at him, "Of course I'm wearing a dress, Bodden is my home. Why wouldn't I wear one?"

"No reason," he continued, "it's just that you look like a woman."

Beverly's face burned, "I AM a woman. What's wrong with you?"

"I always think of you as a knight. I suppose I never saw you as a woman before."

"Are you done?" she asked, irritably. "The princess has important matters to discuss."

"Of course," he said, "forgive my interruption, Your Highness."

Anna smiled, looking like she was trying hard to stifle a giggle. "I have called you all here to listen to your opinions on what we should do next. Who would like to go first?"

Gerald broke the silence. "Do we have word from Arnim yet?" he asked.

"He's been interrogating the enemy commander," Anna responded, "and he'll join us as soon as he has something to report. Gerald, what is the condition of the troops?"

"We've sustained light casualties again, Your Highness. Due to Master Revi here, we've been able to recover most of them, though there are still more to be healed."

Anna turned to the mage, "Master Bloom, how long to heal the rest?"

The mage placed his fingers on his chin, and Beverly saw him echo her father's favourite thinking pose. "I should think I'll have them all healed up by the end of tomorrow, though it will tax my abilities. I would like some time to recover before we march."

"I was thinking of a full day of rest, so that fits in well with my plans. Lord Richard, is there enough food to outfit the army for the march?"

"Unfortunately, no, there is not. I've enough stores to last to Tewsbury if you ration them carefully. I had thought to send riders on ahead to arrange for food to be rounded up in advance of your march."

"Do you have someone you can trust to see to the provisioning?"

"Yes, my brother-in-law, Lord Robert Brandon of Hawksburg. He's a very accomplished man, Your Highness. I've already taken the liberty of writing to him in your name. You have only to give the word, and the dispatch rider will be on his way."

"Thank you, Baron," she said. "I'd like to add a letter to your dispatch rider to deliver to Uxley when he finishes at Hawksburg."

"Of course, Your Highness, I'll ensure it's delivered."

"Excellent," said the princess. "I'll write it out after we finish here. Lady Albreda, I believe you wanted a chance to speak?"

The druid rose from her chair, "I do, Your Highness, though I regret it may not be the most cheerful of news."

"Please proceed," encouraged Anna.

"At the behest of the princess, I have, this evening, cast an augury, to help us decide on our best course of action."

"How accurate are these auguries?" asked Gerald.

Albreda turned to look at him. "An augury tells only what might occur, it is not necessarily cast in stone. There are some that believe they are warnings about what might happen. Others believe it tells what will happen, regardless of attempts to prevent them."

"The Elves have always presumed them to be true," offered Lord Greycloak. "We place great store in them."

"I've never been one to believe in a predefined destiny," said Beverly's father. "I believe we all have the right to self-determination."

"Regardless of what we believe," said Anna, "I think we should at least hear her out. What did this augury portend, Albreda?"

Albreda closed her eyes to recall the words she had spoken while under the spell. , "A shadow grips the land, silencing the Royal House of Merceria," she said. "These words came to me exactly as I have spoken them."

The room fell into silence while everyone contemplated the meaning. There was little space for wiggle room, thought Beverly, the end of the Royal House was extremely specific.

The silence was broken by the princess. "We shall bear your words in mind, Lady Albreda. Thank you."

"If the crown is in danger," said Gerald, "then we should waste no time marching to Wincaster."

"We cannot march until the wounded are tended to," interjected Beverly. "We need every man we can get."

The door opened, and Captain Arnim Caster entered the room. He bowed to the princess, "Your Highness," he said, "I have finished the interrogation of the prisoner."

"Have you news?" she asked.

"Yes, I'm afraid it is as you feared, Highness. The man was colluding with the Earl of Eastwood. The western thrusts were meant to draw the troops away from Wincaster. By now the earl has an army marching on the capital. We must hasten to their defence."

"Thank you, Captain," said Anna. "This at least confirms what we already suspected."

"My men are at your disposal, Highness," said Baron Fitzwilliam.

"Thank you, Baron, but troops are still needed to hold Bodden, lest the Norlanders take advantage of your position. Do you have someone capable of handling the defence of the Keep? I should like to have you accompany the army."

"Of course, Your Highness. Might I suggest the Bodden Knights come with us? They would provide some much needed heavy cavalry for the army. I'm sure Dame Beverly is more than capable of commanding them."

Anna looked at Beverly, who simply nodded. "Very well, we shall place Dame Beverly in charge of the knights."

"How will we tell the Fitzwilliams apart?" asked Revi in a very serious tone.

Gerald looked daggers at him, "You're kidding, right?"

Revi returned the stare with a blank expression.

"That," said Gerald, pointing at the baron, "is Fitz the Elder, and that," he pointed at Beverly, "is Fitz the Younger. Plus, I don't know if you've noticed, but Beverly is a woman."

"A woman? Really? I hadn't noticed."

Revi was far too amused at having baited Gerald.

"That's enough, you two," said Beverly, "Revi, you can be such an arse at times."

"Alas, it is in my nature Dame Beverly, or should I say Fitz the Younger," Revi made an exaggerated bow.

"If you are done," said Anna, "I think I've reached a decision. The army will rest for one day only. That should give Master Bloom time to finish healing the injured. We'll march the morning after tomorrow with what stores we can muster. Beverly, you will command the knights in addition to the light cavalry. Unless anyone has anything else to say, I will leave you to your duties."

The commanders were filing out of the room when Lord Greycloak chose to speak up. "Your Highness, might I offer the services of my troops to gather food? They can scout ahead and hunt for you." He turned to Lady Albreda who had just been leaving, "We will, of course, not hunt in the Whitewood."

"Thank you, Lord Greycloak, I accept your offer of help gratefully, and will inform the king of your assistance," a thankful Anna replied.

The tall Elf bowed deeply, then turned and left with the rest, leaving Anna in the room with Beverly and the baron.

"You had a message you wanted me to send to Uxley?" reminded the baron.

"Yes," Anna responded. "I find myself missing my maid, Sophie. I'd like to send a message for her to meet us in Uxley when we march through. I'll have her bring the carriage with her."

"An excellent idea, Your Highness," the baron agreed, "It will also present well when we enter the city."

"Present well?" said Beverly.

"Why yes, the princess must make an entrance. She is, after all, the victor of two important battles."

"Come now, Baron," said Anna, "don't you think that's overselling it a bit?"

"The truth is, Your Highness, your father, the king, will likely still be dealing with a rebellious earl. Anything you can do to give the impression of your importance will help sway him to include you in his plans."

"You're devious, Father," said Beverly, with a smile.

"Devious and clever," agreed Anna. "All right, Baron, I'll arrive in Wincaster in a Royal Carriage. You've spent more time at court than me. I'll require you to fill me in on what I can expect when we get there."

"I should be delighted, Your Highness. As I once told you in Uxley, I am at your disposal."

The princess wrote out a quick note to Sophie and sealed it with wax. "There you are baron, I shall leave it in your hands."

"Your Highness," he said, bowing. He turned and left the room, calling for the dispatch rider as he did so.

"Your father is a valuable ally," Anna said as she watched him leave.

"Yes, Highness. He only has your best interests at heart."

"Tell me, Beverly, and be honest. What do you make of Albreda's prophesy?"

Beverly thought for a few moments before speaking. "I have to believe it only portends what might happen if we do nothing. If everything in life is pre-ordained, what's the purpose of living?"

"I suppose I hadn't thought of it like that," Anna responded. "We shall have to be especially careful when we're in the capital. The prophecy could relate to the rebellion, but it might also mean someone at court is plotting against the crown."

"I hadn't thought of that," said Beverly. "I shall be certain to mention it to Arnim. He'll want to make doubly sure that the guards are aware of the situation."

"Good, now get some rest. We're going to need your skills in the next few weeks as we march the army back to Wincaster."

"Yes, Your Highness," she said, bowing.

The sounds of celebration echoed through the halls of Bodden Keep as Beverly made her way to the smithy. She had stopped off to gather her damaged armour, and she now found herself thinking of the smith. It had been almost two years since she last saw Aldwin in Hawksburg, and she wondered if her heart would still flutter when she looked into his eyes.

She entered the smithy to observe Aldwin poring over some sketches.

"What are you looking at?" she interrupted him.

He looked up from his work, a smile breaking over his face as he recognized her.

"Going over some plans," he said, "for something special I'm working on."

Her heart felt like it skipped a beat as she gazed into those steely grey eyes, and she couldn't help but return the smile. There was still an unbreakable bond between them.

She walked over to stand beside him, looking down at the sketches.

"What's all this?" she asked.

"It's a plan for a new forge," he answered. "I need to produce more heat."

"What for?" she asked.

"Last year, one of the patrols came across a scar on the ground. A rock had fallen from the sky and smashed through the top of a hill, leaving a furrow in the field below. At first, they thought it was some type of magic."

She moved her eyes from the sketch, to look at his face, seeing if he was joking. His intense stare gazed back, and she felt herself falling once more into those eyes.

"Was it? Magic, I mean?" she tried to keep the conversation going.

"No, it was a stone from the sky. I've heard of this before. I asked your father if it might be possible to investigate it. We rode out, and I took some samples."

"Samples? Of rock?"

"Yes, I think it was a large rock that shattered when it hit, for there were small fragments all over the place. Come, and I'll show you."

He rose from his seat and took her hand, leading her over to a box on the floor. The touch of their hands sent a tingle through her. He knelt down at the chest, releasing her hand. "I gathered up several fragments. When we got back here, I washed them off. They appear to some kind of unknown metal."

He opened the chest to what looked like small chunks of melted steel. Beverly knelt down beside him. "What do you intend to do with this?" she asked, laying her finger on one.

"I plan to forge it into a weapon," he said, "but I haven't been able to melt it. I think I need a higher temperature in my forge."

"How do you do that?" she asked, once again being drawn into his world.

He turned from the rock to gaze at her. "I talked to your father about it, and he gave me the name of a Dwarven smith in Wincaster. I wrote to him about my discovery and his reply was most useful."

"He sent you these plans?" she asked

"More or less," he explained. "He sent me some plans, but I've made a few modifications to them. We've a bit more room to work here in Bodden, so I'm making some adjustments."

"And if you manage to smelt this rock, what then?"

"I'll make it into a weapon, for you of course."

They were crouched by the open box, their faces not more than hands width from each other. Beverly was staring at the rock as Aldwin spoke, and then looked at him, to see his face so close to hers. She leaned forward, and he did likewise, and a moment later their lips met. As they kissed, at that moment, nothing else mattered. There was no war, no invaders, no anything, just the two of them, here in the smithy, together.

Not wanting to, but knowing it had to happen, they separated slightly, but stayed crouched on the floor, neither one wanting it to end.

It was Aldwin who broke the spell. "Did you come here for something in particular?"

"Yes," she said, "I actually came here to get you to fix my armour."

He stood up and held out his hand to help her to her feet. From anyone else, she would have been insulted that they thought she needed help, but from Aldwin, it was purely his kind and caring nature. She took his hand, and they walked back to his workbench.

"Where is it?" he asked.

"Where's what?" she said.

"The armour you need repaired?"

"Oh, it's right here in this sack. It's just the shin guard. It was damaged at Kingsford." She produced the piece of armour from the bag and placed it on the table. She was no longer able wear it for the metal had been so severely damaged it was bent.

He held it up to the light and whistled. "You're lucky you still have a leg to wear this."

"Revi says my shin was broken. I didn't even realize it till my leg gave way after the battle. So, you can fix it?"

"Of course, but I'll have to take some new measurements. I think your legs have muscled up a bit since I made this. Have a seat in the chair over there."

She sat down, and he came over, kneeling in front of her. Gently, he raised her foot and removed her shoe, causing a pleasant warmth to spread over her. Next, he lifted her skirts to reveal her shin, placing his hands tenderly beneath her calf. Her heartbeat quickened, and she strained to control her breathing. Aldwin gently felt her leg, using a leather strip to take measurements.

The touch of his fingertips lightly brushing across her shin made her jump. "That tickles," she said.

Aldwin laughed, "Sorry, my lady, I shall try not to tickle you."

"It's fine," she said, perhaps too quickly. "I liked it," she blushed as she made her admission.

"I'm all done with the measuring," he said, gently placing her shoe back on her foot."

She didn't want him to stop. "Perhaps you should measure the other leg, I might need you to adjust the other side."

He looked up at her, grinning. He kept his eyes locked on hers as he gently lifted the other foot. Soon, his strong hands were tenderly feeling her calf, measuring its girth.

She let out an involuntary groan and then caught herself. She looked at Aldwin in surprise, and they both laughed. He placed her shoe back on her foot and stood up, holding out his hand.

"I'm afraid I've some work to do if you want this done by the time you leave."

"You're right," she said, "I think I'm a distraction."

"You're more than welcome to stay while I work," he invited.

"I'd like that," she replied. "I tell you what, you start working, and I'll go get us some food."

"Good idea," he agreed, "and you need to get the other shin guard if I'm going to adjust it."

She smiled again, kissing him on the cheek. "I'll be right back."

The army was formed up on the road outside the town for the march to Wincaster, the men carrying as much food as they were able without completely depleting Bodden. It would be long, likely two weeks or more, and they must rely on the provisions that the baron's messenger had hopefully procured along the way.

The princess was with the baron, on the road, overseeing the coordination of the army. Beverly made her way out of the Keep, stopping by the smithy to retrieve her finished pieces of armour. Aldwin insisted on putting them on her himself, and they fit perfectly, as she knew they would.

"Your armour has quite a few dents and scratches," he said, "but it'll keep you safe."

They locked gazes for a moment, face to face, neither speaking. Beverly felt she knew Aldwin better than she ever had before, after spending the last two nights talking well into the wee hours of the morning.

"Be safe," he said quietly.

"I will," she replied.

He leaned towards her, and she raised her hands, his arms encircling her waist. They stood, chest to chest for a moment, and despite the breastplate, she felt his heart beating in tandem with hers.

This time, they both moved to kiss, lingering to savour the experience. Neither one knew how long it would be before they saw each other again, but both believed that one day they would find a way to be together. Until then, they silently agreed they would make do with stolen moments.

Once they had separated, Beverly took a breath to calm her nerves. She didn't want to look flustered when she entered the courtyard. She left the smithy without another word, but couldn't help but smile. She was a far cry from the young woman that had departed Bodden all those years ago. The courtyard was filled with Bodden Knights already mounted, and Lightning was waiting for her.

Seated upon her steed, she looked around. It would likely be a long time before she returned to Bodden, for she was sworn to the service of the princess now. She took it all in, re-committing it to memory, though it was hardly necessary. She had grown up here, spent her entire early life behind these walls, and knew every nook and cranny it held. The sound of the light cavalry as they trotted out the gate interrupted her silent farewell, and she gave the order for the knights to advance. Out the gate they rode, to form up behind the rest of the horsemen.

The plan was for the cavalry to bring up the rear while they were close to Bodden. Once they were a day out, they would take the lead, providing a screening force for the rest. They rode by the Great Elm where the princess was sitting upon her horse. Beverly raised her sword in salute as they passed and the princess nodded. The army began to move forward like a giant snake, the Elves taking the lead and quickly disappearing from view. The cavalry advanced, following the footmen in front of them. They had gone no more than a hundred yards when she saw Albreda riding towards them, mounted on a white horse with no saddle, a fact which would have been startling with anyone else, but was somehow fitting for the Earth Mage.

"Lady Beverly," she said as she approached.

"Lady Albreda," Beverly nodded, "this is a surprise. Are you coming with us?"

"I'm afraid not," she replied, "but I come to warn you. You must guard the princess carefully for I fear she's in great danger."

"So you said in the map room," Beverly reminded her.

"It's more than that," Albreda insisted. "She has a part yet to play in the grand scheme of things. You must take extra care in the capital, a shadow lies there."

"You have my attention," said Beverly. "Can you tell me more?"

"I've told you all I know. I can see visions, but I cannot always interpret them. Look after her, Beverly, and yourself."

With that, she moved her horse off the road and galloped to the north.

Beverly turned her attention back to the troops marching in front of her. A couple of the foot soldiers had seen her taking up position behind them and began talking among themselves. A moment later the footmen broke out into a marching song, meant to help pass the time and keep the rhythm of the march.

"T'was the mistress of Bodden, a knight of renown, she fought two great battles and rescued the town. She fought with great bravery which set her apart, who dare marry this lady and tame her wild heart."

It was a catchy tune, and she smiled at the men as she hummed along. If only they knew the truth of it, she thought, they might be surprised.

THIRTY-FIVE

Return to Wincaster

SPRING 960 MC

~

The march was long. It took over two weeks to reach Wincaster, leaving the men exhausted. Even so, they took pride in the fact that they had made three long marches and defeated two armies, a feat unheard of in the history of Merceria. The men straightened their backs with pride as the walls of the city loomed over the horizon. They marched back triumphantly, a sudden spring in their step, harnessing a newfound reserve of energy.

Princess Anna was travelling in her carriage, along with her maid, escorted by the Bodden Knights. As the walls came into view, Anna asked Beverly to ride ahead and take a look, lest the city be in the hands of the rebels.

She spurred Lightning forward, quickly passing the Elves who were leading the advance on the capital. Riding past Lord Greycloak, she called out to him, inviting him to accompany her. The Elven Lord urged his horse onward to match her pace.

As they approached, Beverly saw activity on the walls, though she was not able to discern the details. The closer they drew, the clearer the picture became, and with a sinking feeling in her stomach, she recognized what it was. From the walls of the city were hung cages full of people. Even from this distance she could make out their limbs poking through the bars, flailing about in the air.

Lord Greycloak turned to face her. "Is this the way Merceria typically treats its prisoners?" he asked.

Beverly was disgusted at the punishment, remembering well the same cruel fate dealt out to Olivia. "It's not how I would punish traitors, nor my father, but it is the king's will."

"Surely it would be better to simply execute them," he said. "To punish them in this fashion seems to be of little purpose."

"He's sending a warning to anyone who might go against his rule," she tried to explain. "The message is simple, whoever betrays the crown will suffer this same fate."

"And you condone this?" he asked, looking straight at her.

"I understand it," she said. "I don't condone it, but it is the king's realm, and we must follow his orders. Is it not so in the Elven realms?"

"If I were to give such a command," he stated, "I would be removed from my position."

"Here, that would amount to treason," she said, "and that's the death sentence, usually in an excruciating manner."

"Curious the customs of men," the Elf reflected. "I also notice that the flag on the Palace is at half-mast, has that some significance?"

Beverly, surprised by the Elf's keen eyesight, took a moment before answering, "Are you sure?"

"Indeed, I can make it out plainly, even from here."

"It means a death, likely the death of a royal. The Palace flies the flag of Merceria and the Royal Standard whenever the king is in residence. Can you tell which flag is at half-mast?"

The Elf Lord stared at the Palace which, to Beverly's eyes, was little more than a speck in the distance. "Both," he said with some finality.

"That means a Royal Death," she said. "I'd better ride back and inform the princess."

"Perhaps, when we enter the city," said Lord Greycloak, "I will keep my Elves removed from the king's presence. We will remain camped outside of the city walls, near the woods. You can contact me there should the princess require my services."

They rode back to the princess in silence. Beverly was shocked by the cruel punishment meted out by the king. What would they find when they arrived in the city? The column had halted to allow the men to rest before entering the capital. Beverly rode up to the princess, who was stretching her legs while Tempus relieved himself on the carriage wheel.

"What news, Beverly?" she asked.

"The flag of Merceria still flies from the city, Your Highness. It is safe to enter Wincaster."

Anna looked at Beverly's face for a moment, "What aren't you telling me, Beverly?"

Beverly flushed, "It's not a pretty sight, Your Highness. They've set cages hanging from the walls."

"Cages? What for?"

"I'm afraid they're full of prisoners, Your Highness."

Beverly saw the princess visibly pale as she took in the meaning of her words. "That's barbaric," she said at last.

"Your father likely thought it a suitable punishment for traitors, Highness."

"We both know he's not my father," Anna said quietly, "perhaps that's a blessing. In any event, there's nothing we can do about it. What the king wants, the king gets. Have the troops resume the march. I'd like you to ride to the city gates and make sure the doors are open for us. We'll march the army straight to the Palace grounds and have them form up for the king's inspection."

"I'm afraid there's more, Highness. The flags of Merceria are both at half mast. It appears there's been a death in the Royal Family."

"Just as the prophecy foretold," said Anna. "I wish we'd made better time."

"We cannot lament time which is past. We must look to the future, Highness."

She saw Anna struggling to keep her calm demeanour. "True," she said at last. "Have the army continue the march, we'll find out for ourselves what has happened in our absence."

"As Your Highness commands," Beverly said, wheeling her great warhorse about. "I shall ride to the gate directly."

It didn't take long to reach the gates, which were open, and the guards more or less at ease. She rode up to the soldier standing in the doorway and addressed him.

"You there," she commanded, "Princess Anna of Merceria approaches, what news?"

The guard, startled, stood up straight to answer as he saw her knightly armour. "Prince Alfred is dead," he announced. "Killed a few days ago in battle. I'm afraid I don't know much more."

"Thank you," said Beverly, "can you keep the way clear? We are marching with an army of reinforcements for the king."

"By all means," the man stuttered, "your lord...I mean ladyship."

Beverly smiled at the man's discomfort, for she was used to it. How many other women had had the misfortune to be addressed as a lord, she wondered?

. . .

The army marched through the gates, unhindered by any objections from the guards, making their way through town. Beverly had informed Princess Anna of the death of her brother, Prince Alfred, and was surprised to see the relief on her face. She had no memories of Alfred, she had said, but was afraid it was her brother Henry that had died. Now informed, she was eager to get to the Palace to learn how it had happened.

The carriage rolled up to the Palace, in front of which was a sizable cobblestoned parade ground. Gerald saw to the troops, lining them up as they arrived. Anna called for her other advisors, and entered the Palace itself, following a nobleman named Lord Bradford who had been sent to introduce them. They walked into the great hall, to be met by a crowded audience. The king sat at a large table set up against the north wall, with Marshal-General Valmar on his right and Prince Henry on his left. The rest of the table was crowded with other nobles of rank, while the floor contained lesser nobles and men of import that were gathered to hear the king's words.

The assembly had evidently been carrying on for some time, judging by the half-eaten food on the table, and even as someone spoke from the floor, the king bit into a chicken leg.

Anna had taken the lead, Beverly just behind her, and the rest following. The crowd parted as Lord Bradford instructed them to make way. The throng stepped back even further as they drew closer to the king, creating an open area where the small party now found itself standing.

The room fell into a hush, and Anna whispered to Beverly, who then stepped forward, and in a loud, clear voice announced, "Your Majesty, the army of Princess Anna has defeated the invaders at Kingsford," she paused as the crowd murmured, for no one had heard this news. She waited for the noise to die down and spoke again, "From there, the army headed north to defeat the second invasion at Bodden," she continued, "and now comes to the aid of Wincaster."

She returned to her position behind Anna as they had agreed.

The onlookers were in a tremendous uproar over the news, and the king stood, quieting the crowd. "You have done well, daughter, but I fear you are too late to save your brother. Prince Alfred is dead."

Beverly didn't see Anna's reaction from her position but heard her take a measured breath before answering. "The news saddens me, Father," she said, "I pray that his death shall be avenged."

The king stepped around the table towards her, placing his hands upon her small shoulders. "You have brought good news in our time of sorrow," he said. "Tomorrow, we shall bury your brother, and then the army will move to Eastwood and end this uprising, once and for all."

Anna smiled, and Beverly could almost see her soaking in her father's affection.

"Now you must eat," he said, "and celebrate your victories, for on the morrow we must mourn." He gazed down at the princess, and Beverly was struck by how small she looked in comparison to the king.

He spoke in a quieter voice as the room applauded his speech, "Eat, rest yourself and come and see me when you are done, we have much to discuss." King Andred turned to Prince Henry and bade him look after his sister, and then he strode from the room. Beverly watched him go, seeing the look of grief that was on his face when he thought no one was looking.

Anna made her way through the well-wishers that now closed in on her to offer their congratulations. Beverly grew concerned by their closeness and pushed a path through. Arnim and the others, worried about the prophesy, moved closer to form a protective wall around her. Tempus accompanied her, growling when people got too close. The strange procession made its way to Prince Henry where a chair was already pulled out for the princess. Beverly took her station behind her, alert to any possible danger, while her dog curled up at Anna's feet.

"Good to see you, Squeak," said Henry. "I must say I was surprised to hear you had marched off with an army. I didn't think you had it in you. You're quite a surprise, little sister."

"I did what I had to," said Anna. "I didn't have much choice."

"Still," he insisted, "good job. Father appears most impressed."

"What happened to Alfred?" she pushed. "How did he die?"

"It was a mess. Where do I start?"

"How about when you got to Wincaster?"

"We returned to Wincaster about two weeks after you left for Kingsford," he started. "Just after we arrived, we got word that the earl was marching down from Eastwood. We pulled together all the troops we were able to and marched north to intercept him. We had picked up some troops on the march and were expecting reinforcements from Colbridge and Shrewesdale, but we daren't wait in case he made it to the city walls. Father was surprised to see Dwarves manning the walls, I take it that was your idea?"

"Yes," said Anna, "though it was the Elves that convinced them to join us."

"Father was very impressed," Henry returned to his story, "and so we marched to intercept the earl."

"What happened on the journey?" Anna prompted.

"We marched for three days before we stumbled across the enemy in a thick morning fog. We literally ran right into them. Both armies were on the road and it was completely chaotic. At first, we thought we'd run across one of our own units, but then the fighting started. By the time the fog lifted we were well into it. Even now, I'm not sure of the exact sequence of events, but at some point in time, Alfred led a band of knights in a charge against the enemy. That was the last we saw of him until his body was returned to us."

"Who recovered the body?" Anna asked.

"A ranger named Hayley Chambers," Henry continued. "Father knighted her for it. The body was in a fearful state and nobody knew which blow had killed him."

"So he died fighting?" said Anna.

"I think so, but we'll never know for sure. Father took it hard. He wanted to execute all the prisoners in retaliation."

"I'm guessing someone convinced him not to, judging by the cages on the walls."

"Very perceptive," Henry said. "Valmar talked to him, convinced him not to do it. Some of our men were their prisoners. If we executed their men, they might kill ours. Father decided to punish them instead. For three days he had them tortured, not even bothering to ask them questions. He was in a fearful rage. Now they hang on the walls in cages, to starve to death or be picked apart by crows."

"Grisly," said Anna, and Beverly imagined the look of disgust on her face.

"Yes, but he wouldn't have it any other way. He's a changed man, Anna, something inside him broke that day. Now all he talks about is burying Alfred and sending the army to take revenge."

Anna was quick to pick up on the details. "Send the army?" she said. "You mean he's not commanding it himself?"

"No, he's putting me in charge with Valmar to advise me. I think he really means for Valmar to be in charge, but he needs me to carry the might of the crown."

"How do you feel about that, Henry?" she asked.

Henry shrugged, "All right, I suppose. I want to see the earl brought to justice. Alfred was a pain in the arse, but he was still my brother. His death troubles me. It sends a message that rebels can kill royals with no repercussions. We have to avenge him."

"How many troops are marching?" Anna asked.

"I don't know yet. Father will hold a war council tomorrow after the funeral. He wants you there, by the way, along with any advisors you have."

"I'll be sure to be there," she said.

Beverly saw the prince smiling at his younger sister. "That reminds me," he said, "how did that knight I sent you to work out?"

Anna looked back at Beverly and winked. "I think she's proven to be more than adequate," she said.

A little while later they made their way to the king's drawing room to find him sitting in a large armchair, Lady Penelope standing behind him, massaging his shoulders. Anna entered, with Beverly close behind.

It was Lady Penelope who spoke first, "You don't need a bodyguard here, Highness." She looked straight at Beverly, "You can wait outside."

"It's all right," interrupted the king. "She's earned the right to a body-guard. The knight can stay."

Beverly took a quiet station by the door, not missing the look of contempt that crossed the face of the king's mistress.

"I'm proud of you, Anna," said the king. "You've impressed me. I would never have thought you would command an army."

Anna sat down opposite the king, and from her vantage point, Beverly watched both their faces in profile. "Thank you, Father," Anna said, some-what uncomfortably, thought Beverly.

The king stared at his daughter for a moment. "I suppose in hindsight I should apologize for abandoning you to Uxley, though it appears to have done well for you, keeping you away from the court. You show a strength of character that is seldom seen in someone so young. You take after your mother that way." A slight look of pain crossed the king's face. Perhaps there was regret over the queen?

Anna shifted uncomfortably, apparently not sure how to respond.

"I'm preparing an army to march to Eastwood, as you no doubt have learned," he said. "I think you've earned the right to be part of it."

Anna sat up, suddenly more alert.

"Henry will command," he continued, "with Marshal-General Valmar to advise him. The army will form up in a number of sections, each commanded by its own noble. I'd like you to command the screening force, mostly archers and some cavalry. Do you have a military expert?"

"Yes, several," she replied, "but I would name Baron Fitzwilliam as my official advisor, he has much field experience."

The king nodded his head in approval. "Good choice," he said, "once again you surprise me with your decisions."

Beverly thought Anna was trying to hide a smile, to maintain proper decorum in front of the king.

"I also think it only proper that you take some knights into service. The crown will provide the necessary funds."

Now it was Lady Penelope that spoke up, "Is that a good idea, my lord? She is but a young girl."

"Young she might be, but she's proven herself in battle. If she can lead an army, she can certainly have some knights. Shall we say a dozen or so? I'll leave it up to your people to make the arrangements."

The king turned to pick up a small chalice from the table beside him. Beverly noticed Lady Penelope eye the princess with disdain. This was someone worth watching, she thought.

"Might I ask," said Anna, "what the funeral arrangements are for tomorrow?"

The king took a deep drink, "You'll follow Margaret in the procession, in an open-topped carriage. You should probably have a knight or two beside you while we proceed to the Cathedral. I can lend you a couple of knights if you want."

"No, thank you, I have my own people," said Anna. "What time are we forming up?"

"The procession will leave the Palace at noon. I'll send a servant to your quarters with the details. Now, if you'll pardon me, I have work I must attend to."

The king stood, and Anna recognized this was the signal to leave. She bowed and made her way from the room, Beverly falling in behind her.

Once they were in the hallway, Anna spoke, "Did you get all that?"

"Yes, Highness, where would you like me to begin?"

"I want you to track down Dame Hayley Chambers, for a start. She's the ranger who the king just knighted, and we need some knights."

"Are you sure?" Beverly questioned. "We don't know anything about her."

"On the contrary," said Anna, "I've met her before. I once awarded her a prize for her archery."

Beverly was caught off guard yet again. Princess Anna was so full of surprises.

The next day was a sombre affair as the procession got underway. The body of Alfred, led by a contingent of knights, was driven on an open-topped wagon. King Andred and Prince Henry followed on foot, along with his closest advisors. Princess Margaret came next, riding in an open-topped carriage, followed closely by Princess Anna, who was seated with her maid,

Sophie and Tempus, who stayed at her feet, the ever-alert dog observing the passers-by.

Beverly and Gerald both rode horses, one to each side of Princess Anna's carriage. Beverly had insisted on the extra protection, Albreda's words still fresh in her mind.

The column started at the Palace and began its route through the city that would end at the Cathedral where the nobles of the realm were gathered to pay their respects. The pace was slow, as befitting a funeral, and Beverly scanned the crowds as they rode, on the lookout for danger. The rest of Anna's entourage followed behind, on foot, save for Lord Greycloak. The Elves did not mourn their dead, and he chose to watch from the walls lest the enemy attack while the city grieved.

The procession headed south and then turned westward towards the cathedral, its spires visible over the tops of the houses. Anna was talking to Sophie when Tempus abruptly sat up and barked. Nobody knew what was happening, but an instant later the loyal dog leaped from the carriage to hit the ground just in front of Beverly. Lightning quickly sidestepped, and then the great beast ran forward, towards Margaret's carriage. Anna was calling after him, and Beverly heard Arnim, behind her, calling out.

"The rooftop," he was shouting, "'ware the rooftop!"

Beverly looked to where the captain pointed. A man was crouched on the tile roof, aiming a crossbow at Princess Margaret. She saw him stop moving and pull the trigger. The bolt sang out, sailing across the open distance in what appeared to Beverly like slow motion. Helpless to stop it, she watched the bolt fly closer, and then a large shape sprung up into the carriage. It was Tempus, and he took the full force of the bolt, saving Princess Margaret, and then sagged to the floor of the carriage. Margaret was screaming as the whole street erupted into motion when panic set in.

Anna jumped from her carriage in an attempt to get to her sister. Revi ran past her to help, while Arnim ran for an alleyway.

"Next alleyway," he shouted at Beverly, "there's a ladder to the roof."

She spurred Lightning forward and turned down the alley, to see a ladder firmly fixed to the wall. She leaped from her mount, grasping the ladder halfway up and climbed with all her might. All around her, people were yelling, panicking, running for cover, while soldiers tried to seek out the assailant. The ladder led to a small flat area on the top of the building. There, three people who had been watching the parade from this vantage point, pointed at the adjoining roof as she crested the top. Turning, she saw the assassin nimbly crossing the sloped rooftop, and then heard Arnim shouting from behind him. Running parallel to the other houses until they were closer, she leaped and landed, but her feet slipped on the clay tiling, and she started sliding to the edge of the roof. Grasping frantically, she used a chimney to stop her fall and then hauled herself to her feet just in time to see the assailant running towards her. Seeing her in front of him, he stopped, and peered around, looking for an escape. She saw Arnim who, having just gained the roof was coming up behind the man.

"Surrender," she yelled, but the villain turned and bolted to the other side of the rooftop, intending to jump across the street onto another building. As his feet hit the edge, he jumped, and Beverly noticed that the narrow street below was partially covered by the overhanging roofs. She cursed, for he had a good chance of success, and she could not leap in full armour to follow him.

He thrust himself across the roadway in an all or nothing gambit. Beverly watched as he landed the other side, his waist hitting the edge of the rooftop. He scrambled to gain a purchase, but the thatched roof slipped in his hands. He slid backwards, falling, still grasping at the air as he went, letting out a blood-curdling scream that was only silenced by his impact on the street below. His head hit the cobblestones and shattered, sending blood and bits everywhere. An onlooker standing nearby, splattered with gore, turned and vomited the contents of his stomach, adding to the already grisly scene. Arnim disappeared from the roof and emerged from the alley a few moments later. A small crowd was gathering, and he hastily pushed them back along with the assistance of some soldiers who had filed through from the adjoining street. Beverly made her way to ground level, joining Arnim as he was searching through the man's pockets. He looked up at Beverly, "No way to identify him, he's got nothing on him. I suspect he was a hired hand, a professional."

"Why do you say that?" she asked.

"He took great pains to make sure there's nought on him, not even any coins."

"Why would coins be important?"

"They might indicate he was hired by a foreign king," he said. "You'd be surprised by who might place a death mark on a person."

"Death mark?"

"Sorry, street slang for murder contracts. I've seen enough of them in my time, I used to work on the city watch. I'll get the body back to the temple and have Revi go over it before burial. Perhaps it will reveal something of the man. Did you hear him say anything?"

"No, is it important?"

"Not particularly, but if he spoke, we might have a better idea of his natural tongue. That would tell us if he was a local or not."

"He was trying to kill Princess Margaret, of all people," said Beverly. "Why do you think she would be the target?"

"Probably just the opportunity. Princess Anna was blocked by you and your horse, and the king was surrounded by his knights. It was the only clear shot he had. You'd best get back to the princess, I'll take care of this. I'll fill everyone in later when we've had a closer look at the body."

Beverly made her way back to the alleyway where she had started climbing the ladder. Lightning was still standing there, as obedient as ever. She led him out to the main thoroughfare to see the procession had long since passed. She assumed they had continued to the cathedral for the funeral, but thought perhaps they might have cancelled the ceremony due to the attempted assassination. She mounted her horse and proceeded to ride towards the grand edifice and saw her father riding towards her.

"Any luck?" he yelled, "I hear you were after the beggar."

"He's dead, I'm afraid, fell from the rooftop. Arnim's taking care of the body. Where's Princess Anna?"

"She's at the Cathedral. Revi's looking after the dog as it looks like he bolt was poisoned. Needless to say, the place is swarming with soldiers. The king ordered the bishop to cut the ceremony short."

"How's Princess Margaret?"

"Terrified, but otherwise unhurt. She was quite shaken by the whole ordeal. The king has ordered out the troops to sweep the city streets, not sure what he expects to find."

"Likely nothing," she agreed, "but I suppose it sends a message."

"Yes, I suppose it will, though I'm not sure what the message would be. I'm glad to see you safe, my dear. I must admit I was a little worried about you."

"I can look after myself, Father. You, of all people, should know that."

"I wasn't worried about you getting hurt in a fight, I was afraid you would fall off the roof!"

She laughed as she felt the stress of the day begin to drain from her. "It'll take more than a rooftop to finish me off," she joked with him. "So tell me, do we go to the Cathedral?"

"No, Her Highness wants to meet us back at the Palace. We have plans to make before the march tomorrow."

THIRTY-SIX

The March to Eastwood

THE MARCH TO EASTWOOD

D awn came far too early. They had all stayed up late planning, and then the orders had to be prepared to ensure a timely march in the morning. Princess Anna was given command of the screening force, one of four elements of the army that was marching northeast to Eastwood. The king had appropriated most of the troops she had taken on her march north, and replaced them with mainly archers; two companies of short bowmen along with two companies of the newer crossbows. She retained command of the Bodden Knights, but did not have time to recruit her own. The Elves would march with no other leader, and so she now counted the Elven bow among her contingent. Perhaps the biggest surprise was the addition of a hundred Dwarven arbalesters with their massive metal crossbows and heavy armour. At the last moment, they had refused to march with anyone else. Lord Granitefist, their commander, was a staunch ally of the Elves.

Beverly was impressed with the Dwarves. They were up early and marching before anyone else. Their leader had explained the Dwarven way to her. They were shorter of stature than Humans and thus took smaller steps. To make up for their slower speed, however, they had incredible endurance and would march long hours to make up the difference. Additionally, each Dwarf was heavily armoured in chainmail making them as effective as heavy footmen in battle.

Her father had used the term brigade to explain the organization of this army, an expression that was somewhat foreign to her. The army was divided into four such brigades, each led by its own commander. Anna would lead the screening brigade, while Henry led the main. The other two were named the right and left brigade, and they were commanded by the Duke of Colbridge and the Earl of Shrewesdale, respectively. To Beverly, it was a sensible way to organize an army of this size, but she feared that petty jealousy and currying of favour might interfere with the objective.

Anna had wanted her to find some knights to swear in, but no time had been available for such an activity. She had written letters to all the knights she knew that were not already in service, but it would take time to get a response. Dame Hayley Chambers, the recently knighted King's Ranger, was the only new knight Beverly had been able to recruit to the Princess's Royal Guard.

The screening brigade had marched out of the city on schedule, and now Beverly and Hayley were riding to catch up. The city streets were jammed with troops jostling to leave the capital, and Beverly cursed as she forced her horse through the mass of soldiers.

"Not exactly easy, is it," Hayley commented.

"No," Beverly agreed, "I'm not sure who's in charge of this mess, but it's going to take a miracle to get it moving."

"How far up the road will the princess be?" she asked.

"She left first thing, along with the rest of the Brigade."

"Sorry if I've made you late," the ranger said.

Beverly turned her attention from the street to look at the young woman, "It's not your fault. I didn't have much time to find you. We've been planning all night."

"I'm afraid I'm not much of a knight, I don't even have proper armour, and my horse really isn't very good in a fight."

"The princess knows that, besides, the crown is paying to outfit you. Once this campaign is over, we'll get you some proper armour."

"Like yours? It's quite ornate, who made it?"

She smiled, "Not quite like mine, it's custom crafted, but I'm sure we'll find you something nice. The princess said she knew you, how is that?"

"Hah," said Hayley, "that's an interesting story in itself." She absently brushed a stray hair away from her face. She had long brown hair, in a ponytail, but stray strands always seemed to find their way loose. "I met her at an archery contest in Uxley."

"So you're good with a bow?" asked Beverly.

"Yes, but I'm far too modest to admit it." She looked at Beverly, and they both laughed.

"Why do you carry two bows?"

Hayley tapped the long shaft of wood that lay across her saddle, "This is a longbow, but I can't use it while mounted. My other bow is for firing from horseback."

"Isn't it a little awkward carrying a longbow on horseback?"

"I wouldn't normally do that, but I needed to carry all my belongings with me. I'm hoping to drop it with the baggage train."

"That shouldn't be a problem if we can get through this mess. Who are all these people?" Beverly wondered out loud.

"Those men are with the Earl of Shrewesdale, judging from their colours," said Hayley, "and I think those over there are from the prince's troops. I don't think they've organized any of this."

Beverly swore, "This doesn't bode well. The princess is not going to be happy. They'll never get this lot moving. Come on, we're going to have to force our way through."

She urged Lightning forward, and the crowd parted for the massive charger. Hayley brought her smaller horse into the wake, and they filed through the street, leaving the city by the Northern Gate. The arguing soldiers and wagons clogged the road, so they took their horses off to the side and across the fields to save time.

They soon made up for the delay, and after a bit of riding they caught up to the princess. She was on a horse, and when she saw the two riders approaching, she turned sideways to greet them.

"Your Highness," cried Beverly, "I have your newest knight."

They rode up, and Hayley bowed her head, "Your Highness," she said.

"I'm afraid we don't have much of a ceremony here," Anna said and turned in her saddle. "Baron," she requested, "I need to borrow you for a moment or two."

Baron Fitzwilliam rode over and smiled at his daughter, "Your Highness," he said, turning to the princess, "I am at your disposal."

"I need to swear Dame Hayley into my service, would you do the honours?"

"Certainly, Ma'am," he turned to face the two women. "Who sponsors this knight?" he asked, looking at Beverly.

"I, Dame Beverly Fitzwilliam," said Beverly in a loud, clear voice.

"And who takes this knight into service?" he asked.

"I, Princess Anna of Merceria, do take this knight into service," said Anna.

Fitz turned to face Hayley, who was watching with great fascination. "Do you swear to serve faithfully, to carry out the will of your sworn mistress?"

"I do," said Hayley solemnly.

"Then I now pronounce you a Knight of..." Fitz paused and looked at Anna, "What exactly are your knights called? We can't just call them Knights of the Princess."

Anna showed a surprised look on her face, "Gerald," she shouted, "what should we call my knights?"

Gerald looked as surprised as Anna. He glanced about for inspiration and spied Tempus lying in a patch of sunlight. "Knights of the Hound?" he offered.

Anna smiled. "Knight of the Hound it is then," she said triumphantly.

"Then I now pronounce you a Knight of the Hound," Fitz said, bowing, "How does it feel to be the first one?"

Beverly cleared her throat.

"I believe," said Anna, looking at Beverly, "that she's the second. The distinction of first belongs to Dame Beverly."

Beverly bowed in an exaggerated manner, and they all applauded. The campaign had been long, and the impromptu ceremony had taken their minds off more pressing matters.

As they had done in the previous journey westward, the Elves were out in front. They marched quickly and formed a useful screen against enemy patrols. The Human archers came next, consisting of crossbowmen from Kingsford as well as the bowmen of Tewsbury and Hawksburg. These men had either accompanied the princess in her relief of Kingsford or had been marched to the capital soon afterwards. As such they were hardened and set a brisk pace. The Dwarves followed, marching slowly with their heavy armour and powerful arbalests. The Knights of Bodden brought up the rear of the Brigade, ready to deploy in an instant should it become necessary. Both Beverly and her father had wished for some light cavalry to screen them, but the king had been insistent that the lighter units stay with their liege lords.

Beverly realized that the jostling for political power had already begun. In theory, the duke's men should have been marching behind them, but Beverly saw no sign of his troops. By the time the screening force camped for the night, she had given up looking for them. Her father had taken great pains to arrange supply wagons carrying food and water for the men, but there was no sign of them either. The baron had ridden off to seek them out, only to return a few hours later with news that they were caught in the bottleneck of troops, and would be arriving late. The princess's brigade finished setting up their camp and rested, setting pickets and walking the lines. Anna visited the men to keep their spirits up, and they responded with a fierce pride. They had made fifteen miles the first day, probably not a record, but a decent enough pace. By the time the supply wagons arrived, it was almost midnight, and the men were hungry. It takes a long time to cook large slabs of meat, so the baron had them cut it up into smaller, faster cooking pieces.

Beverly helped distribute the food and ensured everyone got their fair share. The usual grumbling quickly subsided, and the men finally bedded down for the night.

The next morning came far too early, but Beverly had the knights ready to march. They were walking their horses towards the road, before mounting, when she saw Dame Hayley. She was coming in from the south, from the direction of the rest of the army and Beverly veered from her path to intercept her.

"What news, Hayley?" she called out.

"I've just returned from the rest of the army. I'm afraid it's not doing well."

"How so?" asked Beverly.

"They only managed to cover about ten miles yesterday, we gained almost a half day over them," the brunette replied. "I'm on my way to the princess to report."

"I'll join you," said Beverly, turning to the knights. "You men might as well rest the horses, it doesn't look like we'll be in much of a hurry. I'll return before the march begins."

They rode together to find the princess, who was just about to climb onto her horse. She turned as they approached and watched them both dismount. "You have news, Hayley?"

"Yes, Highness, though I won't call it good. The army is making little progress. I tried to talk to the Earl of Shrewesdale, but he was still asleep, and his guards wouldn't let me see him."

"And the rest of the army?" prompted Anna.

"In a similar state, I fear. I did manage to see his Royal Highness, the Prince, he was seated at a large table enjoying his breakfast. Marshal-General Valmar was with him. I tried to tell them they needed to get moving, but the marshal was adamant that it was his decision as to when the men would actually march."

"I see," said Anna. "Did you say Shrewesdale was behind us?"

"Yes, Highness."

"It was supposed to be Colbridge's brigade," she fumed, "This is an absolute disaster, if the enemy comes across us now, we'd be inviting defeat."

Gerald rode towards them, coming from the north, "The men are ready to march, Highness. Shall I give the command?"

Beverly looked over to see the princess staring off into the distance. She was deep in thought and those that knew her had learned better than to interrupt. At last, she brought her attention back to Gerald. "Please send my greetings to Lord Greycloak," she said, "and ask him to advance no more than ten miles. Once he has left, you may march, but only until you reach that limit. The rest of the army needs time to catch up. When they reach their destination, have them set up the camp and mark out areas for the other brigades."

Gerald nodded his head, "Aye, Highness, I'll see that it's taken care of."

"Beverly," continued Anna, "hold your knights here and don't march them until you see the lead columns coming up behind us, that'll give us a better idea of how they're doing. We shall have to match our progress to the rest of the army, or we'll be dangerously exposed."

They all nodded their understanding and then went their separate ways.

Beverly waited with her knights all through the long morning, but the column failed to appear. She conducted some drills to keep their minds occupied, but still, no sign came of the rest of the army. It was as if this small band of knights had been abandoned. Finally, in the early afternoon, she saw a distant dust cloud, the telltale sign of an army on the move. It took quite a while before they came into view.

The Earl of Shrewesdale commanded a force of some three hundred and fifty men, most of which were footmen. At the head of his brigade, the bowmen were moving quickly, but the rest of his men were armoured in chainmail, and Beverly observed them, red-faced and panting, as they were pushed along. There were knights, forming a thin line to either side of the column, running parallel to the road. It was only as they got closer that she realized that they were there to keep the men on the road from halting. Every now and then a knight would yell out at the footmen to keep up the pace or face punishment.

Beverly looked on with disgust at the Knights of Shrewesdale, for they had been responsible for her disgrace years ago. She ordered the Bodden Knights north on the road and was about to follow them when she spotted a familiar face. Telling them she would catch up, she rode over to see the huge knight with an axe strapped to his back.

"Sir Heward," she called out as she approached him.

The great man, startled by the call, looked over at her. He nodded in greeting as she got closer.

"How goes the march?" she asked.

A grim smile creased his heavily bearded face, the thick black hair all but hiding his mouth, "Not as well as I would have liked, Dame Beverly, though I hear your fortunes have risen."

"Indeed they have," she replied, "I am now a Knight of the Hound. I assume you still serve Lord Shrewesdale?"

"I do," he replied, though she thought she detected some contempt in his voice.

She leaned in closer so as not to be overheard, "Is there a problem I should know about?"

He glanced about, but the next nearest knight was out of earshot, "The earl is not the nicest man, as you're well aware. He's had the men marching for hours without a break."

Beverly was surprised, the earl was a cruel man, but even he must realize that the men needed rest if they were to fight eventually.

"I take it," she said, "his knights are here to keep the men in order?"

He nodded grimly, "Yes, there was a lot of grumbling this morning, the men were hungry."

"Hungry? Surely they were fed?"

"The earl believes the men should be able to fend for themselves. As a result, a number of them have begun raiding the local farms."

"Those are Mercerian farmers," Beverly said, shocked. "We can't go about raiding our own people, that'd make us worse than the rebels!"

"He is the Earl of Shrewesdale, one of the king's closest advisors," he replied. "Who would dare tell him otherwise?"

She immediately saw the problem. "I'll mention it to the princess, and perhaps she will have some way to influence him."

"I doubt it," the big man replied, "but you're more than welcome to mention it, just don't tell her it came from me."

"I won't," she promised.

The ride back to the brigade gave Beverly time to mull over her options. The princess would not be impressed with the news, that much she was sure of. What she would do about it was a whole new problem.

She caught up with her knights in time to see the rest of her brigade coming into view. The camp was just being set up, and Hayley had been busy planting sticks to mark out the camping areas for each unit. The knights dutifully trotted to their assigned area while Beverly rode over to the command tent.

Gerald was talking with her father, while Anna was looking over a map, spread out over a collapsible table. The whole scene reminded her of a miniature version of the map room in Bodden. She stepped gingerly over the sleeping Tempus who opened one eye to look at her, and then closed it again.

"Your Highness," she said, nodding to Anna.

"Beverly, you have news of the other brigades?"

"I do, Highness, though I don't think you'll like it. They march, but the men don't look happy. The earl hasn't issued any food to them."

"How can that be? Doesn't he expect them to eat?"

"He expects them to live off the land, Ma'am."

Gerald and Fitz stopped their conversation at the words. "Surely," said Fitz, "he's not that stupid?"

Beverly looked at her father, he was only saying what they were all thinking. "I heard those words from one of his knights," she said frankly.

"What are we to do about it?" asked Gerald.

Anna pulled a sheet of paper from beneath her map, "We can't do anything yet, we have our own problems getting food, thanks to the disorganized supply train." She looked at Gerald and Fitz, "You two have done an amazing job of organizing the supplies, but the congestion on the road is proving troublesome. Unfortunately, there's not much we can do about it. Once we have our own supplies in hand, we can perhaps do something about the earl's lack of planning."

It was not what Beverly had hoped, but it would have to do. Better to get our affairs in order first, she thought.

They made plans for the next day's march. Hayley rode out with some Elves to pick out the next campsite and thankfully, there was still no sign of the rebel earl's army.

Dawn came early, but supply wagons had arrived early the evening before, giving each man time to cook more food than required. This, they would carry with them, in case of further supply problems.

The camp was awash with the sounds of the morning as soldiers ate and dressed for the journey. Tents were disassembled and placed back on the wagons. Baron Fitzwilliam had seen fit to buy up what tents he could for the army, and the men appreciated the use of them, for overnight there had been a light rain, and the field was wet.

The Bodden Knights were just finishing when Beverly noticed a rider approaching. As he drew closer, she saw it was Sir Heward, and he appeared to be in a hurry. She waved at him, and he altered course, riding towards her.

"Dame Beverly," he said, "I must see the princess at once. Will you take me to her?"

"Of course," she replied.

She led him in silence towards the command tent. Anna was finishing her orders as they approached, while others were taking apart the shelter.

"Your Highness," said Beverly, "Sir Heward asks for an audience, he's one of the earl's knights."

"Of course," Anna said, "What can I do for you, Sir Heward?"

The tall knight looked down at his feet before talking, "I'm afraid I must ask you for help, Your Highness," he said.

"How so?"

He raised his gaze to meet the young princess's eyes, "The earl's troops are refusing to march until they're fed," he said.

"And rightly so," said Anna. "How is that a problem?"

"I'm afraid the earl has ordered his knights to force them to march."

"Who else knows of this?" she asked.

"He sent me to assemble the knights," Sir Heward continued, "I am to take them to the campsite and force the soldiers to march."

"You mean kill some men and force the others to march?"

"Yes, Highness, I thought it might be better to come here first."

Anna tapped her chin absently with her fingers, "I would suggest you return to your knights and assemble them," she said. "You might want to take the long way and take your time going to the campsite. We shall see if we can't solve the issue before you arrive."

Sir Heward bowed deeply, "Thank you, Your Highness," he said, "I shall do as you have suggested."

"Beverly," said Anna, "you and Fitz come with me. Gerald, you have command until I return."

"Yes, Highness," replied Gerald, "I'll see to it."

It took less time than Beverly thought it would to ride to the Earl of Shrewesdale's brigade. They had camped in an open field around a loose collection of fires. As the three riders approached, Beverly watched the men gathering in small groups, holding firmly onto their weapons. These men were expecting a fight.

Anna stopped short of the men and dismounted, walking towards the soldiers. She strode towards the nearest fire and warmed her hands.

"It's a cold morning, isn't it," she said to no one in particular.

There was some grumbling from the soldiers, but none advanced towards her.

She was looking around the camp as she spoke, and her eyes rested on a distant wagon. She smiled and turned to face the men. "I'm told you have not been provided with food, is this correct?"

Heads nodded, though no one spoke up.

"What's that wagon over there?" she asked, looking across the fire.

"That belongs to the earl," said one of the men.

"Dame Beverly," she said, "come with me."

They walked over to the wagon and peeled back the tarp that covered its contents. Hidden beneath was the carcass of a freshly killed cow, along with a sack full of bread and some blocks of cheese. Beverly spied a large barrel of wine and a box containing some handpicked vintages. She looked at the princess who merely nodded her approval.

"You," shouted Beverly, "come and take this food, distribute it as best you can. Make sure you cut it up into smaller pieces, or you'll be cooking all day."

She began pulling out the bread, tossing it to the crowd that was quickly forming. The noise level rapidly increased as soldiers realized what was happening, until the cheering was drowning out individual voices. Off to the side, Beverly saw a trio of knights approaching and moved to intercept them.

"What's going on here?" one of them demanded. "That's the earl's property. You'll be hung for this."

"You'd have to take that up with Princess Anna," said Beverly, pointing at the wagon, "she's right over there."

She followed them over to Anna, who was waiting patiently for their arrival. The crowd quieted, and the distribution of food suddenly halted as each man paused to see the outcome of this encounter.

One knight stepped forward, ready to speak, but Anna interrupted them, "I believe it's proper to bow when addressing royalty," she reminded him.

The man was caught unprepared, and Beverly witnessed indecision forming on his face. He finally bowed, and then spoke.

"Your Highness, the earl will not be pleased. These men have stolen his property and they must be punished."

"Let's go and see the earl, shall we?" she said. "Do lead on gentlemen, I have a few choice words in mind."

They turned to lead her to the earl's tent, Beverly and her father following along behind.

Upon entry, the knight walked over to the earl, who was seated and whispered in his ear.

The earl stood up, his face growing red as he did so. "What is the meaning of this?" he demanded.

Baron Fitzwilliam spoke, "You should address the princess as Your Highness, Lord."

Shrewesdale looked at the baron and then took a breath, "Your Highness," he said in a calmer voice, "it is not your place to interfere with the running of my brigade. You have overstepped the bounds of your authority, and I must protest."

"Of course, Lord Montrose," said Anna, "shall we go to Prince Henry and talk to him about it? I'm sure my brother is a reasonable person."

Shrewesdale looked at her and gulped, as the realization of his position hit him like a brick wall. "I...hardly think that's necessary, Highness," he corrected himself. "Perhaps I have overreacted. Still, I would appreciate you coming to me before issuing any commands to my men."

"Oh, but they are the king's men," said Anna. She turned to Beverly, "Tell me again, Dame Beverly, who is the king?"

Beverly strained to hide her smile, "Your father, Highness."

The young princess turned back to the earl. "My father's soldiers have to fight a battle soon against the Earl of Eastwood. They can't very well do that if they haven't been fed, so let me be clear about this. You will ensure you properly feed the men, or I will see to it that both my brother and my father are aware of your incompetence. Is that clear?"

To hear such authoritative words come from such a small girl startled Beverly, and she saw a look of surprise on her father's face as well.

THIRTY-SEVEN

The Enemy Stands

SPRING 960 MC

～

Beverly could not believe it had taken six long days of marching to meet the enemy. Mind you, they had not travelled very far each day, for only the Princess's brigade was up and ready to go at the break of dawn. The soldiers' campfires blazed as the setting sun brought the darkness to life. There would be a battle come morning and then, prayed Beverly, the whole rebellion would be crushed, and the Earl of Eastwood either killed or brought to the king for justice.

His men were camped to the east of the road, looking west. Tomorrow, the king's army opposed them with better than two to one odds. Beverly was suspicious. She looked at the men in the distance and wondered what the earl was planning, for surely he would have been better to retreat to Eastwood and defend from within the city rather than face a foe that outnumbered him.

She was pondering that very thought when a voice interrupted her.

"I suppose you're used to this," said Hayley.

Beverly turned at the sound of her voice, "I see you've strung your longbow, expecting trouble?"

"I don't believe in taking chances," she said. "You never know when the enemy might try a raid."

"We've got pickets up," said Beverly defensively.

"Oh I know," the brunette replied, "but the same can't be said for the rest of the army."

Beverly was startled, could this be true? She shook her head, not really surprised, "If it were up to Valmar, we'd snatch defeat from the jaws of victory."

"Pardon me?" said Hayley. "I don't understand."

"Well, you didn't hear it from me, but the consensus is that Marshal-General Valmar is incompetent."

"Surely not, he's the marshal-general!"

Beverly shook her head and put her hand on Hayley's shoulder, "I'm afraid you've a lot to learn about being in an army. Valmar only commands because he's the king's friend. No one has ever accused him of being a strategist."

Hayley looked across the field. The sun had finally sunk to the west, and the long shadows had disappeared to be replaced by the darkness. Lights had sprung up across the field, and she watched as even more were lit. "There's a lot of them," she said, more to herself.

Beverly turned back to look, "Not as many as you might think, we outnumber them by a significant amount. It has to be a trap."

"A trap?"

"Yes, only a fool would stand and fight here when they're so outnumbered. We must find the princess, she'll want to know."

"Actually, that's why I'm here. Prince Henry has summoned a war council. The princess wants you with her when she goes."

Beverly's eyes went wide, "You should have told me sooner, this is important."

"It's all right, she sent for your father as well, and he's some distance off. You won't be leaving in a hurry."

Marshal-General Roland Valmar lifted the bottle of liquor and scrutinized its contents. "It'll all be over this time tomorrow, Your Highness. Would you care for a drink?" He held the bottle up towards the young prince, but Henry shook his head.

"You're very calm, Marshal-General, I can't say I share the sentiment."

"Nonsense, Highness," he said, "we outnumber the enemy, all that's left is to march forward tomorrow and give him the drumming he deserves. We'll present his head to your father, that'll please His Majesty." He chuckled at the thought.

The tent flap opened, and the servant indicated the others had arrived.

"Well, Highness, it seems it's your time to shine. The leaders are all here."

"Lead on, Valmar," Prince Henry said and followed him into the large tented area.

The Army commanders were sitting patiently awaiting the prince's arrival. Valmar was shocked to see the young princess present. He had gone out of his way to ensure that she did not receive an invitation, but he nodded his head in recognition. His eyes fell upon her knight, the red-headed Fitzwilliam bitch that he so detested. He scowled as Prince Henry began talking.

"We are poised on the brink of a great victory," he was saying. "Tomorrow, we shall defeat the rebellion once and for all and bring the Earl of Eastwood to justice. I now turn it over to the marshal-general to detail the orders."

The group nodded, and Valmar took his place at the head of the table that held the roughly sketched map of the area.

He took a moment to look at the map with a grave face, as if he were thinking deeply. "The enemy," he began, "has deployed here," he pointed with his finger, "but he has left himself vulnerable. We shall commence the attack at first light and finish with him by noon."

It was Baron Fitzwilliam who spoke next, "Marshal-General, I wonder if you might enlighten us with the plan for the attack?"

Valmar looked at the ageing man and sighed inwardly. The baron was said to have some influence amongst the nobility, he'd best treat him with respect. "Of course, Baron," he replied. "We shall engage an assault along his entire front with our heavy infantry. He won't stand. He's been on the run and his men are already defeated. One firm push and his army will disintegrate.

"Are you telling me," said the young princess, "that your plan is to simply advance the whole army to engage the enemy?"

Valmar smiled in his most condescending manner, "That is precisely what I'm saying, Highness. To those of us skilled in the art of war, the answer is obvious. His men are worn out, desperate, they'll crack the instant we engage them."

The princess looked at Baron Fitzwilliam, and Valmar saw an understanding pass between them. This must be put to rest quickly, he thought.

"While I understand your interest, Highness," he said, "you should respectively leave the matters of war to the more capable of us."

She turned to the baron, "How many battles have I been in, Baron?"

"Two, Your Highness," he replied.

"And how many of those did I win?"

"Both of them, Highness," said the baron with a grave face.

"That's right, I must have forgotten. And tell me, Lord Fitzwilliam, how many battles have you been in?"

"I'm afraid too many to count," he smiled.

"And how many of those did you win?"

"Why...all of them, Your Highness."

"Oh yes," she continued, "that's right. How many battles have you been in, Marshal-General?"

Her eyes bore into him, and Valmar felt his chest tighten. This was not going the way he had planned, and now he sought help, casting his eyes around the room in a panic, finally landing on the Earl of Shrewesdale who was busy staring daggers at the princess's bodyguard. "Lord Shrewesdale," he said, "is something wrong?"

The earl tore his eyes from his target to look at Valmar, "Excuse me, Marshal-General, but I must take offense at the presence of this...this person." He pointed at Dame Beverly Fitzwilliam. "This harlot is not fit to be in the company of the prince, and her presence offends all here."

The knight's face reddened, and Valmar saw his chance to deflect the question of his battle experience. "I believe you're right, my lord. But perhaps we should let the prince decide?" He turned to look at Prince Henry. The young man was about to drink from his glass, and he paused as all eyes fell on him.

"I beg your pardon?" he simply said.

"Your father's good friend, the earl, was saying that this knight is not welcome here. Would you agree?" He stared at Henry, knowing the young man would cave in for he was easily influenced. Valmar had taken great pains over the last few days to share the high regard in which the king held him, his hand-picked marshal-general of the army.

"Yes, of course," Henry agreed hastily, "I suppose it's for the best, we don't want to be distracted."

"She's not going anywhere," said Princess Anna, "she's my bodyguard!"

"You are young, Highness," said Valmar, emboldened by his grip on her brother. "This tent is not the proper place for women."

He turned to face Henry in a dramatic fashion. This time he only raised his eyebrows.

"Yes, very well, Anna, you're not needed here, do as the marshal-general says."

"Don't be a fool, Henry," she bit back, "it's a trap. The enemy is trying to lure us in. If we attack tomorrow we'll play right into his hands, can't you see?"

"That's enough!" yelled Valmar. The room fell silent, and he saw the opportunity to remove another detractor. "Baron Fitzwilliam, would you be so kind as to escort the princess back to her encampment?"

"I want a representative at the table," she demanded.

"I'd be more than willing to accept one, provided it's not her," Valmar said, pointing at Dame Beverly.

The princess turned to someone standing behind her and told him to step forward. The red-headed knight slowly took out her sword and passed it to the princess hilt first.

Valmar heard some gasps from the other nobles and moved forward to get a better view. She was speaking quietly, and then the man knelt. "I dub thee Knight of the Hound," she said, "arise, Sir Arnim Caster."

Valmar looked on in disbelief. It was her prerogative to knight whom she pleased, but he was shocked by her choice. As it sank in, he began to laugh. Captain Arnim Caster, the man that Valmar had sent to guard her, the man who worked for him, was her choice to be her representative.

The princess turned to him with a defiant look on her face. "Will that do?" she asked.

"Oh yes," he agreed, "that will do nicely."

"The man is a complete idiot," Anna fumed.

"Agreed," said Beverly, "but what do we do about it?"

"We find proof it's a trap."

"And how do we do that?"

"Tell me, Beverly, what would you do if you were the Earl of Eastwood?"

"I would high tail it back to Eastwood and make us siege the city."

"And under what circumstances would you stand and fight?"

"I wouldn't," said Beverly, and then began to think, "unless I had reinforcements coming."

Anna smiled, "And to do the most damage, where would you have these extra troops arrive?"

Beverly looked westward towards the Deerwood. "I would bring them through that. They'd arrive at our rear for maximum effect."

"Precisely," said Anna. "We need eyes in that wood with some idea of what kind of force we're dealing with."

"With your permission, Highness, I'll go," said Beverly.

The young girl looked at her champion, and Beverly saw indecision written across her face.

"I'll take Hayley," Beverly said, "she can track. We'll be back before morning. We'll learn what's out there."

Anna looked at Gerald, who nodded. "Very well," she said at last, "but be careful, we don't know what to expect."

Beverly looked at Hayley, who nodded her assent. They left the camp a few moments later with their gear.

They rode to the edge of the woods and dismounted. It was approaching midnight, and the full moon cast an eerie glow across the landscape. They entered on foot, the thick foliage clinging to their legs as they made their way through the dense underbrush.

"I have a hard time believing an army could get through this," said Beverly.

"You'd be surprised what an experienced woodsman can do," said Hayley. "They've probably got some guides leading them, and there's bound to be trails nearby we don't know about."

They moved on in silence, and within moments the dense canopy blocked out the moonlight. They waited for their eyes to adjust to the darkness before continuing. Tracking was impossible in the darkness, but an army meant people, and people make noise. If there were troops of any significant number in these woods, they were bound to hear them. They had paused for perhaps the seventh time when Beverly felt Hayley's hand on her arm pulling her down. She strained to hear something, and could just make out talking in the distance.

"Do you hear that?" Beverly whispered.

"Yes, but it sounds odd, we need to get closer."

"What do you mean it sounds odd?"

"I mean the voices sound like another language," said Hayley, "I need to get closer to identify it."

Beverly wasn't sure what this meant. Could it be Norlanders? Unlikely this far south, besides, they spoke the same language as Mercerians, though with an accent. No, this had to be something else.

They crept forward slowly. She followed Hayley, who seemed to glide quietly through the trees. Beverly was sure she was making a tremendous racket, but when she halted, she heard no challenge. The voices were now clearer, low and guttural. She didn't recognize the language and looked at Hayley, whose outline she could just barely discern in the darkness.

"Orcs," whispered Hayley. "They must have come out of the Artisan Hills."

"Why would Orcs help the earl?"

"Coins, most likely. They're not a rich people."

Beverly nodded in understanding, though she doubted Hayley could see her. She had never seen an Orc before, but she had heard of them. They were one of the Elder races, and they once had mighty cities scattered throughout the lands, but that was centuries ago. The race had devolved to the savage warriors that now lurked in the remote hills spread throughout the area.

The two women sat in silence, listening to the sounds echoing through the forest. Beverly strained to see any movement in the gloom. Soon, dark shapes came towards them, and then she heard Hayley curse.

"Damn, they've seen us. We'd better run for it."

The ranger turned to run, and Beverly drew her sword. "Get back to the camp and warn them. I'll delay them as long as I can. Besides, I'll never outrun them in the dark."

Hayley paused for just a moment, no doubt considering her options, but then Beverly heard her footfalls disappearing in the distance as she crashed through the woods.

A dark shape loomed in front of her, and she stabbed with her sword. The tip hit something soft, and she heard a grunt of pain. She was knocked sideways when a strike came out of the darkness, an axe scraping off of her upper arm. She crouched slightly, presenting a smaller target and swung a blow to her right. The blade passed through the thin air, but she heard an Orc jump back as she swung.

She concentrated on her hearing, listening to the sounds about her, judging their movements. A sudden rush to the left and then a low growl had her stepping back and swinging where she had been standing. Her blade glanced off of an Orc who surged past her. Backing up slowly, she hoped she was moving towards the edge of the forest. Her foot snapped a twig, and there was a sudden rush towards her. She jumped to the side and swung her sword in an overhead blow, feeling it dig deep into flesh, almost losing it as the mighty bulk tore past her. She wrenched the blade free just in time to parry a blow. More Orcs approached and they were no longer bothering to remain quiet. A strange keening sound erupted as the Orcs let out a battle cry with others further away taking up the call. Beverly, for once, was glad of the darkness, for she knew it hid her fear.

Orcs are bulkier than Humans, though not to a significant degree. It's not that they were taller, the average Orc only stood about six feet in height, but they had much broader shoulders and a more substantial chest. This gave them more strength, and she doubted that even her armour could stop an overhead axe strike.

She realized she was surrounded, the Orcs were all around her. Without a doubt, this was part of a bigger army. Her only job now was to hold them off long enough to allow Hayley to escape. She gripped her sword with new determination and prepared to die. A yell off to her left caught her attention, and then there was the sound of rushing feet. Orcs might be great warriors, but they are not subtle. She turned to what she thought was the edge of the wood and ran about twenty paces, rotating suddenly to her right. She ducked behind a tree, and she thought she saw a group of them rush past her. Were her eyes playing tricks on her? She gazed into the darkness and saw the outline of a tree. It was a vague outline, but she saw it, daybreak must be coming.

Ever so slowly the forest took form around her as the early light of day began to penetrate the woods, and she realized it was later than she had thought. She cast her eyes about, looking for something that might give her an edge, but couldn't see anything of use. She remained still, pressed against the tree while about her she heard the Orcs crashing through the forest, searching for her. Hearing a loud shout to her right, she turned in time to see a group of three Orcs. One of them had seen her in the early morning light and had shouted his warning. Now the three of them descended on her position as they lifted their axes to strike her down.

She waited as they closed, carefully judging their speed. The lead Orc raised his axe, and she struck out with her sword, stabbing him in the stomach, then quickly stepped back around the tree. The creature howled and clutched himself but the other two, far wiser than their colleague, moved around the tree, one to either side. She ducked in time to see an axe dig deeply into the trunk and then she struck with her sword, a side arc slashing towards his knee, but the Orc was fast and stepped back to avoid the blow. She heard the other one swinging at her from behind, and she dove to the side, trying to put some distance between her and the deadly blade. She rolled to her feet and was up in an instant, her sword held in front of her.

The sound of the fight brought others, and soon all about her, she heard the crash of branches as Orcs rushed to her position. This was it, the final battle. All her life she had trained for combat, and now she put all her knowledge, all her expertise, to the test. She lunged forward, stabbing with the sword, the Orc backing up with the ferocity of the attack. She wheeled on a second Orc and saw the surprised look on his face as she dug the blade into his leg. The creature roared in pain and tried to step back, but collapsed on his injured limb. She ignored him and struck again at her first attacker, leaving cuts on his chest as he back-pedalled in an attempt to avoid her blows. She quickly glanced about and saw a ring of Orcs starting to form around her and knew her fate was sealed. These Orcs would trap her, wear her down, and then finish her off if she didn't do something soon. She saw a small gap in the ring and ran for it. An Orc moved to block her, and she leaped, striking him full in the chest with her knees. The large creature fell with a crash, and she bounded to her feet and ran, as fast as she could. She stopped only long enough to let out a loud whistle and then she turned to face her new pursuers.

There were some loose sticks by her feet, and she used her toe to throw them at her first opponent. As the Orc instinctively raised his arm to shield his eyes, she swung her sword. The blade scraped along his forearm, and he let out a yell, staggering to the side. His companion rush'd forward, bellowing, and struck with his axe, but she sidestepped to avoid the blow and then brought her blade down on the axe's shaft, splintering it. The Orc drew it back up and swung it in a high arc, but the axe head flew off the handle to disappear amongst the trees.

Beverly took another step backwards and prepared to fend off more blows. The Orcs were all coming for her, and she needed to buy more time. She lunged forward, causing the first Orcs to slow, but instead of attacking, she backed up again. The Orcs grew frustrated and yelled and screamed at her. Another Orc rushed forward, this time stabbing with a spear. She side-stepped the thrust and brought her blade down on his back as he ran by her. A blow struck her, but Aldwin's backplate saved her. She staggered forward with the force of it, striking out wildly with her sword to keep them at bay.

Again and again, they kept at her, swinging their axes and driving her backwards. She was getting tired, and as she stepped back, she tripped and fell, landing with a crash into the dead branches that lay scattered throughout the woods. An Orc stepped forward to deal the killing blow, but she rolled to the side, and hearing the crack as the axe sliced through the branches, quickly stood up.

She stabbed again and again, for they were now pressing so close there was no room to swing her sword. Step, thrust, backstep, side thrust, over and over she repeated the moves, her continuous training saving her from having to think about her defence. She felt the energy leaving her and knew the end was close. Backed up against a tree, she was surrounded. This was her final stand.

The Orcs suddenly gave way, and she found herself with room to move. She felt the fog of fatigue and couldn't quite make sense of it, then she saw her saviour. Lightning, her ever loyal steed, had heard her whistle and had come running. The Orcs had backed up at the sound of the approaching horse, and now it ran right up to her. She didn't think twice but grabbed the saddle as he rode past, hanging on for dear life. They tore their way through the woods, snapping branches left and right, but she was safe, the sound of Orc curses dwindling in the distance.

. . .

Marshal-General Valmar took another sip of the excellent wine from his own vineyards. He held it to the light, the early morning sun making the glass sparkle. It looked to be an auspicious day. The army would crush the rebel earl, and he would travel back to Wincaster as the victorious leader. Perhaps he might even get that which he had so long coveted, a title. He imagined himself as a baron but then shook it off, his victory would surely make a higher title more appropriate. Perhaps the king might make him the new Earl of Eastwood?

His thoughts were interrupted by the sound of approaching footsteps. He turned with irritation to see Princess Anna approaching with her entourage. "Ah, here it comes again," he said under his breath. "Princess, what can I do for you?"

"We are in grave danger, Marshal-General, there is another army in the woods behind us, we are surrounded and outnumbered."

"Nonsense," said Valmar, "they're just there to fool us. The real enemy is down there," he pointed absently with his glass.

Prince Henry came into view, and Valmar was about to say something when the princess stepped forward suddenly, knocking the glass from his hand.

"The Orcs are forming up outside the woods even as we speak. If we don't do something soon, it'll be the end of us."

"What's this?" said Henry, "Orcs?"

"Nothing that needs concern you, Your Highness," Valmar said, trying to gain control of the situation. "It's all looked after. Besides, who's in charge here?"

Henry looked from Valmar to Anna, and the marshal-general saw the prince's jaw clenching.

"He is the marshal-general, Anna," he said, "Father trusts him."

Valmar smiled, his influence over the young prince almost complete. "There, you see? Your brother wants me in command."

He turned to smirk at the princess but suddenly felt light-headed. Before he knew it, he was letting out a rather large yawn and collapsed to the ground.

Anna turned to Revi, "Is it serious?" she asked.

The mage bent down over Marshal-General Valmar, "I'm afraid it looks like the sleeping sickness, Your Highness, he might be out for some time."

"How long?"

"At least four hours," he said, and then added, in a lower voice, "even longer if I do a second casting."

Anna stifled her smile and turned to face her brother with a more serious demeanour, "I'm afraid the marshal-general is quite ill, Henry."

Henry started at the marshal-general with a blank look. "But he's in charge of the army, who will give the orders?"

"You're the commander of the army, Henry, not Valmar. YOU will lead them."

"I've never led an army before, I'm not ready. This is all so sudden."

"Henry," said Anna, "you have to take command, there's no time for this."

The prince looked at his youngest sister, pleading in his eyes. "I can't think. What can I do, Alfred died fighting the Earl. I have no battle experience, I can't be the man responsible for losing the crown. Father would crucify me.

"I know what to do," Anna said firmly. "Give me the authority, and I'll take command."

Henry stared at her a moment. Beverly could see the turmoil raging in his eyes.

"You've led in battle before," he said. "I cede command of the army to you."

Princess Anna turned to face the others, "Lord Fitzwilliam, you will command the army that meets the earl. You've fought before, pick the minimum troops you will need for the job. The rest will turn to face our new threat.

"Yes, Highness," said the baron, "and who will command the other troops?"

"That group will be commanded by Gerald, I have complete trust in him."

There were surprised looks around the room. Placing a commoner in charge of the troops was just not done.

Anna broke the silence, "We haven't got much time. Baron, you have command over the Earl of Shrewesdale and the Duke of Colbridge by Royal Decree. If either one complains, send them to me. Detail off the troops you can spare to Gerald, we need them in position as quickly as possible. As soon as Beverly gets back, she'll join Gerald's group."

They dispersed quickly, save for Gerald, who approached Anna, "Are you sure about this? I've never commanded an army before."

She stood in front of him, placing her hand on his shoulder. It was a strange scene, had anybody witnessed it, this young girl giving comfort to a veteran soldier. "I have faith in you, Gerald. You've always been there for me when I needed you. Remember our battle of the mighty weeds? This is just like that, only with a few more enemies thrown in." They both smiled at the memories of the past and knew that no matter what the future brought, they would always be there for each other. Gerald placed his hand over hers, and simply said, "Thank you, Anna."

Gerald left the tent and ran to catch up to Baron Fitzwilliam. The battle for the crown was about to commence.

THIRTY-EIGHT

The Battle for the Crown

SPRING 960 MC

~

B everly sat upon Lightning, leading her troops, while the infantry moved into position. They were in dire straits. While last evening they outnumbered the enemy, now they were trapped between the earl to the east and the Orc army to the west.

"Dame Beverly," called out Gerald, "are your men ready?"

"Yes, sir," she responded formally. She knew he had led men before, even recently, but now he held a grave responsibility. If they lost this fight, they would all die, for the earl would likely not take prisoners.

He moved to stand beside Lightning, casting his eyes once again over the men and Dwarves who took up their positions. She watched him, detecting the lines of worry etched on his face.

"It will work, you know," she tried to ease his anxiety.

He looked up at her, "I hope so, for it's the only chance we have. You remember your orders, Dame Beverly?"

"Yes," she bit back her anger. He had asked her three times what her orders were, but she realized he was just nervous. "You know, you can just call me Beverly," she offered in an attempt to diffuse the air of tension that encircled them.

Gerald humphed, making an unintelligible sound. "That wouldn't be proper," he said at last.

Beverly smiled, some things never changed. "I'll see you soon," she said. "Don't forget the signal."

She gave the command, and the knights started moving. The army was set up parallel to the south road, with a line of troops on either side. The horsemen gathered speed, and soon they were heading south towards Wincaster. One of Shrewesdale's knights, a man named Sir Bartholomew, grumbled behind her, and then a familiar voice roared out, "Shut up, you disgrace for a man, we ride to glory." It was Sir Heward, The Axe, perhaps the one man in Shrewesdale's knights who knew his business.

She had expected trouble when Gerald had asked for Lord Montrose's knights, but Prince Henry had been quite persuasive, and now they joined the other knights under her command. The Duke of Colbridge had gladly given up his knights, but the Bodden Knights had been needed by her father. Even now, as they rode to the south, she worried that her father might face defeat at the hands of the Earl of Eastwood.

The plan had been worked out in the early morning light, even as the Orcs emerged from the distant wood. Her father would face off against the Earl of Eastwood, using the bulk of the army to knock him out of the battle as quickly as possible, while Gerald would fight a holding action against the Orcs until the earl was defeated. It was a risky plan, for Gerald only commanded a small force. He had placed the Dwarves, with their arbalest's in-between his footman. The Elves had been required to aid against the Earl of Eastwood, but the hope was that they could redeploy rapidly to the rear when needed.

It was Gerald who had come up with the strategy for the knights. He suspected that the Orcs lacked cavalry, so they sent the knights south. Hopefully, the enemy would think they were fleeing, or they might redeploy troops to cover them. In either case, it was only a ruse for their real orders. They would ride out of sight and then watch for the signal to return. Beverly would be riding back into the middle of a battle, and would have to choose where to attack based on the situation when she arrived, for there was no telling how the Orcs would fight.

Sir Heward rode up beside her, "The men, they don't mean anything by it, they're just letting off steam."

She turned on him with a steely glare, "Is that why they tried to rape me? To let off steam? There's no excuse for their behaviour."

The Axe stared back, "I might remind you that not all the knights participated, there's still some good men amongst them."

Her face softened, "You're right, Sir Heward, I cannot hold them all to blame for the actions of a few."

"It'll take a firm hand to lead them today, but you have that ability, Dame Beverly," he said.

"I wish I was as sure. I've never led this many into battle before, I'm usually just leading a company. Will they follow me?"

He was silent for a moment before responding, "Aye, they'll follow you, to the gates of the Underworld, if needed. They're ashamed of the stain that a few put on their name. The Knights of Shrewesdale used to mean something. They're eager to erase the past."

"The past cannot be erased," she said. "Believe me, I've tried. We must accept what is done, and move on. Punishment will come to those who deserve it."

She studied Sir Heward's face, he was struggling with something.

Finally, he spoke, "I've seen to it that a number of knights will lead the charge, names you might be familiar with." He retrieved a folded piece of paper from his glove and handed it to her.

"These are the men who attacked me," she remarked.

"Yes, they've 'volunteered' to lead the charge. I'll be riding with the lot of them to make sure they don't run."

She tried to gauge his reaction, "Volunteered? You mean voluntold."

"Some might interpret it that way, but in any case, what does it matter? They will serve the crown and likely get what's coming to them."

"Take care of yourself, Sir Heward, your loss would be greater than all those names put together."

"Oh, I fully intend to, Dame Beverly. I have no wish to die today, but if I must, then so be it."

~

Baron Fitzwilliam began the battle conventionally, by deploying his archers in front as a line of skirmishers. They peppered the enemy infantry to no significant effect, and soon the enemy cavalry appeared, threatening them. This was merely a game of strategy. He was testing the Earl of Eastwood's responses, and they were just as expected. Fitz's next step was to counter the earl's cavalry with a display of his own. He had contemplated this carefully and had derived a plan he thought would surprise the enemy. The earl's cavalry were mostly light troops, enough to harass the archers, but not enough to threaten the carefully arranged lines of footmen. The baron deployed the Knights of Bodden, sending the men with explicit orders, they were to taunt the enemy horse, then pull back to the allied line.

He watched from his vantage point as his knights made their way into the gap between the armies. Would the earl take his bait?

After a brief clash of steel, the enemy horse rode back for their lines, the Bodden Knights in pursuit. Just before his men reached the lines, the rebel's deployed their own knights, for the temptation was just too enticing. Apparently, the earl intended to eliminate the Bodden Knights with his superior force. Usually, knights were held till the decisive moment, but the baron had committed them early. The enemy lines opened up, and the earl's knights surged forth, outnumbering their adversaries by a considerable margin.

Now was the moment of truth. Would the Bodden Knights keep their discipline? He held his breath as he watched, and then exhaled as he saw them turn with precision, making for their own lines. The enemy knights picked up their pace, and it appeared as if the men of Bodden would be overwhelmed. Just as his knights neared the allied lines, they suddenly swerved, riding parallel to the footmen. Fitz gave the command and the Elves, forming the second rank, stepped forward and unleashed a hail of arrows.

Knights are well armoured, but an Elven bow, fired at point-blank range will puncture even the best of armour. With a noise like a sudden hailstorm, the earl's knights were decimated. Horses fell to the ground, crushing their riders. They screamed, both Human and equine, with only about half a dozen riders remaining mounted after the onslaught. The carnage was shocking, but Fitz knew he must strike while the forge was hot. He gave the order, and the infantry advanced, the Elves moving to the flanks. With the enemy knights eliminated, the attack would now commence in full.

∾

"Your Highness, I must object. You are too exposed here," Arnim was adamant.

"There IS no safe place, Sir Arnim, so I might as well make my stand here with Commander Matheson."

"But you are essential to the battle, if you should fall-"

"Then there are others that will take my place," she wheeled on the man. "I appreciate that you're doing your job, but I must be allowed to do mine. The prince is with Baron Fitzwilliam. My presence is needed here."

The sound of chanting drew their attention, and she turned to look at the men formed up in front of her. Her horse gave her the height advantage she needed to see clearly, but as she looked, she silently wished her view was blocked. The entire horizon had turned into one solid line of green-skinned Orcs. They were chanting something, and though she didn't understand the language, the intent was clear, they were coming for blood.

"Hayley, tell me again what you know about Orcs and how they fight?"

"They don't wear much armour, they don't have to, their skin is thick.

They can still be wounded, but a wound that would hobble a man will typically just make an Orc more irritable."

"That's just what we need," said Anna, "irritable Orcs."

"They're impressed by skill. If we impress them enough, they might retire from the field," Hayley offered.

"Really?"

"No, I was just trying to make you feel better. I'm afraid it's more of an 'us or them' moment."

"A fight to the death, then?"

"I'm afraid so."

They sat in silence as the princess digested the news. She watched Gerald riding back and forth behind the troops, uttering words of encouragement. She knew it was all for show, but she had seen the effect it had on the men. After only two battles he had become known as a commander who cared for his men, who took every precaution to protect them. They responded with loyalty, and she knew at that moment that they would hold the line or die trying.

The Orcs began to move, one vast mass flooding across the field, covering the ground like a horde of ants.

"Steady," yelled Gerald. "Steady men, hold your line."

The closer they came, the louder their chants grew until they were deafening. The Dwarves fired off their arbalests, and the front line of green attackers went down. If the princess hoped it would slow their advance, she was sorely disappointed, for the Orcs merely leaped over their fallen comrades and continued the charge. Their chants were replaced with blood-curdling screams as the swarm drew closer.

"Brace yourselves," Gerald yelled just before the Orcs crashed loudly into the shield wall. A tremendous noise as axes tried to smash their way through the shields of the defenders. The shield wall had its weakness, and it was the legs of the defenders. The Orcs soon discovered this, and the line threatened to disintegrate as legs and feet were impaled by spears. The Dwarves rushed forward, crouching, using their shields to protect the legs of the Humans in this gigantic struggle that had emerged. Gerald held his breath as the line was pushed back slightly, but it held. All along it, men and Dwarves were hacking at the beasts that had previously exploited the shield wall's flaw. He saw Orcs go down. The occasional Human fell victim to the attackers, but their comrades stepped in to replace them, holding the shield wall intact. It was like seeing a vision of the Underworld, where men lined up to be slaughtered. His men were pushed back further as they gave up ground to protect themselves from the onslaught. Gerald saw a threat and reacted instantly. "Sir Arnim," he yelled, "bring the bodyguard, they're about to envelop our right flank."

The line had held, but as men fell, it shrank down so that the front became shorter and shorter. Now the Orcs who massed on the right flank had overlapped their defence. A large Orc wearing the skull of an enormous creature was yelling, pointing his staff in the direction of the weakened end of the line.

Revi gesticulated, and the Orc fell over backwards with no sign of injury. Another Orc somehow catapulted himself over the soldiers' heads to land beside the mage, who was entirely taken by surprise. He looked in fear as the large creature swung his mighty axe above his head. The Axe whistled as it passed through the air, and then the Orc collapsed, an arrow through his head. Revi cast his eyes about to see Dame Hayley, her longbow in hand.

Gerald rushed to the flank, driving his mount into the Orcs. He must buy time for the bodyguard to fall into line. In front of him, the Orcs gave way from his mad dash until he heard the yelling behind him. He turned in the saddle to see Arnim joining in the defence, his troops locking their shields together. Gerald suddenly lurched forward as his horse's legs were chopped out from beneath it. The mount fell, screaming in agony and he leaped from the saddle to avoid being pinned beneath its body. The Orcs surged forward, spurred on by his horse's demise, and now he was fighting for his life.

∾

Beverly sat with her knights waiting for the signal. It was nerve-wracking, she heard the sound of battle and knew that men were dying, but everything depended on timing. The horses were all restless, somehow aware that they would be needed to spring into action on short notice. She looked around at the faces of her knights. The experienced ones were sitting calmly, waiting for the coming storm. The untested knights cast their eyes about nervously, not knowing what to expect. She knew many of them would not survive the day and wondered who these brave men were. Sir Heward brought her back from her thoughts with a tap on her arm.

"Is that the signal?" he asked.

She looked to the north to see an arrow streaking into the sky, a flaming arrow that trailed smoke as it climbed. "That's it," she said, then turned to the men. "It's time to do our part, the fate of the kingdom lies in our hands. Onward!"

She started north at a trot, then turned off the road, heading northwest, hoping to come into the enemy's rear. Time appeared to slow down, and she resisted the urge to move faster. Speeding up would tire the horses, and their energy was needed for the charge. Slowly, at an agonizing pace, the noise of battle grew closer. They topped a rise, and she finally saw the action spread out below them in the shallow valley. She watched the two fights, a mere observer at the moment. Her father, to the east, was engaging the enemy line, but the more immediate danger was the green swarm that threatened to engulf the defenders to the west. She halted the knights and ordered them to form-up. It took forever to assemble the knights, very few of them had fought with this type of discipline, and she cursed the very system that the nobility had built. What she really needed was professional cavalry, but she must deal with what she had. Now if only they could maintain the line as they advanced, and reserve their pent-up energy for the last possible moment before impact when they would unleash the full power of mounted knights.

They began the descent into the valley, maintaining their formation. They would strike the enemy from the flanks and rear, cutting down as many as they could. The knights picked up speed, and soon the jangle of the chainmail combined with the horse's hooves drowned out all other sounds. The thunder increased as the horses gained momentum and the Orcs turned to the approaching noise. The very air seemed to shake with the reverberations. Beverly focused on the enemy in front. The charge was committed, there was no turning back now.

The press of knights hit the Orcs like surf on a beach, easily flooding past the front line but slowing down the further they went. There were no formed lines here, just an endless mass of Orcs. Swords rose and fell, blood flew from weapons, knights from high above slaying Orcs everywhere. She saw one knight go down, Orc axes spraying blood as they hacked their victim to bits. Order disappeared as the charge spent itself, becoming a battle for individual survival.

Beverly blocked a fearsome swing with her shield, her arm numbed by the impact. Her sword pierced flesh as she swung out in retaliation. She turned and swung over the back of her saddle, an Orc jumping back to avoid the attack. Another leaped forward to take his place, and she struck him down with an overhead swing. Her shield was nearly ripped from her arm, and she wheeled to see two Orcs attempting to pull her from the saddle. Releasing the shield, they fell back with a crash, while she manoeuvred Lightning to rear up then come crashing down, his hooves driving into the hapless enemy. During this, she transferred her sword to her left hand and gripped her hammer with her right. As Lightning landed, so too did her hammer, penetrating an Orc's helmet, driving into his head.

All around her, axes and spears were striking at her. She parried and thrust, blocking weapons and hitting flesh, but knew that she could not keep this up forever. She urged her mount forward and swivelled her horse to body block an opponent, tumbling them to the ground, taking two others with him. Again and again, she struck, raining blows down on any Orc within striking distance. She felt the prick of a spear as it penetrated her left leg, and looked down to see a spear stuck in her shin guard. The armour had saved her leg, only to have the tip jammed between her limb and the guard, but now the weight of the spear threatened to unbalance her. She struck down with her sword in an attempt to knock it loose but only drew splinters of wood from its handle. An Orc gripped the shaft and yanked, and she felt herself being pulled off her mount. She kicked herself from the saddle with her free leg and yelled at Lightning to run.

Beverly hit the ground, the force of the impact taking her breath away. The spear shaft snapped as the Orc pulled it again and she rolled to the side to avoid the inevitable volley of spear thrusts. She staggered to her feet, realizing she was bleeding from a head wound. She must have hit her head in the fall, and now blood was running through her hair, threatening to obliterate her vision. Wrenching her helmet from her head, she tossed it aside and gripped her weapons, preparing for her final stand.

The Orcs now formed a ring around her, their spear tips pointed inward, preventing any possibility of escape. She took a moment to rip the spearhead from her armour, the enemy watching her closely. None of them advanced, and she wondered if they were going to try to capture her. She swore under her breath, vowing to fight to the end.

The fighting surrounded her, but the sounds were growing further away as the battle progressed. Did the line hold? Was the princess still alive? What of her father? All these thoughts came screaming into her mind, and she shook her head, loosening her hair from its customary braid.

She snarled and stepped forward, striking the spear tips with her sword, then stepped back and lunged to the side, using her hammer to knock another spear aside and stepped into its place, stabbing with a vicious cut to the Orc behind it. There were growls from the Orcs, and then spears parted to reveal a hulking Orc holding a great maul.

The warrior stepped forward, and she knew, in this moment, her fate was sealed.

∼

Baron Fitzwilliam needed to keep the momentum of the attack going, building on the annihilation of the enemy's knights. The successful surprise attack had boosted his brigade's morale, and he knew his men were no longer thinking about being outnumbered. The baron used this newfound bravado to order his men to leapfrog their attacks, beginning with moving the footmen first, then having the Elves step forward with a withering volley, forcing the rebel line to fall back, desperately attempting to get out of range of the lethal bows. With the retreat of the enemy, he employed the footman to advance his line, until they could safely go no further, and then he once again moved the Elves into position. He continued this forward motion, only modifying it slightly to have the footmen stand beside the Elves, in the slight chance that the earl decided to retaliate. The baron's function in this battle was to defeat the earl as quickly as possible, then move to support Gerald against the Orcs. From the Earl of Eastwood's point of view, everything was going according to plan. He need only wait for the Orcs to break through the rear of the king's lines for his plan to succeed. Both leaders were playing a deadly game, where only one would be successful at the end of the day.

Fitz had used the back and forth of the struggle to lull the traitor's army into a sense of complacency in the proceedings. Now was the time for him to strike, to pull the enemy's attention away from the west. The Elves stepped forward a fourth time to send their rain of death down on the enemy, who, predictably, began to fall back. This time, the Elves suddenly parted and instead of the footman stepping in to fill the void, the cavalry, all of it, came thundering through. He had combined both his mounted troops, knights and light horsemen alike, to create a massive offensive that would invoke fear in the enemy long before they realized how many were not fully armoured. It was a huge gamble, for the light cavalry was not designed to fight in battle, but he knew it had paid off when pandemonium erupted as the footmen of Eastwood turned in panic, trying to stave off this new threat.

The light horse had quickly outpaced the heavy mounts of the knights, charging straight through the opposition, breaking apart their formation, preparing the mass of soldiers perfectly for the onslaught of the Bodden Knights. The earl's troops tried to form a defence, but the Mercian Chargers cut a swath through them with a fury like Saxnor himself. Fitz had remained with the bulk of his brigade, waiting for the perfect moment to strike the final blow. The earl himself was attempting to browbeat his men into at a last-ditch defence, and the baron knew this was the time to strike, to use the enemy's fear as an ally. He dispatched half his footman towards the titanic struggle taking place before him, reserving the other half to reinforce the west if his tactic worked. They didn't even get a chance to engage, for when they came within the last ten yards, what was left of the enemy line broke like a flimsy fence against a storm.

~

Gerald blocked a strike with his shield, swung his sword and cut deeply into an arm. A blow to his back hurled him to the ground, the breath knocked out of him. He rolled over, shield in one hand, desperately swinging his sword around to block the next blow, when he felt an axe sink into the shield. While the attacker tugged his weapon in an attempt to free it, Gerald struck with a short, efficient stab that sank into the Orc's belly, and the creature tottered back. Gerald staggered to his feet, but the blow had stunned him. He couldn't tell where his front line was, all he saw was the enemy surrounding him.

An Orc lunged forward with a spear, and Gerald deftly sidestepped and then drove his blade into its forearm. His opponent ran from the fight, the spear dropped to the ground. Years of training and fighting took over and his muscles fought for him. Strike, parry, stab, over and over again came the enemy until a mound of attackers began to get underfoot. He heard a cry and saw an arrow pierce one Orc's eye. Another, beside the first suddenly yawned and collapsed to the ground. He heard yelling and turned to see a line of footmen coming towards him, Arnim in the lead.

"This way!" the guard captain shouted, and Gerald sprinted with what little reserves he had left. The men opened their ranks, and he lurched in, collapsing as they formed back up. He lay on the ground, Arnim standing over him.

"Over here!" someone yelled, and he looked up to see Revi Bloom, waving his hands about in those strange, but now familiar archaic patterns. Gerald felt his senses returning while his head cleared.

"A horse," he yelled, trying to be heard over the din of battle, "I need to see what's happening."

~

The Orc warrior moved about warily, trying to gauge her abilities. Those on the perimeter were content to watch the fight, and so she paced around, like her opponent, waiting for any signs of movement. The moment he tensed, she was ready. He struck with lightning speed, but she was there, meeting his blow with her sword, deflecting his attack to the side. Even so, she felt a numbness as his mighty weapon hit hers. He backed up slightly, nodded his head in approval and then came at her again. This time, she saw him tense and struck out before he did, slashing wildly with her sword, making him step back, and then she swung the hammer, hitting the Orc's knee. It gave out a tremendous howl and collapsed to the ground, grasping his wound.

She waited, fearful that the horde would unleash their collective fury on her, but then spears parted once more, and this time the Orc that stepped forward carried a staff and wore an animal skull on his head. She watched him warily as he approached her fallen opponent.

He touched the tip of his staff to the wounded Orc's knee and incanted in the same language as she had heard Revi speak. This must be a healer, she thought. I've no hope now, they'll just keep healing him.

The Shaman pointed to the ring of Orcs, and the warrior made his way to the edge. The caster looked at Beverly, then turned to examine the remaining Orcs forming the circle.

Beverly's eyes remained locked on him, until he pointed his staff at the ring of Orcs. As her eyes followed in the direction he indicated, they beheld an immense Orc, covered in battle scars. The warrior stepped forward, this one using a wicked weapon that looked more like a giant cleaver than an axe. He swung it with ease and then pulled a second from his back. So, she thought, two weapons, just like me.

They stared at each other for only a few moments, and then both charged forward. Furious blows struck back and forth, each blocking the others attack, and in turn, trying to hit their opponent. Like some strange dance they traded strikes, but neither could land a hit. Beverly was tired, her head pounding from her earlier wound. She felt blood dripping down her face and shook her head to clear it.

The scarred Orc leaped forward, and she suddenly went down, kicking out with her feet. The Orc was caught off guard as her feet struck his ankle, and the great warrior came crashing down, straight onto her sword. The weight drove the sword down, her wrist spasming in pain. She pulled herself out from under the Orc and swayed to her feet, ready for the next opponent.

This time the ring parted and an Orc, unlike any she had seen before, stepped forward. He was wearing a helmet, chainmail shirt, and a torc emblazoned with an arrow hung about his neck. He carried a sword that he held in front of him, point downward, the blade glowing with the faint colour of magic.

Beverly turned to face this new threat and wondered what kind of magic the blade possessed. She had already resigned herself to death and now stood ready, more filled with curiosity than anything else. Nothing could have prepared her for what happened next.

The Orc stepped forward, standing no more than ten feet from her. "You fight well," he said in a heavily accented Mercerian, "we honour your valour."

She blinked, not quite believing her ears.

"What?" she said in disbelief.

"We will give your life and that of your companions, in recognition of your bravery today."

"You're surrendering?" she asked.

"We will withdraw from battle. You have my word as leader of the Black Arrow clan."

She struggled to understand, to mentally grasp the consequences, "You mean you'll leave the battle?"

The Orc ignored her question, "What is your name, Human?"

The Orc sheathed his sword, and Beverly lowered hers, "I am Dame Beverly Fitzwilliam of Bodden, Knight of the Hound, and protector of Princess Anna of Merceria."

"To us, you shall be known as Redblade," he returned, "for your prowess in combat is impressive. Tell your princess that we shall trouble her no more, we wish only to live in harmony."

"I don't understand," persisted Beverly, "why did you come here today?"

"The Earl of Eastwood promised us land, but he is a man without honour. My predecessor was foolish, and now many of my people have died. Even our healers cannot bring back the dead."

"I think I can guarantee that the princess will agree to leave your people alone, once I explain what has happened."

The Orc bowed, "Perhaps one day we shall meet again, Redblade, it would be an honour to fight beside you."

The Orc leader turned to leave, the signal for his warriors to retreat. Horns began to sound nearby.

"Wait, what is your name?" she cried out.

He turned to face her again, "I am Chief Urgon of the Black Arrows," he said.

"Then I am pleased to meet you, Chief Urgon, may you go in peace."

THIRTY-NINE

The Invitation

SPRING 960 MC

The throne room was brimming with nobility as Beverly made her way into it. She looked about, and spying Princess Anna and her retinue, she diplomatically made her way towards them. The mood of the room was sombre, for this very morning the Earl of Eastwood had been hanged, drawn and quartered, the most gruesome punishment Beverly had ever witnessed. Anna was in the middle of a quiet conversation with Gerald as she approached, but upon seeing Beverly, she looked up and smiled.

"Your Highness," said Beverly, casting her eyes about, "where's Tempus? It's so strange to see you without him."

"I thought it best to leave him in my room. I don't want him taking a bite out of the Earl of Shrewesdale."

"I see," continued Beverly, "that you've assembled your retinue. Is the king expected to make an announcement?"

"Undoubtedly." she answered. "He loves the attention, and all hang on his every word. I suspect he'll draw it out as long as possible."

"Where's Revi?" interjected Hayley.

It was Arnim who answered, "He left early this morning with Lily. Said he was going to Uxley, something about the Temple we found there. He had some theories, but didn't go into any details."

"I suppose that's typical for a mage," said Gerald, "being all mysterious." He was about to say more when a hush fell over the crowd. They all turned towards the throne to listen to the king.

The king rose, with Lady Penelope moving to stand just behind him.

"The events of the past couple of months have been most distressing, but we gather here today to celebrate our victory, and to bestow rewards upon those deemed worthy." He paused as the crowd applauded, waiting for the noise to subside before continuing.

"It is with great pleasure that I call forward Princess Anna," he announced in a booming voice.

The crowd parted, and Anna stepped forward, everyone silently awaiting the king's next words.

"Princess Anna," the king continued, "you have proved to be a most loyal daughter, and in recognition of your service to the crown, I bestow full title to the Uxley estate upon you. In addition, henceforth you shall be the Viscountess of Haverston, with all the lands and duties that the title grants."

"I am honoured, Your Majesty," she said in reply, curtsying.

"I would be remiss if I did not also thank others who distinguished themselves in the service of the crown," the king continued, "and so I call forward Baron Fitzwilliam of Bodden."

The baron strode forward, bowing as he approached the throne.

"You have served us well, Baron, and so I grant you an annual stipend to favour you as you have favoured us with your service."

"Your Majesty is too kind," said Fitz, bowing again.

"And the contributions of the Duke of Colbridge and the Earl of Shrewesdale also bear mentioning in the highest possible terms."

The crowd applauded politely. Beverly supposed it was the political thing to do, after all, the king needed the support of his nobles, despite the fact that their contributions were minor.

"I would, of course, like to mention the outstanding leadership provided by Prince Henry. He is an example to us all of the nobility of the crown."

Henry bowed deeply, blushing with his newfound notoriety.

"The title of Earl of Eastwood shall now be retired. In its place, I award the title of Duke of Eastwood to Marshal-General Valmar, whose accounts of the battle led to today's rewards. Our beloved servant has been sent to Burrstoke to recover from his unfortunate illness."

Arnim snorted, and Anna strained to suppress the laughter which threatened to burst forth.

"And now," the king continued, "Dame Beverly Fitzwilliam, show yourself."

Beverly was caught by surprise but quickly recovered. She stepped forward and bowed deeply as she had seen her father do.

The king stared at her for a moment, as if sizing her up. "Dame Beverly," he said, "although you fought in the battle, you failed to bring the Orcs to their knees, allowing them to retreat into the Artisan Hills. This lack of success will, no doubt, come back to haunt us in the future. You are a disgrace to the Knights of the Sword, and are hereby expelled from their order."

Beverly was too shocked to answer and so stared mutely at the king, whose face had reddened as he spoke. Behind him, she saw Lady Penelope smirking at her misfortune.

"I must object, Your Majesty," said Anna, "Dame Beverly was-"

"I will brook no argument," interrupted the king, "my mind is made up."

The crowd looked on in silence, for the king had quickly changed from a magnanimous king to tyrant in the blink of an eye.

As if realizing the spell he held over them, the king scanned the audience. "But we have said enough," he continued, "I now invite you to the celebration in the great hall."

He turned to Lady Penelope and held out his arm. She lightly grasped it, and they walked across the room towards the hall, the crowd following after them.

Anna's group began to follow, but Anna placed her hand on Beverly's shoulder, "One moment, Beverly, I would speak with you."

The others left them alone, and soon the room emptied but for the two of them.

"The king was wrong," Anna started. "We all know how crucial your contribution was, and we shan't forget it. Despite the rewards heaped upon the others, the kingdom knows that you are the true sword of the crown."

Beverly looked upon the young princess, "I was surprised by the king's venom," she said, "but I can live with it. I know I'm unpopular with the nobility, and I can accept that, but Gerald was as instrumental as the others, and he didn't get any recognition at all."

"It's true," agreed Anna, "but the king will not recognize a commoner when the glory can be attributed to a noble. I'm afraid Gerald's background is working against him. In time, he will be rewarded, I will see to it personally. Meanwhile, let me say that you and Gerald both performed magnificently. We didn't do it for the glory, or the rewards, we did it because it needed to be done, and the people of Merceria needed to be spared the horrors of a long, drawn-out war. That's the true reward."

Beverly smiled, "Are you sure you're only thirteen, Highness?"

They made their way into the great hall to be greeted with the sounds of music and merriment. The noise was oppressive, but Beverly found that guests lapsed into silence whenever she approached.

Anna made her way to Gerald, "Gerald, would you like to dance?"

Gerald's eyes widened, and Beverly laughed at his obvious discomfort. "Go on, Gerald," she urged, "it's not as hard as it looks."

Anna led him onto the dance floor to line up with the others. Beverly watched as the music started and the intricate lines began to move.

"He's better than I would have thought," said a familiar voice.

She turned, "Well said, Father. I was afraid he was going to be lost."

The baron chuckled, "He's a surprising man, although nothing really surprises me anymore when it comes to Gerald."

She nodded in agreement and grabbed a glass of wine as a servant passed by.

"I meant to tell you how well you did in the battle, my dear, we couldn't have done it without you. Never mind what the king said. Your mother would be proud."

She felt tears beginning to well up and took a sip of wine to steady her nerves. She had wanted recognition, and it dawned on her that she had always had it from her father. He supported her from the moment she was born, and for that, she would be forever thankful. The king's anger was eclipsed by her father's praise.

"Now, you must excuse me, my dear, I've just spotted your uncle, and I need to talk to him about some cheese."

He made his way across the great hall, smiling as he went. Beverly downed the rest of her wine and placed the glass on a nearby table. Despite the large crowd in the room, she felt alone. It was Hayley who found her a little while later. The brunette was carrying two goblets and handed one to her.

"What's this?" she said. "You're not dancing? There are several young bachelors here who might catch your eye if you let them."

Beverly turned to her new friend, "I'm afraid there's none here that could meet my standards."

"Perhaps you need to lower your standards?" suggested Hayley.

"No, that I will never do."

Hayley shook her head, "No one will ever meet your standards if you don't lower them. You're too picky."

Beverly smiled. She thought of Aldwin, and it brought comfort to her. She knew one day they'd be together, and until then she would have the memory of him to carry her through.

Hayley was about to speak when the music stopped suddenly. The entire room fell into a hush as a group of finely dressed men, strangers to the court, entered the hall.

The crowd parted as they made their way towards the king, stopping about ten feet away.

"Your Majesty," the one in front said, "allow me to introduce myself."
The king nodded in assent, and the man continued.

"I am Lord Edwin Weldridge, the Earl of Faltingham and I have come
from Westland bearing greetings from King Leofric. He apologizes for the
troops that entered your kingdom from our borders and hastens to assure
you that he had no part in the attack. The troops were sent without his
knowledge, and the man responsible has been punished."

King Andred looked the man over carefully. "And what does King
Leofric offer in recompense?"

"King Leofric wishes to make amends and gifts you this." Two members
of the delegation stepped forward, carrying a chest between them. They
placed it on the ground before King Andred, opening its lid for his inspection. Beverly could not see the contents, but the golden hue of light
reflected upon the ruler of Merceria's face left no doubt as to its contents.

Lord Edwin continued, "He invites you to send a delegation to our
kingdom that we might better understand the bonds between our two
realms. We, in turn, shall send an ambassador of our own."

The king stepped forward to shake the hand of Lord Edwin. "I accept
your hand as the hand of friendship," he said, "let it be thus between our
two kingdoms."

The crowd cautiously applauded, and the king called for the music to
resume. Beverly, enthralled by this turn of events, made her way towards
the newcomer, the better to hear what was being said.

As she closed the distance, she found it harder to move, for the crowd
was returning to the dance, and now swirling men and women kept getting
in her way. Eventually, she made it to the other side of the room and saw
Lord Weldridge talking to the king, a bored-looking Lady Penelope in tow.

"I think it's a wonderful opportunity," the king was saying, obviously in
a good mood. "I can have my daughter, Margaret, ready to travel by the
month's end. Would that suit your king?"

"Most certainly," agreed the Westland noble. "I think he will be delighted
to host her. I shall send word immediately so that arrangements can be
made. He will wish to show her every courtesy. Of course, you will send an
honour guard?"

"Naturally, some Knights of the Sword to protect her along with a suitable amount of servants. I shall send an adviser as well."

"I should think that would be perfect," the earl readily agreed.

"Now," said the king with some finality, "let me show you some of our
finest wines."

The two of them wandered away towards a side table, leaving Lady
Penelope fuming behind them. Beverly saw the look upon the royal

mistress's face. It did not indicate a pleasant evening was in the king's future.

Epilogue

SPRING 960 MC

∼

Claire placed the silver tray on the table as quietly as she could. Her ladyship preferred her servants to be seen, but not heard, and Claire needed this position. She took the wine bottle from the tray, carefully placing it on the table along with the silver goblet she had brought.

"That will be all," said Lady Penelope Cromwell. "You may leave."

Claire curtsied, leaving the room quickly. The king's mistress was, perhaps, the most powerful woman in the kingdom, even more influential than the queen some said, and she demanded the highest calibre of service. The nervous servant walked down the hallway, returning to the kitchen only to realize she had left the tray in the room. Silently cursing herself, she made her way back to Lady Penelope's chamber and quietly opened the door. She heard Lady Penelope's voice coming from the room.

"The fighting is over, and I have secured the cooperation of the king. Our plans are progressing well, but there has been an unexpected development."

"Development?" asked a man's voice.

"Yes, an envoy from Westland has come seeking a visit from a royal. The king wants to send Margaret, but I have other plans for her."

"What of Princess Anna?"

"She is a complication that we can do without. I will suggest the king send her in her sister's place. With her out of the way, our control over Henry will be complete."

Claire opened the door wider, straining to see where the male voice was coming from. She poked her head in and gasped, for Lady Penelope was still sitting in front of her mirror, the frame of which was lit up with glowing runes. She was talking directly at the mirror, but the reflection was not that of the royal mistress.

The door squeaked, and Penelope turned suddenly at the sound.

"Do come in, don't be afraid," she said.

The maid stepped into the room and Penelope rose from her seat. Claire tried to keep her eyes from the mirror, but she felt compelled to look.

"Come closer," said the king's mistress, "have a look and see."

Claire stepped closer and gazed into the mirror, but rather than see her own reflection, she saw a completely different room.

"I'm sorry, my dear," Penelope said in a soothing voice, "but I'm afraid you've overheard something you shouldn't have."

The dagger struck quickly, piercing the young maid's heart. Penelope drew it out, its blade hissing as the venom mixed with blood.

"It's so hard to find good help these days."

∾

Share your thoughts!

If you enjoyed this book, share your favourite part! These positive reviews encourage other potential readers to give the series a try and help the book to populate when people are searching for a new fantasy series. And the best part is, each review I receive inspires me to write more in the land of Merceria and beyond.

Thank you!

Mercerian Tales: Stories of the Past, Chapter 1

BODDEN

Summer 960 MC*

~

The wood in the fireplace crackled as Gerald Matheson dropped another log onto the embers. Pausing a moment to watch the ensuing blaze erupt, he returned to the comfort of his chair, satisfied in the knowledge that the room would soon heat up. Princess Anna lay on the floor with her feet to the fire while her back was comforted by the body of her massive hound, Tempus. As she waited for the warmth to curl around her, her body was snuggled into a blanket to ward off the evening's chill.

Baron Richard Fitzwilliam reclined nearby, sipping wine from a tankard while his daughter, Beverly, sat oiling her sword. Dame Hayley Chambers, the recently knighted King's Ranger, was chatting with her quietly, as the fire sparked back to life.

"It's almost like old times, Gerald," commented Fitz.

Gerald smiled, "Not quite, my lord; we've all gotten a little older."

A small laugh escaped the princess, "Not all of us are old, Gerald."

"Are you sure," said Fitz, before Gerald could respond to the princess's good-natured banter, "that you don't want me to accompany you to Westland, Highness? The Knights of Bodden would be only too happy to act as your escort."

"No, Baron. Much as I appreciate the offer, you're needed here to protect the border. I don't want to come back to Merceria, only to find it overrun. Besides, I've got Beverly and Hayley here, along with my other new knights; I'll be safe enough."

The room quieted, and then Beverly put down her sword. "Remember when you used to tell me stories in front of the fire, Father?"

Anna, who only a moment ago was laying tranquilly on her beloved pet, perked up. "Stories? Do tell."

"Baron Fitzwilliam used to tell all manner of stories to young Lady Beverly. She loved them," explained Gerald.

"I love stories, too," a now animated Anna, gushed. "Would you be willing to regale us with one, Baron?"

"Well," said Fitz, as he absently stroked his beard, "what kind of stories do you like?"

Anna sat up, turning to face the others with a sparkle in her eye. Even Tempus' ears picked up. "I like all kinds of stories."

"You realize," said Gerald, "once you start, there's no stopping. You'll be telling stories all night long."

"What if we took turns?" suggested Beverly.

"Oooh, even better," begged Anna.

"I'm afraid I don't remember any of the stories I used to tell Beverly. It's been many years since we had a young girl in the Keep," responded the baron.

"How about when you first encountered Albreda?" asked Beverly. "I've often wondered how you two met each other. I understand it was some time ago."

"Now, that," said Fitz, getting into the spirit of it, "is an interesting story, an interesting story indeed. It all started back in '33 when I was still a young man…"

∾

Continue the adventure in Heir to the Crown: Book 2.5, Mercerian Tales: Stories of the Past, now available at your favourite retailer.

How to get Battle at the River for free

Paul J Bennett's newsletter members are the first to hear about upcoming books, along with receiving exclusive content and Work In Progress updates.

Join the newsletter and receive *Battle at the River*, a Mercerian Short Story for free: PaulJBennettAuthor.com/newsletter

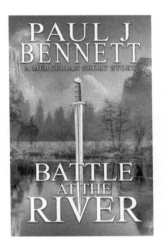

An enemy commander. A skilled tactician. Only one can be victorious.

The Norland raiders are at it again. When the Baron of Bodden splits their defensive forces, Sergeant Gerald Matheson thinks that today is a day like any other, but then something is different. At the last moment, Gerald recognizes the warning signs, but they are outnumbered, outmaneuvered, and out of luck. How can they win this unbeatable battle?

If you like intense battle scenes and unexpected plot twists, then you will love Paul J Bennett's tale of a soldier who thinks outside the box.

A few words from Paul

When I started writing the original book in the series, I knew I wanted to tell a unique story, the story of the heir to the crown as witnessed by those around her. The first significant influence on her life was Gerald Matheson, but in Sword of the Crown, the focus shifts. Gerald is still in her life, but now Beverly takes centre stage. Ultimately, Beverly must overcome opposition, as well as her fears to become the warrior that she needs to be. In order to fully understand the character of Beverly, I had to develop a richer background to her father. His story has inspired Mercerian Tales: Origins, which will be published later this year.

It is easy to write a story about a hero who conquers all, but in real life, there are often obstacles that can only be overcome with great effort. Like many real women today, Beverly faces ostracism and sexism, but triumphs due to her abilities and sheer determination. I tried to make her relatable, so you, the reader, could understand her motivations, for we are all a product of our upbringing. Despite her setbacks, she carries on. Even so, she doesn't get the recognition she so richly deserves. Will she ever gain the acceptance of the crown? You will have to wait and see.

Beverly's story is not over, for the heir to the crown is soon to travel to Westland where cultures clash in the next book 'Heart of the Crown'. Now, with the kingdom safe, she and her companions embark on a trip to a foreign land, where everything is different, and danger lurks in the most unsuspecting places.

I also want to thank those who have been an integral part of bringing this new tale to fruition. Christie Kramberger, who once again created a cover that is amazing. To my small group of dedicated beta readers who have been instrumental in ensuring that there are no plot holes or character introductions forgotten: Brad Aitken, Stuart Rae, Andrea Kenny, Nancy Wolf, Amanda Bennett, Laurie Bratscher and Stephanie Sandrock. Thank you also to Brad Aitken, Jeff Parker and Stephen Brown for bringing the characters of Revi, Arnim, and Jack to life. (More about Jack in 'Heart of the Crown').

Although she did not want me to, I must thank my wife, Carol Bennett. I am so happy that she enjoys doing all the things that I don't, such as editing, marketing, social media and promotions. Without Carol, there would be no Heir to the Crown! Carol, I want to say one thing to you: "Hun, wear this hoody and know that it is as if my arms are holding you."

Finally, I want to thank you, the reader of this book. Without you, there would be no series, no need for future books. I enjoy reading each review that you post, and it truly makes my day to see what you liked most about my stories. Please take a moment and tell me what you enjoyed in 'Sword of the Crown' by posting a review on your favourite retailer's website. If you would like to be kept up to date on what is happening in the world of Merceria, please subscribe to my newsletter, Paul J Bennett Newsletter or follow me on social media:

Lightning Source UK Ltd.
Milton Keynes UK
UKHW010029071120
372942UK00001B/222